Royal WEDDINGS

...Through the Ages

Seven Phenomenal Royal Love Stories!

What the Duchess Wants by **Terri Brisbin**
Eleanor, Duchess of Aquitaine and Henry of Anjou
(future Henry II), 1152

Lionheart's Bride by **Michelle Willingham**
King Richard and Princess Berengaria, 1191

Prince Charming in Disguise by **Bronwyn Scott**
Prince George and Caroline of Ansbach, 1704

A Princely Dilemma by **Elizabeth Rolls**
George, Prince of Wales (future Prince Regent/George IV)
and Princess Caroline of Brunswick, 1795

The Problem With Josephine by **Lucy Ashford**
Napoleon and Marie-Louise, 1810

Princess Charlotte's Choice by **Ann Lethbridge**
Princess Charlotte and Prince Leopold, 1816

With Victoria's Blessing by **Mary Nichols**
Queen Victoria and Prince Albert, 1840

Royal
WEDDINGS
...Through the Ages

TERRI BRISBIN

MICHELLE WILLINGHAM

BRONWYN SCOTT

ELIZABETH ROLLS

LUCY ASHFORD

ANN LETHBRIDGE

MARY NICHOLS

MILLS
BOON

Mills & Boon, an imprint of Harlequin (UK) Limited,
Eton House, 18-24 Paradise Road, Richmond, Surrey TW9 1SR

ROYAL WEDDINGS...THROUGH THE AGES
© Harlequin Books S.A. 2011

The publisher acknowledges the copyright holders of the individual works as follows:

What the Duchess Wants © Theresa S. Brisbin 2011
Lionheart's Bride © Michelle Willingham 2011
Prince Charming in Disguise © Nikki Poppen 2011
A Princely Dilemma © Elizabeth Rolls 2011
The Problem With Josephine © Lucy Ashford 2011
Princess Charlotte's Choice © Michèle Ann Young 2011
With Victoria's Blessing © Mary Nichols 2011

ISBN: 978 0 263 89752 4

013-0312

Printed and bound by
CPI Group (UK) Ltd, Croydon, CR0 4YY

CONTENTS

WHAT THE DUCHESS WANTS

TERRI BRISBIN

Terri Brisbin is wife to one, mother of three and dental hygienist to hundreds when not living the life of a glamorous romance author. She was born, raised and is still living in the southern New Jersey suburbs. Terri's love of history led her to write time-travel romances and historical romances set in Scotland and England. Readers are invited to visit her website for more information at www.terribrisbin.com, or contact her at PO Box 41, Berlin, NJ 08009-0041, USA.

Previous novels by Terri Brisbin:

THE DUMONT BRIDE
LOVE AT FIRST STEP (short story in *The Christmas Visit*)
THE NORMAN'S BRIDE
THE COUNTESS BRIDE
THE EARL'S SECRET
TAMING THE HIGHLANDER
SURRENDER TO THE HIGHLANDER
POSSESSED BY THE HIGHLANDER
BLAME IT ON THE MISTLETOE (short story in
One Candlelit Christmas)
THE MAID OF LORNE
THE CONQUEROR'S LADY
THE MERCENARY'S BRIDE
HIS ENEMY'S DAUGHTER

And in Mills & Boon® Historical *Undone!* eBooks:

A NIGHT FOR HER PLEASURE*

* linked to The Knights of Brittany trilogy

Did you know that some of these novels are also available as eBooks? Visit www.millsandboon.co.uk

Prologue

City of Paris, Île-de-France, 1151 AD

'Whoever named him Geoffrey the Fair had the right of it.'

Eleanor, Duchess of Aquitaine and Queen of France, tried to ignore the comment, whispered from behind her by one of the many women attending Louis's court, but it was difficult to ignore the truth. The next comment caught her full attention.

'They say his son is seeking a wife.'

God forgive her, she did look just then at the two men standing off to one side of Louis's hall, awaiting their turn to speak to the king. Sitting up straighter, she adjusted her veil and smoothed her gown. They were both excellent specimens of manhood: proficient warriors, proven leaders, with more-than-pleasing physical attributes. And anger sat on their features, highlighting both their similarities and differences. Eleanor watched as they gathered their allies around them, discussing whatever matter brought them to Paris and to face the King of France.

Searching her memory, Eleanor realised that two matters brought Geoffrey, the sometimes-rancorous Count of Anjou, and Henry, his heir, to court—to see to the investiture of Henry as Duke of Normandy and to deal with one of Louis's own stewards whom Geoffrey accused of taking part in the plundering of the marches of Anjou.

Fighting words from a fighting man and one who expected the king's justice on the matter.

She wondered if this was wise since Louis tended to side with Eustace of Blois and Henry was pushing next to claim his rights to the English throne, one to which Eustace was his rival. The House of Anjou now stood under sanction from the church for their treatment of Louis's man, something the king's religious advisor thought would soften the count into releasing him. Instead of reacting as most would have—quaking in fear of the damnation of their immortal souls—the count had simply accepted the guilt of his actions and dared the old priest who'd pressed for their excommunication for more!

Eleanor's own man, Godfroi of Poitiers, had explained the intricacies of this case with her, since Anjou and Poitou were historically either enemies or allies and Godfroi had knowledge of their ongoing relationship. Still, they stood waiting, almost challenging Louis to take them on and give them their say.

At the beginning of their marriage, Eleanor would not have hesitated to offer her counsel to Louis in matters such as these, but now, things were so very different for them. Her own advisors were seeking ways to end their marriage and every step she took and each word she spoke were scrutinised *ad infinitum* and *ad nauseam*—something that had grown tiresome years ago. Eleanor glanced over at her daughter Marie and watched as she admired the Angevins too. Glancing around, she noticed that not a woman in the room, save the three older nuns who attended from the abbey she and Louis sponsored, missed a move the father and son made.

A match between Marie and Henry had already been refused because Abbé Bernard declared such a marriage too close in relationship. Watching her daughter's reaction, Eleanor wondered if she'd given up on the possibility or was nursing the romantic idea of a love lost. When the man who prevented that marriage entered, the entire crowd grew silent as he limped his way through the throngs who watched.

When Abbé Bernard reached the dais, he turned and blessed those watching but purposely turned his back to the Angevins! Now loud complaints and grumbling echoed through the crowd until Louis raised his hand to bring it to a halt. Knowing his predilection for every word the abbé uttered and his natural antagonism towards the count and his heir, she wondered at Louis's decision to hear the matter of the abbé's sanction in public.

Finally, Louis stood and motioned to his chancellor, who escorted the men away to his office where the king could speak with them. Eleanor stood and decided to accompany her husband. These Angevins were intriguing and she wanted to learn more about them after seeing them in person. Although Louis frowned at her, he did not order her away, so Eleanor followed along and entered the chambers he used for just this purpose. Surprisingly, the abbé did not join them, though several other bishops did, along with a few trusted nobles who had common borders with Anjou and the other provinces held by that family.

Louis waited for her to be seated before offering chairs to the others and then the discussions commenced. Geoffrey articulated their arguments succinctly and Eleanor fought a smile at how well he did so. Though his son remained at his side, the young man said nothing, simply watching and absorbing and studying every word spoken. He missed nothing, not even her observation of him, and he offered a discreet tilt of his head to acknowledge her attentions.

'Twas then she began to notice things about him. Though young, he had the body and stature of a warrior and she remembered he'd been knighted by his great-uncle David, the King of Scotland. Power and confidence flowed in his veins and throughout him, making it impossible for her not to watch him now. He nodded at several points made by his father, but did not speak. Although he disagreed with Louis's position on several items, only his stance betrayed it and mayhap she was the only one watching so closely as to see it.

More than an hour passed and still they argued over the disposition of Anjou's prisoner, whom he refused to give up without guarantees of action from the king. Ministers huffed and puffed and the Angevins stood their ground. No amount of threats or cajoling seemed to sway the opinions of the count and the duke. Then suddenly, angry words were spoken and the Angevins left!

Eleanor had never seen the likes of this before—a noble

leaving in the middle of a parley, refusing all offers and demands and walking away without any resolution. She could tell from Louis's expression that their behaviour surprised him as well, for his mouth tightened into a thin line and his brows gathered in a fierce frown. But, before they left the chamber, the duke caught her gaze and winked, giving her every sign that this was purely a manoeuvre meant to gain them leverage against their opponents.

The French nobles were insulted and demanded Louis take action, but he forestalled any repercussions with a word. Those in the chamber began to leave, both to see to their own issues and to spread the word of the outrageous behaviour they'd witnessed. With a nod to Louis, Eleanor found her maidservant and ladies waiting for her in the corridor and sought out her chambers.

Later that night, after sending the women away and discussing the day with her trusted advisor, Eleanor decided to enter into private communications with the Angevins. She believed she could aid them in moving across this quagmire safely and they could, in return, be the very thing she sought—someone, a nobleman, strong enough to offer a soon-to-be divorced queen sanctuary....

Or something more than sanctuary...

A future that would see Aquitaine and Poitou joined to Normandy and Anjou in an alliance stronger than either thought possible.

More than that, the possibility that teased her far into the night and into the next days, weeks and months was one of finding a husband worthy of her and all she had to offer.

Could Henry Fitz-Empress be that man?

Chapter One

City of Poitiers, Duchy of Aquitaine, spring 1152 AD

'Why do I feel as though I am simply moving between prisons?' Eleanor twisted the edge of her sleeve between her fingers and glanced over at the man before her. Luckily, the fabric was already pleated so her rough handling of it did not make it look worse for it.

Godfroi had been the commander of her personal guard for years and had remained behind in Aquitaine during most of her marriage to Louis, defending her home and her lands. At least, he had until she'd needed him these past difficult years. Now, she entrusted him with the most delicate of tasks—negotiating the possibility of marrying the Duke of Normandy.

'Perhaps because you are?' he replied, his droll and sometimes bold sense of humour apparent even in this serious situation. 'But then does a queen truly expect her life to be otherwise?'

Eleanor sighed, looking away from his astute gaze. Duchess or queen, the expectations of others guided and ruled her life. Born from bloodlines that could trace back to Charlemagne, *duty* had been the first word she'd learned and would be the last concern when her life ended. These doubts, voiced to someone she trusted with her life, were only momentary lapses in the musings of an otherwise confident woman.

'Tell me your impressions of him, Godfroi. Not what everyone at court said. Not the ones I gathered from our brief encounter and those few missives between us in Paris last year. Tell me what you have learned of the man I would have as husband and lord.'

'He is very different from Louis.'

She laughed then and turned to face him. 'There are not many men who are like Louis.' Eleanor searched Godfroi's face to see if he had been being sarcastic or serious. 'My first husband would have been more content in a monastery than in his palaces. He could have spent every moment in prayer and would not have had a wife who placed the demands of the flesh on him. How is this Angevin different from that?'

'Twas the root of the whole matter when she considered it.

Her marriage to Louis Capet had been for dynastic reasons and power and had brought together her properties with his, creating a kingdom that was double in size to his lands alone. She'd brought wealth and titles to the match and a body ready to produce heirs. Unfortunately, daughters were all they'd created between them, along with scandal, war and discontent. Meeting up with her vibrant uncle during the crusade to the Holy Land had made her think again of all that she'd given up to live as Louis's wife and to suffer from the scorn and diatribes of all his counsellors and bishops. Ultimately, it had been her daughters, now under his custody and control, who were the key to her freedom and her annulment.

'He is filled with a breathless and ruthless enthusiasm for life. Henry could never be controlled by the church or others. His life spent waiting for the crown of England has been spent in honing his skills as a warrior and a king. And I suspect that you will not have to force him into demands of the flesh.'

Only Godfroi could say such things without being impudent, but his words answered her concerns about things of a personal nature. Eleanor was exhausted by the constant demands of Louis's ministers and his church cronies, and though the worst had passed away, others had not relented in their condemnation of her and anything and everything she did or said. They'd even blamed her for the debacle in the Holy Land!

'Truly?' she asked, waiting to see if she could bring the hint of a blush to this imperturbable man. Eleanor realised that there were repercussions to that kind of husband as well. The heat of a blush entered her own cheeks and surprised her. She'd lived a full life and was a mature woman of thirty years and she thought more worldly than a blushing maiden approaching her first marriage bed.

'Just so, Your Grace,' Godfroi replied, tipping his head to her.

'I would meet with him before I agree to this match,' she said.

'That could be difficult now. His brother and others so lately seeking your hand as well.' They'd attempted to kidnap her so that she'd had no other choice was a better description of the matter. Henry's brother, Geoffrey the Younger, had ambushed her just before she'd reached Blois, then Thibault of that city had chased into her own city of Poitiers. She may no longer be Queen of France, but she would not accept second-born sons much lower than she was in status, name or wealth to husband!

'Make it so, Godfroi. I have only met the man in the presence of others. I would assess him in privacy and speak with him candidly without others to hear the conversation.'

If Godfroi thought it was a mistake, he did not say. He simply bowed to her and left to make it happen. Such was his way. She knew he would keep her best interests in mind while negotiating this new marriage, just as she did not doubt Henry would impress her as much in a private discussion as he had when he appeared with his father before Louis demanding to be invested as Duke of Normandy. For once in her life, she held the reins in her hands. For once, she would exercise control not afforded to most women in this world.

For once, Eleanor, Duchess of Aquitaine and former Queen of France, would make her own decision.

Henry paced.

When the son of Empress Matilda and her second husband wanted something and it did not come to hand, he paced. Henry had waited and fought for the English crown and it yet remained out of his grasp. Now, he wanted Eleanor and all she brought and she sent her warrior instead.

'She said what?' he demanded, not believing the words spoken by the man playing messenger to a seemingly reluctant woman.

'The queen—'

'No longer.'

'The duchess would like to continue the negotiations in person.'

He roared out his anger and frustration, effectively clearing the chamber of all who would take cover from him at times like this. More effective sometimes than a mild request, he used it when needed. Times like this when he did not wish to appear too conciliatory or needy, or when there were issues to discuss that were better done without an audience.

But need her, he did.

And the man facing him now seemed to grasp all that he would hide from others, and more.

'Speak,' he ordered. Henry walked around the perimeter of the chamber as he listened.

'She seems to favour your suit over others,' the knight admitted quietly. Henry sensed it was a difficult disclosure for this man sworn to the duchess's personal safety and honour. 'Over others who have tried to force the issue.'

Henry considered the words and their intended result. He remembered meeting the then Queen of France at her husband's court last autumn. Though well-mannered and quiet as befit the wife of the monk-turned-king, her vitality and thirst for life was barely constrained and he recognised the kindred spirit within her. All knew her story, but he wondered where the truth lay. Meeting the knight's gaze, he studied the man.

'Have you fallen under her spell as well as the others?

Do you love your lady as her uncle did?' There were even rumours about his own father and Eleanor but he would leave that unspoken now. 'Do you share such scandalous nights as she did with him to warrant forcible custody by her rightful husband?' he goaded.

The man moved so quickly that he rivalled Henry himself and surprised him. In only a few seconds Henry found this Godfroi of Poitiers confronting him, so close that he could feel the man's exhalations on his face.

'Spiteful stories spun and told to shame and humiliate her.' He swore something truly insulting and yet inventive in Latin under his breath. 'I thought better of you than this, Your Grace.'

The title spoken like another curse, Henry did not know whether to call for his guards or be ashamed.

'The bishops have spoken of little else in their sermons from nearly every pulpit in France. Her shameful behaviour in Antioch that caused the Holy Crusade to fail and that caused God to curse her husband with only daughters.' Henry watched as every word was like a blow to this warrior's own honour. 'Surely the shepherds of God's church know the truth?'

'They shepherd not God's church, Your Grace. They see to their own aspirations and ambitions. Much as they do in your England.' Henry smiled then and stepped back from Godfroi. He had the same concerns about the power of the church in the secular world.

'And to what do you aspire, Godfroi of Poitiers? If you do not aspire to have the queen for your own, what benefit is overseeing these negotiations to you?' Every man had his price and Henry sought to know this man's since his part in this was crucial. 'A title? Land? Why do you remain loyal to this woman when so many have abandoned her?'

'I aspire to fulfil my sworn duty to my liege lady. That is all. I would see her placed with a husband strong enough to see to her dower lands and to her person.'

'And your price?'

Godfroi sputtered then and turned away, a bold move for a knight in the presence of a duke and soon king of all England.

'When I am content that her future is settled, I will enter the service of God.'

Henry was not easily surprised but this man had managed it. Giving up all worldly goods and taking vows of poverty, chastity and obedience were not what he would have expected to hear. 'You are not an old man and yet you would give up the world and all its pleasures?' Godfroi looked surprised by Henry's question, but accepted it.

'My wife died a few years ago, Your Grace, and I have no intention of remarrying. And, in spite of her first husband's leanings, the duchess has given me permission to resign from her service and enter God's.'

Henry did laugh then, both at this man's manner and words, for he did not mince either and Henry would like such a man in his own service. Appeased by the answers and understanding that this knight would stand behind him and not between him and his lady, Henry nodded.

'Make the arrangements. I will plead my own case to your duchess.'

Godfroi left the duke with his advisors and returned to Eleanor with the arrangements for his visit. He wondered as he told her of them whether this was a good idea or not.

He'd watched the previous marriage, one that had been questioned as to validity from its start, begin, flare and then crumble. His lady now had the opportunity that most women only dreamt of—to choose her husband—and he wanted to counsel her well. After meeting Henry, Duke of Normandy and Count of Anjou, Godfroi knew they would make a spectacular match.

Together they would claim huge areas and wealth and control more of France than their liege, King Louis. Once Henry made good on his efforts to claim England as his, and Godfroi did not doubt that he could and would, they would be a force to be reckoned with in all the world.

Godfroi smiled then, thinking of the woman Eleanor, and he knew that Henry would be a better match for the highly educated, intelligent, shrewd, worldly, passionate woman she was than Louis could ever hope to be. Oh, there would be problems—most likely loud and raucous problems—but there could be great passion…and love between these two.

He had no doubt that their names and the story of their lives together would carry down through generations and history; he just prayed he would survive it all.

Chapter Two

Eleanor sat in a simple chair and watched him enter the solar. A room decorated for comfort and pleasure to her own tastes, it did not have a dais or high throne as the great hall did. The women attending her embroidered or worked on tapestries and gave her command to ignore him a valiant if unsuccessful effort.

Accompanied only by Godfroi, he strode into this nest of women and walked about as though he already owned it. Arrogance filled every step, but at the same time, he wooed and won every woman there. He greeted each of them, bowing gallantly before them, asking their names and inquiring about their positions in her court. Only when he'd spoken to each of them did he turn his attentions to her.

She lost her breath at the intensity of his gaze on her!

Their last encounter had been in the midst of a formal court event and Louis had been at her side. Although she never missed the opportunity to appreciate male beauty, her behaviour that day had been the most circumspect of her life for the end of her marriage was under consideration and she'd do nothing to interfere with that. So, she'd watched him from beneath her lashes, noticing his strong warrior's body and close-cropped curly reddish hair and shrewd grey eyes. More than that, he exuded a love of life like the one she kept hidden these past years.

His gown, though of expensive fabric, was plain and unadorned and he wore a short cloak over it as was his habit. Henry did not wear expensive jewels nor try to impress others with such accoutrements; he used the force of his will and his drive to take all that was his to capture others.

'Your Grace,' he said as he approached her. 'It is kind of you to receive me.'

She wanted to laugh, for Godfroi had given her a rather colourful report about Henry's actual response to her demands for this meeting. That he tried to be gracious, even if only in public, made her smile. Rising, she offered her hand to him. They would meet as equals, for other than her sex, they were equal in status...for now.

'And you are gracious in attending me here, Your Grace,' she said as he took her hand and kissed it. It would have been just like any other respectful gesture had he not paused and kissed not only the top of her hand but also the inside of her wrist.

She shivered, though his mouth heated that sensitive spot and Eleanor knew she let a soft gasp escape.

He looked at her without moving his mouth and the deliberate touch of his tongue on her skin made her body heat from within. No stranger to bed-play, Eleanor understood and felt this as the foreplay he meant it to be.

Bold. Sensual. Male. Challenging her to accept him.

Without breaking their gaze, she nodded and her women and Godfroi left quickly and quietly. And then they were truly alone.

Henry still held her hand in his and decided not to release it. He liked the way she'd gasped when he'd kissed her wrist. He liked the frank appraisal of her eyes as he'd entered the chamber, all the while appearing as though she ignored his presence. He especially liked the way her body blossomed beneath his mouth.

Since she was nigh on thirty, he thought to find a woman long-tired of the marriage bed, especially after spending the last score of years in the bed of a man who preferred praying to sexual play with his wife. But instead it pleased him immensely to find a woman whose appetite for life and all it offered equalled his own. Her beauty, sung about by troubadours and spoken about by bards across the land, was not an exaggeration. She retained the glow of youth, the one that drew men to her like bees to honey. When she pitched her voice lower and softer, his body reacted as though she slid her hand over his naked skin.

'I thought to meet with you before negotiations proceeded any further, Your Grace,' she murmured, allowing him to continue his intimate caress of her hand. He smiled then, inhaling the scent of roses she wore.

'You wanted to inspect me to see if I was acceptable to the Duchess of Aquitaine.' He dropped her hand and stepped away. 'So, Your Grace, what say you? Do I meet your requirements?'

If he thought she would blush or act the demur maiden, he was mistaken. The bold caress of her gaze heated his

blood; she looked on him as if he were some sweet prepared by the cook for only her pleasure. He wanted to peel
off the carefully arranged garments she wore, loosen the
floor-length braid of her golden hair and taste the sweetness she offered over and over until they could not move or
breathe.

But what she did next surprised him, for it was a boldness he hoped for yet dared not dream could happen. It also
confirmed that not all the stories he'd heard of the errant
queen of the Franks were falsehoods. Eleanor crossed the
distance between them, took hold of his shoulders and
kissed him.

Her lips were soft against his and he stood motionless
for a moment, savouring the feel of it. Then he reached up
to cup the back of her head, causing the bejewelled circlet
holding a gauzy veil in place to fall onto the floor. Henry
took control then and kissed her back, opening his mouth
and tasting her deeply. She pulled away for a moment
and studied him, the tip of her tongue skimming over her
bottom lip in a most enticing manner. When he thought she
would end it, instead she leaned back into him and lifted
her mouth to his once more.

His body reacted as he expected it would when faced
with temptation such as this and he would have taken her
there and then, save for the fact that it would most likely
cause her to back out of negotiations completely. Captur-
ing her and claiming her physically would only work as a
strategy if he could do it outside her own city, as his brother
and the others had so recently attempted. And even if they
allowed this pleasurable interlude to seek its ultimate end

with him planted deep within her warm flesh, it would not result in the marriage he wanted.

And something deep inside him wanted her to want this marriage and him as much as he did.

He could try to fool himself that it was only the lands and titles and power that made him want her, but watching her as queen and knowing how accomplished, learned and skilled she was and the personality she would bring to him as his wife, Henry knew he wanted her for much, much more. When their mouths touched and he felt her passion rising and her body soften against his hardness, he knew theirs could be a successful match and marriage.

Eleanor the queen had been impressive. Eleanor the duchess was desirable. But Eleanor the woman was irresistible!

Henry held her close and slid his hands around to her back, possessing her mouth and letting her taste of his desire for her. He wanted to touch more of her and began to caress the curve of her hip. Just when he would have moved his hand up, a loud knock came on the door and Eleanor jumped back, putting distance between them. A carefully planned move, he was certain, to allow her enough time but not allow him too much.

Well played, Eleanor!

Godfroi opened the door at her word and was the first to enter. As her women filed in, he admired her strategy even as he noticed that her lips were now swollen from their kisses. Before turning to face the others, she reached up a trembling hand and touched her mouth. Desire ripped through his blood and he wanted to kiss all of her until she quaked with pleasure under him. Feeling smug at the reaction he was able to provoke, Henry strode to the door confident that she would be his. But, as he bid her farewell, it took only a moment for her to take the matter back into her control.

As he leaned over to kiss her hand, determined this time for it to be the respectful gesture it should be, Henry heard her husky whispered words.

'You will do, Your Grace.'

Henry met her gaze and let out his laughter, not stopping as he walked from her chambers and not until he rode from Poitiers's gates.

As will you, my fair Eleanor. As will you.

Chapter Three

'Your Grace!'

Both Godfroi and Henry's counsellor, William, called out the words at the same time, sending it echoing through the large chamber where the negotiations were being held. Once she'd decided that Henry would be the man to see to her fortunes and to herself, the discussions had begun in earnest and in secret. Time was scant and they needed to move forward quickly before Louis learned of their intent and tried to stop it out of fear for what their alliance could mean to him and his rule.

Henry had tried again to argue for control over Aquitaine to pass to him and Eleanor had let slip a rather rude epithet, one she'd heard many times while in the company of crusaders and one she thought explained her position on Henry's demand exactly. Those of a gentler disposition assisting in the discussions apparently did not appreciate the candour of the word or her use of it.

Henry...well, Henry seemed to laugh it off, accepting

her foibles during these discussions, whether it was her use of this particular word or her ongoing refusal to acquiesce to his demands. He watched her in a way that took her breath away, but she was coming to know that he did everything with an intensity she'd never known in a man before. Though he never repeated, nor did she, the kisses or caresses of that first meeting, she could tell by the way his grey eyes darkened when he was thinking on matters of the flesh.

At times, he seemed to undress her with that intense gaze, and she could swear she felt his fingers sliding over her clothing, loosening and untying laces, peeling away layers, until her very skin burned in anticipation. Though she had enjoyed the pleasure found in the marriage bed, Louis had looked on it as a chore and something he must do. He was never unkind in those matters, but did not like to linger or explore or spend more time than was necessary to accomplish his goal—spill his seed within her and then pray she would bear a son.

Now though, every time Henry touched her, and he seemed to do so with increased frequency and ardour, her body readied itself for him, for more. From the look he gave her now and the way he slid his tongue along his lips as though preparing himself to taste something sweet, she hoped these discussions would finish quickly. For the shallow woman everyone seemed to think she was did indeed live within her and that woman was ready to invite him to her bed…now…outside the vows of marriage.

Could he read her thoughts? Was she as transparent as her favourite silken veil? It must be so, for he watched her and then laughed to himself.

'Forgive me, good sirs,' she said, nodding to each of the counsellors. 'I but forgot myself momentarily in my enthusiasm to bring these discussions to a pleasing conclusion.'

Though certain that Godfroi and William were thinking of a successful marriage contract that benefited their own lord or lady the most, she was thinking of another conclusion, one that would have Henry in her bed...

'Your Grace?' Godfroi said quietly, waiting for her to stir from the lustful reverie that seemed to overtake her when in the same room with the duke. 'Mayhap if Your Graces take a walk around the garden, William and I could come up with the suitable wording?'

In other words, pray thee leave and let those less involved handle these personal matters.

'Your Grace?' she said, looking at Henry. 'What say you to Godfroi's suggestion?'

Henry nodded. He never remained still for long and being closed up in this room for these hours must grate on him. The suggestion made him smile and he held out his hand to her.

'An excellent one, Your Grace,' he said, leading her to the door. 'The sun is most agreeable this day and a brief respite would do us all good.' It sounded so polite, like any other courtier's expected reply, until he whispered under his to her. 'They wish to be rid of us both, Eleanor. Let us away before they decide otherwise!'

He took her hand firmly in his, entwining their fingers, and then he ran down the corridor, forcing her to keep pace with him. Their maids and menservants were caught by surprise and were dozens of paces behind them—Henry's clear intention—when they arrived at the gate of the garden. Laughing and out of breath, she could only allow him to pull her into the garden and then watch as he locked the gates against the rest of them.

Her guards called out to her, always mindful of the dangers that yet existed for her, but she answered them, and soon it was just Henry and her...alone.

'Walk with me, Eleanor,' he asked prettily.

How could she refuse such a request when done nicely? She held out the hand he'd released and they walked, though briskly, around the perimeter of the manicured gardens. She loved this one best and would miss it when she went to live in...

'Where will we live?' she asked.

'So you think these matters will be worked out, then?' he asked, stopping for a moment and then walking again.

'I have never been to Rouen,' she said, ignoring his question and continuing as though everything were settled. Because it would be. 'Is it warm there?'

'Rouen is a beautiful city, but there are others in Normandy if you do not like it,' he offered. Now it was her turn to be surprised by such an offer.

'But it is the seat of your duchy. Surely the duke and duchess should reside there.'

He pulled to a stop and faced her. 'My mother maintains a household in Rouen.'

'Is that a warning or an invitation?'

Since the Plantagenets, as Henry's father called themselves, and the Capets tended to be enemies, Eleanor had had no opportunity to meet the extraordinary woman who had nearly claimed England as her own and now sought it for her son.

'I think you would find her interesting,' he explained, the respect for his mother evident in his voice and tone. 'She has had many interesting experiences similar to yours and you might find her helpful in establishing yourself as the Duchess of Normandy.'

His mother had been the Empress of Germany during her first marriage and from a very young age, much as Eleanor had married and become Queen of France.

'I would like to meet her,' she admitted.

Strong women in power were so few in these times when inheritances were more and more going only through male heirs. Eleanor knew that she was in fact only a placeholder for the titles of Aquitaine and Poitou and would relinquish them to a son, if she had any. Though Henry pushed for it, she would not, however, relinquish her rights to those if they married. She had held them through her marriage to Louis and as that relationship ended.

'There is another similarity between the two of you, Eleanor.' His voice was lighter, teasing her, and she tried to think of another thing she could have in common with the empress. 'After marrying older men in your first marriage, you have both taken on the challenge of marrying someone much younger in your second.'

Eleanor laughed then, for Henry leaned in closer and teased, 'I hope you hold up as well as she did.'

He failed to mention how much his mother hated his father and she hoped that was not something that would also happen between them. The conversation continued with neither of them even questioning that a match between them would not occur.

'We may spend much of our time moving between

our holdings, especially when I am finally successful in claiming my birthright in England. Have you ever travelled there?' he asked, guiding her to a bench while he stood, or rather paced, nearby.

'Nay. Many other places but not across the Channel.'

And she had travelled far and well during her lifetime— as far as the Holy Land and through many countries and territories as they returned. Eleanor had seen many wonders, peoples and lands from the very exotic to the familiar. But she'd never gone north to England. As Henry's wife, she would be expected to visit there and rule with him, once he attained the throne.

'What is your favourite place in England?' she asked, trying to learn more about this man she would marry. 'Other than the battles, of which I have heard a little, when did you spend time there?'

She did something then that she did well—Eleanor listened. Her teachers had taught her that there was much to be learned in both the words chosen and the words left unspoken and now she watched as he became very excited, telling her about his time in England with his uncle, becoming a knight just two years past. He spoke of his teachers and his time in England as a child, spent with his mother's half-brother, the Earl of Gloucester.

The Duke of Normandy was a passionate man—his plans to claim his birthright, his refusal to bow to the whims of Louis, indeed his willingness to take a path that many could and would call treason, and even just his interests in fighting and hunting and hawking, all spoke of his enthusiastic approach to everything in life. And the manner in which he constantly found ways and opportunities to touch her spoke of his passion of another sort.

When an hour or more had passed, Eleanor sat on a bench in a secluded alcove of the garden. Henry lay with his head on her lap, entwining his fingers with hers as they spoke. She laughed, more than once, at his impertinence and arrogance and she could not remember the last time she'd felt so very light-hearted or was filled with such anticipation about any event in her life.

Though Louis would remain her liege lord for her lands and titles in Aquitaine and Poitou, a marriage to Henry would return her to the same status, perhaps even higher, than her now-former husband and any new wife he might seek. Louis most likely did not wish to do so, though finding a new wife, begetting a male heir, was something his ministers and advisors, both religious and secular, would pursue vigorously. In order not to be shamed by this new social order, marriage to someone equal to or higher than Louis would be necessary.

Eleanor sighed then, realising the political efficiency of this proposed match bore more weight than she had first considered. Much as she'd like to think it could be about other matters or issues, it would not be. She was a woman of rank and privilege and as such would never be free from the responsibility to marry well.

'That does not bode well for my suit,' Henry said softly as he reached up and gently moved a few loosened strands of her hair out of her face. He turned his hand and caressed the exposed area of her cheek as he smiled. 'Is there ought I can do to remove the frown from your brow, Eleanor?'

If she closed her eyes and listened only to the sound of

his voice, she could almost believe they were simply a man and a woman. Her biggest concern lay in the most dramatic difference between the two men she would call husband— Henry's appetites, for all things exciting, would bring her into a life very different from the one she had with prayerful Louis. She'd watched all of her life while sexual affairs changed the world around her and she suspected—nay, she knew—Henry would never be limited to one woman in his bed.

All she could hope for was his regard, his respect and possibly his love, even while she knew she would share his body with others.

'I think you will break my heart, Henry.' She shared her deepest fear. 'I think you will break it often.'

Regret entered his grey gaze and Eleanor read the truth there—Henry knew their life would not be easy and that her fear would be realised. Men of power and status lived a certain life with perquisites and expectations. Women other than their legal wives were always part of that life. Though not a large problem as Louis's wife, Eleanor understood that it would be a part of any marriage with Henry, especially as young and vigorous as he was. When he opened his mouth as though to speak against such accusations she placed her finger over his lips to stop him. Better not to make promises she knew could not be kept over time.

'But we will manage this, will we not?' she asked.

'Better than manage,' he whispered, and he guided her head down so he could touch his mouth to hers. 'We will be spectacular together, Eleanor. Spectacular.'

The kiss that followed his words gave her hope of such

things. He tangled his hands in her hair and one kiss led to another and another until she could think of nothing else but having this man as her husband.

Chapter Four

City of Poitiers, Duchy of Aquitaine,
18th May 1152 AD

The day dawned bright and sunny as days in her favourite city often did in the midst of spring. Gentle breezes flowed around the city, rustling the flags that flew high on the walls of Poitiers. The colours of the Duke of Normandy interspersed with her own decorated the castle and the cathedral, announcing to all their future lord's arrival. Eleanor leaned her head back and inhaled the fragrance of the blossoms of May.

She would never tire of this place and its beauty. She was of this land and of these people and it would always be part of her soul. Did he feel the same about Normandy or Anjou? Or England? Was there a city or province that called to his blood the way Aquitaine did hers?

Her gaze moved over the people gathered along the sides of the road as her carriage made its way from the castle stronghold to the cathedral where the marriage would take place. Though no announcement had been made, word had spread and her people came to wish her well. Waving to her as she rode past, they smiled and some of the children even tossed flowers at her.

Negotiations had concluded that afternoon they'd spent in the garden and now they would wed. The ceremony would be much smaller than personages of their consequence might have been expected to hold but the circumstances around this marriage warranted it. They and their advisors understood that the king could take offence to it since they did not ask for his permission, as those sworn to their liege lord should have.

She sighed then, catching the attention of the two women who accompanied her inside the carriage. Constance and Eloise smiled and she allowed them to continue to think she thought on Henry and his many attributes—attributes they'd discussed for hour upon hour these past days. A woman on her wedding day should not be thinking on the possibilities of coming war and retribution claimed by a king.

After discussing this same issue with Godfroi and other advisors, Eleanor suspected that Louis's true opinion about this situation was that, though he'd released her from their marriage, she should not seek another on her own but wait for him to arrange one. In her mind, she could see his reaction, his usual Capet calm regard exploding into something completely different. She'd seen it once, in Antioch, when accusations were made against her behaviour towards her uncle. She had no doubt that the news of her marriage to

Henry and the merger of all of their lands and titles would enrage him as little else could.

'Madam,' Constance said. 'We are approaching the cathedral.'

Eleanor nodded and arranged her gown so that she could climb down more easily. The horses drew to a halt and the crowds cheered. Peering through the window, she saw Henry walking down the steps of the cathedral towards her. In an unusual gesture, he was coming to her.

She smiled and allowed the others to climb down first to assist her. As they moved a few steps away, Henry appeared with his hand outstretched to her. He smiled and bowed to her and her people cheered loudly. His garments were of the finest cloth and he wore a heavy gold chain around his neck. A signet ring was his only other jewellery but the large ruby in it spoke of its value. His red hair gleamed in the bright sunshine and his eyes sparkled as he helped her out and gathered her at his side.

He kept his arm around her waist and guided her up the stairs to the door of the large church. It was inappropriate and daring, but she loved the gesture. She, the Duchess of Aquitaine, did not enter as a supplicant to this marriage. They entered together, as equals, and he even had the audacity to pause at the doorway, turn to face the crowd and then kiss her before them!

Eleanor was still laughing and breathless when they reached the altar and, try as she might, it was difficult to regain the composure expected of a duchess on such an occasion. Instead she and Henry shared glances and even gentle touches as the ceremony commenced. Although this wedding was nothing when compared to her first one, there were sufficient witnesses of significant standing to ensure its validity. And the Bishop of Poiters and several others attested to the lack of obstacles in making this marriage.

Eleanor found herself nervous just then, as the last clause of the marriage agreement was read aloud and it was time to exchange vows with this man...vows that would make her his property, under his control and no other's. Her throat tightened for a moment and she swallowed against it.

'Here now, Your Grace,' Henry whispered. 'Be of stout heart and take me as your own.'

He squeezed her hand then and nodded and it both relieved her fears and warmed her heart. He'd noticed the unaccountable nervousness and tried to assist her. If he would continue to do that, she had great hopes for their life together.

Henry felt her hand tremble ever so slightly and squeezed it, willing her to look at him. Eleanor of Aquitaine, a woman who had travelled the world and seen a holy crusade, was nervous about marrying him? He would never have thought it possible. But then, until just a few months ago, he would never have believed such a marriage possible either. Now, as she smiled at him and he saw some softer emotion flicker deep in her blue eyes, he was glad his beliefs had been so misplaced.

When she'd arrived before the church and he'd heard the people chanting her name and his, his heart had raced with excitement and anticipation of their joining. He watched as she prepared to climb from the carriage, smoothing the blue gown that matched the colour of her eyes and adjusting the shimmering veil that covered her long hair, hair left unbound as though a virgin bride.

The blatant desire in her eyes as their gazes met only served to confirm that virginity could be overrated and that a woman of experience had much to offer. The passion that awaited them both would be as exquisite as she was and his body shook from the power of his response to her. Only hours remained until they were one in name and in body and he hoped he could resist acting the barbarian and carrying her off to his bed before the festivities concluded!

Her boldness, her vitality, her sense of humour and adventure, all called to him. Her beauty and her innate passion riled his blood. She would be a fitting wife for him and he was glad of it. The bishops, surrounded by the wafting smell of burning ashes and candles, consecrated their union by praying blessing after blessing for them and offering a seemingly endless litany of prayers. Henry grew anxious to reach the end of this ceremony. 'Twas sacrilegious possibly, but he wanted her called wife so that he could have her to himself—and that could only happen when they were declared married.

With each passing prayer, he drew her closer, enjoying the feeling of her body near his and the knowledge that she was minutes away from being his. At last, the final benediction was prayed and, as they knelt next to each other, Eleanor squeezed his hand in response.

She was a fitting match for him and would be the wife he would need at his side during these next crucial years as he claimed England at last and forged his own kingdom. Everything he needed in a helpmeet, everything he wanted in a future queen and everything he wanted in a woman he found in Eleanor.

As he helped her stand and listened to the bishop's words declaring them man and wife before God, Henry felt the laughter bubbling up from within and he let it out. It echoed through the large open spaces in the cathedral and then hers joined his as they raced down the long centre aisle towards the doors and the rest of their lives together.

Reaching the doors, he paused only long enough for the guards to open them before drawing Eleanor into his arms and kissing her the way he wanted to, beginning to make her his and to claim her passion for himself. Then, waving off those who would help, he lifted her onto one of the matching horses that stood waiting for them and climbed onto the other.

Trumpets flared and drums beat. Their names were chanted by the crowds and echoed down the cobbled streets of Poitiers as they made their way slowly back to the castle where they would celebrate with a feast and dancing for the rest of the day. Eleanor's every move was filled with elegance and grace, as she nodded to her people, now his, and accepted their adulation as though it was more than simply that expected of a people for their liege. She was accepting their love.

Though his men surrounded them as their honour guard, Eleanor's own troops led their way along the streets. An example of what their marriage meant, this merging of Normandy and Aquitaine, Angers and Poitou, would create something new and different among the powers on the continent. Henry smiled and waved as people called out his name.

As he turned back, he caught sight of Eleanor smiling at him and, for a moment, they were not duke and duchess or count and countess. They were not heirs or heiresses. Instead they were simply Henry and Eleanor, a man and a woman, married and beginning the rest of their lives together. In that instant, Henry offered up a prayer for all those things every man must wish for at such a time—many years together, a happy life and the blessing of children.

Eleanor nodded at him, seeming to understand and share his feelings, and Henry knew all would be well between them. Reaching over, he held out his hand and took hers. They rode the rest of the way with hands joined.

'Twas hours later when Henry announced an end to the feast and sent Eleanor off with her ladies to prepare for their marriage bed. Though his men and those he called friends called out bawdy words and offered challenges to him, he brushed them off and arrived at Eleanor's chambers alone. A formal bedding ceremony was expected, but Henry had ordered there be none. She would be his wife for the rest of their lives, for Henry had no intention of repeating Louis's mistake in letting such a treasure escape. He would never repudiate their marriage or the woman herself and he had no intention of exposing her loveliness to the gawking gazes of others.

As arranged, she was alone when he entered, her women leaving just as he closed the door behind him. Uncertain of what to expect or where he would find her, Henry lifted the candle he carried and saw her in the bed. He lost the ability to think in that moment, for the sight of her sitting there among silken pillows and sheets, with only her hair covering the creamy flesh and feminine curves, was too alluring to resist.

What should not have surprised him was the way she watched him as he walked across the bedchamber to stand before her. If he thought she would watch him with less intensity or interest than he watched her, Henry discovered differently in a very short time. He remembered the moment he caught her staring at him in Louis's court last autumn and saw the frank assessment in her knowing eyes. The same gaze greeted him now and he wondered how bold she could be.

Henry paused at the side of the bed, placed the candle on the table to join the others there and began to untie the laces on his tunic and shirt. She never said a word, but she missed nothing. He lifted his arms and tugged the garments over his head, allowing her to watch.

He could feel the heat of her gaze move over his flesh and his body reacted to her frank scrutiny by readying itself for what was to happen. Eleanor shifted in the bed but said nothing. Then a slight smile curved her lips and she nodded, giving him permission to continue! He laughed then and reached for the belt around his waist. Watching her reaction caused his heart to pound and his blood to race through his veins, heating every part of him.

Henry bent down and removed his boots and stockings before loosening his trews and pushing them down and off. Standing, he faced Eleanor and let her look her fill for he intended to do the same of her before the night was done. If he thought she would look away or not carefully examine his manliness, he was wrong, but the true surprise came when she spoke.

'As I said some weeks ago, Your Grace, you will do.'

He would have sputtered out some words but her gesture forestalled him. Eleanor lifted the sheets, gifting him with a view of her full breasts and narrow waist. When she opened her legs and offered him a place between them, he accepted the passion and the woman she offered.

Only some hours later, when their ardour had been spent by several bouts of pleasure together did he respond to her words.

'As will you, my sweet Eleanor. As will you.'

Epilogue

Eleanor, Duchess of Normandy and Aquitaine and Queen of England, smiled as the baby was handed to her husband. Henry had wanted sons and this was the third they'd produced—something even she had wondered would be possible when they'd married five years before. After having only daughters with Louis Capet, the doubt had lived deep within her. The births of little Henry and this son had eased her grief over losing the firstborn of Henry's get and now her contentedness in the marriage she'd sought with the House of Anjou increased. Henry examined the baby and then nodded his joy at her.

'I agree with your choice, Eleanor. Richard is a fine name for my son,' he said. He handed the baby back to his nurse and sat on the bed, next to Eleanor, sliding their hands together. 'I am pleased, wife.'

Eleanor understood that part of her husband's pleasure

involved tweaking the nose of her former husband, who could not seem to have a son. Word would be sent out announcing the arrival of the latest son in the Plantagenet family and she could imagine Louis's reaction.

'As am I, husband,' she said, accepting the kiss he offered.

'He will make a fine heir to Aquitaine,' Henry declared as boldly as ever, knowing that the decision was hers and not his to make.

'He could,' she answered, not consenting or rejecting the idea as yet.

Five years before he had relented in his demands over this issue, but, like a dog with a juicy bone, he could not let it go. Though he'd gone on to make his claim on England the year after their marriage and then assumed the throne there another year after that, Henry still wanted Aquitaine. Even having England within his grasp did not cause him to let go of her claim of control over her provinces.

Now though, he was happy with this new heir she'd given him and would be gracious in her refusal. He realised it even as she did and so she eased her stance the tiniest bit.

'Richard Plantagenet, Duke of Aquitaine,' she said. 'It does have an appealing sound to it.'

Henry leaned in close and touched his mouth to hers, gently squeezing her hand as he did so.

'You will do,' Henry replied. Kissing her again, he gathered her close and held her in his arms, mindless of anyone else in the chamber. 'Aye, you will do, Eleanor.'

* * * * *

Author Note

As we all know, the marriage of Henry and Eleanor would last for decades and be one of the best known of all of the royal matches in British history. From their legendary squabbles which split apart the Angevin empire (and were the basis for dramas like *The Lion in Winter*) to the extraordinary long life of Eleanor (she died in her eighty-third year), who tried to hold it all together for her sons, their story was filled with all of the things that families deal with even now—love, betrayal, support, estrangement, restoration and competition.

The fates of the Capets and the Plantagenets remained intertwined and connected for generations. In love or in war, theirs was a constant competition for control of lands and titles in what would become modern France.

Though Eleanor is often demonised in the histories of the times, blamed for everything that ever went wrong in the life of Louis Capet, I cannot help but believe that history is not kind to extraordinary women who step outside the boundaries of society's expectations of them. And I chose to see Henry as an enthusiastic young man, about to set out to pursue all of his dreams, in search of a woman who could be his equal. If he decided later that he did not want such a woman, we can't blame her for it!

As their marriage progressed, Henry and Eleanor produced eight (or possibly nine) children, sons and daughters who inherited various parts of their family empire or who were married off to strengthen bonds with other important and powerful families. Most readers tend to remember only two of them—Richard and John. Divided by contention and favouritism, Henry's sons were never content and eventually saw almost all of their lands on the continent lost and only England remain under their control.

But, at the beginning of it all, a marriage between an older woman and a younger man, a duchess and a duke, a count and a countess, began, I believe, with enthusiasm, anticipation and a bit of love. I hope you enjoyed the story of their royal wedding.

For readers seeking more of the historical details about this time period and this particular marriage, let me suggest two of the books I use when writing in this time period: *The Knight, the Lady and the Priest: The Making of Modern Marriage in Medieval France* by Georges Duby, and *Eleanor of Aquitaine and the Four Kings* by Amy Kelly.

Those readers familiar with my previous historical romances should recognise the man who facilitates the delicate negotiations between Henry and Eleanor—Godfroi. In *The King's Mistress*, he is known as Godfrey and has indeed entered God's service. By the time of that story, he is abbot of a large monastery in northern England and counsellor to the hero, Orrick of Silloth-on-Solway, as well as to an older but not much wiser Henry II of England. It was fun for me to go back and see how Godfroi helped in this marriage. He is, of course, a fictional character, created for these stories and not based on any real person, though I suspect there must have been someone like him who helped things along.

Happy reading!

Terri Brisbin

LIONHEART'S BRIDE

MICHELLE WILLINGHAM

Michelle Willingham grew up living in places all over the world. When her parents hauled her to antique shows, Michelle entertained herself by making up stories and pondering whether she could afford a broadsword with her allowance. Currently she teaches American History and English, and lives in south-eastern Virginia with her husband and children. She still doesn't have her broadsword. Visit her website at: www.michellewillingham.com or e-mail her at michelle@michellewillingham.com

Previous novels by Michelle Willingham:

HER IRISH WARRIOR*
THE WARRIOR'S TOUCH*
HER WARRIOR KING*
HER WARRIOR SLAVE ^
THE ACCIDENTAL COUNTESS %
THE ACCIDENTAL PRINCESS%
TAMING HER IRISH WARRIOR *
SURRENDER TO AN IRISH WARRIOR *

Also available in eBook format in Mills & Boon® Historical *Undone!*:

THE VIKING'S FORBIDDEN LOVE-SLAVE
THE WARRIOR'S FORBIDDEN VIRGIN
AN ACCIDENTAL SEDUCTION %
INNOCENT IN THE HAREM
PLEASURED BY THE VIKING

* The MacEgan Brothers
^ prequel to The MacEgan Brothers mini-series
% linked by character

Did you know that some of these novels are also available as eBooks? Visit www.millsandboon.co.uk

Prologue

Pamplona, the Kingdom of Navarre, 1187

'I didn't know if you would come,' Richard said, reaching for her hand. He had removed the chain-mail armour he'd worn earlier and wore a blue silk tunic trimmed with fur. His dark mantle rested over his shoulders, and even in the moonlight, Berengaria could see the cool grey of his eyes and the reddish glint of his hair.

'What choice did I have?' she accused. 'You stole my ring at the tournament when you kissed my hand.' Holding out her palm, she sent him a warning look. 'I want it back.'

'I wanted an excuse to see you again.' He sent her a slow smile that quickened her pulse. Opening his hand, he revealed the emerald and gold ring. 'Is this what you want?'

When she tried to seize it, he curled his fingers over his palm. 'Come closer, and you shall have it.'

'Do not play games, Your Grace. I've no interest in them.'

'If that were true, you wouldn't have come. You'd have sent a servant for the ring.'

'And you'd have refused to return it.'

He drew closer, pressing the ring into her hands. 'Do you think me such a villain?'

'I don't know who you are.' Though her hands were gloved, she could feel the heat of his skin. Something about this man intrigued her, slipping past her defences like the warrior he was.

Don't stay, Berengaria warned herself. *Leave now.* Her father, King Sancho, would be furious if she knew she was standing in the garden with the Duke of Aquitaine, the son of King Henry Plantagenet of England.

'I want to know you,' Richard said slowly. 'No woman has ever dared to speak to me in the way that you do.'

'No,' she whispered. 'You aren't my betrothed husband and never will be.'

'You're right.' His hand moved up to her cheek, and when she tried to move away, he held her in place. 'Berengaria, you remind me of Eve. You tempt me with the tartness of your tongue. The flashing of your dark eyes.'

She shivered slightly, and her mind warned her again to move away. But his voice held her captive, while his thumb edged her cheekbone. 'I admire your spirit.'

Richard tipped her face up to look at him. Then he leaned in closer, resting his forehead against hers. 'You should know that this is your last chance to walk away untouched. If you stay, I'm going to claim a kiss.' He released her and stood motionless, waiting for her decision.

Her mind cried out for her to flee, even as her feet remained rooted in place. Richard was not a man who was free to court her. He was already betrothed to another woman.

But she wanted to experience the forbidden taste of a

kiss from a man who wanted *her*. Not her kingdom, nor her wealth, for he could have neither. Richard knew what it was to be caught in a world full of rules, a world in which they had no freedom.

His lips covered hers, and at the first moment of the kiss, she forgot all the reasons why this was never meant to happen. Richard rested his hands upon her hips, drawing her body nearer. 'Close your eyes,' he said softly. 'You're not a princess anymore. And I am not a duke.'

She obeyed, and the barriers seemed to vanish between them. Against her mouth he murmured, 'If you were my betrothed wife, I'd steal away from my duties to seize moments like this. And you'd never tell false compliments to me, would you?'

'Your arrogance is great enough, my lord.'

'Richard,' he corrected. This time, he captured her lips like a ruthless invader. There was nothing kind or polite about the kiss. She opened her mouth, shocked at the wild feelings that coursed through her. He trapped her face between his hands, kissing her as though he wanted to shred all of her defences and find the woman beneath.

Though inwardly she knew that he had an insatiable need to win, to conquer, she hardly cared. The rush of need provoked a tremulous response inside her. She couldn't catch her breath as he plundered her mouth. And when she began to kiss him back, he softened the intensity. Warm and wet, his tongue slid inside her mouth. He drew her hips against him, and she could feel the hot length of his arousal against the folds of her skirts. The knowledge, that he wanted to claim her body, made her tremble. She clung to him, so afraid of the feelings that ran untamed within her.

'Innocent,' he murmured against her skin. 'I knew it when first I saw you.'

She caught her breath as his mouth travelled over her cheek. 'I must go now.'

'You should.' But he didn't release her from his embrace, and she wondered what he intended. His palms moved up her spine, and when he kissed her again, she sensed that this was farewell.

But now, she had a memory to call her own. One that her father could not govern or take away from her. And as she kissed him for the last time, Berengaria thought to herself, *I'm glad it was Richard.*

Chapter One

Off the coast of Cyprus, April 12, 1191

Liam MacEgan hated ships. Though he'd spent many years of his life exploring the waters of his native Éireann, being trapped aboard a wooden vessel for months was somewhere between purgatory and hellfire.

It was your idea to go on Crusade, he reminded himself. He'd believed he was embarking on an adventure, to see the Holy Land and fight to free Jerusalem. His family had been firmly opposed to it. His father, King Patrick of Laochre, had demanded that he face his responsibilities as a future provincial king.

But he'd needed an escape from his homeland. He'd grown up listening to the stories of distant lands, told to him by his uncle Trahern. He longed to see the glittering foreign cities and taste new foods. He needed this last chance to see the worlds that were forbidden to him...to feel the sting of desert sand against his face...to learn the secrets of exotic women.

And so, defying his family's wishes, he'd slipped out one night and arranged passage to France, to join in the service of the King Richard, *Coeur de Lion*.

Liam stared out at the fierce blue of the Mediterranean, and a bittersweet tang of homesickness caught him. The sky was a dark grey, and clouds rolled in the distance. He was dimly aware of a woman moving along the side of the boat, just behind the oarsmen. Her long dark hair was covered by a veil, but the length of it stirred in the sea winds.

Adriana, daughter of the Vicomte de Manzano, was one of the Princess Berengaria's ladies. She was a dark beauty, with olive skin and raven hair. He watched as her hands curved over the wood of the ship, and she turned back to stare at the waves.

He wanted to go and talk to her, but he sensed it would be an intrusion of her time alone. Her eyes lifted to the darkening skies, as though she were afraid.

Instinct made him glance behind him, and he spied the Count of Berduria staring at the young woman. The unrestrained lust on his face made Liam cross over to Lady Adriana's side. Though she shied away from him, he said in a low voice, 'Don't be afraid. I came to offer my protection, not to disturb you.'

When she sent him a confused look, he added, 'The count is watching.' At that, Lady Adriana settled her gaze back upon the sea. Liam wasn't certain whether or not she wanted him to stay. 'Would you rather I left you alone with him?'

'Stay,' she whispered. 'Unless your intent is the same as his.' She shivered in the wind, rubbing her shoulders. Liam unfastened his cloak and settled it around her shoulders. It was meant to offer her warmth, but it also sent an unmistakable message to the count.

She pulled the cloak around her. 'You're one of King Richard's men, aren't you?'

'I chose to fight at his side, aye. But I am not his vassal.' He refrained from mentioning anything further, not wanting to admit his own rank. During this journey, he'd told no one that he was an Irish prince, save King Richard. He wanted to experience life as a common man, as a soldier. It had meant giving up the luxuries he'd come to enjoy, but in return, he'd seen a side of life that his family had tried to protect him from.

'Has King Richard spoken of the princess?' Adriana asked. 'My lady Berengaria worries that he seems so... distant, ever since the new betrothal.'

Liam shrugged. 'His Majesty is preoccupied with the journey to the Holy Land. He's eager to fight for Jerusalem.'

'What of the Princess Alys? He broke his betrothal to her only a few months ago. Does he desire to reconcile—?'

'Given that his father took Alys as his mistress and she bore him a daughter, rest assured, King Richard had little desire to take her to wife.' Liam sent her a sidelong glance. 'Berengaria didn't tell you?'

Adriana shook her head. 'She didn't know. Queen Eleanor never spoke of why the betrothal was broken, but it was she who brought Berengaria to become the king's bride.'

'And what of you?' Liam asked. 'You intend to travel wherever the princess wishes to go? Even to the Holy Land?'

She nodded. 'She has no choice, any more than I do.' The young woman clasped her hands together.

'You could marry or return to your family,' he suggested. 'Jerusalem is dangerous for a woman.'

'Not for me.'

He stared at her, and she sent him a confident smile. 'I have four brothers. I know ways to protect myself.'

'How?' He moved closer, until his knee brushed the edge of her silk gown.

The tip of a knife touched the soft skin above his throat. 'Like this.' Adriana's dark brown eyes were dancing with amusement. 'You wouldn't be likely to harm me now, would you?' She removed the blade and offered it back to him.

Son of Belenus, it was his own blade. She'd somehow stolen it from his belt without him even sensing her.

'How did you do that?'

Her face transformed with a knowing smile. 'You should know better than to underestimate a stranger. I am one of the princess's guards, just as you protect His Majesty.'

It was rare for a woman to surprise him, but he found himself fascinated by Adriana. Her full mouth drew his attention, and her scent reminded him of aromatic spices, like a heady mulled wine.

'Men are often distracted by a woman,' she said. 'Just as you were.'

'You are a distraction,' he agreed. Her expression shifted, and he saw the wariness in her eyes. She wanted nothing from him; that much was evident.

Stepping back, he asked, 'What if your enemy overpowered you? Your strength would be no match for an attacker's.'

'I rely on myself. And I protect the princess when there

is need of my blade.' She squared her shoulders and re-moved his cloak. 'Take this back. You'll be cold.'

'It's far colder than this in my homeland. I'm accustomed to it.' He nodded toward the aft side of the ship. 'Are you wanting me to escort you back to the princess?'

'Not yet.' Lady Adriana took a deep breath. 'She gave me leave to do as I please for the next hour. I'll go back soon enough.' She donned his cloak once more, and the wind buffeted the sails, the sky turning ominous. Within minutes, the rain began to fall. The change in the weather was enough to send the count away from his pursuit. The lady lifted her face to the droplets, smiling wryly. 'Isn't it my ill luck to have rain during the only moments of free-dom I've had?'

Liam ignored the rain and studied the waves. The seawa-ter reflected the grey skies, and as they continued eastward, the waves were rising. 'You should go below, *a chara*. The storm is going to get worse.' Already the oarsmen were fighting the winds, their arms straining to keep control of the ship.

As if in response to his warning, the vessel lurched, and Adriana went flying. Liam caught her before her head could hit the deck, and he steadied her on her feet. 'Are you all right?' She nodded, but he kept her hands at her waist for balance. 'You need to go back to the princess. I wouldn't want you to be swept overboard.'

Her face had gone pale, and she glanced out at the waves. 'How far are we from land?'

'Don't think about that now.' Aye, it was likely that if the ship capsized, they might drown. Liam was a fair enough swimmer, but it was spring and the water would be uncom-fortably cold.

Adriana removed his cloak and handed it to him. 'Take me back to the princess.' Liam donned the garment and walked behind her as she returned to the princess's tiny chamber.

'Stay with Her Royal Highness,' Liam said. 'And tell her not to be afraid.' Even as he spoke the words, he knew they were unconvincing. He was struggling to remain on his feet, and when the ship tossed again, Adriana struck the wall hard.

She rubbed her shoulders, wincing at the pain. 'I'll be all right,' she said before he could ask. 'But promise me something.'

Liam rested his hand against the wall for balance. Adriana stood only inches away, her dark hair resting over the shoulder of her crimson gown. He waited for her to speak, though his gaze was caught by her lips and soft skin.

'If the ship is going to sink, I want to know. We may lose the king's treasure for the Crusade, but I don't want him to lose his bride.' She knew, as he did, that this ship was one of two that held the king's gold and treasure to fund the Crusade.

'If the storm seizes the ship, I'll do what I can to help the sailors,' he said.

Adriana dipped her head in a nod. 'What is your name?'

'Liam MacEgan.'

She studied him, and her expression held doubt. 'You're not like the other men I've seen aboard this ship.'

'Why?'

'You don't behave as though you serve the king. You carry yourself like an equal.'

'Perhaps I am his equal,' he said in a low voice.

Though her gaze said she didn't quite believe him, there was enough hesitancy in her face to suggest that she knew he was not as he seemed to be.

'I'll come for you if the storm worsens,' he promised. Lifting her gloved hand, he pressed his mouth upon it. 'Guard your princess. And I'll guard you.'

But the worry didn't dim in her eyes. If the storm worsened, as he suspected it would, there was a very real chance that all of them would die.

All through the night, Berengaria clung to her bed, praying. She hadn't slept at all, but she clenched the gold-and-ruby-encrusted cross necklace Richard had sent as a gift. Though she'd given him her own token, she didn't know if he valued it in the same way. Her fingers ran along the edges of the jewels, as if they held the warmth of Richard's hands.

She still couldn't believe he had asked for her hand in marriage. Within a matter of months, her life had been utterly changed. Queen Eleanor had escorted her to Sicily, and later, the king's sister, Queen Joan of Sicily, had joined their party as her new companion while Eleanor returned home. The months of travelling were gruelling, but Berengaria's greatest fear was seeing Richard again.

Her predication had come back to haunt her: *You aren't my betrothed husband and never will be.*

How wrong she'd been. Her father had seized the marriage offer from Richard, leaving Berengaria to wonder whether it was Queen Eleanor's idea...or Richard's. She'd been unable to stop thinking about the stolen kiss in the garden. He'd awakened such feelings within her, tremulous thoughts that made her blood quicken.

On their arrival in Sicily, he'd stood awaiting the ship. And later that day, he'd arranged for a private meal with her.

'For once, I can make a royal alliance that pleases me,' he'd said.

Though Berengaria wanted to believe him, her doubts held strong. The table was set so that her chair was at his left, and during the meal, he'd touched her hand several times.

'My lord, why? There are dozens of princesses who would make a stronger alliance for you. Some wealthier than I.'

'It's true that your dowry will help our Crusade. I won't lie about that.' He kissed the knuckles of her hand. 'But I remembered you, long after our ways parted. I wanted you then, just as I do now.'

Her nerves tightened as Richard pulled her to stand. He remained in his chair, his hands sliding about her waist as he drew her to sit on his knee. He was taller than most men, and it brought her face even to his. 'Was I wrong to ask you to wed?'

His steel eyes held hers, and she shook her head. 'I don't suppose a marriage with you would be any different than any other king.'

'It would, *ma chère*. And you know this already.' He brought his hand to caress her cheek. 'I prefer a wife who can speak her mind. One who desires me, as much as I want her.' His fingers stopped at her chin. 'I demand your honesty, Berengaria. Is it your will to be my bride?'

She covered his hand with her own. 'I've never been permitted to choose my husband.' Fear trebled her heartbeat as she lifted her face to his. 'But although you intimidate me, there is no other man I've wanted.'

His mouth curved in a smile. 'Were it not Lent, I would wed you this day.' He brushed a light kiss against her mouth, and she shivered at the sudden rise of heat within her. 'As it is, we'll wait until after Easter and marry before I bring you to Acre.'

She wasn't looking forward to their travels to the Holy Land. Though she understood that this Crusade meant everything to him, she knew that as his queen, she would be the target of assassins.

'I've never been so far from Navarre before,' she admitted. 'And I can't say that I wish to live so close to the war.'

His face hardened. 'You doubt my ability to keep you safe?'

'No. But if you are away fighting—'

'I protect what belongs to me,' he asserted. Taking her hand, he led her away from her ladies and his attendants. A tall Oriental screen, decorated with flowers and birds, stood in the corner. Richard took her behind it, giving them what privacy he could.

'Berengaria,' he whispered, framing her face with his hands. 'From the first moment I saw you, you cast a spell over me.' His hands slid down her cheeks, and the caress made her breath catch. When she touched his hands with hers, he leaned in for a kiss.

Just as before, the brush of his mouth was searching, kindling a response that she didn't understand. He drew her against the far wall, the wood pressing against her spine as his mouth moved away from her lips, down to her throat.

'There's no reason for you to be afraid,' he said against her skin. 'Not of the Saracens. And not of me.'

She ventured a shaky smile, catching his hands. 'I can't stop my fear. Whenever I'm near you, I can hardly breathe.'

He moved in, pulling her hips to his. 'That isn't fear, *ma chère*. It's desire.' His mouth moved to her throat, kissing her softly. 'I don't want you to breathe. I want to possess every part of you. And were it not a sin, I would claim you tonight.

'We'll wed in the Holy Land,' he swore. With another smile, he added, 'You'll have to travel on a different ship than me, Berengaria. Otherwise, I won't be able to keep my hands from you.' He stole another soft kiss and released her. He brought her the gold-and-ruby-encrusted cross necklace, fastening it around her throat. 'Take this token, and think of me when you're asleep at night.'

Berengaria held on to the necklace, tracing the rough gold. The ship heaved in the water, and she gripped her skirts, terrified of being flung across the room.

'Are we going to die?' she whispered to her lady-in-waiting, Adriana.

The young woman came and gripped her hand. 'The king's man assured me that he would let us know if we were in danger. It's just a bad storm.'

Though Berengaria wanted to believe it, instinct told her otherwise. The king's sister, Queen Joan, reached for a strand of rosary beads, dropping to her knees in prayer.

A loud knocking resounded at the door, and her gaze snapped toward the sound. Adriana hurried to answer it, and a tall man stood at the entrance. He had dark blond hair and grey eyes, and he wore a black cloak fastened with a brooch the size of her palm.

'My lord MacEgan?' Adriana addressed the man.

Berengaria saw the look that passed between them, and it escalated her fear. 'Are we going to sink?' she interrupted.

'We're near the coast of Cyprus,' MacEgan said. 'The captain is going to divert the ship towards the shore, so that if the worst happens—'

'—we can swim to the shore,' Berengaria finished.

She turned away from them, her eyes burning. She couldn't swim at all. If the ship capsized or sank, she was going to die. Her hand clenched into a fist around the necklace, and she tried to quell the terror that rose up inside.

Then, a loud cracking noise resounded, and the ship tipped violently.

It was less than an hour before water came pouring within the ship. Adriana's feet were soaked, and she left Berengaria with the king's sister while she went in search of MacEgan.

He'd kept his word, and she trusted that he would tell her the truth. She saw him rowing alongside the other sailors, his arms straining against the oars as the men fought against the sea's power. Adriana took one of the ropes and wound it around her arm as she moved forward. On one side of the ship, she saw half a dozen men bailing water with buckets.

As soon as he saw her standing there, MacEgan yelled at one of the men to take his place at the oars. He fought his way toward her and gripped another rope to hold his balance.

'I told you to stay with the princess!' he yelled over the roar of the storm.

Adriana's arm wrenched with the motion of the rope, and MacEgan pulled her back, unfastening the rope and guiding her to him. His grey eyes glared at hers. 'You could have been tossed overboard.'

'We're going to die anyway, aren't we?' Her hands were shaking, her clothing soaked from the rain and the seawater.

Liam kept her in his arms, warming her shoulders. 'Not if I can help it.' He nodded outside. 'We're only a few miles from the shore.'

'And we're sinking.' She gripped his shirt, her feet frigid in the cold water. 'We don't have time to reach land.'

He kept his hands around her waist, and she made no effort to push them away. 'Listen to me.' His voice was commanding, reaching inside her to push back the fear. 'If the worst happens, swim as hard as you can toward the shore. I'll find you.'

Her hands were shaking, and she felt his arms come around her, as if to offer shelter from her fear. 'I won't let anything happen to you,' he murmured.

Despite the freezing water and rain, there was a steady warmth in his embrace. Her instinct was to trust him, to let herself believe that there was a man whom she could believe in…unlike her father and brothers, who had betrayed her.

'Now return to the princess and Queen Joan,' he insisted. 'And we'll get as close to the shore as we can.'

She held on to his forearms, as if she could take a piece of his courage with her. Then, unexpectedly, he leaned down and touched his lips to hers. 'For luck,' he said.

He left her standing there, while he went back to the others.

The ship was going down. Liam knew it with a surety in his blood, but he'd be damned before he'd let the sea claim him. The vessel shuddered, and it was reaching the breaking point. They couldn't bail the water out fast enough, and now it was only a matter of time before they abandoned the ship.

He let out a curse as another wave soaked the deck. A moment later, the women appeared, their gowns sodden above the waist. Adriana led them forward, holding Princess Berengaria's hand. Queen Joan followed behind, gripping a strand of rosary beads.

Liam gathered the women together and pointed toward the shore. 'We're doing what we can to stay above water as long as we can. But if the sea takes us, try to make it towards land.'

The princess's face was white, her hands gripped together. 'I can't swim.'

He gave a nod and surveyed the others. 'What of the rest of you?'

'I can,' Adriana said. Queen Joan nodded as well.

'Try to stay together,' Liam urged. To the princess, he added, 'If the ship breaks apart, hold on to the largest piece of wood you can find. It will keep you afloat.'

The vessel started to tip as the lower quarters filled with water. Liam heard their shrieks, and saw Adriana lunge toward one of the younger maids, who was pulled under by the force of the water. She caught the girl's hand, struggling to hold on, but the sea fought to keep its prey.

'Adriana, no!' Berengaria cried out. And then both women disappeared beneath the water.

Chapter Two

Liam fought to catch the women, but it was too late. His lungs burned as he swam underwater, his eyes unable to see them in the darkness. He swept his arms through the water, reaching for them. His fingers touched wood, but no flesh. He dived deeper, kicking hard through the water, and suddenly his hand gripped a length of silk.

He pulled hard, the water fighting against him to drag the woman down. And when at last he managed to bring her head above water, Adriana coughed, her body shaking. He saw that she was still holding the other woman's hand, and when he pulled the maid above water, she was lifeless, her limbs unmoving.

His efforts to revive the maid met with no success, and Adriana broke down in tears.

'You tried,' he said, holding her tightly. 'Her life was in God's hands.'

'I thought I could save her,' Adriana whispered, her body trembling hard. 'Before the water took her under. '

He let her cry, holding her against him. Her arms embraced him, and strangely, it brought him his own sense of calm. In her courage, he saw a piece of himself. She'd gone after the young maid with no fear, never minding that she'd nearly lost her own life in the effort.

Liam helped bring Adriana to the side of the ship. Berengaria gripped a large rope, but terror lingered in her eyes. 'When the water fills the remainder of the lower chambers, the ship may split in half,' he told her. 'If that happens, be ready to let go of the rope or you might be pulled under. Hold on to any piece of the deck you can find.' The princess's face was white with fear, and Adriana took her place at Berengaria's side, Queen Joan at the other.

'MacEgan,' came Adriana's voice softly. He looked into her dark eyes, and she steadied herself. 'You saved my life.'

'I kept my promise,' he answered, 'to let nothing happen to you.' But even so, the sea had claimed one life. He only prayed it would be the last.

Within minutes, Berengaria watched in horror as the ship split apart, the wood fragmenting beneath her feet. She held fast to the side of the boat, but she was plunged into the frigid water without warning. Her head went below the surface and she tasted salt.

She struggled, trying not to panic, when an arm caught her waist and forced her above the surface. She took a deep breath, and saw MacEgan holding her. He swam away from the wreckage, guiding her toward a large section of the ship. 'Hold this,' he ordered. Her fingers dug into the wooden surface, and she gripped it with all her strength. Then Adriana joined her, while Joan floated on a piece of wood further away.

She lost track of time, but Adriana never left her side. Her lady-in-waiting fought to swim with the current, bringing them closer to shore. From time to time, Liam adjusted their direction, swimming alongside them. Though he ensured that each of the women were safe, Berengaria didn't miss the way he was watching Adriana. There was an intensity in his eyes, as though the young lady meant something to him.

Her heart faltered, for Richard had looked at her that way on the first day they'd met. Sometimes a single flicker of interest was all that was needed to give rise to the seedling of love.

Will I see him again? she wondered. She rested her head against the wood, her body exhausted from the immense force of the storm. Along the edge of the sea, the sky had grown lighter, the rose of dawn painting the edge of the grey water. And after endless hours, her feet touched the sand.

An unexpected laugh broke forth, and she beamed at her lady-in-waiting. 'Adriana, we're going to live.' They struggled towards the shore, their skirts weighing them down, while Liam escorted them forward.

The storm had ceased, and pieces of blue sky broke through the clouds. The waves had grown calmer, though Berengaria still struggled to keep her balance in the waist-high water. Ahead, she saw the Count of Berduria, who had reached the sandy beach before any of them.

Within moments, men on horseback emerged along the shoreline, their armour gleaming in the sunlight. Liam drew close to the women. 'Don't trust them,' he warned. 'We don't know anything about the Cypriots.'

Berengaria's smile faded, and the chill of the water made

her nerves grow uneasy. A few yards away, Queen Joan was walking out of the water towards the shore.

'Do not tell them who you are,' Liam warned, but the young woman made no indication that she'd heard him.

He started to move toward the queen, but Adriana caught his arm. 'Be careful, MacEgan.'

His grey eyes studied hers, and he covered her hand with his. 'Wait here.'

He made his way towards Joan, and Berengaria eyed Adriana. 'He means something to you, doesn't he?'

Adriana didn't answer, nor did she pull her gaze away from MacEgan. 'I only met him a day ago. And yet it feels like far longer.'

'He *is* handsome,' Berengaria admitted, 'but not as handsome as Richard.' Her voice held more melancholy than she'd intended. Inwardly, she worried that she would not see the king again. She might die a maiden, before ever becoming a bride.

'Were it not for him, I would have drowned,' Adriana whispered.

Berengaria took her lady's hand in hers, and they walked together towards the shoreline. Although MacEgan was trying to bring Queen Joan closer to them, she ignored him and kept walking away.

The Count of Berduria had reached the men and was speaking to them. Although they remained mounted, Adriana tensed.

'Something's wrong,' she predicted. Her hand went to her leg, where Berengaria knew her lady-in-waiting kept a knife. 'MacEgan was right. Stay close to me.'

She didn't understand what bothered Adriana so, and when she asked, the woman replied, 'If you saw a shipwreck, wouldn't you try to help the survivors? These men are only watching.'

With a glance behind her, Berengaria saw that three other ships had also been blown off course and were anchored less than a mile from the shore. 'Should we try to reach those ships?'

'Not yet.'

Both of them watched as the count spoke to the men. His tone held arrogance, but Berengaria thought she heard him speaking Greek to the men. Queen Joan had already reached the shore and was preparing to join the count. The woman marched forward, her bearing filled with pride. The count pointed to her, and then to Berengaria and Adriana.

'Don't tell them,' Adriana whispered, as if pleading for the man to remain silent.

But it was too late. To her horror, one of the armed men unsheathed his sword and plunged it into the count's chest. The nobleman sank to his knees, falling against the sand while his lifeblood spilled out.

Saints deliver us. Berengaria covered her mouth, shocked by what she'd just seen. Queen Joan grasped her skirts and fled back to the water. Liam called out for her to come toward them, and he reached them a moment later.

Berengaria couldn't stop from shaking, and from the gleam in the soldiers' eyes, she didn't know if she would become a prisoner or die the moment she emerged from the water.

'The count told them who you are,' he said grimly. 'Our best hope is that they take you hostage.'

But Berengaria knew that MacEgan's life was in greater danger than her own. Already these men had killed the count, so it was clear they had no use for the men. 'You need to swim hard towards the other three ships anchored off the coast,' she ordered. 'If you reach one of them, you can sail back and alert Richard.'

'I can't leave you here alone.'

The horsemen started to ride forward, and their time was running out. 'You must,' Berengaria insisted. 'If what you say is true, then they won't kill us because they'll want to use our lives to bargain with Richard. If you stay, your fate will be the same as the count's.'

His face hardened, but she saw her words were breaking through to him. 'Go, MacEgan. I am commanding you, as your future queen.'

An unnamed expression crossed his face, and she remembered that he was Irish, not English. Correcting herself, she added, 'Please. Go to Richard.'

Before he could move, the soldiers charged forward with their horses. Armed men surrounded them, with spears and swords raised as a visible threat. Berengaria held her breath, not knowing what to do now. The soldiers reached for MacEgan, but he made no effort to fight.

In the Norman tongue, he commanded, 'Obey their orders.' His eyes met Adriana's, and she saw the softer assurance within them. 'I'll return to you. I swear it.'

MacEgan moved so fast, Berengaria barely had time to get out of the way. It took only seconds for him to drag a soldier down from his horse, smashing his fist into the man's face. When a second man tried to stab him with a spear, MacEgan grasped the weapon, twisting it free of the soldier's hands. Now armed, he seized the first soldier's horse and rode the animal hard along the shoreline, forcing the others to follow. Three men remained behind with her and Adriana, one of them seizing Queen Joan.

Berengaria held her breath as MacEgan reached the deeper water. He stood on the horse's back and dived into the waves, disappearing from view. Adriana clung to her, hot tears breaking free.

'Don't be afraid,' Berengaria whispered to her lady-in-waiting. 'I believe him. He'll find a way to send a rescue.'

But when they didn't see him resurface above the waves, she feared the worst.

The Isle of Rhodes, April 22, 1191

'Where are they, Sir Bernard?' King Richard demanded.

The knight's face paled. 'We—we don't know, Your Majesty. There are twenty-five ships missing, and unfortunately, Princess Berengaria's was among them.' He lowered his head in regret. 'We believe the storm may have blown them off course.'

'There were two hundred and nineteen ships, Bernard.' Richard fought to keep his temper under control. 'And you mean to tell me that not one of them saw where Berengaria's ship disappeared?'

'I'm sorry, Your Majesty. But we'll send out ships to search for your bride—'

'Out,' Richard ordered, pointing towards the door. The knight fled, like the coward he was. Right now, Richard's temper was about to break loose. Crete and Rhodes were meant to be rendezvous points, where they would stop for a few days en route to Acre. But his betrothed wife wasn't on either island.

She might be dead, her body resting at the bottom of

the Mediterranean Sea. He expelled a breath, imagining Berengaria's dark hair, her lovely eyes and form. He'd been looking forward to marrying her, understanding what sort of woman lay behind the unbridled honesty. He hardly knew her at all, but her spirit intrigued him.

Outside, the sky was clear, the sun bright and warm. The deep azure water nestled against white sand, an idyllic place to walk with a lover. He traced the emerald ring that lay upon his smallest finger. She'd given it to him in Sicily, a token that had aroused strong memories of the night he'd first taken it from her. Seeing it now only fuelled his anger. He would find her, no matter how long it took. She belonged to him.

He gestured for a servant to summon one of the ships' captains. If no one could find the women or the ships containing the treasures for his Crusade, he would stop on every island en route to Syria.

But when the captain arrived, he bowed and pleaded, 'Your Majesty, we have news of the princess.'

Moments later, the Irish prince, Liam MacEgan, emerged from among the men. The man looked as though he hadn't slept in days, and bloodstains marred his face.

'They are at Cyprus, Your Majesty.' MacEgan drew closer, lowering his voice so that only Richard could hear. 'Soldiers took the women captive.'

'Come.' Richard wanted no other men to hear what MacEgan had to reveal. He brought the man within his chamber and ordered, 'Tell me what you know.'

'The Cypriots murdered the Count of Berduria,' the Irishman explained. 'Afterwards, Princess Berengaria bade me to seek help, so I swam to one of the ships nearby, and we sailed west. We found your galleys here.'

Richard's gaze narrowed. 'You left the women un-guarded.'

MacEgan met his gaze with no fear. 'Your bride gave me a direct order to seek help. Would you have me disobey her?'

'If her life is harmed in any way, I'll take yours.' Richard used his height to his advantage, staring down at the Irish prince.

MacEgan didn't back down, but chose his words carefully. 'The women will be safe enough. The princess's lady-in-waiting is as good as any trained guard. I've seen it myself.'

Though Richard didn't like it, he didn't doubt that Isaac Ducas Comnenus, the Emperor of Cyprus, would want to use Berengaria to further his own purpose. The man was allied with Saladin, and it was rumoured that they had drunk each other's blood, as an oath of loyalty.

The idea of his betrothed wife falling into the hands of the emperor was unthinkable. Richard stared hard at MacEgan.

'Tell no one that Berengaria and the queen were taken captive,' Richard warned. If anyone learned that his be-trothed wife was in the custody of the enemy, they would believe that she'd been violated, whether or not it was true. He wanted nothing to threaten their marriage alliance.

'Let them believe that Berengaria and the queen re-mained on board one of the other ships. Tell them that the emperor invited them to disembark, but they refused.'

MacEgan nodded, understanding the implications. 'No one will know.'

'I will send you with a group of men to attack the coast

of Cyprus. Find the women, and bring them back to me alive.'

Richard returned to his place by the window, dismissing MacEgan. His gaze fixated upon the sea. If Isaac Comnenus had threatened Berengaria in any way...God help the man. For Richard would tear him apart.

Limassol, Cyprus, May 1191

Nearly three weeks had passed, and there was no sign of Liam MacEgan or the king. Adriana had seen the princess's hope fading from her eyes, as they realised that they would remain prisoners of the emperor. Although Isaac Comnenus had not bound them in chains, they were locked in a chamber guarded inside and out. There was no privacy at all, and though she tried to shield the princess from the humiliation, there was little Adriana could do. The guards cast lots for the right to guard the interior of the chamber where they hoped to catch a glimpse of them.

Queen Joan never stopped complaining. From the moment they'd been taken captive, she'd made outrageous demands, for which the emperor had mocked her. When she'd insisted upon softer beds, he'd sent her a length of silk, removing the only mattress in the room. That night, they'd huddled together on a wooden floor, with nothing but the silk.

Joan had refused to humble herself, and they'd endured weeks of stale food and uncomfortable living conditions. But it was the princess who concerned Adriana the most. Berengaria had grown so thin over the weeks, her face pale while she stared for hours on end at the sea outside their barred window.

'We're not going to be rescued, are we?' she whispered. 'The crusaders who came on those ships…they're dead, aren't they?'

The remaining two ships had arrived only hours after their imprisonment, but the emperor had seized control of them, taking the king's treasure and murdering the men. From their window, they'd seen the bodies of the crusaders, displayed like bloody prizes of war.

Adriana tried to reassure the princess. 'The emperor knows Richard will come. He wouldn't bother with guarding the shore otherwise.' She crossed the small room and pointed to the hills where the Cypriots were bringing down carts filled with wood and stone. Over the next few hours, the men set out large stones, chests, doors of wood and all manner of building materials to fortify the beach.

One of their guards stepped in front of the window, barring their view. Though he could not speak their language, his message was clear. Adriana hesitated before moving back, sending him a slight smile as she withdrew.

The distraction was enough, and she stole his curved knife, hiding it behind her back. If the Cypriots were preparing for battle, it meant that an invasion was imminent.

The door to their chamber swung open, and a young maiden appeared, trailed by two of her ladies. She gave a sharp order to the guards, and they obeyed the command, leaving the room. In heavily accented French, she said, 'I have been ordered to bring the princess and the queen to my father.' Adriana remained against the wall for a moment, slipping the guard's curved blade beneath the girdle at her waist, just behind her back. Neither Joan nor Berengaria moved forward, but while the guard was focused upon the noblewomen, Adriana donned the princess's cloak to hide the knife.

'Why does he want to see us?' Berengaria asked, her voice calm. But Adriana knew that the soft voice hid the young woman's fears. All of them knew that they had been kept alive only to be used as hostages...or worse.

The young girl shook her head. 'I do not know.' She wrinkled her nose when they drew closer and added, 'I will arrange for you to bathe and refresh yourselves before you are presented to him.'

Berengaria cast a worried look back at her, but Adriana nodded. The girl's offer was made in good faith. To the princess, she said, 'If they intended to kill us, they would not bother with the way we look now.'

'That's what I am afraid of,' Berengaria said.

She closed her eyes, and Adriana went to her side. 'He probably wants to prove to Richard that we are well, despite the captivity.'

Berengaria reached for her hand and Adriana took it. As they followed the girl down the winding stairs, she took them into a walled garden. The warmth of the sun and the lush fragrance of jasmine flowers lifted her spirits, though she was more reassured by the weapon she'd hidden.

As the girl brought them up another set of stone stairs, Adriana drew Berengaria to a stop and pointed towards the sea. There, she spied the sails of nearly a hundred ships.

'They've found us,' Berengaria breathed with thankfulness.

Adriana wondered if Liam MacEgan had alerted the king. Or whether he was still alive. She remembered the light kiss he'd stolen for luck, and the memory darkened her heart with regret. The handsome Irishman had been like no other man she'd met. Brave and strong, he was one she'd wanted to know better.

When the young girl took them within her own chambers, she arranged for them to bathe in privacy and offered them clothing in the Cyprian style. Though Berengaria refused to wear the foreign garments, Adriana agreed to try them. The soft diaphanous fabric was like nothing she'd ever felt against her skin. She wore a cream-coloured anteri tunic and soft salvar trousers. Though it was strange, not to be wearing skirts, she liked the clothing.

'You must feel like a concubine,' Berengaria teased. 'I can't imagine wearing clothes like that.'

Queen Joan stiffened, smoothing her own silk gown. 'I prefer not to look like a savage.'

The princess's mood dimmed at Joan's words. Adriana adjusted a fold of her clothing and admitted, 'It's more comfortable than what we were wearing earlier.' But she had other reasons for wearing the new clothes. If she needed to defend the princess against an attack, the lighter trousers gave her more freedom of movement.

The girl led them from her chamber to a large, open pavilion. The sun had grown hotter, and though Adriana tried to see if any of the ships had come closer, the walls were too high to view them.

The emperor awaited them upon a throne inlaid with gold, while servants waved palm branches over his head to provide cooler air.

With the help of a servant who translated, the emperor announced, 'The invaders have come for you. My men have seized the treasures that were within your ships, and your king must decide which he wants returned to him. His gold...or his bride.'

Berengaria's face changed, and there was anger within it that Adriana had never seen. The princess stood tall, and whispered in the Norman language, 'Adriana, when they take us back, I want you to make your escape. Tell the king what has happened to us. Make certain he knows where we are.'

'I'm not leaving your side,' she insisted. She couldn't rely on Joan to protect Berengaria, not when the queen might say something to offend the emperor.

'They'll use us for bargaining. But I worry about your life.' The princess reached out and squeezed her hand. 'Forgive me, but you have no value to them. They may use you as an example.'

Though Adriana didn't like it at all, she understood what the princess meant. No doubt Isaac Comnenus would display the queen and princess, using them as leverage to get what he wanted from Richard.

'I don't want you to die,' Berengaria insisted. 'I'm afraid for you, if you stay.'

Adriana bowed her head in acquiescence, but inwardly she knew if anyone discovered her, she would be killed. Either way, her life was in danger.

Isaac looked displeased with their private conversation, and he ordered his men to separate them. Adriana was dragged away from the princess, who gave her a nod of permission.

As the guard brought her back towards the courtyard, Adriana studied their surroundings, wondering how she could possibly break free. Her gaze settled upon some of the women who had veiled their faces.

And then she knew exactly what to do.

* * *

Just before dawn, Liam MacEgan rowed alongside the other men, bringing the smaller boats closer to the shore. The beach was covered with obstructions meant to prevent them from using war horses. It wouldn't stop Richard, however. Already, several of the smaller boats were within distance that the horses could swim to the shore. Liam's task was to bring the soldiers close enough to clear a path.

The archers launched a shower of arrows upon the Cypriots, and from the chaos, it was clear that they'd taken them by surprise. When they reached shallow water, Liam unsheathed his sword and charged forward with the others. His blood raced with fear and the thrill of fighting. He'd been trained by his father and uncles since he was old enough to hold a sword, and as he faced his enemy, it soon became clear that these men were not warriors.

Farmers and merchants, they'd been ordered by their emperor to defend the land…but without weapons, they were dying by the hundreds. Liam stopped attacking and moved into a defensive posture. Only if they made the first move would they taste his sword.

As they moved past the enemy, they climbed uphill toward the city. The grey morning light was starting to illuminate the ancient Roman ruins dotting the landscape. Nearer to the centre lay the fortress where Liam suspected the princess and queen were held captive. Adriana would be among them.

The image of her face remained strong within his mind, with her beautiful dark eyes and slim form. She had more courage than any other woman he'd met, for she was a survivor. He'd hated leaving them here, but without Richard knowing their whereabouts, there could be no rescue.

When they reached the fortress, it appeared to be con-

structed around the ruins of an old basilica. Liam ordered
his men to fall back, and they retreated behind one of the
stone buildings. He needed to study the defences, to de-
termine the best approach. Aye, they could likely make
it through the front gate, but without knowing how many
guardsmen were waiting, it could endanger his men un-
necessarily.

He lifted his gaze to the upper segment of the fortress,
for he suspected the princess and queen were being held in
a fortified location. He hadn't told any of the men about the
prisoners, only that they were to seek information about the
emperor's defences. Just when he had decided to lead his
men along the outer walls, he heard the sound of a confron-
tation nearby with men shouting orders.

He gestured for two of the men to follow him while the
others retreated along the left side of the fortress. Liam ran
lightly, his hand resting upon his sword. Ahead, he spied
a veiled woman running through the streets. Two guards
pursued her, and it was clear that their speed was overtak-
ing hers. He was torn between helping the woman and remaining focused upon their mission. But when the woman
saw them, instead of fleeing, she ran straight towards them.

She didn't make it. One of the guards grasped her by the
veil and jerked her backwards. When the man unsheathed
a curved blade, Liam didn't stop to think, but charged forward, a roar tearing from his mouth. The guard's attention
shifted just long enough for Liam to drive his own sword
into the man's gut.

Shocked eyes met his, but the blade fell from his enemy's hand and he let go of the woman. When the other
guard caught up, he took one look at his fallen companion
and fled.

A curse slipped from Liam's mouth. Their chances of infiltrating the fortress would be gone as soon as the man alerted the others. He sheathed his weapon, and held out his hand to the woman. He couldn't have been more surprised when she suddenly threw herself into his arms.

Berengaria's heart beat so fast, she could hardly catch her breath. The emperor had ordered her and Queen Joan bound with silken ropes, and neither of them had slept last night while they awaited Richard's arrival. From the hundreds of ships that lined the coast, Berengaria had no doubt that the men would come soon.

The question was, what would the emperor do with them, once the king's men arrived? Though she wanted to believe that Richard cared enough about her to bargain for her life, she didn't know.

It seemed like almost a dream when she'd seen him last in Sicily. But his kiss lingered with her still. She stared out into the blinding sun, twisting her fingers around the chain of the jewelled cross that hung hidden beneath her gown.

Hours passed, and she ignored the food and drink that were offered to her. From deep within, she reached for courage. If Adriana were there, her lady-in-waiting would offer words of encouragement, insisting that they would be rescued. And though she knew that her friend had managed to escape, using the blade she'd stolen from their guard, she was afraid of what would happen if they caught her. They wouldn't hesitate to take her life, in return for the men Adriana had wounded. Berengaria closed her eyes, hoping to God that the young woman was still alive.

The noise of battle rose within the air like the rumbling of thunder, and Berengaria's heart raced as crusaders surrounded the fortress. She lost count of the dozens of armoured men who poured through the gates and tried not to stare at the death and destruction that was happening all around her.

At last, she spied Richard. He was mounted on horseback, fully armed, and his chain mail glinted with gold and silver. Tall and strong, he rode forward, his sword cutting down the men who dared to oppose him. She understood now why they named him Lionheart, for not once did he flinch in battle. When he finally spied her, she couldn't stop the smile that broke forth. The look in his eyes was filled with relief, and she wanted nothing more than to race forward and fall into his arms.

But something reflected against her eyes, forcing her to look up. It was then that she saw the dozens of archers with their bows drawn…aimed directly at her and Joan.

Chapter Three

Liam kept Adriana close to his side. It hadn't taken long to find the princess and queen, given Isaac Comnenus's desire to display them. Richard had responded by bringing the full force of his army to attack Limassol, and his warships had moved into position, surrounding the Isle of Cyprus.

Isaac was going to lose this battle, and he knew it. The only question was whether or not they could rescue Princess Berengaria and Queen Joan in time.

Though Liam didn't like bringing a woman into battle with him, neither could he leave Adriana behind. She had a blade palmed in her hand, and she remained at his side. Unlike most women, she didn't cower at the sight of blood or death. Instead her eyes were alert, her body poised to fight if needed.

He'd never met another woman like her. She fascinated him, and when this was over, he intended to pursue her openly.

When they reached the centre of the fortress, Isaac Comnenus had grown pale. Liam suspected that the emperor hadn't known how vast Richard's forces were. It had taken only a matter of hours to take Limassol, and now the man's life lay in the king's hands.

With the help of a translator, the emperor came forward to speak with Richard. 'An invasion was not necessary. We could have negotiated a truce between us.'

Liam saw the king's mouth twitch, as if Richard were struggling to hold back his temper. 'And why would I seek to negotiate with a man who seized my betrothed wife and my sister, stealing our treasures and murdering my soldiers?' He gestured for two dozen of his men to come forward, surrounding the king.

'If I signal my archers, your women will die,' the emperor responded.

'If you harm them, so shall your daughter die.' Richard nodded towards the back of the fortress where several soldiers held a young girl captive. She was sobbing with fear, knowing that her life lay in the soldiers' hands.

The emperor's face reddened with fury. And then, when he gave a signal, Liam glanced up to see the archers poised. Adriana wrenched the shield free of his arms, and he watched in horror as she threw herself in front of the princess and queen. Half a dozen arrows embedded within the wood, and Liam followed her lead, seizing another shield to protect Berengaria and Joan.

God above, Adriana could have been killed. She hadn't hesitated to offer her life for the princess's, and he hadn't known how it would feel to see her in such danger. Both of them held their shields steady, protecting the women.

Arrows shot through the sky, taking down the emperor's archers, until at last the fighting ceased within the fortress.

Isaac was now the king's prisoner, and Richard had taken possession of Cyprus.

'Don't move,' Liam ordered Adriana. 'This isn't over yet.'

She ventured an unsteady smile. 'I'll be glad when it is.'

'Your Majesty,' the emperor begged, 'I wish there to be peace between us. As compensation for your losses, I will offer twenty thousand gold marks. In addition, I offer my only daughter as your hostage and I will join my men with yours to fight on Crusade.'

Soldiers gripped Isaac's arms, and Richard moved in, towering above the man. 'We will discuss the terms later.'

'Not in irons, Your Majesty. I beg of you, do not place me in irons.'

A strange smile came over the king's face when he unsheathed a dagger at his waist, slashing through the silk bonds of Berengaria and Joan. 'As you will,' he agreed. And when the emperor had been taken into custody, Richard flashed a smile to his knights. 'Have his chains made of silver.'

The king moved forward and Liam drew back with Adriana. Her body relaxed against him, and he held her near as Richard took Berengaria into his arms, kissing her. The warmth of Adriana, the softness of her hair against his cheek, felt right. And when she touched her fingertips to her own lips, he wondered if her thoughts mirrored his own.

The next day, Berengaria's stomach felt like a thousand wings were fluttering inside it. Adriana had spent hours helping her to bathe, dressing her in a gown of blue silk embroidered in silver. Her hair was parted in the centre with a transparent veil of the same length, covering it in the style of a *mantilla*. Upon her head rested a diadem with several bands of jewels and *fleurs-de-lis* with enough foliage to resemble a double crown. At her throat, she'd chosen to wear the ruby-encrusted cross that Richard had given. And as a gift to her future husband, she'd given a gold belt inlaid with jewels.

'You look beautiful,' Adriana pronounced, stepping back to arrange Berengaria's train. Soon, it was time for her to join the king.

When she saw Richard riding to greet her at the chapel of St George, Berengaria couldn't stop her smile. His Spanish steed had a bejewelled golden saddle with two lions upon it, and the horse's bit was also made of gold. He looked so handsome wearing a satin rose tunic bound by the golden belt she'd given him, while a striped silver tissue mantle rested about his shoulders. A silver sheath encased his sword of Damascus steel with a golden hilt.

Upon his head he wore a scarlet bonnet, brocaded in gold, with figures of animals. As he dismounted, he walked forward with a truncheon in one hand to show his power over the Cypriots. His reddish-gold hair glinted in the bright sun, while in the distance, the sea gleamed like a sapphire.

As he took her hand in his, her heart filled up with happiness. No other man had ever made her feel this way, and she couldn't have dreamed of a more beautiful island to be married upon. The warm air held the deep scent of jasmine from the vines growing up the stone walls.

I could love him, she realised. And from the answering look on his face, she felt honoured to be his wife.

After they spoke their vows, the Bishop of Evreaux offered blessings upon them and finished the mass. Berengaria took Richard's arm, and she was then anointed and crowned Queen of England and of Cyprus.

The cheers of the men resonated throughout the old fortress, but Berengaria didn't care about her new title. She had eyes only for the man who had rescued her from harm, the one who took her hands in his.

'I'm glad you didn't have to wear chain-mail armour to our wedding,' she teased. Richard leaned in and stole a kiss, drawing her close. The warmth of his mouth and the eagerness of his passion made her cling to him as though he could steady the beating of her pulse.

'I would wear sackcloth and ashes, if it meant having you as my bride,' he answered. His hands moved over her spine, as if he couldn't wait to touch her in the privacy of their chamber.

'All my life, I've never been allowed to choose anything for myself,' Berengaria admitted. 'Having you as my husband is a gift I never expected. But had I been given a choice, it would have been you.'

Richard grasped her waist, and he lifted her up until her face met his. All around them, she heard the sounds of celebration, the feasting and drinking…and the laughter of their people.

'It won't be easy when we journey to the Holy Land,' Richard admitted. 'But now that God has given you back to me, I must complete the vow I've made.'

She touched his face with her hands. 'And no matter what comes, we'll be together.'

The moon hung bright in the sky, and Adriana walked barefoot, with Liam's hand in hers. She carried her shoes in her other hand, revelling in the intimate feel of the silken sand against her soles.

They walked in silence for long moments, until Liam led her up the side of a hill. In the distance, he pointed to a large rock rising from the sea.

'A legend says that the goddess Aphrodite rose from the sea, near that stone.'

'The goddess of love,' she murmured quietly, sitting back against the grasses.

Liam joined her, and the look in his eyes made her shiver. 'She wouldn't compare to you.' His hand moved up to push a lock of her hair aside, and Adriana felt her blood rising like the tide of the sea.

He laid her back against the grass, his hands resting against her wrists. 'The first kiss I gave you wasn't the one I wanted to claim.'

'Then show me what you wanted,' Adriana bade him.

When he kissed her, the first touch of his mouth was like a fire she'd never before tasted. His hungry lips plundered hers until she could no longer catch her breath. With his tongue, he tasted the softness of her mouth, inviting her to open for him. And when he invaded the softness of her mouth, her body responded with need.

His hands moved over her shoulders, down to her waist, and when his body moved atop hers, she felt the length of his desire.

'Who are you, Liam MacEgan?' she murmured against his mouth. 'You're like no one I've met before.'

'A man who desires you more than anything in this world.' He rolled onto his side, and her legs twined with his. She didn't care that this was improper, for there was no one to see. Her own family had sold her into the princess's service, and their betrayal left an emptiness inside her. But Liam had filled up the loneliness, offering a hope she'd never expected.

She lifted her arms around his neck, pressing her breasts against his firm chest. 'When we reach the Holy Land, you'll be gone from me.'

'I'll fight for a time,' he admitted, 'but I'll not let you go.' He bent and took her mouth again, coaxing her to cast aside her inhibitions and take him as her lover.

'You'll go back to Ireland when this is over,' she said, 'and I'll remain with Queen Berengaria.' She didn't like to think of it, though she knew there was no other choice.

'If it is your will, I can take you with me, back to my homeland.' He rested his cheek against hers, pulling her into a tight embrace. The confidence in his voice, the assurance that the king and queen would follow his own wishes, struck her as impossible.

But Liam MacEgan had never behaved like the king's servant. And the more she thought of it, Richard had never treated him as such.

'You're not a merchant or a serf, are you?' she ventured. 'You're more than a warrior.'

'Does it matter who I am?'

'I wouldn't care if you were a beggar,' she admitted. 'I would take you for the man you are.'

'And what if I were a prince?' He raised up, touching her shoulder as his grey eyes stared into hers. 'Would that bother you?'

In his face, she saw a sudden tension. It was true, she realised. This man was not a commoner, but a man of royalty...just as Richard was.

'It would only bother me if you left me behind,' she said softly. 'I want to know the man you are.'

He sat up and brought her into his lap, holding her close to stare out at the sea. 'My father is King of Laochre, a small kingdom within Ireland. Not a High King,' he admitted. 'But I have responsibilities to our people. I came seeking an adventure.' He brushed a kiss against her temple. 'But instead I found you.'

She laughed softly. 'If the past few weeks are any evidence, every day with you will be an adventure.'

'But I'll keep you safe,' he offered. 'I give you my solemn promise.'

She lifted her mouth to his, giving him the answer hidden inside her. And when he enfolded her in his arms, she could imagine nothing but a future with him…the prince of her heart.

* * * * *

Author Note

Sometimes truth is stranger than fiction. When I began researching the story of King Richard I and Berengaria, the journey towards their wedding day had all the elements of an adventure. A shipwreck, crusaders being captured, and the King himself overthrowing the ruler of Cyprus to rescue his bride... It was enormously entertaining to research the true-life details.

It is widely believed that Richard was introduced to Berengaria years before they were married, and that there was an attraction between them. However, my sources could not quite pinpoint the exact year when he visited Navarre. I have taken a slight historical licence in predicting the year when he might have met her. Queen Eleanor of Aquitaine did bring Berengaria to Sicily to meet with Richard and to arrange their betrothal. Richard caused a controversy with King Philip II of France when he set aside his betrothal with Alys, the King's sister. Alys was the ward of Richard's father, King Henry II, and it is rumoured that

Henry seduced her and that she bore him a child. Richard did not want to offend Philip; but neither did he wish to wed his father's mistress.

Richard set off from Sicily to go on Crusade with over two hundred ships. A storm blew some twenty-five ships off course, one of them containing the King's future bride Berengaria and the King's sister Queen Joan of Sicily. It took some time to track down the missing ships, and they later learned that the vessels were wrecked off the coast of Cyprus.

Many sources stated that Berengaria and Joan remained on board their ship and refused to disembark when invited by the Emperor of Cyprus, Isaac Comnenus. I did take historical licence in this story by having them taken captive by the Emperor—as was the case with several shipwrecked crusaders who became the emperor's prisoners.

Richard did lead an attack upon the island and successfully took Cyprus. The Emperor sued for peace, offering twenty thousand gold marks and his own daughter as the King's hostage. In return, Isaac begged the King not to place him in irons. Richard agreed, and then had special silver chains made for the King, in order to keep his 'promise'.

Richard and Berengaria's marriage, unfortunately, did not have a happy ending. Their separation due to war and the King's captivity made it a childless marriage. In addition, historians argue over whether or not Richard was bisexual. Berengaria is known as the only Queen never to set foot upon English soil while her husband was King.

The character of Liam MacEgan is the eldest son of King Patrick of Laochre from my *MacEgan Brothers* series. You can learn more about the MacEgan books by visiting my website at: www.michellewillingham.com. I love to hear from readers and you may e-mail me at michelle@michellewillingham.com or by mail at PO Box 2242 Poquoson, VA 23662 USA.

For further reading, my sources for this story included: *Richard the Lionheart: King and Knight* by Jean Flori; *Richard I* by John Gillingham in the Yale English Monarchs series; *Lives of the Queens of England From the Norman Conquest with Anecdotes of their Courts* by Agnes and Elizabeth Strickland; *The Crusade of Richard I 1189-92*, selected and arranged by T.A. Archer, in the 'English History by Contemporary Writers' series.

Michelle Willingham

PRINCE CHARMING
IN DISGUISE

BRONWYN SCOTT

Bronwyn Scott is a communications instructor in the Puget Sound area and is the proud mother of three wonderful children (one boy and two girls). When she's not teaching or writing, she enjoys playing the piano, travelling—especially to Florence, Italy—and studying history and foreign languages. You can learn more about Bronwyn at www.nikkipoppen.com

Previous novels by Bronwyn Scott:

PICKPOCKET COUNTESS
NOTORIOUS RAKE, INNOCENT LADY
THE VISCOUNT CLAIMS HIS BRIDE
THE EARL'S FORBIDDEN WARD
UNTAMED ROGUE, SCANDALOUS MISTRESS
A THOROUGHLY COMPROMISED LADY
SECRET LIFE OF A SCANDALOUS DEBUTANTE

And in Mills & Boon® Historical eBook *Undone!*:

LIBERTINE LORD, PICKPOCKET MISS
PLEASURED BY THE ENGLISH SPY
WICKED EARL, WANTON WIDOW
ARABIAN NIGHTS WITH A RAKE
WICKED EARL, WANTON WIDOW (featured in
SCANDALOUS REGENCY NIGHTS anthology)

Did you know that some of these novels are also available as eBooks? Visit www.millsandboon.co.uk

Chapter One

Herrenhausen Palace, Hanover, Germany,
autumn 1704

Kings, even future kings, could be a lot of things but not refused. Yet it seemed Hedwig Sophia, the Dowager Duchess of Holstein-Gottorp, had done just that.

'She has declined a proposal from the future King of England?' a flare of characteristic temper mingled with disbelief in young Prince George's voice, his dismay evident in the slouch of his posture as he collapsed inelegantly into a chair. Not all of his dismay was over the refusal. Most of it was over having come from the delectable Lady Marie-Thérèse's warm and accommodating bed.

One thought kept running through his head: He'd given up a bout of morning lovemaking for *this*? Who did the duchess think she was to refuse him? He had excellent prospects these days. It wasn't merely his own arrogance that suggested such a conclusion, it was empirically true.

He'd always been assured of succeeding his father as the Elector of Hanover, but now his prospects were settled far beyond that, his future ascension to the British throne assured thanks to Queen Anne.

Aging and wanting to ensure there would be no more Catholics on the English throne, Queen Anne had decreed the throne would pass to George's grandmother, Sophia, the Dowager Electress of Hanover, by right of her being James I's granddaughter and a Protestant. After her, the throne would go to his father and eventually to him.

He was a king-in-waiting, and while he waited, his wife would have the privilege of being called the Princess of Wales, the first one to bear that title in two hundred years. That alone would be an honour, to say nothing of the title his wife would bear later: queen consort.

It would have been enough for any number of the eager women in the Hanover Court. He didn't exactly lack for female companionship in or out of the bedchamber.

Yet it apparently wasn't enough for the Dowager Duchess of Holstein-Gottorp. George fished in the pocket of his waistcoat for a miniature he carried of her. He'd stopped by his chambers for it on a last-minute whim when he'd received the summons. He knew the envoy from the duchess was here. He'd been expecting good news. It had seemed a nice touch to have her picture on him at the moment of acceptance. It would make a romantic gesture to pull out the miniature, an intimate detail for the envoy to convey back to the dowager duchess about George's reaction upon hearing the glorious news.

To his mind, the decision was *au fait accompli*. Not only was Hedwig Sophia a dowager duchess, she was the daughter of Charles IX of Sweden, a princess in her own right.

She of all people knew the power of what marriage to him offered.

When he'd arrived at his father's study, the envoy had gone. His father had looked at him with steady eyes and delivered the news. She had declined the match.

'Who does she think she'll get better than me?' George groused, spearing his father with a hard look. Usually he and his father disagreed on most points. But on this, they'd been fairly aligned. His father's own unhappiness in marriage had spurred a desire to see his son's marriage better settled.

George gave the cased miniature a flip and studied the portrait inside. The dowager duchess was pretty enough with her dark hair and dark eyes. Both features upheld her reputation for intelligence. She'd already born one son before her husband had seen fit to die, freeing her of what was rumoured to have been an unhappy marriage to which she had not freely consented.

By no means was he in love with her. Love before marriage had no real place in a political alliance, and usually didn't have a place afterwards. But he was certain she would have been a credit to him and, in turn, he believed in his own arrogance that marriage to a young, attractive man like himself would have been far less of a nuisance than her prior husband.

George's father shrugged a shoulder. 'I would not perceive her refusal as a personal criticism. The envoy mentioned there are other contenders for her hand. From the way he spoke of them, I do not think she means to marry again, not you or anyone else. She's too busy enjoying herself with a young noble at the Swedish court. But it's unlikely she means to marry him either.'

Well, so be it. George shut the miniature with a forceful click. As with many things in his life, he was most concerned with events from his point of view. He was nearly twenty-five, and the heir to Great Britain part aside, he needed a wife, preferably one that he liked at least a little. Ideally, one that he liked a lot. It would have surprised his father to know the thoughts running through his son's mind at the moment. He might have grown up knowing the expectations of a political marriage but that didn't stop him from acquiring expectations of his own. Surely, some affection, some mutual regard, was possible.

George stood and tugged at his waistcoat, pulling himself together. What was done was done. Hedwig Sophia had refused. 'I thank you for informing me, Father. It's time to move forward from this and start thinking afresh about who might suit.' He gave his father a short bow and exited.

The prospect of returning to Marie-Thérèse had diminished in light of the news. He wanted to be alone, to think about what had happened and what he'd do next. A walk in the gardens would help clear his mind and re-establish a sense of clarity. He was level-headed enough to understand this: his disappointment over the refusal stemmed from the obstacle it created, not from any fond affection. He'd never met the dowager duchess. All he knew of her was contained in reports from diplomats and the small miniature. He was merely disappointed that his goal of marriage had been thwarted.

Having embraced the idea of marrying, George was set on seeing it accomplished with his usual dogged determination. Once he'd committed to a concept, he was seldom swayed from his course whether it was the wisest or not.

George stopped by a fountain to watch the rhythmic

trickle of water into the basin. Soon it would be winter and the fountain would freeze until spring. Not unlike his marital expectations, he thought wryly. It would take at least the winter to search out another alliance.

He threw back his head and laughed at his own impatience. It was something of a revelation to him that, future king or not, he was no different from other men of his age, full of the fires and passions of youth. From the lowest farmer to the most powerful ruler, every man had an empire to rule and that empire was the one he created himself—his family.

It seemed unfair that when he rode through the Hanover villages he saw men younger than he, with far fewer prospects than his, with pretty young wives waiting for them at home and chubby round-faced children to toss in the air while he had riches to command, titles to offer and yet he had no wife.

George threw a small pebble into the basin. He would make a new start tomorrow. He would commission a miniature or two of himself. He knew himself to be not unattractive with his fair hair and square-jawed features. People often said the strong set of his chin hinted at the strength of character beneath. He was of a middling height, although some said 'short,' but that was a matter of opinion. He preferred 'middling.' But what his stature might lack, the youthful physicality of his body supplied, a fact to which the courtly ladies of Hanover could well attest. Perhaps he'd hire a portraitist as well. The miniaturist would show off his face but he secretly thought in vainer moments his legs were one of his best features with their supple calves, muscled from hunting and horses.

Having a plan soothed his disappointment and he headed

back into the palace. His bride was out there, somewhere, he just had to find her. In the meantime there were ladies waiting or ladies-in-waiting, if one preferred.

The Elector of Hanover drummed his long fingers atop the desk. George had taken the news much better than he'd expected. He was just as disappointed with the news as George. In his opinion, the duchess was precisely what George needed in a wife—a young woman with intelligence who would long be at his side, helping him govern with a borrowed intelligence George's directness lacked. But there would be others to choose from. But who would be best?

His thoughts sifted through conversations and letters he'd exchanged with his mother, the dowager electress, over the past few years. There was one name his mother was fond of interjecting into matrimonial discussions. If only he could remember. Ah, yes, Caroline of Ansbach, if he recalled correctly.

There was a moment of elation at remembering the name. Then he recalled why he'd not seriously pursued the offering in the first place. Caroline's brother was the Margrave of Ansbach. She had no significant dowry and no family connections to make up for the lack of personal wealth. In fact, she'd been orphaned at the age of eleven. If it hadn't been for her late mother's friendship with the Electress of Brandenburg, Caroline might have faded into ignominy.

Therein lay Caroline's one redeeming asset. The elector remembered now. The Electress of Brandenburg had become the Queen of Prussia three years ago, making Caroline the official ward of King Frederick, a mighty connection indeed. Well, the elector thought with a private smile, if you were only going to have one political connection, it might as well be that one. It was time to revisit the Caroline question.

Chapter Two

'Is that your final answer?' Frederick, King of Prussia, speared the young woman in front of him with a dark gaze. She held his stare, menacing though it was. He was her guardian, and in the ten years she'd been his ward, his dark eyes and long face had been nothing but friendly. Today that was not the case. Barely disguised anger and disappointment seethed below the surface of his countenance. It took no small amount of courage to offer her response.

'Yes.' Caroline fought the urge to glance down at her hands but that would be a show of weakness as she uttered the last. 'I do not wish to marry the King of Spain.'

Caroline sat alone with the king and queen in a private receiving room set aside for the royal family. Frederick rose to pace, giving full vent to his spleen. 'The archduke is heir to the King of Spain—he will be the next Holy Roman Emperor.'

'Titular.' Caroline managed her objection in a single word.

Frederick rounded on her. 'Titular? What in the name of all that is holy does "titular" mean?'

'He is the *titular* King of Spain. It is a probability that is not as ironclad as they've been represented,' Caroline argued.

'Is that the only reason you refuse?' Frederick all but growled.

Caroline swallowed and sighed. They all knew it wasn't the true reason for refusal. The archduke's suit had been pressed since the summer in full force. Charles was considered by most of the royal world an 'amiable prince' and he'd courted her earnestly, even sending his own priest, Urban, to answer her theological questions. The visits with Urban had left Caroline in tears, however, and had not solidified Charles's claim for her hand.

'He is a Catholic and I am not, nor will I be,' Caroline said resolutely.

Frederick shot his wife a hard look. 'Who should I blame for this interference? This smells of a Hanover plot to prevent the marriage.' By 'Hanover plot' he meant the queen's mother, the Dowager Electress Sophia, a powerful, opinionated woman.

Caroline shook her head vigorously. 'The plot is all mine. I will not convert.' It was true that her friend, the philosopher Leibniz, who acted as factotum for the Hanover Court, had helped draft her official letter of refusal. But the decision was all hers, based on the convictions she'd shaped after years of being with Sophia-Charlotte at her intellectual court in Lutzenburg.

'Not for all the riches Charles offers? I know you to be an ambitious girl, Caroline,' Frederick coaxed, softening just a little. 'A marriage with Charles would fulfil that ambition.'

She heard the unspoken message: marriage to Charles was far beyond what a girl of her background aspired to. Caroline was well aware the princesses of Ansbach had a history of marrying minor lords or other local gentry and fading into the family tree unrecognised. To be the Queen of Spain far exceeded the achievements of her house to date.

It was not her ambitions alone that would be fulfilled. She heard the other unspoken message as well: 'After all we've done for you, will you not do this one thing for us?' But she could not relent.

'I am sorry, I cannot,' Caroline said simply. 'I have only one soul.' It would not be possible to love a man who did not respect her faith. Without that, marriage to Charles would be an empty alliance, an absolute betrayal of herself, no matter how amiable he was reputed to be.

It did not take long for Caroline to realise the king would not forgive her for what he saw as her stubborn and foolish decision. In his anger, Frederick was inclined to make staying in Berlin miserable. Caroline understood his disappointments but could not agree with him. He staunchly believed that princesses did what they were told, and if that meant converting, they converted. It was the axiom by which he ruled his own daughters. Princesses were to be flexible and adaptable. She had proven to be neither.

If this period of difficulty had taught her one thing, it was that she must face the prospect of marriage in the near future. There were those who claimed her a beauty; Charles of Spain had certainly thought so. He'd been ardent in his pursuit of her but he'd never truly thought of her intellect, nor had he truly believed she'd have the learning to resist the persuasions of his priest. That last assumption had upset her greatly. In theory, she'd understood at an early age the nature of political marriages, the idea that she was a prize to be won.

In practice, she'd not quite understood what that meant until recently. Perhaps she'd believed her lack of dowry would protect her from the game of royal alliances. That had proven to be a mistake. The King of Prussia's ward would not escape notice.

Being a prize did not settle well with her. She was more than a beautiful spoil of politics. She'd been given a great gift of education at Lutzenburg where Sophia-Charlotte had allowed her to sit in on debates even at a young age. She did not harbor misguided romantic expectations about marriage, but she did hope to be a partner to her husband, to enjoy his respect and admiration. In turn, she hoped to visit the same affections on her husband.

Charles of Spain was only one prospect. She was twenty-one now, of perfectly marriageable age. There would be others and soon. She knew Sophia-Charlotte had long harboured desires of a marriage to her son Frederick William. Nothing had come of those desires yet. Caroline was not particularly fond of Frederick. It worried her that in the wake of refusing Charles, the king and queen would re-examine the potential of marrying their son. There would be no refusing another future king a second time.

Her once very certain world was now full of uncertainty.

By December, Caroline had come to the conclusion that remaining in Berlin would take the decision to marry out of her hands. With a sad farewell to Sophia-Charlotte, Caroline packed her travelling trunks and set out for her childhood home in Ansbach. At Ansbach, she'd have her doting brother's protections. She silently vowed she would marry the first interesting Protestant man who came along.

Chapter Three

Herrenhausen Palace, Hanover, spring 1705

It was with great excitement that George answered his father's summons on a warm spring morning. The leaves were green, the sky was blue, early flowers were blooming in a profusion of colours throughout the Herrenhausen gardens. Spring was in the air and in his veins. George could nearly feel it thrumming in his very pulse. He was acutely aware of being a man in his prime and the vigour of youth coursed through him fast, hard and hopeful, and not without reason.

With the coming of spring and the thawing of the ground had come the thawing of his matrimonial hopes, which had predictably frozen with the roads. Winter made courier runs irregular at best. At least his hopes had frozen on a high note, giving him something to sustain him through the long winter. His grandmother, the dowager electress, had put forth a name as a prospective bride and a glowing description of the young woman's virtues. Caroline of Ansbach. George had never met her but thoughts of her lovely attributes had kept his mind and heart much occupied through the cold German nights. Now it was time to see what would become of those hopes.

His father barely waited until they were alone in the grand office of Herrenhausen Palace before he said the words George had waited the winter to hear. 'I think it's time to go to Ansbach.'

'Perhaps I might take grandmother's ring,' George ventured hastily. He'd long imagined how this meeting might play out. This would be an honest courtship between two people. In this matter, he would represent himself. He would see her and judge her on his own. She would be able to do likewise. It would be an enormous compliment to her that he wanted her to judge him on his merits, not the merits described in letters from political dignitaries.

For this courtship, there would be no more diplomatic intermediaries, no more letters written between negotiators in far-off lands, as it had been with Hedwig Sophia. This would be a true wooing. He'd come to the conclusion over the winter that his bride must suit him before she suited his kingdom. He didn't want only a queen. It would be years before he inherited the throne but a wife would be with him always.

His father made a sharp wave of his hand. 'No, do not take a ring or anything that marks you as the Prince of Hanover. I think you must go incognito. You have never met her and it would be best not to declare yourself until you're certain the two of you will suit.' The elector counselled caution.

His father laid out the case for disguise. 'I think it will

lessen the chance of a *mésalliance*.' George heard years of regret behind those words. His father's marriage had been fraught with constant interpersonal strife which had led to abject abandonment and numerous infidelities that perhaps could have been avoided if his parents hadn't been so ill-suited. What had looked like a solid alliance on paper had not borne out in reality.

Still, in his enthusiasm to finally be doing something at last after a winter of inactivity, George countered readily with the optimism of youth. 'I understand your hesitation, Father. I assure you, I'll act with prudence and not rush to a hasty conclusion.'

His father shook his head. 'It is more than that. You are a man full grown. You will know your own mind. It's not your mind that worries me. It is the minds of Spain and Prussia I'm concerned about.' His father dropped his voice. 'If the King of Prussia hears we're courting his ward he will move decisively to block the marriage.'

Something primal and competitive stirred in George's blood. This was not going to be a mere courtship; it was to be a challenge. The idea's appeal was growing by the moment.

He'd never shied away from an adventure but first there were questions. 'From whom do you get this news? I thought grandmother mentioned the princess had refused the King of Spain?' His father was not by nature a grand political strategist. George knew his father to be like himself—straightforward and oftentimes blunt, expecting others to see things in a similarly direct manner. Nuances and consequences often escaped his father simply because he didn't contemplate them.

'From the prime minister,' his father disclosed.

George nodded. Count Platen could be trusted to know such a thing. 'What does he think of the match?'

'He does not object, but he is emphatically neutral about it.' His father shrugged as if the prime minister's lack of exuberant approval did not bother him.

'And grandmother? Surely she will sway Count Platen to raptures of ecstasy over it.' In his conversations with his grandmother, George knew her to be exceedingly supportive of the match. She would be a superior ally in this matter.

But his father's response surprised him. It was quick and curt. 'Your grandmother is *not* to be told. We cannot risk anyone getting wind of this before anything is settled. I would not want to stir the King of Prussia's irritation without reason if the girl is not to your liking.'

George nodded. There was wisdom in that. Grandmother *was* a gossip. Discretion would be the watchword for his campaign. Once or *if* things progressed to a certain degree, there would be little the King of Prussia could do about it. 'Then it is settled. I will go in secret to win my princess.'

The more George thought about it, the more appealing the idea became. The medieval romance of it intrigued him. It would be in part a rescue to save his Protestant princess from the clutches of the Catholic king. But mostly, it would be an adventure—a prince in disguise off to seek out a woman capable of honest love.

The very stuff of legends.

Exactly what he wanted.

The intensity of that want had caught him unawares. Slowly, George closed the lid of his travelling trunk, letting the realization sweep over him. He stared out the long windows of his chambers into the gardens contemplating what it meant.

He absolutely did *not* want Caroline swayed by the enormity of his future prospects. He wanted her to love the man, not the future king. He wanted her to be different from the myriad women who traipsed through his bedchamber awaiting the pleasure of his royal prick so that he might give them something in return. Not that that was the only reason women came to him. After all, he was reasonably assured he had some skill in the bedchamber that had nothing to be with being a king.

When had he become so incredibly bored with the routine exchange of sex for favours? It wasn't as if he hadn't understood the game. He simply wanted something different, something more than a sex-based negotiation between the sheets.

Well, he'd find out soon enough. They were set to depart that night. For all his thoughts about this being a princely quest for the virtue of love, he had no illusions about the fairy-tale nature of his journey. He hoped Caroline was likeable. He hoped he would be able to see potential for genuine regard as they weathered the years together. He was not expecting love at first sight, only the hope that affection might grow from mutual appreciation of each other as real individuals, not merely titles. Still, from where he stood, that was hoping for quite a lot.

By midnight, all was ready after months of careful planning. As spring had hurtled towards June an elaborate ruse had unfolded to protect the prince's identity. George knew it well. He would travel as a Hanoverian noble who had gone to Nuremberg with plans to meet friends. But since his friends had not arrived and Nuremberg was not to his liking, he'd decided to venture on to Ansbach. To make the plan authentic, George would travel with only one other companion and his valet. They would all travel under aliases. George would be Monsieur de Busch. His companion, the privy councillor von Eltz, would be Baron von Stede.

George and his companions mounted their horses, making quick farewells to the small party gathered in the palace courtyard and set out on his bride-quest. The goal was before him. He was determined to succeed on this adventure, come hell or high water or even the King of Spain himself.

Chapter Four

Ansbach, June 1705

'I'll say this much for him, Charles is *most* persistent,' William Frederick, current Margrave of Ansbach, said with a laugh. He patted his sister's hand where it lay tucked in his arm as they strolled the tree-lined *hofgarten*. Caroline appreciated his attempt at levity and favoured him with a smile. It felt good to be out of doors after the dismal winter. It was a warm, beautiful day; the lime trees lining the promenade perfumed the air with the faint scent of their fruits. She was determined to enjoy it in spite of her growing predicament.

'I did not expect him to try again. I thought my refusal was most definite.' Caroline shook her head in disbelief. It had been a shock to them both when the last letter from Charles's advisors had found its way to Ansbach. It was a strong reminder that she could not escape her woes entirely. If she did not marry Charles, she'd have to marry someone else just to escape him. She was beginning to think Charles would not give up until she was wed to him or to another.

'Perhaps we should have understood how the situation would look from his perspective,' her brother suggested gently, obliquely veiling his reference to the death of Caroline's dear friend, the Queen of Prussia, in January.

It had been a horrible blow to her and she'd grieved the winter away, so much so that she knew William had feared for her own health.

'I see Charles's thoughts plainly. Instead of letting me mourn my friend in peace, he believes her death has changed my situation. He's committed to capitalising on what he thinks must surely be my reduced circumstance,' Caroline said with no little feeling. She was still appalled that Charles would use such an advantage to push his suit. 'If he could see things from my perspective, he would know such manoeuvrings does not raise him in my estimation. Instead he looks like an ill-mannered boor.'

William laughed. 'And all the while he's back in Spain thinking he's put on quite a show of devotion, hoping, no doubt, to persuade you with the tenacity of his sentiments.'

Caroline smiled. There was a great deal of humour in William's observation. The very image of the great Archduke Charles pacing his quarters and worrying over how to best convince her of his heartfelt regard brought a bubble of laughter to her lips. 'It's amazing men and women ever get married at all with such different opinions about how to woo the other.'

'Don't worry, you'll find someone,' her brother reassured her. 'Just because Charles presses his suit is no reason for you to rethink your decision. You're welcome here for as long as you like.'

It was a brave statement. She was grateful her brother had been willing to open the family home to her even though it meant sheltering someone who'd displeased the King of Prussia. Caroline was conscious of overstaying her welcome and putting her brother in real political jeopardy. The King of Prussia was a powerful enemy when one was only the margrave of a petty principality.

'I will never forget your kindness to me, William.'

'That's what brothers are for, my dear. But enough of this talk—the day is meant to be enjoyed.'

They had not gone far when a page caught up to them, excited and breathless. 'There's a visitor, Your Highness.'

Caroline felt a moment's trepidation. They were not expecting anyone. She exchanged a worried look with her brother. Had Charles made good on his offer to send his priest again after she'd politely but firmly written there was no need? Or worse, had the King of Prussia sent one of his minions to press the case?

'He says he and his travelling companion are noblemen from Hanover,' the page offered between gasps. 'He has letters of introduction from the prime minister in Hanover.'

Caroline felt the growing knot in her stomach unravel and ease. It wasn't Charles, then, or Frederick. Frederick was not favouring Hanover presently. She knew he blamed his mother in-law, the dowager electress, for inspiring her rejection of Charles's proposal.

By the time she and William arrived to greet the newcomers, Caroline's trepidation had been replaced by excitement. Unexpected guests brought a certain spark of spontaneity to the quiet life at Castle Ansbach. While she was appreciative of William's hospitality, Ansbach could not compete with the glittering society found at the

Prussian king's court in Berlin or the intellectual circle of
Lutzenburg.

The guests did not disappoint—a Baron von Stede and a
Monsieur de Busch. Both were mannerly and well-dressed,
but it was Monsieur de Busch that held Caroline's attention. His friendly brown eyes were warm and set amidst
the clean, square features of his face. If one was observant,
one would note his eyes were more than friendly. They carried a hint of the daredevil, a characteristic that begged for
further enquiry. Caroline had to admit she was intrigued
by the adventurous sparkle she saw there when he looked
her way.

But what she liked most was the strong straight length
of his nose, which drew the eye and fastened one's gaze
on the whole of his visage. He was clearly a young man
of some means if not position. His coat was of a celery
brocade with gold trimmings accompanied by an elaborately embroidered waistcoat beneath. And yet, he was not
so ostentatious as to be foppish. The gold watch chain he
wore tastefully sported a single fob, Caroline noted with
approval as they all moved out to the castle's private courtyard for refreshment.

Caroline quickly arranged to have cool drinks served,
pleased to also note that Monsieur de Busch and his companion were easy conversationalists. Monsieur de Busch
had them laughing in no time. 'For fear of sounding as if
I'm angling for an invitation to dinner,' he began, 'I must
say I've heard of the striking art in the dining room and
would very much like to take a look at it.'

William chuckled. 'Stay for dinner, please. Stay for the
night or for a few nights if it suits your plans. My sister and

I live quietly here and I daresay you'll liven things up for her.' William tossed her a quick wink. 'She'll never admit it, but my court is much subdued compared to the courts she comes from. I fear she grows bored but is too polite to say it.'

Monsieur de Busch fixed his gaze on her; the daredevil spark flickered knowingly. 'Perhaps I could persuade you to offer me a tour of the castle?'

Caroline found herself smiling. A handsome man was always a welcome novelty.

She was positively enchanting! George ushered her ahead of him into the dining chamber of the palace, manfully noting the gentle sway of hips as she passed. Grandmother had not exaggerated the beauty of Caroline. Her hair shone like spun gold in the sunbeam-lit dining room; her blue eyes were pleasantly expressive when she spoke, to say nothing of her figure, which by any account was all a man could desire. Right now he was having a deuce of a time keeping his mind and eyes on the crystal chandeliers of the dining room while she talked. He'd much rather look at her.

'There's also the minstrel gallery.' She made an elegant gesture towards the little balcony that presided over one end of the room. 'On special occasions, musicians entertain our guests during supper.'

'And tonight, *mademoiselle*? Will tonight be special enough to warrant minstrels?' George ventured a light bit of flirtation.

She smiled, blushed becomingly and lowered her pretty blue eyes. George thought the gesture was out of a sense of good breeding rather than any genuine shyness. Good.

He didn't want a timid wife. 'Perhaps my brother might be convinced to have a small party. It's not often we get such entertaining guests.'

Ah, he would take that as a small token of her approval. It was a promising start. She was moving again down the length of the room to a doorway and George surreptitiously followed the light sway of her movements.

'This is the porcelain saloon,' she said, stepping inside a room off the dining area. 'This is where all the margraves keep their collections of china.'

'Lovely, absolutely lovely,' George murmured, his eyes politely on the porcelain.

The tour led them back out into the cloistered courtyard, where, to George's delight, the conversation turned more personal. It gave him an excuse to look at her and note everything about her—the excellent fit of her gown, the tasteful pale blue cameo she wore at her neck, the small pearls at her ears, all of it.

'What brings you to Ansbach?' Caroline asked after she'd shown him the west façade.

Personal interest is good, George thought, and he launched into his prepared story. 'Baron von Stede and I were to meet friends in Nuremberg. They are journeying on to Italy and we thought a reunion of sorts would be in good order.' Here, he paused and shook his head. 'But we must have missed them. We waited a few days in Nuremberg but to no avail.' He paused here and leaned forward conspiratorially with a wink. 'Perhaps we should have waited longer, but between you and me, I did not find the city appealing. We decided to come on to Ansbach before heading home.'

She smiled at his light confession and held his gaze with a mischievous look of her own. 'Between you and me, I must confess I am very glad you did.'

Chapter Five

Caroline dressed carefully for supper that evening. The meal was to be an entertaining affair. She'd coaxed her brother into bringing in some local musicians to fill the gallery and had sent a hastily modified menu to the kitchens to accommodate their guests. Everything was in ready for a lovely evening except herself.

It was silly, really, this indecisiveness over which gown to wear. Their guests were two unanticipated noblemen. She was acting like they were visitors of state. But she'd be lying to herself if she didn't admit Monsieur de Busch raised a few flutters in her stomach. They'd spent the afternoon walking the grounds and talking as if they were old friends. Not once had the conversation lagged between them as it often did between strangers. Monsieur de Busch was charming as well as good-looking and they'd laughed together. The feel of her arm linked through his was natural, as if it belonged there, as if *she* belonged there. By the time she'd departed to make the arrangements for supper, she felt she'd known him far longer than the space of an afternoon.

That was why she was having trouble dressing for supper. She wanted to look her best. Caroline discarded the fifth gown on her wide bed before inspiration struck. She'd wear the rose silk trimmed in silver. That decided, Caroline sat still long enough for Fräulein von Genninggen to do her hair. For a finishing touch, Caroline added a tiny silver tiara to sit discreetly atop the elegantly arranged curls and one of her favourite necklaces, a cameo *habille* of coral on a matching ribbon. Despite her lingering toilette, Caroline made it to the drawing room promptly at seven o'clock.

'There you are, my dear,' her brother greeted her, drawing her into the little circle of conversation. Their guests were already there and she felt Monsieur de Busch's eyes on her. If she'd entertained any worries that the delightful afternoon was an aberration, they were quickly dismissed. In evening attire, Monsieur de Busch was elegant charm itself.

'Enchanté, vous êtes très belle.' Monsieur de Busch bowed gallantly over her gloved hand, displaying courtly manners.

'Merci.' Caroline favoured him with a short curtsey and her brother tactfully moved away a slight distance, engaging Baron von Stede in a conversation about politics at Hanover.

'Nous sommes seulement,' Monsieur de Busch said in a low voice that hid a light smile at her brother's kind manoeuvrings. 'Perhaps you might tell me about the artwork in this room.'

'Are you a student of art?' Caroline asked, enjoying the chance to continue their conversation in French.

'Why would you think that, *ma chérie*?' Monsieur de Busch's eyes twinkled.

'You've made several enquiries about the artwork here.'

Monsieur de Busch leaned close and she could smell the clean scent of his evening toilette, herbs and a hint of sandalwood. It suited him. 'You study the art, I study you,' he flirted.

Caroline blushed but didn't look away. 'Are you trying to seduce me, sir?'

He placed a dramatic hand over his heart. 'Do you think I would dare such a thing with your brother mere feet away?'

Caroline laughed. 'I think you would dare a great many things, *monsieur*, if it suited your purposes.'

He drew her hand up to his lips and kissed her knuckles. 'In this case, you are most certainly right. I bow to your superior wisdom, princess.'

Caroline shook her head in feigned exasperation, trying to ignore the jolt of awareness that shot up her arm at his touch. 'You, sir, must be a sore trial to the ladies of Hanover.'

He winked. 'They don't have any complaints and, I wager, neither would you.'

Caroline cleared her throat and redirected the conversation to the art on the wall. 'This painting is an original.'

'Is it? I would say this room has quite a collection of originals. The thing about originals is that they can't be found anywhere else in the world.'

Oh, this was bold and heady stuff indeed. She could debate the merits of physics and religion from dawn to dusk, but these flirty games of Monsieur de Busch's were out of her depth. For all her academic worldliness she was well-aware *he* was out of her depth. She was not so naïve to think he spoke mere words. He found her attractive. Eyes that had been warm and mischievous this afternoon were hot and knowing this evening. There was no sense in pretending she did not understand what the veiled reference to 'originals' meant. 'I am honoured, sir, by your compliment.'

'As am I,' Monsieur de Busch replied, the chocolate coals of his eyes burning hot with unmistakable desire of a man for a beautiful woman. Then he smiled, dispelling the moment before it could disintegrate into awkwardness.

Caroline toured him about the room, stopping to point out various paintings and mural work, speaking in French the whole time. At one point, Monsieur de Busch broke into fluent but heavily accented English.

'Are you trying to impress me with your command of languages?' Caroline laughed, responding in English herself. 'We've spoken German, French and now English.'

Monsieur de Busch was all mock seriousness. 'Hardly! If I was, I'd be telling you how lovely you are in Dutch and Spanish, not to mention Latin.' He leaned closer in a conspiratorial fashion and whispered, 'But usually women like jewels better than my flattery.'

They laughed over this and made light of it, but Caroline tucked the piece of knowledge away in her thoughts. This guest from Hanover was learned. While it was not uncommon for the nobility to be fluent in French and German, there were plenty who didn't have more than a passing acquaintance with the other languages. She was suitably impressed.

Caroline was suitably impressed over dinner too. Monsieur de Busch and his companion comported themselves well. Talk was mainly social and political, an exchange of news from Hanover and the court at Berlin. Only one odd thing occurred during dinner and it was minor. Although the court at Berlin was the Prussian king's court and admittedly the most glamorous of the German courts, Monsieur de Busch was eager to steer the conversation away from it. He commented instead on the musicians in the gallery. 'Music during dinner is inspired. It makes the meal so soothing.' He turned to Caroline specifically. 'I've met the composer Handel. He's quite talented. You should have him write a piece for your dinner parties.'

Caroline smiled. 'I met him at Lutzenburg. He is indeed talented.' But that was the wrong way to take the conversation for both of them. For Monsieur de Busch, it would only lead back to the Prussian court and for her it would dredge up painful memories of losing Sophia-Charlotte. Caroline took a sip of wine. 'Tell me about the entertainments at Hanover? Are you at the elector's court much?'

Monsieur de Busch merely shrugged. 'The elector's court is manageable but it lacks the grace of Ansbach.' Caroline did not miss the compliment.

The meal passed amiably and there were cards to follow. As the evening turned late, Monsieur de Busch asked if she might accompany him on a short walk about the gardens before retiring.

'The night air is revivifying.' Monsieur de Busch breathed deeply as they stepped outdoors. He turned his head up to the sky. 'Just look at those stars.'

Together, they sought out constellations, although Caroline noted his knowledge of astronomy was not nearly as developed as hers.

'Well, not all of us can study with the great Leibniz. I assume that's where you come by your vast knowledge of the skies,' Monsieur de Busch said affably, not the least bit bothered that he'd been outpaced in this arena.

'Yes, we are regular correspondents still. He's been both friend and mentor to me through the years, although I do not know when I might see him again....'

Monsieur de Busch's hand closed warmly over her own, his voice soft. 'I am sorry for your loss. I have gathered the queen was dear to you. I understand losing her meant much not only as the loss of a friend but the loss of access to another life, one that you enjoyed fully.'

In that moment, Caroline's heart went out to the Hanoverian noble. He'd understood her loss in a way she'd not been able to convey since the queen's death and she was moved beyond words he was the one to recognise it.

He stroked the tops of her knuckles with his thumb, a slow languid gesture that sent a lovely trill up her arm. 'I did not come out here to conjure up sad memories, my dear. I've come out here because I find myself enraptured with the company of Ansbach and I am loath to leave. But I would not impose myself on you, if my company were not also to your liking.'

He was asking her permission to stay. Caroline saw the request and so much more in the carefully courtly worded statement. He wanted to stay, because of her. She wanted to dance about the garden and give an undignified yelp of delight. But he'd been so very gentlemanly in his request. She must respond in the same.

'We would be delighted to entertain you here at Ansbach for as long as you wish,' Caroline replied.

'That would be eternity.' Monsieur de Busch gave a wry smile and stepped forward, drawing her gently to him. 'Let us seal our agreement with a kiss and the stars shall be our witness.'

His arm was about her waist, drawing her against him, his mouth taking hers in a soft kiss that deepened as it lingered. It was the perfect kiss to offer a lady who'd not been oft kissed in her lifetime—gentle and sensuous but not so arrogantly passionate to scare off an untried girl. Caroline sank into it, a breathy gasp of approval escaping her. She revelled in the feel of the hard planes of his body. Beneath the layers of coat, waistcoat and shirt, Monsieur de Busch was a well-made man. The King of Spain might send diplomats to woo on his behalf, but this man wooed for himself and that was a heady novelty indeed; to be drawn into a man's embrace and kissed thusly without considerations for diplomatic agreements and political alliances was quite the elixir, and for the moment, Caroline gave herself to it beneath the stars of Ansbach.

Chapter Six

Her brother was waiting for them when they returned. Baron von Stede had already gone up to his rooms. Caroline gave a vague thought to whether or not one could look 'kissed.' She hoped not. Monsieur de Busch took very correct leave of her that belied no suggestion of the exchange that had taken place in the garden.

'You like him,' William commented once they were alone. He smiled as he said it. 'It makes me glad to see you happy again.'

'He has proven to be good company,' Caroline offered, not wanting to give too much away, but inside she was a jumble of emotions, all of them good. 'We've only just met. It is too soon to rush to any conclusions.'

It was the logical stance to take. They didn't know anything about him beyond the introductory letter from Count Platen. They didn't know his prospects, his family, nothing. Not that it necessarily mattered. Princesses of Ansbach could usually marry as they wished. They were not known for making grand alliances. But there was still the King of Prussia to consider. Not all princesses of Ansbach were wards to the king either. Nonetheless, Caroline hummed a little tune as she went upstairs. Against all rational thought, she couldn't help but think Monsieur de Busch might be the one.

She might be the one, George thought as he prepared for bed. It would be hard to sleep. There was so much to contemplate. Princess Caroline had far exceeded his grandmother's descriptions. She was beauty incarnate and had intelligence too. Even from their conversations today he could tell her education far outstripped his own. His education had not been neglected in the least, but while he *knew* things, she *thought* about things. He was not a thinker in that regard. He was a man of plans and actions.

Beautiful and intelligent, she graced her brother's home with serenity. He'd noted the quick arrangements she'd made for dinner. He'd had only to mention the musicians and she'd seen it done, seemingly effortlessly. He could already imagine her gracing the tables of his state dinners, of her re-creating an intellectual circle like Lutzenburg in his own court when the time came.

It was also clear that she was kind and well-liked. Her brother held her in genuine affection. In short, Princess Caroline was a paragon. A passionate paragon if what had transpired in the garden was anything to go on. He was glad for it. It seemed, in coming to Ansbach, he had found what he was looking for—both a queen and companion. Even so, it surprised him mightily.

In all honesty, it had been the adventure which had appealed to him. He'd coached himself not to expect too much from Princess Caroline. Mutual respect had been the goal.

Love at first sight was far beyond any expectation. He'd been wrong about that. Apparently it was possible after all.

But he'd been right about one thing. It was hard to sleep that night.

He allowed himself three more days in Ansbach. He counselled himself to seek a road of caution in spite of his early elation, a rare option for him. He did not view himself as a cautious fellow, nor did he hold the concept of caution in high esteem. If he saw something he liked, he went after it.

That was precisely what he did. He turned his three-day stay into a whirlwind courtship, spending every moment at Caroline's side. They strolled the Hofgarten together. She toured him through the medieval streets of the town. They rode out into the countryside to picnic with von Eltz, her brother and other friends William invited.

During the day, he could touch her in small ways—a hand at her back, an arm to steady her across rocky terrain. But in the evenings he could kiss her beneath the stars in the garden. He revelled in the idea that he was the first to teach her the art of such intimacies. She was virtuous as a princess should be, but that did not stop her from taking pleasure in their garden interludes which she seemed to enjoy as much as he.

As much as he imagined himself in the role of chivalrous knight, it was not a role he'd lived out. Most of the women he associated with at Hanover's court were happy to oblige him in all ways. Kisses always concluded in something more and usually in bed. But there was no question of that here. Princess Caroline was not a woman to be taken outside the benefit of marriage and that proved to be his greatest trial. As his time at Ansbach drew to a close, he was hard-pressed to exercise restraints on his ardour.

On his final evening, George presented her with a fine cameo necklace. They were alone in the garden. It had become their ritual.

'It's beautiful,' Caroline murmured, her blue eyes filling with emotion. She drew a finger along the raised contours of the cameo's silhouette. 'How did you know?'

George smiled. 'I noticed that you've worn a different one each day of our visit.'

'I collect them.'

'Then I am especially glad I chose it for you. I hope you will keep it as a token of my affections, and in appreciation for your hospitality to two strangers.'

'Perhaps this is also a parting gift? Will I see you again?' Caroline asked. It was a question they'd been dancing about all day. George could not answer the question without exposing himself and he did not want to spoil their remaining day with talk of farewell. He wanted to take the image of her laughing in the sun with him back to Hanover to sustain him until he did see her again.

'Partings are not necessarily forever,' George said softly. 'I will see you again.' But never as Monsieur de Busch. The next time they met, he would be the Hanoverian prince. When he'd donned this guise, he'd never thought he'd regret giving it up. It came as something of a surprise to find that he did. But when Caroline came into his arms, his worries were allayed. She cared for the man he was, not the king that would be revealed. She would not care if he turned out to be more than a charming man from Hanover.

Chapter Seven

George wasted no time in returning to Herrenhausen. He went straight to his father without bothering to change out of his travelling attire, relieved to find his father still at home and not yet departed for Pyrmont, where he liked to take the waters.

'It was love at first sight. She was all grandmother said and more,' George announced without preamble, standing in his father's study.

'The trip was good, then?' his father enquired with good humour, laughing at his son's high colour and apparent hurry. Part of George wanted to answer his father's calm demeanour with a calmness of his own but he found he couldn't.

He was probably smiling like an idiot. He didn't care. It was a charmed life he was living these days. First, his father's surprising affability after years of a strained father-son relationship, and now having found Caroline. The Fates were certainly favouring him.

'And for her?' his father pressed, amused at his son's

high spirits but still possessed of a measure of caution. 'It's not enough for only one of you to love the other.'

'For her as well. I think she will want to marry with all possible haste, as do I.' George's mind went back to their last private moments in the garden. She'd not wanted him to leave.

His father nodded. 'Very well. We will see what can be done. But—' he raised a cautioning finger '—we will need to proceed with prudence and always with an eye towards the Prussian king. If we are too hasty, it will look like we're trying to steal a march on him and, of course, we'll want to ascertain that the King of Spain has broken off his suit.'

His father was lost in thought for a moment, the mental wheels of his mind creating lists very different of the sort being created in George's mind. 'We'll need to send a discreet envoy. The fewer people who know about this, the better, until things are officially settled.'

'Send Baron von Eltz back in his guise as von Stede,' George said abruptly. 'She will recognise him and know that he speaks the truth.' He was wishing he could go himself, wishing he could be there to allay any reactions Caroline might have.

'That's a good suggestion. He's already familiar with everything we've done so far.' His father shot him a humorous look. 'You might be interested to know that people who noticed your absence are speculating as to the reason. Some suggest you've followed the entourage of the Princess of Hesse and her lovely companion.'

George laughed. 'At least they acquit me with good taste. But they will be wrong. My intentions are firmly fixed on Caroline.'

'Then I will send von Eltz back to Ansbach as soon

as our position is in order.' His father stuck out his hand across the desk. 'Congratulations, son, I think you have made a good choice in this.'

For the next few days, Herrenhausen was a hive of covert activity. Details were arranged with von Eltz, secretaries drafted the appropriate letters of goodwill to the margrave and the elector continued to pack for his trip to Pyrmont.

Von Eltz made ready to leave. The elector made ready to leave. George settled in to wait, something he was not admittedly skilled at. More than ever, he was glad to have taken his father's suggestion about visiting Caroline incognito. Their splendid but whirlwind courtship provided him memories that were vivid with colour and recalled with private laughter. Ever since his declaration, the 'personal' aspect of wedding Caroline had been transmuted into an act of the state. He was glad not to have met Caroline first under those conditions, where everything was stiff and formal. They would have walked the gardens of Ansbach with a retinue following behind. There would have been no laughter, no time for joking; everything they'd done would have been on display and then analysed and dissected. It would have been a play acted out on Hanover's political stage. Like a play, it wouldn't have been real.

This wasn't real, this couldn't be happening, Caroline thought for the hundredth time as she led Baron von Stede up the stairs to her private receiving chambers. The phrase ran through her head, a litany of disbelief that had been summoned up upon von Stede's arrival at Ansbach that afternoon.

To her great disappointment, von Stede had arrived alone, suggesting he'd left his companion at Nuremberg, trying once more to make contact with their Italy-bound friends. But it wasn't that simple. Von Stede had been invited in, tea had been offered. Her brother was glad to see their recent company again. She noticed von Stede had been stiff, his demeanour far more formal than it had been on his previous visit. Caroline had thought it might be due to the absence of his more outgoing friend, but she was admittedly biased. Everything had seemed less colourful in the wake of Monsieur de Busch's departure.

Then von Stede had looked over at her and said intently, 'If it is to your liking, I would like a private conversation with you. I have news of our mutual friend that I'd like to share. He sends his greetings.' Among other things, Caroline was sure but that surety didn't cause her pulse to race any less.

With all the calmness she could gather, Caroline led von Stede to her apartments and closed the door. They were not entirely alone. Her chaperone, Fräulein von Genninggen, placed herself at a safe distance near the long windows of the room.

Caroline took a seat in a chair and folded her nervous hands in her lap to keep them from betraying too much. 'I trust our friend is finding Nuremberg more to his liking this time through.'

This comment seemed to catch von Stede by surprise. He lifted an eyebrow in enquiry.

'It is only that he remarked to me that he found Nuremberg a bit dull,' Caroline offered.

Von Stede made a gracious nod of his head. 'I believe that, these days, all else pales by comparison to your company. Which is why I am here.'

'A very neat segue, sir,' Caroline said. 'Please feel able to speak freely.'

Von Stede cleared his throat and gave a jerk of his head to indicate the fräulein's presence was disagreeable to him. 'Perhaps the fräulein would be good enough to await us somewhere else.'

It was to be entirely private, then. Caroline understood and sent the fräulein out of the room.

'First, I need to inform you that our friend is well and sends his most sincere regards. I also need to inform you that the name Monsieur de Busch is entirely fabricated. The man who came to you as Monsieur de Busch is George Augustus, the Electoral Prince of Hanover.'

This was definitely not real. This was the stuff of fairy tales, of princesses rescued by knights in disguise. When she'd thought she was kissing a nice baron, she'd been kissing the electoral prince, a future king of Great Britain.

'I do not mean to distress you.' Von Stede was looking at her strangely, as if she might become overwhelmed by the news. Perhaps he was regretting sending Fräulein von Genninggen out of the room.

'I had no idea,' Caroline managed. Now, of course, it made sense—the polyglot accomplishment of languages including English which he'd need in his new country, the courtly manners, the desire to not discuss the court at Berlin. There'd been little signs that he was not a mere baron.

She recovered herself quickly. Sophia-Charlotte had taught her to be gracious and controlled in all situations. 'I am honoured that he's remembered me enough to send a personal messenger.' She looked sharply at von Stede, another thought occurring. 'I assume you're not merely Baron von Stede either?' It was the perfect opening for him to declare himself and Caroline desperately wanted to know with whom she was doing business.

Von Stede bowed. 'I am Baron von Eltz, privy councillor to the Elector of Hanover. I have been sent by the prince's father to ascertain your agreeability to a proposal of marriage by the prince.'

There it was, wrapped in the fancy words of court negotiations, the simple proposal of marriage. Her dashing baron wanted to marry her. Caroline's heart sang but she could only answer, 'I am agreeable to the offer. I will speak to my brother this evening. He will know what steps need to be taken next.' She knew very well what the next steps were but she also knew her role in this. It was time for the men to make the arrangements and write up the contracts. It was time for her to be a bride.

Chapter Eight

Von Eltz gave a cough. 'I must also probe into a matter of some delicacy before we proceed. Are you free to pursue this alliance?' He paused here, looking for the right words.

Caroline divined his intent and took pity on him. 'The King of Spain has no claim on me. I have recently sent a note to not bother with the meeting his councillors and others requested in Nuremberg.' She smiled at the irony of it. 'The prince is not really in Nuremberg, is he?'

Von Eltz returned her smile, chuckling a little at the dark humour that the King of Spain's envoys might accidentally meet up with the prince after all of Hanover's contretemps to avoid discovery. 'No, the prince is not in Nuremberg. He's in Hanover, chafing at the bit for a wedding as soon as it can be arranged.'

'Then you may tell him I will come to him with all haste possible, although there is much to be done.' She was amazed she managed to sound so decorous. Her pulse was racing with the thrill of it and she thought she'd fairly burst with the joy of the moment. If it were up to her, she'd leave this minute, but princesses did not act impulsively.

Von Eltz bowed graciously. 'I will leave you with a final admonition, princess. This must be kept as secret as possible. It is the prince's wish.'

'His wish is my own, from this day forward,' Caroline pledged. Even if the privy councillor hadn't requested it, Caroline would have urged secrecy anyway. With such happiness close at hand, she didn't want to risk any interference from the King of Prussia.

As soon as von Eltz left her alone in her rooms, Caroline danced across the floor in her happiness, her skirts sweeping about her, her arms outstretched. She knew hearts should not be factored into alliances and ultimately this was an alliance, but her heart *was* engaged just a little. She would be a fool not to admit it. She had found a prince among men, quite literally.

Caroline did her duty. She spoke to her brother and, in turn, he did his duty requesting the presence of the Landgrave of Hesse-Darmstadt to draw up the settlement of property between brother and sister.

To her great relief, the drawing up of contracts did not take long. The landgrave, her own councillor and von Eltz did an admirable and expedient job, although the waiting seemed interminable for her. She was more than ready to see George again.

Von Eltz tried to allay her growing impatience with rides in the countryside where he'd share bits of news from George enclosed in the official dispatches.

On the ninth of July, George wrote that his grandmother, the dear, had been surprised by the announcement of their betrothal because she had known nothing about the plans in motion and in many ways it had been her plan from the start. It seemed to Caroline that it was quite fortuitous. She could not have Sophia-Charlotte as a mother, but she could have Sophia-Charlotte's own mother as a grandmother-in-law.

By the twenty-first of July, Caroline was assured the betrothal was now considered an 'open secret' at Hanover's court. It would become public knowledge at a dinner hosted by the Elector of Hanover within the week.

By late August, her trunks were packed, her entourage ready for the journey to Hanover and the royal wedding that awaited her there.

It had all been accomplished with remarkable speed, although at times the speed had seemed to diminish to a snail's plodding. Looking back, she could see the whirlwind truth of it. In June, she'd had no inkling of who a future husband might be, nor had she even been looking for one. She'd merely been resigned that there would be one. Now, eight weeks later (and that was being generous with the calendar; a stickler for details would claim it at seven), she was off to marry the future King of England, a prize so far beyond the scope of her House as to be unthinkable.

Caroline smiled to herself as they set off on the journey to Hanover. He was not only a future king. She was off to marry a man who made her laugh, who knew within a span of days and without asking that she liked cameos, who liked her the way she was—Protestant and intelligent. That was worth more than any crown. She knew in her heart that if Monsieur de Busch had asked for her hand, she would have given it.

Their marriage would not be perfect. Of necessity, kings and queens led imperfect lives and marriages; the very nature of how the alliances were arranged guaranteed that. She was not naïve enough to think she and George would escape those limitations. No, it would not be perfect but they would be happy.

Late August 1705

There was no more perfect way to ruin a wedding than a death in the family. George cursed his bad luck and paced the reception hall of Herrenhausen, where the relevant parties were gathered. The kind Fates had turned their backs for just an instant and the impossible had happened. His grandfather, the Duke of Celle, had died suddenly. He hadn't been sick. He'd been out hunting, for heaven's sake. It was nothing more than a chill. A man hale enough to hunt shouldn't die from a chill. At least he should have the courtesy of dying after the wedding festivities.

'We'll postpone the wedding, of course,' said one of the councillors. Others agreed. But that was unacceptable to George.

'Why "of course"?' George broke in briskly.

The councillor who'd suggested it stammered, looking for an answer. 'It's customary,' he managed. 'When there's a death, impending celebrations are put off.'

'But in this case, it is almost impossible to stall the preparations. The princess is en route to us.' George had a flash of brilliance. 'In many ways the wedding is no longer an impending event, but already under way.' He glanced at his father. 'The contracts are set, the bride is on her way, preparations have been made.' Everyone was listening to see where he was going with his argument. 'It's one thing to cancel events that haven't occurred yet, but it's another to cancel events that have begun. We cannot expect Princess Caroline to idle away her days in Hanover waiting for a wedding she's been promised.' The very mention of this request being for Caroline's benefit swayed the argument in his favour.

Once the announcement of their engagement had been made, George had discovered just how wonderful people found his choice. Everywhere he went it seemed someone had a glowing compliment to make about his future wife. It filled him with pride and with great longing to be with her again. Mentioning her was a stroke of genius. The room began to murmur. It would be unfair to Caroline, one advisor assented. Others nodded.

George shrewdly launched his other salvo in a quiet voice now that the seed was sown. 'After all our efforts, we certainly don't want to risk losing her to the Prussian king. If we delay, he might find a way to oppose the contracts. He is her guardian after all....' George let the last trail off into whatever implications individuals might draw.

At last his father spoke up. 'I think, in this case, we might set aside mourning for the duke for a few days.' He shot a sharp glance at George. 'But you have to understand the festivities will be curtailed greatly, three days at most. The wedding itself will need to be a quiet affair.'

George maintained a sombre expression as he managed, 'Yes, Father, I understand entirely.' He understood that he'd won. There would be time later for pomp and pageantry. Right now he only cared about making Caroline his. His young blood burned hot at the prospect. Another thought occurred to him.

'I think it would be best if I rode to meet their travelling party and inform them of the new plans,' George said, careful not to word it as a request but as a statement. The entourage from Ansbach would be halfway to Hanover. It would be a chance to see Caroline informally before she arrived at court. Perhaps even a chance to be Monsieur de Busch again before he had to be the king.

'Monsieur de Busch is downstairs, my lady,' Fräulein von Genninggen announced. 'He's requested an audience with you in a private parlour.'

Caroline looked up from her needlework, her fingers starting to shake. 'He's here? Of course I'll see him. I'll be down right away.' Just as soon as I tidy my hair, change my dress—oh, I must look a mess, Caroline thought. Travelling was difficult on a person. There were never enough facilities for a proper bath.

George is here! Her heart sang. It was most unlooked for and yet most welcome. Unless he brought bad news? The fear that something had happened prompted her to forgo an elaborate toilette. She was downstairs and in the parlour within five minutes. She was in George's arms thirty seconds after that, just as soon as they were alone.

'It's not bad news?' she enquired, worried eyes searching his face.

'Bad news with a happy ending,' George told her. He sat down on a bench and pulled her onto his lap. 'I've ridden out mostly because I missed you. But also because my grandfather has died. It was very unexpected.'

Caroline's heart sank. Deaths meant mourning. The wedding would be postponed. She waited to hear the disappointing words.

'The wedding will have to be a quiet one. But at least it

won't be postponed.' George smiled. 'I could not bear that. The summer apart has been torture already.'

Caroline let out a breath of relief. 'A quiet wedding is fine, George. It only matters that we are together. Perhaps it's better to begin our married life on a calm note.' She looked down at her hand where it rested against his chest, his heart beating beneath it.

'I am eager to know you, George,' she ventured. 'I want to learn what you like, your favourite colour, your favourite hobbies. Our time at Ansbach was too short and yet it's enough to know I care for you.'

'If you like, we can start tonight,' George whispered huskily in her ear before stealing a long kiss that recalled starry nights at Ansbach and promised a future full of adventure.

He came to her that night under the secrecy of darkness. She was ready for him. She'd left her hair loose, brushed until it shone like spun gold in the candlelight of her room, and she wore a white gown of linen embroidered at the hem with tiny green flowers. She was fully aware the linen was not a barrier to eyes, the candlelight illuminating her body through the shift.

It would be better this way, they'd decided over a private dinner of red wine and boar, to be together as man and wife in the relaxed intimacy of the inn. Here, there would be no expectations of the kingly marriage bed. Here, they would just be themselves, two lovers exploring each other's bodies. The very thought of it had made her rush through dinner.

The door opened a fraction and George entered silently, shutting the door firmly behind him and locking it. He was dressed simply in white shirt and buff breeches. He was already barefoot.

'Boots are nothing but a nuisance.' George smiled, following her eyes to his feet but his eyes didn't stay there long. He was obviously entranced with her. 'Boots are a nuisance and you are beautiful.'

Caroline smiled, uncertain what to do next. How did one proceed with a lover? But George had it all well in hand. He caught her to him and kissed her. Would you like to undress me, my dear?' he whispered against her neck.

It was an easy enough task and one that she revelled in. There was a certain thrill in revealing her lover's body inch by inch as the shirt fell away and she gazed at his chest. In the prime of youth, he did not disappoint. The muscled chest she'd guessed at through layers of clothes did exist in truth. It tapered down to a lean stomach and hips. Here she hesitated, her hands resting on the waistband of his trousers.

He helped her with the trousers until he stood unabashedly naked before her, his arousal jutting proudly. She blushed profusely. But he laughed. 'You should look your fill, and take pride that you can rouse me so thoroughly. This is what you do to me.'

So she did look. The male body was wondrously made, and for all her education at Lutzenburg she recognised she was woefully uneducated in this arena.

He took her to bed then, pulling her shift over her head and looking longingly down the length of her body. He cupped her breasts and kissed each of them by turn, causing her to tremble with the pleasure of such attentions. He kissed her belly, his hands framing her hips before he rose over her, kissing her full on the mouth. Oh, this was exquisite! She clutched him to her, her legs spreading in-stinctively to bring him closer. She felt him nudging at her entrance and she strained against him, her body begging him to take her. Then he was there, inside her, bringing with him a stab of pain, a shock only because there'd been so much pleasure.

He stilled and let her body relax around him. But she was anxious to find the completion her body craved. She arched her hips against him as she took him in her arms and brought his mouth down to hers, a moan of satisfaction escaping his lips. They were moving together now, finding a twin rhythm in their mutual need for each other, a need that surged around them, enveloping her in its intensity until she thought she'd shatter from the force of it.

And shatter she did.

George gave a final thrust, his own pleasure evident in the pulsing throb of him inside her, and she broke, posi-tively broke, into a kaleidoscope of sensations that wrapped about her as she spiralled slowly back down to earth. For all she knew, she'd not known this, not ever dreamed this was possible.

'You're mine now,' George murmured a long while later, his hand idly stroking the length of her hair.

'Yes, I am yours.' She turned in his arms to face him. She was his in a way that far transcended contracts and diplomats, thrones and titles.

'I think you're a very brave woman, Caroline.'

'Why is that?' She smiled up into his face.

'You have given up your home to make a new one in another's court. Eventually, you'll give up your country for a land you've never seen. I don't think just any woman can do that. You have my admiration.'

'And you have my devotion. I don't think about what I'm giving up, George. I am thinking about what I'm gaining in return and that's you. Not your crown, not that blasted list of titles I saw in the contracts, just you.'

George kissed her, long and lingering. 'I hope I can live up to your expectations, then. That's a lot of pressure to put on a man.' He laughed.

'Don't worry.' Caroline caressed his face. 'You already have.'

'My family doesn't have the best track record at marriage.' George chuckled at her optimism. His father had repudiated his mother years ago and locked her in a tower.

Caroline shook her head. 'Mine doesn't either. My mother didn't have the luxury of choosing with her heart.'

'It won't be perfect,' George whispered.

'No, but we'll be happy.' Caroline sighed contentedly.

'Yes, I believe we will.'

Chapter Nine

Caroline stood at the entrance to the chapel at Herrenhausen Palace and smiled softly, surveying the quiet beauty of the setting laid out before her. Candles lit the chapel and the interior basked in the warm glow. Summer flowers adorned the aisle, lending a faintly sweet fragrance to the air. One could hardly guess from looking at the chapel that she'd arrived just that afternoon with George riding beside her.

There were those who might comment on the haste, but it only added to the romance and mystery that surrounded public accounts of their betrothal. If the setting was simple, it was also romantic. Those in attendance seemed to sense it too. Gathered in the pews were her people from Ansbach and George's family, perhaps a small number of guests compared to what might have been if circumstances had been different. But Caroline didn't mind. The intimate evening wedding seemed the perfect cap to the whirlwind courtship that had consumed her summer.

Now, dressed in her best, a gown of deep French blue trimmed in white lace and embroidered with white flowers at the hem, a bouquet of orange blossoms clutched in her hand, she was ready to go forward.

Her prince waited at the aisle's end, looking well-groomed and stately in his coat with its wide cuffs turned back to show the lace of his shirt. Smiles of approval met her as she walked forward, although she gave them the barest of notice. Everyone was fond of saying George had gotten the better end of the bargain, claiming she was the finest princess at court. Caroline would nod and laugh lightly at these comments, but in her heart she knew she had done well in this arrangement. She was to have a king and a companion and the latter was worth more than anything court councillors could list in their marriage settlements.

George smiled fondly at her and took her hand, squeezing it affectionately. 'Everyone is wondering what I did to win such a lovely bride,' he whispered.

'You were yourself.'

'Sort of.' George laughed and earned a sharp look from the priest, who wanted to get on with things.

Caroline wanted to get on with things too. Their apartments at the palace were waiting for them. Tomorrow there would be a ball and there would be congratulations to receive but tonight would be just for them.

George lifted her chin for a kiss and it was done. Together they walked down the aisle and took their first steps into their new life, confident in their newly created union.

Outside the chapel, George halted and drew her to him, kissing her far more soundly than he had at the altar moments ago. His eyes danced as he released her.

'You're up to something,' Caroline teased. 'What are you thinking? I can practically hear the wheels of your mind spinning.'

'I am thinking a king can be a lot of things, even happy.' And he kissed her again just to prove it.

* * * * *

Author Note

I was thrilled to be asked to be part of the *Royal Weddings* shorts to celebrate the wedding of William and Kate. The hard part came, however, in the selection of a royal wedding. I wanted to do a real wedding that actually resulted in a happy marriage. I settled on George II and Caroline of Ansbach for two reasons. First, she's a fascinating woman in history about whom little is known, and second, one item kept showing up in the accounts we have of them: they were relatively happy together and their marriage is considered in general to have been a success.

Here are some facts: Caroline and George had several children together. Most of them lived to adulthood. Except for approving of his marriage to Caroline, George's father continued to have a strained relationship with George. At one point, George and his father had a public fight at the baptism of one of George's sons and his father evicted him and Caroline from St James's Palace in London. Yes, George kept mistresses throughout the marriage. But when

Caroline died in 1737 after thirty-two years of marriage, it's reported that George vowed at her death bed to never marry again.

As a man and a king, George was considered to be attractive in his youth and likely to take a dare. He liked a challenge. One of the distinguishing factors of his biography is his claim to fame of being the last British monarch to personally lead troops in battle. He was considered daring and impulsive but possessed of a temper. While he was fluent in several languages, intellect was not his forte. It was generally held even during their reign that Caroline was the brains behind the throne. There were many accounts of Caroline serving as the Regent of England while her husband was abroad visiting Hanover. Some say she served as temporary regent up to seven times during their reign. Caroline quickly understood that her husband's interests were her interests. Their happiness and mutual affection depended on the two of them championing the same causes. Historians credit this insight to the success of their marriage. She never sided against him.

Not much is written about Caroline's early life. I did find useful resources in a book entitled *Caroline the Illustrious*, written back in the early 1900s, and a 1997 release of *King George II and Queen Caroline*.

It is true that Caroline was a popular bride choice. The King of Spain was very insistent in his courtship and her refusal of the future Holy Roman Emperor distressed the King of Prussia greatly.

It is true that George visited her incognito and immensely enjoyed his visit in June at Ansbach. He is reported in dispatches sent to Queen Anne in England to have told his father upon his return, 'It is love at first sight.' And that he wished to marry immediately.

It is true that his grandfather died right before the wedding and dispatches to England from England's representative at the Hanover Court reported the wedding would probably be moved back several weeks for mourning unless Prince George contested the decision. His father and grandmother left the decision entirely up to him. He did indeed argue to hasten the marriage and he did ride out to meet Caroline's party halfway to tell her the news.

Places where I embellished…

I do not know what Caroline wore to her wedding. From my research, I came across only one account of the wedding ceremony itself and that was in the English envoy's dispatch. I based my description on the general tradition of the time which was to wear one's best clothes to be married in. It was also customary at the time to wear white as a sign of half mourning but I elected to put Caroline in blue since the historical record suggests that everyone left off mourning behaviour for three days to celebrate the marriage. It was also tradition to carry orange blossoms as a sign of purity.

George did ride out to meet the party halfway on its journey to Hanover. Did he and Caroline consummate their relationship then? I don't know. Maybe not. However, we do know that George felt the need to 'restrain his ardour' (a direct line from research I found) during his visit to Ansbach since he could not reveal his true identity or the true nature of his visit. They'd also just spent the whole summer apart and Caroline made all haste to Hanover, even waiving all 'unnecessary ceremony' to hasten the marriage. So, they were in earnest and this particular story is foremost a romance.

Two final historic points of note:

There was one unromantic report that George slept through the wedding but, since I could not collaborate it, I chose to overlook it.

It was not clear which palace George visited in Ansbach when he courts Caroline in disguise. It may have been the hunting lodge or White Castle in Triesdorf, or it may have been the main palace in Ansbach. The book *Caroline the Illustrious* says he was received at the palace—which would be the main palace at Ansbach. The book *King George II and Queen Caroline* states he found Caroline in residence in Triesdorf but does not name the residence specifically as the hunting lodge or the White Castle. I chose to put their meeting at the main palace in Ansbach.

George II did have a love for the arts and opera. To reflect that, I centred their early conversations around the art of the margrave's palace which was known for its painted ceiling and the porcelain saloon. Since I had a description of the main palace and some of its interiors, setting their courtship there worked well with George's love of art. It was difficult to find any significant descriptions of the Triesdorf residence that would have been accurate for those years.

It is clear that George was devoted to her in his own way. There are reports from the first months of their marriage that he hardly left her side and that their friendship was fond to look upon. There are also accounts of Caroline catching smallpox in 1707 and of George staying beside her much of the time, endangering his life and falling ill with the disease himself. There are also other stories about their devotion to each other that equally affirm their mutual regard in a marriage that lasted thirty-two years until Caroline's death. However, there are reports as well that Caroline learned George's faults in short order as well. He was not a perfect man.

There's so much more I'd love to share here, but I hope you enjoyed this story. Please know that I tried to be as true to history as possible and did so to the best of my abilities.

For more information and fun facts about Caroline and George's courtship, check out my blog at www.bronwynswriting.blogspot.com or look for me on Facebook or at the eHarlequin blog.

Bronwyn Scott

A brief guide to players and terms:

King Frederick of Prussia: previously the Elector of Brandenberg before becoming King of Prussia in 1701, he is the official guardian of Caroline of Ansbach. His court is in Berlin. He is married to Sophia-Charlotte, Caroline's greatest mentor.

Queen Sophia-Charlotte: previously the Electress of Brandenberg before becoming queen. Married to Frederick, she is mentor and substitute mother to Caroline. She took on responsibility for Caroline when Caroline was eleven. Queen Charlotte's court of intellectuals gathers at Lutzenberg Palace just outside Berlin. Her husband spared no expense for the creation of this gathering place.

Sophia, Dowager Electress of Hanover: related to all the relevant players in this story. She is the granddaughter of James I. After Queen Anne, she is the closest Protestant claimant to the English throne, hence the succession through her line to George I and II. She is mother to Sophia-Charlotte and to the Elector of Hanover (George I) and grandmother to George Augustus (George II). She is well acquainted with Caroline, and is the first to suggest George marry Caroline, although she is not involved in any of the actual planning.

The Elector of Hanover: later to become King George I, father to George II.

William of Ansbach: the Margrave of Ansbach and brother to Caroline. William and Caroline were both children of John of Ansbach from his second marriage.

The Duke of Celle: George Augustus's maternal grandfather.

Margrave: a title that dates back to medieval times and is given to a governor (usually military) or lord of a border province in Germany. It is also used as a 'hereditary title' for certain princes in the Holy Roman Empire. In the case of William of Ansbach, the title is hereditary. He became margrave after the death of his father and his older stepbrother.

Elector: a member of the German electoral college in charge of electing the emperor of the Holy Roman Empire (previously known as the Roman king). Very early in the organization of the Germanic tribes, the position of elector was indeed elected from the tribes. However, by the days of George I the position had become hereditary and was passed from father to son. Heirs to the electors were called electoral princes. By all accounts the title 'elector' was highly respected and came with great power. An elector outranks a margrave, in case anyone was wondering.

A PRINCELY DILEMMA

ELIZABETH ROLLS

Award-winning author **Elizabeth Rolls** lives in the Adelaide Hills of South Australia with her husband, two soccer-mad sons, two dogs and a cat. She also has four alpacas and two incredibly fat sheep, all gainfully employed as environmentally sustainable lawnmowers. Elizabeth has what most people would consider far too many books, and her tea and coffee habit is legendary. She enjoys reading, walking, cooking and her husband's gardening. Elizabeth loves to hear from readers and invites you to contact her via e-mail at books@elizabethrolls. com and visit her website at http://www.elizabethrolls.com

Previous novels by Elizabeth Rolls:

THE UNEXPECTED BRIDE
MISTRESS OR MARRIAGE?
THE DUTIFUL RAKE
THE UNRULY CHAPERON
THE CHIVALROUS RAKE
HIS LADY MISTRESS
THE PRODIGAL BRIDE (in *A Regency Invitation*
anthology)
A SOLDIER'S TALE (in *A Regency Christmas* anthology)
A COMPROMISED LADY
LORD BRAYBROOK'S PENNILESS BRIDE

And in Mills & Boon Historical *Undone!* eBook:

A SCANDALOUS LIAISON

**Did you know that some of these novels are also
available as eBooks? Visit www.millsandboon.co.uk**

Chapter One

Easter Sunday, April 5, 1795, St James's Palace

'Severn! A moment, if you will!'

Christopher James Beaulieu, Duke of Severn, turned at the summons to find Lord Malmesbury, his face white, closing the door to Prince Ernest's private apartments in St James's Palace.

'Of course, Malmesbury,' said Severn, keeping his features blank. 'Something I can do for you?'

'Can you turn the clock back nine months?'

Severn blinked...having just seen His Royal Highness, George, Prince of Wales, burst from his brother's apartments. 'Nine months?' His mouth twitched. 'Has a happy event just occurred in there? Who's the father?'

Malmesbury cast a harried look around in case any of the bewigged and liveried royal footmen stationed in the corridor had heard, and glared at him. 'Levity, my lord duke,' he snapped in an undertone, 'is out of place!' He wiped his brow with a handkerchief and, keeping his voice low, said, 'I have just had the—' he gulped '—honour of presenting Princess Caroline of Brunswick to His Royal Highness.'

Severn could only conclude that to ruffle Malmesbury's diplomatically serene feathers so badly, the introduction had not gone well. Of course, the fact that the prince had fairly galloped down the corridor...

'I beg your pardon, Malmesbury,' he said. 'I saw the prince. He seemed, er, distracted. Muttered something about being duped and he must see Her Majesty immediately.'

Malmesbury groaned. 'I have but a moment—the king wishes to see me. Severn, he repulsed her!'

Severn thought it possible his lower jaw might not recover from the shock. He, too, shot a glance at the footmen. Stolid and unblinking, they gave not the least hint that they had any idea of what was going on. He wouldn't have wagered a groat on that. Not after Prinny's idiocy. 'He repulsed the princess?'

'Yes!' Malmesbury gripped his arm, drew him away from the footmen. 'Repulsed her, announced that he felt unwell and demanded a glass of brandy!'

And Severn thought he knew all there was to be known about making a disastrous marriage of convenience. 'Er, is there something wrong with the princess, or is it just that His Highness is being—' He hesitated, searching for a diplomatic phrase.

'—is being a damned fool?' suggested Malmesbury. 'A little of both perhaps. The princess is not, I fear, overly acquainted with the use of soap.'

Severn wrinkled his nose in sympathy with his future king as Malmesbury continued. 'But she *has* improved vastly, and appears willing and eager to conform, but *not* if the Prince of Wales continues in this wise! After he left she complained that he was not as handsome as the portrait she was sent, and that he was fat!'

'He *is* fat,' said Severn. And it was highly likely that the portrait sent had been flattering in the extreme. At least *he* hadn't made the mistake of relying on a portraitist's fancy; he'd thought he was extremely well-acquainted with his bride before offering, let alone marrying. Which just went to show how mistaken one could be...

Malmesbury didn't even glare. 'Lord, what a mess. Severn, if you can, try to see the prince. Represent to him the...the folly of continuing to insult his bride. She is not, I fear, of a governable or tractable temper. This, on top of sending Lady Jersey as lady-in-waiting to meet her at Greenwich.'

'He didn't!'

'Oh, yes, he did,' said Malmesbury. 'Apparently the queen was behind it. *And* the blasted woman was late! Lady Jersey, that is—not Her Majesty.' His teeth actually ground. 'Furthermore she had the temerity to attempt to sit beside the princess in the carriage. Claimed the motion made her unwell if she sat facing backwards!'

'Well, quite apart from Prinny's rudeness in sending his mistress to receive his bride,' said Severn, 'why the devil did Lady Jersey accept the appointment if she can't sit in a carriage backwards?'

Malmesbury's smile was pure acid. 'I asked her that myself. Anyway, look, Severn, if you can talk with the prince, try if you can to get him to see reason. He likes you. And haven't you recently married?'

'I returned from my honeymoon yesterday.' And he didn't want to talk about it to anyone, least of all Prinny. 'I'm surprised you knew anything about it.'

The baron nodded. 'Oh, yes. Someone mentioned it in a letter. The thing is, he might listen to you. Voice of experience and so forth.' Malmesbury looked apologetic. 'After all, there are parallels, if you will forgive my bluntness.'

Severn forcibly relaxed his hands. 'At least His Highness is marrying to settle his *own* debts,' he said coldly. Then, at Malmesbury's steady regard, he sighed. 'Oh, very well. I'll try what I can do, but I'm not making any promises.' Prinny, when he had a bee in his bonnet about a woman, was deaf to anything remotely resembling reason. And if Lady Jersey was pulling his strings about the princess... Nor was the queen happy about the match, having wanted her son to marry her own niece, not the king's.

Malmesbury gripped his hand. 'Thank you. I promised her father, the duke, that I'd do my best for her, but it's rapidly turning into a disaster.' He strode off down the corridor towards the king's apartments, with a final injunction cast over his shoulder. 'Just do your best, Severn.'

Chapter Two

His best. Severn contemplated that as he entered his Grosvenor Square mansion three hours later, and handed his hat, gloves and cane to the butler. 'Thank you, Blythe. Have brandy sent to the library, if you please.'

After his meeting with the prince he needed it. His best had not been anywhere near good enough. His Royal Highness showed absolutely no sign of being capable of listening to reason where the Princess Caroline was concerned—it was the king's fault in pressing for a marriage, Malmesbury's fault for not realising how unsuitable the woman was and getting him out of the match gracefully but instead bringing her to England, the princess's fault for being so utterly repellent!

'She reeked, Severn! Simply reeked. And all Malmesbury—blast his impudence!—could do when I positively begged for brandy—I felt faint, Severn, faint!—was bleat that I'd better have a glass of water!'

In the library Severn stared at the portrait of his father, resplendent in the silks and lace of his generation, an angel of ill-fortune, looming over the chimneypiece. 'What a mess,' he said. 'Why the hell do fathers have to interfere in the marital decisions of their sons?' He sank into the chair at his desk and buried his face in his hands.

His head snapped up again as a throat cleared in a very pointed sort of way.

Oh, hell!

His wife, having clearly just arisen from the wing chair facing the window, stood, book in hand, her expression unreadable, but her chin tilted just a little higher than normal. His heart kicked at the sight of her, but he kept his expression indifferent. Perhaps she hadn't quite heard. It wasn't as if he'd been speaking loudly.

'I beg your pardon, my lord duke. I did not hear you enter. I hope you do not mind if I borrow your book?' Her voice was quite even, not the least sign that she realised she had just heard herself comprehensively insulted.

'They are your books now too.' He looked at the one she was holding. 'What are you reading?'

'Goethe.'

'What?'

'You object?'

'Of course not! I just didn't know you could read German.'

'And French, and Italian.'

She was better educated in that respect than he was. 'An accomplished wife.'

'As you wished. Or so I thought.'

Oh, damn. She had heard.

'You will excuse me?' She started for the door, her deportment perfect, correct in every particular.

'Madam…' He rose, went towards her, hands held out. 'Linette, I did not mean—'

She changed course, quickening her step and skirting his outstretched hands. The slight hint of panic in her step, the sharply indrawn breath, halted him as nothing else could have. 'No matter, sir. Fathers can be inconvenient creatures, I am sure. Good day.' She reached the door and was through it in a froth of muslin skirts.

Returning to his chair, he dropped his head back into his hands and swore. He hadn't even thought that she might be in here. Women were supposed to prefer drawing rooms to libraries, weren't they? But his new duchess loved books, judging by the pile she kept beside her bed, and he had politely made her free of the library when he brought her home yesterday. At least it had been his wife, rather than a maid dusting. Although he wasn't entirely sure which would be worse—the servants' inevitable gossip, or his bride's stony face over the dinner table.

Dinner… *Oh, hell!* It was Easter Sunday; they'd invited his immediate family, and her grandmother, for dinner. It might have been possible to speak with her, apologise, over dinner if it were just the two of them. He would have no hesitation in dismissing the footmen and dining alone with her. Impossible with guests. He'd have to speak with her before dinner.

Chapter Three

Linnet, Duchess of Severn, having ordered a bath in front of the fire, wondered in what way her undoubtedly bourgeois behaviour had disgusted her aristocratic husband. Grandmère had made it all perfectly clear, instructing her on how to conduct herself in such a grand marriage. Clear enough until one tried to actually *do* it. It didn't help that he called her Lin*ette*, rather than *Lin*net; Grandmère had been very clear that being named after a bird was not at all proper.

Leaning back in the bath, she closed her eyes, listening to her maid, Bolt, moving about beyond the screen, laying out her evening clothes. She was never, or rarely, alone and yet she had never been so lonely in her life.

She had never thought that she would have no one to talk to. Really talk to. She certainly couldn't talk to Bolt, who had been her mother-in-law's maid and clearly disapproved of her new mistress. She had thought that she would be able to talk to Severn, that they could be friends, even though he had not married her for love. But it seemed that Grandmère had been right....

'No demonstrations of affection... You must use his title always... Any display of vulgar enthusiasm will betray ill-breeding, and give him a disgust of you... A lady of consequence lies still and accepts her duty; she submits to her husband's attentions quietly.'

She hadn't realised how difficult it would be to don the cloak of formal decorum. It didn't feel at all like the gracious ease of manner that her grandmother told her was necessary; it felt stiff, and cold. Papa had always encouraged her to be affectionate, open in her manners. Not vulgar, of course, but relaxed. But she supposed Grandmère must know more about the aristocracy than Papa had. In fact, Papa had never intended such a grand match for her at all.

'Marry a fellow you can trust to be honest with you.'

She swallowed. Severn had been completely honest with her about his reasons for offering for her hand—debts. His father's crippling debts which, without her fortune, would have sunk the dukedom. He had been open about it all, not paying her flowery compliments, nor pretending that he had fallen head over heels in love. She shivered; he had not behaved at all like her cousin, Joseph. Joseph had fooled her completely. Courting her, paying compliments, buying her extravagant gifts, which it turned out had put him even further into debt. He had been all tender consideration, with the false light in his eyes a beacon to lure her to disaster. She had been so lonely with Papa gone, had wanted someone to love so desperately. Apparently Joseph didn't even much like her....

'But, Father, she's so plain! And she reads too much, dull as ditchwater!'

'She's worth a fortune, boy. Enough and more to pull you out of the River Tick. That makes her a beauty, especially if you blow out the lamp. And there'll be time enough to school her out of annoying habits once you're safely married, and the money's tied up. She'll have to obey you then.'

Plain. Very well, she knew she was plain. Without the curling iron, which she hated, her hair was dead straight. And, with or without the iron, it was an unremarkable mousy colour. Not unlike the plumage of her namesake. Her eyes were a dull brown, and although her complexion was good, it was marred by those horrible freckles. As for her breasts, well, it was a good thing her stays pushed up what little there was. And Severn... She closed her eyes. Severn was beautiful, if you could call a man beautiful— those gorgeous eyes, the deep burnished gold hair and a face like...like a Greek god! And he was strong, but so gentle with it.

'She's bran-faced, Father, not to mention as flat as a board!'

'Take a mistress, then, once you've got a brat on the chit. Just marry her and secure the money.'

She grabbed the washcloth, soaping it vigorously. Eavesdropping was shameful, of course, not at all the behaviour expected of a lady. She had known it then, and if that hadn't been enough to prove to her that eavesdroppers rarely heard any good of themselves, then this evening had proved it. Not that she had meant to eavesdrop on either occasion. Still, sometimes it was better to know the truth even when it hurt. She had refused Joseph's offer the following morning, accompanied by a few pithy quotes from the conversation she'd overheard, and removed from her uncle Bartholomew's house to her grandmother's within the hour.

There had been nowhere else to go. Her father's will stipulated that until she married, or turned thirty, she must reside with either her uncle Bartholomew or her French *émigré* grandmother.

Madame la Marquise de la Marchèrand had received her willingly, if coldly. Even her enduring disgust at her daughter's elopement twenty-three years earlier with a wealthy English merchant did not blind her to the advantages of chaperoning a young lady worth two hundred and fifty thousand pounds.

'*Soit.* So be it. We will contrive. Bad blood, *oui.*'

Her Gallic shrug said it all.

'*Et pas de beauté.* You are no beauty. But with such a fortune, here in England—a land of shopkeepers!—it will suffice for many.'

The old lady had sniffed disdainfully.

'In *la belle* France it would not be so. Such a *bourgeois* connection, it would be *incroyable.* Unthinkable! But while there may be none in this nation fit to ride in a carriage with the French king, there will of a certainty be many suitors for such a fortune.'

As opposed to suitors for plain, bourgeois Linnet Farley.

Instead of pointing out that the last French king and his queen had lost their heads two years before and their young son remained imprisoned in the Temple, she had submitted to Grandmère's decrees, preferring brutal candour to lying sweetness. If all she could expect was to be married for her money, then she would do it with her eyes open and choose for herself.

And she had. She had chosen Severn, almost from the minute of meeting him. Severn, whose smiling blue eyes had offered friendship…or so she had thought.

She blinked away the hotness behind her own eyes, grabbed the washcloth and soaped it. It would all be perfectly fine, if only she had not permitted herself to believe that Severn felt something for her. That beyond his pressing need for her money to pay off his father's debts and save his family, there had been a genuine liking for her. There had been something in his smile, something affectionate, almost a caressing, that had always left her warm, tingly and slightly breathless. She still felt that way, only now there was that cool reserve in his voice, a certain distance when he spoke to her.

Ignoring the lump in her throat, she washed herself. She had hoped it was just discretion after that dreadful time Grandmère had caught them together and she had been in his arms, about, she had thought, to be kissed. And very willingly too. After that he had been all that was polite and proper, keeping a decent distance at all times.

Even on their wedding night. Oh, he had bedded her. Gentle, careful and considerate, he had made her his wife. With the lights out. Just as Uncle Bartholomew had suggested to Joseph. And left her room as soon as he had assured himself that he had not hurt her too much in taking her virginity. It was the same each time he came to her, and each time she found it harder and harder to just lie still and silent beneath him, her heart pounding, her body shivering with the need to move against him, with him. It was even harder not to ask him to stay afterwards, to hold her for just a little while. She dared not. Apparently Grandmère had been right; it was folly for a lady to wear her heart on her sleeve. It was better off kept safely away from sight, if not intact.

She could no longer hear her maid, which suggested that it was probably time for her to be out of the bath, ready for the hated curling iron. Sitting up, she braced to stand; the outer door opened, and she froze.

'Your mistress is here?' That deep, quiet voice that brushed every nerve.

'Yes, Your Grace.'

'Out.'

The door closed, and he spoke again. 'Madam?'

Madam wondered that the bath didn't evaporate in steam, she was blushing so hotly. 'I'm…I'm here, sir. In the bath.'

Chapter Four

Walking in on his wife in her bath had not been part of his plan. No wonder the damned maid had scuttled out past him, cheeks scarlet and eyes brimming with suppressed speculation. Why couldn't Bolt have said something? If his mother had been in her bath, the wretched woman would have seen him off breathing fire!

'Was there something you particularly wished to tell me, sir?'

He shut his eyes, wishing to God he could shut off his imagination as easily.

'Er, yes. Yes, there is.' He'd think of it in a moment, when his brain stopped dwelling on how she might look in her bath—silky brown tresses pinned up on top of her head, just waiting to be tumbled around her shoulders…all soft, and rosy, and…moist.

'Yes?'

'Ah…' He floundered. What had he wanted to say? He grabbed at the first thing that floated past. 'You've remembered that we have guests tonight?' That hadn't been it, surely?

'Yes. Your family. Grandmère.'

Who knew that a faint French accent could be so damned erotic?

'I would not forget such a thing,' she said.

'Er, no. Of course not. Um, oh, yes.' He dragged in a breath. How the hell was a man meant to offer his wife an apology for something he hadn't really said, when all he could think about was how damp and rosy that wife would be in her bath, and how soft and warm she'd been in his arms last night.

Soft, warm—and still frightened of his lovemaking, he thought. She lay so still, it was as though she was afraid to move. It was nearly killing him to keep it slow and careful for her, let alone leave her bed afterwards, but the thought of distressing her any more was untenable. Patience. That was the key. Bed her gently, keep himself under control.

He let the breath out, banishing all thoughts of either dragging his wife from the tub or joining her. 'I wished to assure you that my...remarks in the library earlier did not refer to our...situation.' He frowned, thought about that. 'Our marriage,' he corrected. He wasn't going to have a situation. He was going to have a marriage. He hoped. Right now it was probably a situation.

'Oh.'

Oh? What the hell did that mean? 'No,' he affirmed. 'I was speaking of—' He broke off. Dammit! Under no circumstances could he discuss the prince's private affairs, not even with his wife. 'Well, I was not speaking of you...

that is, us.' Lord! If he had a horse that lame, he'd have to shoot it.

'Oh. I see.' Apparently his wife would shoot the poor, gimpy-legged creature too. 'Well, thank you, sir. Um, if that was all, perhaps you might send my maid back in? I should be getting out to dress. And…and I need the towel.'

The towel hung in plain view over a dainty lyre-backed chair. If it was anything like the towels he used, and it had damn well better be, then it was silky soft, but he'd wager it wasn't as soft as his wife's skin.

He was moving before he'd so much as drawn breath. 'Permit me.'

'What? *No!*'

The towel was already in his hand as he rounded the end of the screen. There was a frantic splashing as his furiously blushing wife drew her knees up to wrap her arms about them and hide her breasts, but he had one brief glimpse of heaven—wet, creamy, rose-tipped breasts and the delicate curve of her waist. It was enough; she was utterly delectable.

He shut his eyes and held out the towel. 'There you are.' There she was indeed. Soft and damp and naked. And he had his damned eyes shut.

'Th-thank you.' The tinkle of water told him she'd stood. He shut his eyes even tighter, reminding himself of all the reasons he shouldn't open them. She was a new bride. Still shy, maidenly. She shrank from the idea of making love with a lamp lit; last night he'd tried leaving a candle alight, but she'd reminded him, in a wooden little voice that had torn him apart, so he'd blown it out, drawn the bed hangings to banish even the firelight.

The towel was taken from his grasp by a hand that seemed to tremble, and he fought the ignoble urge to open his eyes and see his wife, this woman whom he knew only by touch, and taste, a little.

Against all physical possibility, he hardened even more. Hell. If she saw that— With a strangled curse, he turned away, walking stiffly back around the screen.

'I'll send your maid back in, madam.' He hesitated. The queen was not the only mother in London furious about her son's choice of bride. Perhaps a tactful warning? 'My mother, by the way, is likely to be early.' Just because in this house, of all houses, she could arrive early to fluster her hostess without raising the slightest censure. Just to be able to moan a little more about his appalling marriage if her daughter-in-law was not down to receive her. All the while accepting an allowance made possible by the despised daughter of trade. And foisting Bolt on the poor girl. Just as the queen had forced Lady Jersey on Princess Caroline.

'Ah, you know if you wished for another maid…there is no need to keep Bolt, just to please my mother.'

'Oh.' She sounded stunned. 'Yes, of course. Thank you, sir.'

Chapter Five

Linnet stared at the gown laid over the chair. Dull grey silk, high-necked and long-sleeved; it was positively dowdy. It was one her mother-in-law had chosen as being appropriate. And Bolt had been her mother-in-law's maid, in attendance when the gown had been fitted...and of course Bolt knew who was coming to dinner.

'That isn't the gown I asked you to lay out.' She had asked for the muslin in soft lavender, embroidered with silver.

The maid sniffed. 'No, Your Grace. But I thought it would be more appropriate.'

She was in mourning after all...but then, despite the downcast eyes, she saw the gleam of triumph in the maid's expression. Linnet stiffened. She had nearly succumbed meekly to her maid's decree. Quite possibly to her mother-in-law's decree. Her father-in-law had been dead six months, she had never even met him and lavender was perfectly acceptable for half-mourning. She drew in a breath.

Listening to advice was one thing; being dictated to was another.

'But then I do not pay you to think for me, Bolt,' she said coolly. 'The gown I requested, if you please.'

Mouth primmed, Bolt obeyed. Slowly.

'And, Bolt?'

'Yes, Your Grace?'

'This gown—I find that I do not like it at all. You may keep it.'

Dressed in the lavender muslin, with its elbow-length sleeves, Linnet stared into the mirror, wondering if she had taken leave of her senses. Oh, it was pretty enough. In fact, she thought it might be the prettiest gown she had ever had. But it was so daring! The low-cut, high-waisted bodice, and filmy clinging muslins of dress and petticoat, showed every curve. Not that she had many curves. She swallowed. It was one of the few gowns she had chosen for herself one afternoon when she had shopped with Severn's older sister, Lady Farnsworth, just before her marriage.

'Excellent choice. Kester will like that one.'

Severn hadn't seen it yet. She hadn't dared. She took a deep breath. If she changed her gown she would be down late. Worse, Bolt would have won. And she still had to choose the right jewellery.

'Yes. I like it. My jewellery case, if you please. And my gloves. Oh, and the turban that matches this gown.'

The knock at the door startled them both.

Severn walked in. Gorgeous, utterly elegant in satin evening breeches, black coat and a grey-and-lavender waistcoat, a single pearl nestled in his cravat. And then the man of fashion stopped dead in his tracks staring at her, his jaw dropped in a most unducal and inelegant fashion.

Despite the blush that scorched her cheeks, Linnet kept her chin up. 'Am I late, Your Grace?' She knew she wasn't. Perhaps he simply wanted to assure himself that she was suitably attired.

For a moment he said nothing. Just stared, his gaze burning, intent. Then he took a visibly shaky breath. 'No. Not at all. I…I came to give you these.' He held out a long slim box covered in shabby green velvet.

Biting her lip, Linnet took the box and opened it.

'Ohhh!' she breathed. Pearls glimmered up at her, and in their midst a great amethyst winked in the lamplight. Her hands shook as she lifted the necklace out. She couldn't speak. The pearls hung in a great rope, caught together by the amethyst which was surrounded by tiny diamonds, a smaller loop of pearls hanging below. It was lovely, beyond lovely, but the lump in her throat defeated her.

She looked up at Severn, saw a muscle in his jaw twitch. 'Out.'

For the second time in as many hours, Bolt scuttled from the room under ducal decree.

'I had them reset, but if you don't like it—'

'I like it,' she whispered.

He frowned. 'Are you sure?'

'Oh, yes.'

'Then, may I—will you permit me to put it on for you?'

Wordless, she nodded. He hadn't said anything about the gown. Yet.

He stripped off his gloves and came to her slowly, and took her hands. For a moment he was motionless, then his hands skimmed up her arms, her bare arms. Slowly. While her knees shook and her mind melted in pleasure. He paused at the silver embroidered sleeve, and then for an instant one long forefinger slid under the sleeve. The lightest caress on her hidden flesh, yet she had to stiffen herself and swallow to hold back the gasp of pleasure.

A gentleman wants a virtuous wife and mother. Not displays of wanton abandon. Over and over she reminded herself, pretending the deep, aching need wasn't there.

With a sigh, he shifted his hold to her muslin-clad shoulders, turned her to face the dressing mirror and lifted the necklace to slip over her head. Cool and silky, the pearls slid against her skin, the great central amethyst ablaze between her breasts, just above the bodice. She shivered again as his fingers feathered along her jaw.

'The…the pearls are lovely,' she managed to get out.

'I've seen lovelier,' he murmured, and bent to brush a kiss where his fingers had trailed. 'Perhaps a kiss, sweetheart?'

Everything inside her melted, yearned, as she instinctively turned towards the temptation of his mouth. Their lips met, hers trembling, his warm, firm, moving gently on hers so that they parted on a sigh.

Abruptly he straightened. Stepped back. 'That gown—' His voice sounded odd. 'I've not seen that before, have I?'

'No.' Oh, God! Here it came. Was he going to tell her it was shameless? That she was to change? And she had kissed him, for heaven's sake! Would he think *her* shameless? Yes, he had meant to kiss her, but she had done it for him.

'Did you choose it?' Still that odd, strangled voice.

'Yes.' Defiant suddenly, she lifted her chin. 'But Lady Farnsworth thought it was pretty.'

He shut his eyes. 'I may have to kill Louisa.'

Her heart sank. 'You don't like it, then.' He had shut his eyes when he'd handed her the towel too.

The blue eyes opened, their expression unreadable. 'The gown is very pretty. Most fashionable.' His voice was practically a growl. He reached into a pocket of his coat for another velvet-covered box. Handing it to her, he said, 'You had better put these on.'

She stared. His hand was shaking.

'Earrings,' he said, clearing his throat. 'To match the necklace.'

Taking the box, she opened it. More amethysts winked up at her, each with a dangling teardrop pearl. Carefully she put them on, fumbling. 'Thank you, Severn,' she whispered.

He frowned again. 'You are sure you like them? I thought, well, we are still in mourning for my father, so colours, except for purple, are out, but I didn't know what you liked, so if you don't—'

'I love them,' she said firmly. Carefully she picked up the turban that matched her gown and set it on her hair, and pulled on her white kid gloves. Tentatively she smiled at him. 'Is it time to go down?'

He looked at her quizzically. 'You don't want to check yourself in the looking glass?'

Her stomach lurched. 'Is something wrong? Have I forgotten something?'

He stared. 'No. Not a thing. You look lovely. Come.' He held out his arm. Shyly she set her hand on it and he led her from the room.

Chapter Six

They beat the dowager duchess to the drawing room by a flight of stairs, hearing her below in the hall, bemoaning the inconvenience of a Sunday night dinner to her unmarried daughter, Lady Sophia.

She entered the drawing room in the wake of Blythe's announcement. 'The Dowager Duchess of Severn, Lady Sophia Beaulieu.'

The dowager's mouth drooped petulantly. 'Oh. I feared you would not yet be down, Miss Far— Dear me, what should I call you now? Oh, yes—Linette, is it not?' She raised a lorgnette and examined Linnet from top to toe. Then lowered the glass with a faint sigh.

Linnet managed a smile. 'Welcome, *madame*. And Lady Sophia. How do you go on?'

Rustling black silk, the dowager waved a languid hand. 'Quite well, I assure you. If one may be well in such a poky establishment as that to which we are reduced.' She cast a sorrowful eye around the drawing room.

'You chose the house yourself, Mama,' said Severn. 'And

if you feared we would not yet be down, then I wonder you chose to arrive so early.'

Linnet blinked. Severn sounded positively snippy. Seeing the dowager about to take offence, and fearing for the success of the evening, she rushed into speech. 'But of course your mother may arrive whenever she likes, and welcome, Severn,' she said firmly.

Baulked of prey, the dowager permitted herself a little smile. 'Sophia, pray—my vinaigrette.' She sank onto a sofa.

Behind her, Linnet heard Severn's teeth grinding.

The Marquise de la Marchèrand arrived next, closing followed by Lord and Lady Farnsworth.

The marquise greeted her granddaughter with a deep curtsey, before subjecting her to a penetrating examination.

'The gown… It is in the modern style, but not—'

'I like it.' Beside her, Severn sounded rather like a bear.

The marquise shrugged. 'Naturally, if *monsieur le duc* approves, there is no more to be said.'

Lady Farnsworth dispensed with ceremony, greeting her new sister-in-law with a hug and approving look. 'Hmm. I said that gown would be pretty. You seem very well. Kester looking after you?'

Linnet blushed.

Lady Farnsworth just smiled and turned to her brother. 'I thought you'd appreciate that gown, Kester.'

Only Linnet was close enough to hear his response. 'Yes, I do, and I'll kill *you* later.' Lady Farnsworth laughed and stood on tiptoe to kiss his cheek.

So, if he really did like the gown, why did he want to kill his sister?

Farnsworth shook her hand. 'Evening, Lady Severn. Shan't ask how you're going on—you look famously. Severn's a lucky devil. Told Louisa that in the carriage.'

She liked Lord Farnsworth, even if her grandmother did dismiss him in acid tones as the grandson of a country physician. He was blunt, kind and made no secret of the fact that he thought his wife was brilliant.

'Are we all here?' asked the dowager. 'Perhaps we should go down to dinner. Where is Blythe?'

Linnet hesitated. She ought to make the announcement that they would go down, but Severn's younger brother, Lord Guy, was not yet arrived.

Lady Farnsworth dealt with her mother smartly. 'For heaven's sake, Mama! You are not the hostess here now, you know. Besides, Guy is not here yet.' She glanced at Linnet. 'I'm assuming you invited him because you're too polite not to do so, but since he usually ignores family invitations—'

'Lord Guy Beaulieu,' intoned Blythe, admitting a fashionably dressed young man with the same bright hair and blue eyes as his brother and sisters.

'Unless he wants something,' muttered Lady Farnsworth to Linnet.

Lord Guy bowed over Linnet's hand. 'How d'you do, ma'am?' He smiled charmingly. 'Sorry to be late. My fellow forgot to remind me in time.'

'You're not late at all,' said Linnet politely.

Lord Guy passed on to his brother. 'Evening, Severn. I say, any chance of a quick word before dinner?'

To Linnet's surprise, Severn shook his head. 'No. No chance at all.'

His lordship looked petulant. 'Oh, I say. Really—'

The dowager drew herself up. 'Now that we are—'

'Blythe, now that Lord Guy is here, please have dinner served,' said Linnet, speaking across her mother-in-law and shuddering internally for being so rude, but hoping to avert further arguments. To her surprise Grandmère gave a slight, approving nod. '*Bon, ma petite.* You begin to assert yourself.' She dealt the dowager's glare a gracious smile. 'You and I, *madame*, we must remember that it is our children to whom we must now defer. *Non?*'

Severn moved gracefully to the marquise. 'Madame, I doubt you have ever deferred to anyone in your life.' He offered his arm. The dowager's glare redoubled and Linnet began to wonder if they would survive the evening without bloodshed.

Smiling, Farnsworth strolled up to Linnet. 'Now I'm a lucky devil,' he said. 'I get the new bride.' He sent his wife a wicked grin.

Lady Farnsworth choked back a laugh. 'True enough. Guy, you take Mama in, since Kester is taking Madame de la Marchèrand.'

Lord Guy looked annoyed.

'It's that or Sophie,' his elder sister informed him.

Lady Sophia stared around. 'What? Isn't anyone else coming? You mean there is no gentleman to take *me* in? How shab—'

Severn's glare had her swallowing her remarks. 'This is a family dinner, not a grand occasion, Sophie,' he informed her. 'You may consider yourself lucky, since you are not out until next year, to be invited at all. But next time we'll invite Cousin Randolph for you.'

Lady Sophia scowled. 'But I would be out this year if Papa hadn't died! It's not fair! Why can't—?'

'Oh, come along, Soph,' said Lady Farnsworth, over her sister's complaint. 'You'll have to make do with me in Randolph's absence. Or go up to the old schoolroom.'

Lady Sophia did not look at all as if this pleased her, but she shut up and took her place with her elder sister.

Farnsworth choked. 'Randolph's sixty. Divinity Fellow at Oxford,' he explained to Linnet in an undertone. 'For God's sake take me in to dinner before one of the Beaulieus murders another!'

Chapter Seven

Surveying the guests ranged around the laden table, Kester nearly groaned. He must have been insane to have suggested a family dinner like this. It would have been better to invite a few extras. Then his family might actually behave itself.

Instead Mama was putting on her best die-away airs over the soup to impress the marquise, who looked completely unimpressed. Guy was sulking because he had been denied his 'quick word.' Kester knew what *that* was all about—money. Even if Farnsworth hadn't warned him, he would have known. Guy assumed that now the family was afloat again, he could apply to his ducal brother for an endless supply of the ready to pay his mounting debts. Well, he couldn't. Linette's money was not going to be wasted on idiocy.

Sophie was sulking, too. She had obviously assumed that at least one eligible young man would have been provided for her entertainment.

Briefly he wondered how the family dinner at St James's

Palace was progressing. Had the prince thought about what he'd said? That he needed to give his bride a chance? Would the princess find a single friend at that dinner table beyond poor Malmesbury?

He could only thank God for Farnsworth and Louisa, happily chatting to Linette at the other end of the table. Even if he *did* intend to murder Louisa over that damn gown. How the devil was a fellow supposed to remember to eat when his wife sat glimmering in silver-shot muslin, with a confounded amethyst between her breasts? Had she really meant to—?

'Severn!'

He turned to look at his mother. 'Yes, Mama?'

She adopted a wounded air. 'I've spoken to you three times, Severn. No doubt you have more important things on your mind, but...'

Dead right, he did. Such as whether or not his wife had really meant to kiss him when he gave her the necklace? If he hadn't stepped back...well, he didn't think that dinner would have been served at all, let alone on time—

'Severn!'

He jerked his attention back from that blasted amethyst. 'Sorry, Mama. What did you say?'

'I was saying,' said his mother, in a slightly louder voice that had everyone turning to listen, 'that since your wife evidently prefers her *own* jewels to the family collection, you might give Sophia the pearl set. If not for your father's death, she would have come out this year, and—well, Severn, the pearl set would be most becoming to your sister!'

Even separated from her by fifteen feet of mahogany,

Kester saw the shock and embarrassment on his wife's face. In that single unguarded instant he saw the insecurity, the hurt. And then it was gone. Hidden behind the polite, demure façade.

'Of course, if Lady Sophia—' she began.

'No.' He didn't bother to sugarcoat his words. *Is something wrong? Have I forgotten something?* She was already unsure of herself and damned if he'd permit anyone, even his mother, to belittle her. 'Those *are* the Beaulieu pearls, Mama. I had them reset especially for Linette. They are *hers*. Until *she* chooses to hand them on to my heir's bride.'

His wife was simply scarlet, and he could have cheerfully murdered his mother for embarrassing her. He drew a deep breath and beckoned to a hovering footman. 'Champagne for everyone—a half-glass for Lady Sophia.'

He waited until everyone was served and then rose.

'To my bride,' he said simply, lifting his glass. Their eyes met, hers so soft and—damn it—were those tears? Was it so surprising that he'd defend her? Had she really thought that he'd let his mother insult her?

'Well, I'm sure that's very pretty,' said Louisa, setting down her glass. 'And the pearls are lovely. Just right, Kester.' She gave him an approving nod. 'But is it true what Farnsworth tells me—that Princess Caroline arrived this afternoon and the Prince of Wales actually sent Lady Jersey to meet her?'

Kester looked at his brother-in-law, who shrugged. 'That's what I heard, Severn. Seems a mad start, but who knows? Prinny can be such a fool at times.'

'I cannot think why you should say such a thing,' snapped the dowager. 'Lady Jersey is a particular friend of mine, and I am sure she is a most fitting person to greet the princess. Why! She is the daughter of a bishop!'

In the light of Sophia's presence, Kester could hardly point out that, as the Prince of Wales's mistress, Lady Jersey was hardly living up to her ecclesiastical origins.

Guy, however, laughed. 'For God's sake, Mama! She's Prinny's mistress, and everyone knows it! Smack in the eye for the bride though. Wonder what she's like? And can he marry her after Mrs Fitzherbert?'

'Guy!' Kester rapped it out.

His brother scowled. 'Oh, don't be so stuffy, Severn! Everyone suspects he actually married Mrs Fitzherbert.'

Kester caught his wife's gaze. She looked stunned. No, unfamiliar with his world, she might not have known. But she probably knew he'd been at the palace this afternoon. Would she say something about that?

'Poor Princess Caroline, if it is all true,' she said quietly. Her eyes met his searchingly.l Kester swallowed. Dammit. Did she think he would insult her like that? Take a mistress when without her he would have lost everything?

'Well, it's not as though he can possibly be in love with her,' said Sophia indifferently. 'It's an arranged marriage. Everyone knows *that*!'

He opened his mouth to scarify Sophie, but his wife was speaking again.

'I dare say such things are common,' she said. 'That does not make them right. And he could still be polite, even if he does have a mistress.' Kester blinked at the suddenly fierce note in her voice. 'She has come all this way, to a strange land to live amongst strangers,' she went on, 'away from her family and friends. How hard can it be for a prince to be polite? And…and kind!' Her chin went up a notch. 'Even in an arranged marriage, courtesy is important.'

The marquise nodded. '*Exactement!* Why, when la Reine Marie-Antoinette came to France, *le dauphin* was most gracious to her. As befitted his breeding.'

Kester had an odd feeling that his wife was not thinking about the martyred French queen. Sometimes you did not have to cross seas or continents to find yourself in regions marked Here Be Dragons.

Chapter Eight

Linnet heaved a mental sigh of relief when the conversation veered from the prince's impending marriage. Since it was only a family affair they used the small dining parlour and were seated at a round table so the talk could range freely.

She made several efforts to coax Lady Sophia out of her sulks, asking about the plans for her Season next year, but received the most gloomy of replies, amidst bitter glances at the pearls. Sophia expected hardly to enjoy herself at all—how could one, when everyone knew how *low* they were sunk? She would be unlikely to receive as much as a single offer! Since Linnet was aware that a decent dowry had been set aside for Sophia, she knew this was nonsense, unless of course the dowry was not sufficient to compensate for Lady Sophia's petulance.

Lord Guy was not much better. He supposed he was enjoying town. Not much fun when a fellow was kept so dashed short though. And of course, being in mourning a fellow couldn't *do* much. Still it was better than being down at Camley Priory. And he had been put on to a sure thing just yesterday, if only Kester would oblige! Not as though *he* was short!

Linnet noted that Lord Guy kept his voice low enough that his remarks did not carry to the other side of the table. She also rather thought that although Lord Farnsworth was chatting with his wife across the table, they were both very much aware of the tenor of Lord Guy's conversation.

'*You* could have a word with Kester though, could you not?' Lord Guy said to her, as though he had only just thought of it.

Lord Farnsworth's eyes snapped into focus and his mouth opened.

'No. I'm afraid not, Lord Guy,' said Linnet gently. She smiled at his chagrined face and looked across to his lordship. 'Is the dinner to your liking, my lord?'

'Excellent,' Farnsworth assured her. 'Most entertaining dinner I've been to in years. You must come to us next week. Meet a few people, eh? Louisa will see to it now that you're fixed in town.'

'I should like that very much,' she said. An invitation. Even if it was given out of family obligation and kindness.

By the time Linnet rose to lead the ladies out and leave the gentlemen to their wine, her head ached. But the drawing room was almost worse than the dinner table.

Lady Sophia opened hostilities. 'It's not really so surprising that the prince has a mistress,' she said, sipping her tea. 'After all, most men do. Even Kester, I should think. He was very interested in Lady Anne Davison last year. Everyone knew.'

Linnet nearly dropped the teapot into Lady Farnsworth's lap. She had met Lady Anne, a charming widow, shortly before her marriage. The dowager had made the introductions.

'What rubbish!' said Lady Farnsworth. 'Just a drop of milk, thank you. Sophie, your manners are disgusting! It's just as well Mama can't bring you out this year if you can't hold your tongue!'

'I do not say that Severn *does* have a mistress,' said the dowager. She flicked a glance at Linnet, whose stomach churned. 'But he has certainly done so in the past, and it would not be anything at all surprising if he were to continue to do so.' Another pitying glance at Linnet.

Linnet forced her features to remain blank. Yes, she had considered this possibility when she had realised Severn was likely to offer for her. Considered it and accepted the likelihood. She had thought she would be able to cope, that common sense would be enough. She had been a fool.

'Most gentlemen do,' continued the dowager. She primmed her mouth and sipped her tea. 'Dear Linette would be well-advised to bear in mind that a *lady* does not notice these things.'

'Which does not explain how you and Sophia come to be noticing them,' said Lady Farnsworth dryly.

Her mother glared. 'I *meant* that a lady does not make a fuss, or fall into the dismals when her husband strays, as he inevitably does.'

'I can assure you that when Farnsworth takes a mistress, I shall not fall into the dismals, Mama,' said Lady Farnsworth. 'I'll be too busy beating him about the head with his own duelling pistols!'

'*Really*, Louisa!' The dowager looked pained. 'That would be most improper.'

Linnet couldn't help it; she laughed out loud, despite the aching pain of wondering if Severn would stray.

Lady Farnsworth turned to look at her. 'I doubt you'll need them, but Kester keeps his in the bottom of his armoire. Or he used to. If you can't find them, let me know. I'll lend you Roger's.'

'It is not at all the thing for *madame la duchesse* to be beating her husband around the head,' pronounced Grand-mère. 'In that—' she nodded to the dowager '—Madame is perfectly correct. However—' and she looked down her nose in scorn '—I think it is most vulgar to speculate upon whether or not *monsieur le duc* has, or may perhaps take, a mistress in front of his bride. At the court of Versailles, such manners would not have been tolerated.'

The door opened and the gentlemen entered. Linnet's stomach dropped. Had Severn heard any of that? Whether he had or not, she would survive this evening with her head held high. She gritted her teeth and smiled.

'Tea, Lord Farnsworth?'

Chapter Nine

After bidding his mother and Sophia farewell, Kester looked at Louisa and Farnsworth, who were the only guests left.

'I suppose you think I ought to be grateful you didn't make a dash for it an hour ago.'

'Yes,' said Farnsworth. 'I do. Damned grateful. What's all this nonsense about Prinny and the Princess Caroline?'

Kester cleared his throat. 'Can't discuss it. Sorry.'

Louisa snorted. 'Really, Kester! You must be the only person in town who *won't* discuss it. Were you, or were you not, at St James's Palace this afternoon?'

'Yes. And that's all I'm going to say.' He looked over at his wife. She appeared pale, sad. What the devil had the ladies been talking about earlier? When he'd brought the gentlemen up the conversation had died instantly, and Linette had looked as though someone had struck her. 'Why don't you go up? I'll see these two out.'

She looked hesitant, but Louisa spoke up. 'Yes, don't stand on ceremony with us.' She went over and gave her sister-in-law a hug. 'Cheer up. Mama never behaves at family dinners. Don't pay any attention to her nonsense—we none of us do.'

'Which particular nonsense was Mama spouting over the teacups?' asked Kester as he accompanied Louisa and Farnsworth downstairs. 'Did it have something to do with the court of Versailles?'

Louisa glanced at Farnsworth, who shrugged. 'He's your brother.'

'True,' said Louisa. 'Very well.' She looked at Kester. 'Do you, or do you not, have a mistress?'

Farnsworth spluttered.

Kester stopped dead in his tracks. *'What?'*

Grabbing his sister by the wrist, he dragged her down the last few steps and into a small parlour off the front hall, to the evident surprise of the footman on duty.

Slamming the door behind them, he turned on her. 'What the hell do you take me for, Louisa? A complete—' He broke off as the door opened to admit Farnsworth. '—brute?' he continued as Farnsworth closed the door.

'Are you going to kill her, or just beat her?' asked Farnsworth equably.

Beyond flinging him an irritated glance, Kester ignored that. 'Are you aware,' he demanded, glaring at his impossible sister, who had strolled across to peruse the bookshelves, 'that if it hadn't been for Linette agreeing to marry me, we would have lost practically everything due to Papa's damned folly? *Everything.*'

'Slightly more aware than Mama, I should think,' said Louisa, over her shoulder. She pulled out a book. 'May I borrow this?'

'Yes, curse you!' Kester dragged in a breath, reaching for control. Damn it! He could scarcely think for wanting his wife, worrying that she might be regretting their marriage—how the hell could he possibly want a mistress? 'And you believe I wouldn't at least give her my loyalty?' He wanted to give her far more than mere loyalty.

'Of course not,' said Louisa. 'But Mama planted the seed. Or rather Soph did, and then Mama dropped a load of manure on it and watered it in. You might want to do some weeding.'

Farnsworth looked pained. 'Such a crude way of putting it, Louisa. May I presume to offer a word of advice, Severn?'

'What?' said Kester.

'Don't let this take hold. Even if she doesn't believe it now, every time a woman so much as looks at you, particularly Anne Davison—'

'Curse it, Farnsworth! I haven't seen La Davison for months!' He'd broken off the connection when he'd decided to court the marquise's unknown granddaughter.

'—she's going to worry. Even if you don't love her.'

'What the hell would you know about it?' snarled Kester.

'Make sure she knows that your loyalty at least is given,' said Farnsworth. 'And make sure our world knows that too. Otherwise, they will tear her to pieces.' His mouth thinned. 'Just as Princess Caroline will be torn to pieces if Prinny doesn't conduct himself as a gentleman.'

He went upstairs slowly, thinking. Understandable that the prince resented the situation. He hadn't been happy about being forced to marry either. But that was not his wife's fault. Nor was it the princess's fault. Only a cur, or a spoiled princeling, would take that resentment out on his bride, or permit his family to make her life hell.

Besides, he *liked* his bride. More than liked, if he were to be honest with himself. Only something had gone wrong, and he would have to put it right.

He found his wife in her bedchamber, still dressed, but she had discarded the turban and stripped off her gloves. With her hair hanging down in long soft curls, she looked terribly young and vulnerable. He swallowed. That dratted amethyst was still riding in pride of place. He'd look like an idiot if he challenged a jewel and shot it for being precisely where *he* wanted to be.

'Oh. My lord. I was about to ring for my maid.'

'Don't.' He thought about that. 'Please,' he added. 'Why don't you come through to my sitting room? There's a brandy decanter there and a couple of glasses. If you don't need one after that evening, I do.'

One thing they weren't going to need was her maid. He took off his own gloves, stuffed them in the pocket of his coat and held out his hand. 'Come.'

Slowly she laid her small hand in his much larger one. He drew her up, resisting the urge to kiss her. For now. Instead he led her to his rooms.

'This,' he said, turning to face her in the middle of the sitting room, 'has got to stop.'

She paled. 'What? I don't understand, my lord duke.'

He groaned. 'No. You don't. I mean this formal idiocy we've taken refuge in. It has to stop. I'm damned if I'll spend the rest of my life being my lord duked by the woman I—' he cleared his throat '—share my bed with!'

She opened her mouth.

'And don't call me Severn either. Not when I'm about to—' He broke off and cleared his throat again. 'Not when we are private together. It's Kester.'

'Kester.' His name had never sounded so sweet.

'Yes.' He reached out to take her hand. 'Yes, Linette—'

Her hand stiffened in his. 'That's not my name.'

He blinked. He might be a duke, but he *could* read, and he'd seen her name written several times, heard her grandmother speak it too. 'What?' He drew her over to a sofa and sat down, taking her with him. How the hell had he got her name wrong?

'It's *Lin*net, not Lin*ette*.'

The small hand tried to pull away, but he held tight. 'Why the devil didn't you tell me, then?' he asked. How the hell had he been married for a month and not even known his wife's name?

She blushed. 'Grandmère always said that Linnet was not a proper name, that Papa was ignorant and Maman must have meant for me to be called Linette.'

'And did she?'

'No. When Papa came to her room after—' she blushed even deeper '—after I was born, there was a linnet singing outside. They called me after the bird. Of course Grandmère didn't like that either—that her only grandchild should be called after a common, drab little bird.'

'I like linnets,' he said, caressing her palm.

Her hand trembled. 'Grandmère said it was not proper for a duchess to be called after a bird either.'

He was beginning to think that Grandmère had said entirely too much. 'She probably also said that I was not fit to ride in a carriage with the French king,' he pointed out. His wife's grimace confirmed his guess, but he left that. He was beginning to get a glimmer as to what might have gone wrong between them.

Grandmère. Here Be Dragons. Had the marquise also said something about how a lady should conduct herself in bed?

He knew Madame had very definite ideas on what befitted an aristocrat. It had not occurred to him that her influence over her granddaughter was quite so strong. Although if she had convinced him that his bride was a young lady of delicate sensibilities who would be disgusted by passionate lovemaking... Damn it to hell! He'd been a fool. Combined with his mother's attitude...dragons indeed.

'Do you remember that house party in Kent?' he asked. He'd found Linette—*no, Linnet*—alone in a parlour. Always before they had been strictly chaperoned, and here she was, alone. All shy, welcoming smiles, she had not repulsed him when he'd taken her in his arms. If he'd kissed her then...

She blushed again. 'I thought you were going to kiss me,' she said.

'I was,' he said. 'Completely senseless. But your grandmother came in.' He'd wanted to kick the prickly marquise into the middle of next week. 'Would you have minded?'

Her blush deepened. 'I wanted you to kiss me.' A pause. 'That was why I was there.'

Shock hit him. 'You were waiting for me?'

'Yes.' Still scarlet, she hung her head. 'But I didn't mean to trap you!'

He touched her chin, lifted it. 'Bold minx. I had no idea

you planned it. And I certainly never thought you were trying to trap me. Not your style at all.' He frowned. 'But the next time I saw you...' He sighed. Her grandmother. The old lady had summoned him, castigated him roundly for endangering her granddaughter's reputation. Shamed that he'd been essentially caught dallying with an innocent at all, let alone the girl he was rapidly falling in love with, he'd offered marriage on the spot.

If the marquise had shamed him, a reasonably experienced twenty-nine-year-old...

'I barely escaped your grandmother with my skin,' he said. 'What did she say to you?'

'That my...my behaviour was so vulgar, I would lucky if you could be prevailed upon to marry me. That even my fortune—'

He put his hand over her mouth. 'Stop.' Beneath his fingers the tender lips quivered, igniting him. 'I was not *prevailed upon*,' he said. 'I wanted to marry you. You. Linnet Farley. Yes, I had to marry money, but believe me, the knowledge that I would also have *you*—' He dragged in a breath. 'I could have waited. Compounded with the creditors. I did *not* have to marry the first heiress I saw if I didn't like her.'

'You didn't?' Something tightened in his chest at the note in her voice.

'No. But I didn't see just any heiress.' His hand cupped her chin again. 'I saw you. And I didn't want to wait. Now...' He lifted her chin, his other arm sliding around her, drawing her close, close enough that her fragrance slid through him, winding about his senses. 'We're going to turn the clock back.' He undid his cravat in a few careless jerks, tossing it God knew where.

'What?' Her breathless voice skimmed his nerves. She was going to be even more breathless before he had finished.

'I've found you. All alone in a private parlour,' he murmured. Her eyes widened as he shrugged out of his coat. 'What do you think I'm going to do?'

Her lips parted.

'That's exactly right,' he said, taking her into his arms and kissing her.

He had kissed her before. Of course he had, and she had liked it. But it had not been like this, all heat and demand. Always before he had been gentle. Careful. Restrained. This was different. Now he was hungry, all fierce possession, taking her mouth with tender ruthlessness, surging within to stroke his tongue against hers. And she felt it; clear to the place between her legs where he would come into her, she felt it as fiery delight, and moaned, stroking her tongue back against his. His arms tightened.

Briefly he released her mouth. 'Yes.' His husky voice slid over her senses. 'Let me pleasure you. Show you.' And he took her mouth again.

He could do whatever he liked to her, as long as he didn't stop touching her. Kissing her. Consuming her.

He didn't. One hand closed over her breast and even through gown, chemise and stays his touch seared her. And where the upper curve of her breast was exposed, his touch lingered, tracing the delicate skin.

He released her mouth, only to murmur her name, and feather kisses over her throat, pausing to lick hotly at the scrambling pulse, then finding the upper curve of her breast.

'Damned amethyst,' he muttered, pushing it out of the way. 'I've been thinking all evening about challenging it to pistols at twenty paces.'

'You have?' It was a shaky gasp. Amazing that she could think, let alone speak.

'God, yes. Jealous as sin.' His hand slid over her waist, lower, lower, until he could slip it under her skirts and skim it up her leg, past her stocking and garter.

'Say my name,' he whispered, against her breast.

The insistent knock at the door took some time to really penetrate. It probably only did so because Kester raised his head from her breast and stopped stroking her thigh.

'Hell and the devil!' he muttered. 'Damned servants— you'd think they'd know that when a duke is closeted with his duchess at this hour, then he's not at home to anyone but her!'

Releasing her, he strode, unbuttoned waistcoat and all, to the door, opened it a crack and demanded, 'What the devil are you about, Blythe?'

The butler's murmur was unintelligible, but rather than dismissing him, Kester groaned. 'Very well. I'd better see him. Tell him I'll be down in a moment.'

He shut the door and turned back to her. 'It's poor Malmesbury. Probably wants to know how I got on with Prinny.' His gaze lingered. 'I'll be back as soon as I can get rid of him. Why don't you get into bed?'

Linnet gazed dazedly at the door as it closed behind him. *Get into bed?* Whose bed? He'd brought her to his own rooms though, and ravished her half out of her senses. Surely that meant... She drew a deep breath. Yes. She hurried from the room back to her own apartments.

Chapter Ten

Malmesbury was pacing the library when Kester entered.

'Sir?'

The baron swung around. 'Severn. I apologise for calling at such an hour—' His gaze took in Kester's dishevelled state and something that might have been a smile flickered around his mouth.

Kester cleared his throat. 'Not at all, sir. I collect it is something urgent.'

'Urgent enough,' said Malmesbury. 'The prince is talking about calling off the marriage! Saying the only woman he will ever love is Mrs Fitzherbert, and—'

'Did he marry her?'

'God knows, and it doesn't matter. If he did, it was invalid according to the law and cannot be upheld, since he had not the king's permission. Which, given Mrs Fitzherbert is a Catholic, would never have been granted. The point is the embarrassment that will ensue should he now refuse to marry the princess! After all my work instilling a sense of the importance of what was before her into the princess, the prince has undone all that good by his folly.'

He turned again to pace. 'Her father warned me that she could be intractable, and it appears she has decided to give as good as she gets. Nothing could be more disastrous for her! And now that Lady Jersey is in charge—God help us! She takes every opportunity to aggravate, Severn.'

'You wish me to see the prince again?'

'Please. For what good it will do. I fear even if you can bring him around, the princess is now so intransigent that *she* will go out of her way to offend *him*. Her behaviour at dinner tonight!' He covered his eyes briefly. 'Flippant, rattling, and she threw out the most vulgar hints about Lady Jersey!'

Kester perceived that he was indeed not the only one to have endured a ghastly family dinner that evening. 'Is it too much to hope that Lady Jersey wasn't present?'

Malmesbury groaned. 'Of course she was present! Not that it would have made any difference—she would have heard everything over her breakfast otherwise. Severn, you *must* see the prince again.'

'Perhaps I should see the princess instead.'

Malmesbury almost smiled. 'Perhaps. What I need is a sympathetic woman of high rank who can talk to her without Lady Jersey being able to interfere.'

He halted before Kester. 'I'll not keep you from your bed any longer, Severn.' His mouth twitched. 'Thank you for seeing me. And pray, give my regards to your wife.'

Kester's cheeks heated.

'I shall look forward to meeting her,' continued Malmesbury. This time he actually smiled. 'You look happy, Severn. I could wish your example might inspire the prince. Goodnight.'

Kester returned to his private sitting room to find that the bird had flown. Muttering a curse under his breath, he headed across the room for his bedchamber—for God's sake! What had he been thinking, telling Linnet to just get into bed? Of course she had gone back to her own—

'My lord? I mean, Kester?'

He stopped dead in the door leading to his very large bedchamber, turned around and wondered if his heart had stopped too.

His wife stood just inside the door that led through to *her* sitting room.

Of course she had gone back to her own bedchamber. He took a deep breath. She had changed for the night and returned. With a book. He supposed if Malmesbury hadn't left when he did, she might have found a use for it. As it was...

She looked at him, an expression of uncertainty on her face, the slender column of her throat rising from the high-necked nightgown, bare toes peeping from beneath.

'Yes,' he said, before she could ask. 'This is exactly where I want you.' God help him, that demure nightgown was as erotic as the evening gown. Or perhaps it was just her. And him. No matter. He strode back across the room, swept her up, startled gasp and all, heedless of the book crashing to the floor, and headed for his bed.

Chapter Eleven

Linnet found herself tumbled onto the ducal bed, the duke tumbling after her, rolling over and over with her locked in his arms until they reached the middle of the vast counterpane. She ended beneath him, a willing captive, held by his hard, hot weight and by the surrender of her own heart. He smiled down at her, brushed his mouth over hers and began to unbutton her nightgown. 'Naked,' he said softly. 'Not a stitch between us, and I'm not putting the candle out either.'

She flushed. 'But I'm not…pretty—'

'No,' he said. 'You're gorgeous. And you are mine and I want to see you. You're not going to hide from me any longer, sweetheart.'

And all the time those buttons were coming undone, until her nightgown hung open and he stripped it from her. Moments later he had shed the last of his own clothes and took her in his arms. Naked. Not a stitch between them. Hot skin to hot skin. Firelight and candlelight a dance as sensuous as his fingers at her breast.

Slowly, he rose over her, gazing down, and she trembled

at his expression. Hot. Hungry. One hand still fondled her breast.

His mouth, all hot demand at her breast, drawing it deep into the heat of his mouth. Delight shot through her to where his thigh held her legs apart and she felt his hand slide down over her belly and cup her. There. There where she was aching and needy and wet for him. There where emptiness cried out so that her hips lifted, dancing and pleading for more. And he gave her more, teasing and stroking, finding a place where all pleasure was centred, pressing so that she cried out as lightning struck from where he suckled to where he caressed her so tenderly.

'You like that,' he murmured against her breast. 'Say it, sweetheart.'

'Yes,' she panted. What did *he* like? 'But you—I want to please you.'

He drew back a little, lifted his head. 'Touch me, then,' he said.

Her breath came in. 'Touch you?' Even as she spoke her hands spread over his back, finding and loving the lithe muscles, loving that his body shuddered. No longer did she think it was distaste. She knew that pleasure now.

He still caressed her, but lightly. Watching her. Letting her explore and possess. And she did, discovering his chest, that the small male nipples could tighten, that he liked it as much as she did. Finding the taut curve of his buttock, the length of thigh.

With a groan he caught her hand, brought it to his mouth and kissed it. Then slid it down the front of his body to…

'Touch you there?' she whispered.

'God, yes.'

All velvet heat and steel, he pushed into her hand as she sat up and leaned over him. The firelight danced, lit his eyes, slid over his tautly muscled body in golden shadows. Shamelessly, she explored, discovering all the textures, the sleek, hard shaft, that leapt to her touch, finding that she loved his response, loved that she could please him. That pleasing him made *her* ache even more, there where they would join. And all the while his hands roamed her body, possessing her, loving her. And he watched, his eyes hot, hungry. Hot and hungry for *her*. Plain Linnet Farley, who had never thought a man would look at her like that.

'Enough,' he groaned, moving her hand away. 'My turn,' he said, and slid his hand back between her thighs, rolling her beneath him again. And this time it was different. Now that she wasn't trying to hide from her own desire, it was different. Beautifully, splendidly different.

'Kester, please!' She pushed up against his hand, fierce, urgent in her need. But he kept the caress light, maddening.

'You want more?' His husky voice breathed delight in her ear.

'Yes!'

'What? What do you want, Linnet? Open your eyes. Look at me. Tell me.'

She forced her eyelids open. He was there, above her, firelight and shadow gilding the planes of his face, his mouth hard with restraint. She could feel it in him. He was holding back as though leashed. Waiting. Waiting...

Waiting for her.

'You,' she sobbed. 'I want you. Everything.'

The leash snapped, all restraint gone as he came to her on a surge of power and wild possession. Her body leapt to meet him, to welcome him, and then he was there, pushing deep inside where she wanted him. Around her, above her, part of her.

Clinging to the last rags of control, Kester shuddered at the hot, wet clasp of his wife's body, trying to remain still, to give her time. But she moved under him, all silken fire in his arms, and need raked him.

'Linnet.'

Unable to help himself, he began to move, the world contracted to the space around them. Contracted to her soft gasps as he loved her, to the feel of her body matching his rhythm, to the silk of her hair spread on the pillow, its fragrance all around him and through him.

Braced on one elbow, he reached down between their bodies, found the taut nub and stroked. Her cry seared him and he circled it, feeling her body tighten around him at each thrust, hearing her desperate sobs as she swirled closer to the edge. He felt her body shatter around him, pulse after pulse as she broke and fell, and he went with her, his consummation a white-hot wave crashing over him.

Chapter Twelve

Somewhere in the middle of the night she awoke to warm darkness lit only by the dying glow of the fire and realised that she had fallen asleep in his bed, that she was—a furious blush heated her cheeks—nestled in his arms, her lower limbs shamelessly entangled with his.

Heavens! What must he have thought of her? Carefully she began to extricate herself, only for the arms holding her to tighten to steel, and the powerful thigh wedged between hers to shift possessively.

'Where do you think you're going?' he murmured in her ear.

'I fell asleep,' she said.

'You certainly did.'

A gentle nip at her ear scattered her thoughts. Determinedly she attempted to order them again. 'So, shouldn't I be going back to my own bed?'

'Definitely not,' he said, and, rolling her beneath him, showed her exactly *why* not.

* * *

She awoke finally in soft grey light to find her husband sitting up in bed looking at the volume of Goethe she had dropped the previous night. His long fingers were carefully smoothing a page which had become creased.

She watched him for a moment. He did not appear to be reading; in fact, she was reasonably certain that he didn't read German. But he was staring at the book, deep in thought. She ought to be embarrassed. Here she was at dawn, *still* in her husband's bed, and stark naked. He was naked too. Beautifully and utterly naked. And he apparently thought *she* was beautiful. He had spent a good portion of the night making her feel beautiful too. And wanted. And wanton. He hadn't minded at all. Quite the opposite.

He looked across at her, and smiled. A tender, intimate sort of smile that had her snuggling closer against his body.

His reaction shuddered through him, and he slid an arm around her. 'You said you read German, Linnet.'

She blinked, slightly surprised. 'Yes.'

'Do you also speak it?'

She nodded. 'Fairly well. I had an Austrian governess for a few years. Why?'

'Just something you might be able to help me with later.' He put the book aside, slid down in the bed and reached for her. 'For now, I have something much more important to do.'

'Kester, are you sure about this?' asked Linnet as he handed her out of the carriage in the courtyard of St James's Palace. 'It seems mad to me. Why would a princess want to talk to me?'

Kester led her across the courtyard. 'Because you speak

her language. Because you'll listen. And you won't make nasty little digs at her expense.' His hand tightened on hers where it lay on his arm. 'And perhaps because you're *you*.'

'But what if she refuses to receive me?'

'Then I'll send you home in the carriage,' he said. 'But she won't. I sent a message via Malmesbury. Apparently she trusts him. He is your devoted friend for life, by the way.'

'And what about Lady Jersey?'

His grin was wicked. 'You outrank her,' he said simply. 'Just remember that. By the way, she is known as That—' He leaned down and murmured the rest in her ear.

Her jaw felt positively dislocated. 'She isn't!'

'Oh, yes, she is,' he assured her. 'An appellation more fitting for the kennel than a bishop's daughter, I agree, but believe me, it suits her. Remember that too, and don't trust her any further than you can spit!'

'A lady,' she informed him, 'does *not* spit.'

'There are quite a number of things a lady isn't supposed to do.' And his lazy grin sent curls of delight along her spine. He bent down to speak softly in her ear. 'You did quite a few of them last night, and I'm looking forward to the rest.'

Chapter Thirteen

Princess Caroline Amelia Elizabeth of Brunswick-Wolfen-büttel eyed her visitor with patent disfavour. Bright blue eyes were narrowed between white lashes.

'I haf dis note from Malmesbury.' She held up the note. 'Vy should he t'ink I vish to meet *another* English?' Her blue eyes narrowed. *'Hein?'*

On the other side of the room, Lady Jersey tittered, and murmured something to another lady.

'Perhaps he thought you might like someone to speak with privately, *madame*,' said Linnet in perfect, if careful, German.

The princess's remarkably delicate mouth went from pout to smiles in an instant. She clapped her hands. 'He's not such a fool after all!' she said in the same language. 'That one—' she made a dismissive gesture at Lady Jersey '—interferes with everything I say or do, but she can't if she doesn't know what I'm saying.'

'You think not?' murmured Linnet. Lady Jersey was bearing down upon them, her expression haughty.

'I am sure you mean it for the best, Your Grace, but if Her Highness is to learn our language and ways, it is best for her to hear and speak only English!'

You outrank her... Remember that.

Linnet looked the countess up and down, just as Grand-mère would have done. She frowned, as if puzzled. 'Oh, yes. Lady Jersey, is it not? I am sure Her Highness is learning a great deal of English, and most...*interesting* ways from you.'

Lady Jersey drew in a sharp breath. 'Impudence!' she snapped.

Linnet raised her eyes. 'She is learning that from you too? How very dreadful. Please excuse—'

'Go.' The princess accompanied this command with a flip of her hand at the countess.

Lady Jersey retreated.

The princess's bright blue eyes sparkled. 'That was fun,' she announced, reverting to German with a broad smile that unfortunately revealed less than perfect teeth. 'She won't like you now. You know that, don't you?'

Linnet smiled back. 'What a shame. Did you enjoy your journey, Your Highness?'

Apparently not. Princess Caroline related everything that had gone wrong, from the weather—frightful—to avoiding French troops—annoying—and finally having a tooth drawn in Osnabrück—painful. 'My page took it down to Malmesbury,' she said cheerfully, 'but I think he did not much like it.'

Probably not.

The princess changed the subject. 'Tell me—there is a place called Richmond, is there not?'

'Two,' said Linnet. 'One in the north, but I think you must mean the village just outside London on the river.'

'Yes, that is the one. My mama spoke of it often. She was very fond of it. My papa had built for her the little pavilion quite away from the court in the country by the River Oker. Such a pretty place.' Her expression turned wistful. 'She called it Little Richmond. I should like to see the real one.'

'I am sure you could. It is not very far, perhaps ten miles. You could order a carriage.'

The princess shook her head. 'Later. I have to be fitted for my wedding gown. Tell me—have you met the prince?'

'Er, no. I...I believe my husband is upon terms of friendship with him.'

This was greeted with a snort. 'Then I pity you! Such a one cannot have pleasant friends!' She jerked her head at Lady Jersey. 'That one! Do you know what she *is*?'

Linnet drew a breath. 'Yes.'

'Then your husband is friends with a man who offers such an insult to his bride! Is he of the same sort?'

'No,' said Linnet. She knew beyond all doubt that she spoke the truth. 'He would never treat me like that.' He had made that very clear to her last night.

'I have my linne to sing for me, so there will be no birds of paradise.'

The princess frowned. 'You are quite young. How long have you been married?'

'A month.'

'A month! And did he take you for love?'

Honesty was all that could help here. 'No. It was for money. But he is...all that is kind, and honourable. And I am happy.'

The princess leant forward and took Linnet's hands in hers. 'Then I am happy for you. I think perhaps it will not be thus for me and I shall like to think that there is one Englishman who treats his bride rightly.'

'Ma'am,' said Linnet, 'I am sure that once His Royal Highness comes to know you... We—my husband and I—have both had to adjust.'

'He dislikes me,' said the princess simply, releasing Linnet's hands. 'But we will be married in two days and one day I will be queen. It is enough. You will come to my wedding?'

'I... Yes. I believe we are invited.'

'Good. Then it shall not be just Malmesbury who is my friend. Tell me, have you met this Maria Fitzherbert?'

For a woman who spoke little English, the princess had certainly made herself familiar with all the pertinent facts of the case very quickly. But then, her own mother-in-law had gone out of her way to put certain facts, and fictions, in her way.

The princess scowled. 'His Royal Highness may have a mistress and two wives, but should *I* stray, why then I may be executed!' She thumbed her nose and made a rude noise. '*That* for their rules. My Lady Jersey wishes me to learn English customs. Well, I shall—from her example!'

'But, ma'am, if you were to behave perfectly, then everyone would see that it was not *your* fault—' She broke off, realising that she had come within a whisker of criticising the Prince of Wales directly to a woman, who, however wronged she might be, Linnet was not certain she could trust.

'Not my fault he has two wives and a mistress?' The

princess shrugged. 'Perhaps. I can try. That is what Malmesbury wants, but I doubt it will change anything. And if I am to try, then he must also.'

'I tell you, Severn, I'll not marry the woman! The thing is impossible!' The prince took another swig of brandy. Kester sipped his own and maintained his patience. 'She's not even pretty! *Nothing* like her portrait, and she smells, Severn. Smells!' The prince sank onto a chair, eyes closed, nearly weeping. 'How they can ask it of me, when I have already taken to my bosom the most dear, the most exquisite, flower of womanhood! *She* is the only woman I shall ever love.'

The question remained—had the prince actually taken Mrs Fitzherbert to wife, however illegally, or merely to bed? At least, he assumed the prince was not referring to Lady Jersey. One would have to be a great deal more foxed than His Highness to refer to the countess as an exquisite flower of womanhood.

'Sir, you must see that to refuse to marry Princess Caroline now would constitute an intolerable insult. Although she is the king's niece, infamy must attach to her name, and whatever your personal...reserves...she has done nothing to deserve that.'

The prince opened his eyes and gazed piteously at his friend. 'Severn, I thought you would understand. You! Who have been forced into the same appalling situation by your father!'

Kester let that pass. Now was not the moment to explain that his marriage of necessitous convenience was becoming something rather more. Especially when he had not said as much to his bride. 'Precisely, sir. So I know that such a marriage can work if both parties to it are willing to try.'

And it would have worked, he realised. Because he would have remained loyal to his wife under any circumstances, and she was too true and honest to do anything but her best.

'Both parties, you say, Severn? Yet I have no such confidence that the princess intends anything of the sort! Her behaviour—it passes all bounds! At dinner last night— I blushed for her, Severn. Positively blushed!'

'And could she perhaps have had some provocation?'

'Provocation?' The prince bridled. 'Certainly not!'

Kester stripped off the verbal kid gloves. 'Sir, you repulsed her when you met, and demanded a glass of brandy.'

'Damn Malmesbury's wagging tongue!' the prince replied sharply.

'You told me so yourself, sir.'

'I was in shock, Severn! Shock! And I blame Malmesbury entirely. He should have seen at a glance that the woman was unsuitable and avoided the match! Besides, she could not possibly have heard me ask for brandy—Malmesbury and I were on the far side of the room!'

'Nor was sending Lady Jersey to meet the princess necessarily the wisest choice,' persisted Kester.

The prince glared. 'Her Majesty the Queen approved the appointment!'

Which only went to confirm, as if he needed confirmation, that royalty could be as foolish as the next human.

'And speaking of Lady Jersey,' went on the prince, 'the princess actually informed me today that she knew *all* about the intimacy of my friendship with Lady Jersey.

Slanderous, Severn. Even if she *had* been sent anonymous letters on the subject, a lady should affect not to know such things!'

'That makes it very convenient for us gentlemen, does it not, sir?' said Kester, not bothering to mask the sarcasm.

The prince drew himself up. 'I believe this interview is at an end, Severn,' he said.

'As you wish, sir,' said Kester, bowing.

'You will, of course, present my compliments to your bride, Severn,' said the prince in frigid accents.

'Of course, sir. She will be gratified.' A lie if ever there was one, but necessary under the circumstances.

'I shall look forward to meeting her, of course,' said the prince sweetly. 'I understand from Lady Jersey that she was an extremely wealthy young lady, but nonetheless passably pretty. I daresay she will attract a great deal of attention as she goes about in society.'

Kester stiffened slightly at the malicious glint in his future sovereign's eye. He knew a threat when he saw one. Somehow he reined in the urge to violence, and spoke in the laziest tone he could muster. 'As you say, sir. I fear though that I shall be one of the most unpopular husbands in London.' The prince blinked, and Kester let his tone harden slightly. 'I have a feudal, positively feudal, dislike of sharing.'

'Er, quite, Severn. Quite. Good day to you!'

Chapter Fourteen

Kester was directed to one of the withdrawing rooms where he found Linnet waiting for him alone.

'Are you ready to leave?'

'If you please, sir.'

He offered his arm and murmured, 'Wait until we are private.'

She nodded.

Together they traversed the corridors and finally reached the courtyard where their coachman was waiting. Kester handed her up and leapt in beside her. A footman closed the door, got up behind and the coach started.

'What do you think?' he asked.

She sighed. 'I think, if the prince would but be polite, and…and not flaunt his mistress in her face, that she would at least try to be conciliatory, but—'

'There's little chance of that,' said Kester. He took her gloved hand and held it. 'You are a very lucky bride. You know that, don't you?'

She looked at him with that glimmering smile he had seen for the first time last night. 'Oh?'

'Yes. If I behaved like Prinny, Louisa would beat me bloody for you!'

The smile deepened. 'Behave like that, my lord duke, and Louisa will have to stand in line.'

Wednesday evening, April 8, 1795

Linnet, Duchess of Severn, sat alone in her pew, watching as others of the nobility crowded into the Chapel Royal. Further along the pew other guests glanced at her surreptitiously, then turned away with ill-concealed smiles and shrugs.

'Trade', she heard whispered. *'Severn's heiress.'* None of them spoke to her.

She assumed Kester would rejoin her when he could, but the Princess Caroline was already waiting at the altar, chatting merrily to the gentleman that a kindly middle-aged lady seated behind Linnet had said was William, Duke of Clarence.

The lady leaned forward again. 'Do you know where Severn has gone?'

Linnet shook her head. She and Kester had barely sat down when a very handsome gentleman in regimentals, younger than herself, had come to murmur in Kester's ear and escort him out.

'I'm Lady Blake,' said the middle-aged lady. 'This—' she prodded the elderly gentleman dozing beside her '—is Blake. Obviously you are Severn's bride. Permit me to wish you very happy. Louisa Farnsworth told me all about you. She says it's an excellent match.'

Linnet blushed. 'Thank you.'

Lady Blake gave her a tap on the shoulder. 'You'd better look forward, my dear.'

The princess had broken off her chatter to Prince William and was staring straight at Linnet, her head cocked to one side. As Linnet looked towards her, she smiled broadly, raised a gloved hand and waved. Then turned back to her conversation. Further along Linnet's pew there were more stares, and murmurs of astonishment.

Lady Blake nodded. 'There. She saw you. I hear you gave Frances Jersey her own again the other day. Good for you. Any woman who can give *her* a set...'

Linnet lost track of what she was saying. A tall, familiar figure was hurrying down the nave towards her, hat tucked under his arm.

Lady Blake broke off and glanced over her shoulder. 'Ah. There he is. Just in time.'

And he was there, slipping into the seat beside her, reaching for her hand. 'Lady Blake,' he said with a smile. 'How do you do?'

'Very well, Severn,' said her ladyship. 'I've presented myself to your bride. Congratulations. Your mother is an idiot. Bring your bride to see me tomorrow. Blake!' She sat back in her seat, giving her husband a hearty nudge in the ribs. 'Wake up, do, Theodore!'

'Hmmph! What? Just had my eyes shut for a moment. Too bright in here!'

'Is everything all right?' asked Linnet softly, turning to her husband.

Kester grimaced. 'I have to tell you, you nearly got Roxburghe to sit beside you.'

'Roxburghe?'

'Duke thereof,' said Kester in a very low voice. 'Prinny is as drunk as a wheelbarrow. Roxburghe and Bedford are supposed to be supporting him in his ordeal, but he decided at the last minute that nothing would do but that *I* had to uphold him. Literally. That's why young Brummell came to fetch me.'

'But you're here.'

'He was talked out of it. Tradition decrees bachelors. Probably Roxburghe is wishing *he* was married right now. Good Lord! What is the princess wearing?'

Lady Blake leaned forward. 'What her grandmother wore for *her* wedding day by the look of things. The queen's idea, I understand. And of course Frances Jersey backed her up—anything to make the poor girl look like a dowd!'

Kester rolled his eyes. 'Linnet, don't let my mother tell you what to wear. Ever. Listen to Louisa instead. Even if I do find her suggestions distracting.'

Brass and the organ sounded and the entire congregation turned at the entrance of the prince.

His Royal Highness looked terrible. Almost, Linnet thought, as if he had been crying. Unthinking, her hand stole out, seeking... At once it was taken in a firm grasp. She let out a breath. Kester moved a little closer, sheltering her. Reassuring her. Whatever the outcome of this royal marriage, theirs was going to be happy.

At the altar the bishop began the service. 'Dearly beloved, we are gathered here together...'

'That's Moore,' murmured Kester. 'Archbishop of Canterbury.'

The archbishop's voice rolled on, intoning the prayers. '…and therefore is not by any to be enterprised, nor taken in hand, unadvisedly, lightly, or wantonly—'

The prince rose to his feet jerkily, looking around in what appeared to be desperation. A murmur rippled through the chapel, as though a great beast stirred, sniffing a meal.

'Heaven help us,' breathed Kester. Linnet tensed. What was the prince doing? Surely he wasn't going to leave! The king came forward, spoke quietly, and the prince sat down again, his head lowered. Linnet felt sick. What must the princess be feeling at this display?

The service continued without hitch. Until they reached the part about just causes…and the archbishop's voice slowed. 'Therefore if any man can show any just cause why they may not be lawfully joined together, let him now speak, or else hereafter forever hold his peace.' He stopped, and laid down his book, gazing, it appeared, at the king.

'What the devil is Moore about?' came a gentleman's voice from behind them.

There was a snort. 'Making quite sure, if you ask me.'

Linnet thought that was Lord Blake, because she heard a woman saying, 'Shut up, Theodore! You're in church!'

After a moment His Grace of Canterbury continued, apparently reassured.

But it seemed he still had doubts when they reached the Prince of Wales's vows. '…and forsaking all other, keep thee *only* unto her, as long as ye both shall live?'

'I do.' The prince's response sounded as though it had been obtained under torture, and the archbishop laid down his book again.

Beside her, Linnet felt Kester stiffen.

The archbishop repeated the question. Murmurs sprang up again, nearly drowning the prince's response.

Kester leaned down to her. 'He's not taking any chances, is he?'

Behind them someone was heard to say, 'I'd wager Moore's risking a second murder in his cathedral at this rate. Damned impertinence!'

After a moment the marriage continued to the end without further sensation. The ring was given and accepted, the blessing pronounced and, for better or worse, the Prince of Wales and Princess Caroline were husband and wife.

Chapter Fifteen

'I'm telling you, Severn, he scarce spoke to her at all on the way here from the chapel,' said the Duke of Leeds.' They were squeezed into a corner of the drawing room in St James's Palace at the reception. Leeds shook his head. 'I was right in front of them. And she's really quite amiable. I can't understand him!' He smiled at Linnet. 'Anyway, Lady Severn, a pleasure to meet you, and it's plain to see that Severn here is happy. You will excuse me? I'd best return to the, er, *other* happy couple.' With a bow, he left them.

'They aren't going to be happy, are they?' said Linnet very quietly, watching the princess. Kester followed her gaze. The princess seemed in high gig, chatting and laughing. Beside her, the Prince of Wales looked like a man about to face his own execution. Even as Kester watched, she spoke to her husband. Politely. Cheerfully. His Royal Highness turned away, his gaze seeking and finding Lady Jersey.

Kester gritted his teeth. Impossible that the princess had

not understood what happened during the ceremony, but apparently she was going to try....

He sighed. 'Probably not. But we are, aren't we?'

His bride looked up, her eyes wondering. 'Yes. Because you're far too honourable to treat your wife like that.'

His heart twisted. 'Honourable? Perhaps. And no, I'd never insult my wife, no matter how I felt about her. But I have to tell you, love makes all the difference between duty and joy.'

She became very still, but her hand on his arm trembled. 'Love, my lord?'

He nodded. 'Yes. Love. You are my wife, Linnet. My duchess. Will you be my love also?'

'Yes,' she breathed. 'Oh, yes.'

* * * * *

Author Note

Anyone who knows anything about Regency England probably knows that the marriage of George, Prince of Wales, to Princess Caroline Amelia Elizabeth of Brunswick-Wolfenbüttel in April 1795 was an unmitigated disaster. Forced by the king into a legal marriage so that Parliament would clear his debts, when he had already contracted an illegal marriage to the Catholic widow Maria Fitzherbert, the prince married his first cousin without ever having laid eyes on her until three days before the wedding.

Princess Caroline's arrival in England, the cousins' first meeting and the wedding ceremony are as I have described them, and Lord Malmesbury was a real person and where possible I have used his own words, or a close approximation. Frances, Lady Jersey, was the prince's mistress at the time and she was appointed as lady-in-waiting. Everything else is fiction, although as historically accurate as I can make it.

Readers who would like to know more about the marriage and Caroline of Brunswick may like to consult Flora

Fraser's excellent biography, *The Unruly Queen*, as I have done. *The Disastrous Marriage*, by Joanna Richardson, also has useful information, if taking perhaps a rather romanticised view of the Prince of Wales's frequent to-ings and fro-ings between mistresses! My story covers only the three days between the first meeting of the cousins and their marriage. More than enough time for Kester, Duke of Severn, to sort out his own marital difficulties and convince his bride that he wants more than just her money.

Elizabeth Rolls

THE PROBLEM
WITH JOSEPHINE

LUCY ASHFORD

Lucy Ashford, an English Studies lecturer, has always loved literature and history, and from childhood one of her favourite occupations has been to immerse herself in historical romances. She studied English with history at Nottingham University and the Regency is her favourite period.

Lucy has written several historical novels for Mills & Boon® and has also been published under the name of Elizabeth Redfern. She lives with her husband in an old stone cottage in the Peak District, near to beautiful Chatsworth House and Haddon Hall, all of which give her a taste of the magic of life in a bygone age. Her garden enjoys spectacular views over the Derbyshire hills, where she loves to roam and let her imagination go to work on her latest story.

Previous novels by Lucy Ashford:

THE MAJOR AND THE PICKPOCKET
THE RETURN OF LORD CONISTONE

Did you know that some of these novels are also available as eBooks? Visit www.millsandboon.co.uk

Chapter One

Paris, March 1810

'This wedding is going to be...' The Emperor Napoleon paused. His courtiers froze. 'This wedding is going to be *absolutely perfect*,' Napoleon went on at last. 'In every way!'

With his strident voice still echoing all around the great hall of the palace, the emperor of half of Europe fussily started pulling on his gloves.

'The wedding. Perfect. Of course, Your Imperial Majesty. Sire...' Eager bows were being swept by the assembled servants: the stewards and the butler, the housekeeper and the Groom of the Chambers. Napoleon Bonaparte fixed them one last time with his eagle eyes, then strode purposefully out of the Tuileries Palace in a flurry of grooms and footmen to his waiting carriage.

Meanwhile, up in the shadowy gallery, a whispered admonition could be heard.

'Fleur, do try to stop sniffling,' pleaded Sophie. 'It's a wonder the emperor didn't hear you!'

Eighteen-year-old Fleur dabbed at her eyes. 'I'm sorry, Mam'selle Sophie. But it's just so romantic! To think that our emperor's riding off to Austria to claim his bride, who's the same age as me. And in two weeks, she'll be here for the wedding!'

'Indeed, and we've got plenty to do before then,' promised Sophie. 'The new empress's rooms to be made ready, for one thing.' Sophie, as the senior seamstress, had told little Fleur they could leave their work for just a few moments, to watch the emperor's departure. But now she rather wished she hadn't. For when Napoleon said 'perfect,' he meant it.

Fleur chattered all the way back to the bride-to-be's chambers. 'As soon as my darling Henri is back from the war, then we will be married too! Not that ours will be a grand affair, Mam'selle Sophie, but, oh, doesn't everyone love a wedding?'

Sophie was already threading her needle, and picking up a section of the pink silk draperies they were embroidering for the four-poster bed. And she was thinking, with a heavy heart, *Love a wedding? Not me. In fact, I'm positively dreading this one!*

Only two weeks, and the Emperor Napoleon would be marrying the Archduchess Marie-Louise of Austria in celebrations that were to be the envy of the world.

But there was one problem. And it was up to her, Sophie, to solve it, or her beloved papa would be utterly ruined.

Three hours later Sophie was hurrying through the crowded arcades of the Palais-Royal, home to drinkers, gamblers and prostitutes.

A gaudily dressed whore brushed past and cackled, 'You'll never get custom dressed like that, love.'

A man grabbed Sophie's arm, leering. 'Oh, I don't know, she's quite pretty under that drab cloak....'

'Get off me,' Sophie warned. His visage was hideous: his front teeth were missing—not unusual, because quite a few citizens had knocked out their own front teeth so they weren't forced into the army.

Fleur had explained it to her. 'They can't rip open the cartridge without any teeth, you see? But my Henri, he's brave—he wouldn't do a thing like that. Oh, I cannot wait to be his wife!'

Sophie shoved the half-drunk man away. Weddings, weddings. She pressed on to the corner where the Paris artists gathered, some of them with their easels set up, others with their pictures spread out for passing trade. *Here goes.*

'Can you help me?' she asked the nearest of them. 'I'm looking for an artist called Jacques.'

He roared with laughter. 'Jacques what? There'll be thousands of artists named Jacques in Paris, love!'

'If you'll give me a chance to finish, he's from a place called Claremont!' Sophie's voice by now was rather desperate. 'I heard he was wonderful at portraits, and I heard he was cheap!'

'That,' drawled a masculine voice just behind her, 'depends on what the commission is. And who is paying.'

She whirled round. A man stood there, looking down at her, and she felt her throat go rather dry. He was in his late twenties, and his dark, overlong hair and clothes were those of a devil-may-care artist. But his bearing, his composure, spoke of something altogether different—of arrogance, even. His features were clean-shaven, and striking; his mouth was sensual, his eyes dark as his hair.

She drew a deep breath. 'Are you Jacques the painter from Claremont?'

'My name is Jacques, I come from Claremont, and portraits are my speciality.'

'Then, Jacques—' Sophie summoned the *hauteur* she had learned in the palace '—I may have a proposition for you. But first I require proof of your talent!'

He drew out of his pocket a small sketchbook and flicked it open with his strong lean artist's hands. 'See for yourself, *mam'selle.*'

On every page was a watercolour portrait. Each one glowed with life and detail.

'Oh! They are beautiful,' she breathed.

He looked amused. 'So people say. Your proposition?'

She met his eyes steadily. 'I happen to require some work done. On several portraits that need certain...adjustments.'

'Adjustments?' His dark eyebrows arched.

'Yes!' she declared. 'But the work must be done discreetly, and I cannot afford to pay you much....'

'It sounds,' said Jacques of Claremont, 'as if you're offering me a commission I could very easily turn down flat.'

He saw the colour rush to her cheeks, and he thought, Why, she is *pretty*. More than pretty. With those high cheekbones and those thick-lashed blue eyes, she could, if she chose, be a beauty.

But clearly she didn't choose, with her hair scraped back in a spinster's cap, and those faded clothes. And now she was nervously clasping her hands. 'Please, I will do my best to make it worth your while. But if I could just *show* you what I require? In confidence?'

'In confidence, of course,' he agreed gravely. 'Your name is?'

'That doesn't matter! May I show you—*now*—the work that needs to be done, *monsieur*?'

'Of course.' He saw her face brighten with hope. 'And then,' he went on, 'I can tell you my price.'

Her face had fallen again, so expressive. She was lovely, he thought, quite lovely! She hesitated, then lifted those wide blue eyes almost in defiance. 'Very well. Monsieur Jacques, we need to go to the Louvre.'

The Louvre Palace? Where the imperial wedding would take place, so very soon? Jacques blinked. He gave a bow. 'Lead on, *mademoiselle*.'

As soon as Jacques had arrived in Paris, he'd quickly realised that the wedding dominated *everything*. The *modistes* and tailors were working every hour they could to keep up with the demand for finery from the rich. The mayor of Paris had hired all available artisans to work on the completion of the Arc de Triomphe, through which the imperial procession would pass on the great day. The military were constantly on parade, practising their ceremonial marches. Musicians were being sought from all quarters to fill the Champs-Élysées and the Tuileries gardens with melody during the celebrations. As he followed the well-spoken but rather desperate woman who was his guide along the rue de Rivoli towards the Louvre, Jacques noted with wonder that even Paris's streets were being swept.

She pulled up before the great public entrance of the Louvre, where crowds of visitors hurried to and fro.

'We'll have to pay to get in today,' he warned her. 'Can't your business wait till tomorrow, when the place is open to the public for free?'

She glanced up at him, agitated. 'We cannot wait. Please, follow me.' She hurried up to the curator guarding the door, who waved her through with a nod and a smile.

So she was known here, registered Jacques. Intriguing indeed.

Chapter Two

As she led him inside, Sophie's heart was pounding rather frantically. Not just with the nature of her task—though *that* was formidable enough—but because she hadn't imagined, for one minute, that he would be so very—what? So very masculine? Of course you knew he would be a man, you idiot! So very handsome, then. Most irritatingly handsome. And he was laughing at her, which wasn't surprising in the least. Her heart thumped. He would laugh even more once he knew the tremendous mess she was in.

The Louvre's interior was crowded, because a huge new mural of Napoleon's victory at Marengo had just been put on display. Everywhere in here, there were reminders of Napoleon the conqueror, Napoleon the law-giver, Napoleon the emperor. And soon…Napoleon the bridegroom.

She paused momentarily at the entrance to the Long Gallery, a vast, vaulted hall which would hold more than a thousand guests for the wedding ceremony. 'This is the way we must go,' she told Jacques rather curtly.

He was still looking around. 'Isn't this the route the royal couple will take?'

She nodded tersely. *Please. No more questions, not yet.* Then, from amongst the crowds, a grey-haired curator came hurrying up to her. 'Mam'selle Sophie! You'll have come, of course, to report on the Marengo painting to your father. How is he?'

Jacques saw something tighten in her rather lovely face.

'He is improving, Thierry, but—' she glanced quickly at Jacques '—he is fretting about the wedding plans. He will not, unfortunately, be better in time for the ceremony.' She was aware of Jacques watching her steadily. 'I see the Marengo picture is a great success!' she went on brightly. 'Although really I expected it to be in the Salon Carré, with the other paintings of Napoleon's victories.'

'So did I, Mam'selle Sophie, but the Salon Carré is locked at present because, of course, it's being prepared for the wedding ceremony itself.' He spoke in hushed tones. 'And the preparations have been thorough. For as you know, if anything were to offend our noble emperor—' he swallowed nervously '—he would express his disapproval rather strongly.'

Napoleon was famous for his rages. Jacques noticed Mam'selle Sophie turning distinctly pale. But then that bright, forced smile was back on her face. 'I'm sure, Thierry, I can tell my father that everything is exactly as it should be.'

'You can indeed, Mam'selle Sophie! Pray give him my best wishes!'

She marched onwards and Jacques followed her, along the great gallery, past the throngs clustered round the new painting. Then the crowds thinned, and they were at the Salon Carré, where only a few candles could be seen burning dimly through the ornate wooden latticework of the great door. She looked at him almost in entreaty, he thought, an entreaty for silence; then she glanced round, reached in her pocket…and unlocked the door.

How the devil did she have the key? mused Jacques. Certainly she was in no mood for idle chatter. Instead she led him swiftly into this vaulted inner sanctum, where two gilded bronze thrones stood behind a magnificent carved altar.

All around the room were yet more paintings, of exquisite quality. She beckoned him in further, and hurriedly went to lock the door again.

'You are rather taking my breath away, I must admit,' he said. 'Who exactly are you?'

She pushed back the hood of her cloak. That hideous spinster's cap fell back also, and he saw that some of her tightly pinned dark hair had come loose and was twining round the slender column of her throat. He could also see that her waist was of hand-span slenderness, and her breasts were heaving rather agitatedly, indeed quite delightfully, beneath her tight, high-necked bodice.

'I will be honest with you, Jacques.'

'You are taking a risk,' he said, 'trusting a stranger.'

Her small chin jutted. 'If you choose in any way to take advantage of my trust, I will call out, and say that I found you in here, intent on theft. Your punishment would not be light.'

His eyes glinted. 'Please continue to trust me, Mam'selle Sophie.'

She flinched at his use of her name, but went on. 'Very well. I am a servant—chief seamstress, in fact—at the Tuileries Palace. And my father is a deputy curator here.' Her musical voice, he noted, was steady, but he could see the anxiety, the fear almost, that shadowed her lovely blue eyes.

'I see,' he said. 'And both you and Thierry seem rather afraid of the emperor finding anything in here to provoke him on the day of his wedding. Is there any chance of that, *mam'selle*?'

She drew in a deep breath. 'At this point, Monsieur Jacques, I must take you yet further into my confidence.'

'Let me guess.' The artist—Jacques—had been looking around calmly at all the treasures in here, but now he turned to her, his dark eyes steady. 'You're planning a daredevil robbery, aren't you?'

'Please do not be ridiculous!' Sophie clasped her hands together tightly. Ever since she'd set eyes on this man, she'd felt awkward, self-conscious. And it was absurd! She was a twenty-three-year-old woman, and used to dealing with the haughty staff of the Tuileries, sometimes even the emperor himself! 'There is no question of any wrongdoing whatsoever,' she went on emphatically. 'But the problem, such as it is, means that some work has to be done in here in utter secrecy. As I've said, if word of this gets out, then I am in trouble. But so are you, and I take it that you are probably in various sorts of trouble and penniless anyway, living as you do!'

She saw an answering flash of something else in his eyes then. Humour? Was he still finding all this *amusing*?

'So,' Sophie went on, fighting down the fresh thudding at her heart, 'so, I will pay you what I can, which is not much. But my father, as deputy curator, has a certain amount of influence, and he will see, once our transaction is completed, that you get commissions in plenty. Do you agree, before I tell you what I require?'

His eyes flickered over her, lazily, yet in a way that somehow made her pulse race. What was he *doing*, looking at her like that? She tried to stubbornly outstare him, yet found herself utterly distracted by his implacably male figure, his hands, his mouth—oh, Lord, that impossibly wicked mouth, that surely was curling even now, in a smile of derision....

She fixed her eyes rather desperately on the rakish stripes of his waistcoat. He drawled, 'Promises are empty things. You said you will pay me what you can. I'd like to know how much.'

Her voice was a little unsteady now. 'I cannot afford more than two hundred francs.'

He folded his arms. 'That,' he said with faintly concealed contempt, 'is pitiable.'

'It's not much, I know!' Her distress was open. 'But the commissions—my father will make sure you become known, in circles you can only dream of, aristocratic circles!'

He folded his arms, and leaned his wide shoulders back against a gilded pillar that was crowned by a marble bust of Napoleon. *Bother* Napoleon, Sophie thought in a sudden outburst of fury, bother him!

'An offer I can resist, believe me.'

'Oh.' Her disappointment made her almost crumple.

Then he shrugged, an easy, lithe movement that somehow made her heart do a strange little flutter. 'But I'll make a suggestion, shall I? I'll tell you what my fee will be. But only when you've told me exactly what you require me to do.'

She bit her lip. 'I've told you. I have so little money, I cannot pay you more!'

'Who said it would be money, *mam'selle*?' he drawled. 'Indeed, all it will cost you is a few minutes of your time, believe me.'

Her mind reeled. Whatever it was, she had to accept. She was desperate.

'My task?' he prompted gently.

She moistened her dry lips and met his eyes directly, almost proudly. He liked that.

Then she said, 'The problem, you see, is Josephine.'

'*Josephine?*'

She nodded. And so they began their tour of the salon that was to be Napoleon's wedding chapel.

'Here, here and here are portrayals of Napoleon's first wife, the Empress Josephine,' Sophie said to Jacques, finding an inner calmness now that she was—she hoped—getting somewhere. 'The official portraits of the former empress were removed, of course, as soon as Napoleon was divorced from her. But unfortunately it was overlooked that Josephine, at Napoleon's request, was often portrayed in other paintings, for example in the crowd scenes, you will see here. Or *here*—' she pointed to a classical lakeside scene '—as a nymph.'

He leaned closer to inspect it. 'She's a little old for such scanty attire.'

'She was a great beauty once,' Sophie said, rather sharply. She had always felt a sneaking sympathy for Josephine. The reason for the divorce, her father always said, was not the number of tempestuous affairs that both Josephine and Napoleon indulged in, but the fact that Josephine had been unable to bear the emperor a child. 'Anyway,' she went on, 'beautiful or not, she was painted in everywhere to please him.' Her face fell again. 'So we need someone, rather urgently, to paint out Josephine.'

'And paint in the Archduchess Marie-Louise?'

'Unfortunately, that would not be possible, since no one has seen her.'

'Haven't they?' Casually drawing out of his pocket his small sketchbook, he flicked through several pages to show her a beautiful watercolour of a young woman with fair hair and a pleasant face, wearing a tiara and necklet of pearls. 'The archduchess,' he said.

She gasped. 'You have been to Austria?'

'A few months ago, yes.' He smiled. 'I'm a wandering wastrel. I pick up commissions where I can.'

'I'm surprised you've not been commissioned by the emperor himself,' she said rather tightly.

'Napoleon? Oh, he goes for the rather grander artists. In fact, he commissioned Canova to do a marble statue of him, as Mars the Peacemaker, but it's still in Rome—I saw it there. Canova is proving awkward about transporting it to Paris, partly because of money, and partly because Canova objects to Napoleon's far-from-peaceful conquest of his homeland, Italy.'

'Oh! I would love to see it!'

'I'm sure you would.' He smiled wryly. 'Napoleon is ten feet high, and stark naked.'

Her cheeks flamed. Whistling, Jacques started strolling round in the dim candlelight, examining the pictures for himself, his hands in the pockets of his shabby black frock coat. She was stunned by him. Made a nervous mess by him. He was so handsome. So...*at ease.*

He swung round and caught her staring. 'Some of these paintings in here are by David,' he said. 'He is the official court artist. Why not get him to do it?'

She clenched her teeth. 'Because we cannot afford him!'

'But surely the curators were given sufficient funding for such things?'

'All gone.' This time her voice shook, just a little. 'All gone, except for two hundred francs.' Which was, in fact, her life savings.

The man called Jacques was drawing nearer. She backed away, and came into collision with a pillar. 'You know,' he said, 'you really are rather beautiful. You must allow me to paint your portrait some day. As for this work—if I agree to do it, how will I get access?'

'You will have noted that I have a key,' she said rather tightly. 'I can let you in here every evening, though we must not take long, because the guards come round on the hour. We will have to be here, say, after six, then leave before seven. Will you do it?'

'How important is this to you, Sophie?'

'It means everything, Monsieur Jacques,' she answered quietly.

* * *

Two days ago her father had explained it to her from his sickbed.

'The paintings,' he muttered. 'Of Josephine. They must be dealt with. But there is no money....'

Her heart had lurched. 'Surely it's not your personal responsibility, dear Papa? Surely Monsieur Denon will have seen to it?' Denon was the chief curator of the Louvre, a stern, soulless man.

Her father had shaken his head. 'That's the trouble, my dear. Monsieur Denon asked *me* to see to it, a month ago. He gave me money, but I spent it, on the restoration of other paintings. I quite forgot about Josephine! If I told Denon now, I would lose my job. And I love my work, Sophie, I love all the paintings....'

'I will see to it,' she'd said resolutely. 'Trust me.'

And now came the question. Was her father's job and happiness worth putting herself in the hands of this disdainful stranger?

The question had already been answered. She had no choice.

Jacques had merely nodded at her earlier answer and was already examining another of the paintings. 'Incidentally,' he said, turning to her, 'how did you hear about me?'

She clasped her arms across her bosom. 'My father follows the gossip of the artists' quarter, and heard there was a talented portrait painter called Jacques, recently come from Claremont. He said you were known to enjoy a challenge.'

'How true,' he answered. He was watching her carefully. 'I like payment also. And the time has come, Mam'selle Sophie, for me to name my price.'

He was drawing nearer. The dim candlelight softened the harsh planes and angles of his handsome face, but it also lit sparks in his smouldering dark eyes. A wicked little pulse began to beat rather dangerously in all her nerve endings.

She tried to stand firm. 'Name it, then.'

He was looking again around the softly lit chapel. 'How many pictures need altering?'

'Six—no, I counted seven!'

He let his hand rest very lightly on her shoulder, and she jumped as if a burning brand had touched her. He was smiling down at her now. 'Well, then. For each hour I spend painting here, I want, in return, a kiss.'

She reeled. 'No. That is despicable. That is a mean, mean trick!'

Someone was coming, along the gallery outside, towards this chapel. They both heard it at the same time. Heard the key in the big lock turning, the squeak of hinges as the heavy door slowly swung open.

Her terrified eyes flew up to Jacques. She whispered, 'It's Monsieur Denon. He must not know!'

As quick as lightning, Jacques grabbed hold of her wrist and pulled her down with him behind the altar, crouching there with her in the shadow of the lavishly embroidered altar cloth. Old, fat Denon came in and stamped around, muttering, 'Strange. I would swear that I heard something. Must be those rats from the river. The sooner this business is over, the better. Be damned to Napoleon. Be damned to the whole wedding!'

He marched off again, slammed the door shut and locked it. And Sophie suddenly realised fully her predicament. She was huddled in the dark on her hands and knees, and gently round her shoulders lay the muscular arm of the most handsome man she'd ever met in her life. She ought to spring away, but she couldn't for the life of her move. His arm was holding her tight; his body was pressed close to hers. The clean male scent of his skin, of his hair, made her senses sweetly swim. And he was shaking, she realised—with soft laughter.

'I know Denon,' he whispered. 'He travels a lot, doesn't he? Scouring Europe for art treasures for Napoleon. But he doesn't seem too keen on his imperial master at the moment.' He was laughing again. '"Be damned to Napoleon,"' he said in a perfect imitation of old Denon's grumpy tones. '"Be damned to the whole wedding!"'

Then she was laughing too, because of course it was utterly absurd, finding herself here beneath the sacred marriage altar with a stranger who was going to paint out poor Josephine. Especially when she was nothing to Jacques at all! Just a rather absurd seamstress from the palace, whose request must strike him as ridiculous.

But then she saw that those compelling eyes were watching her with a mixture of amusement and—could it be desire? A kiss. He'd said he wanted a kiss, for every hour he spent on the task. Suddenly her situation didn't seem funny at all. Her pulse quickened and she licked her lips, which were dry with anxiety. He was murmuring huskily, 'An apt time to take payment in advance, I think.'

He was drawing her to her feet and holding her so close that she had to tilt her chin to look into his eyes. He slipped his hands around her waist and drew her even nearer, with gentle but relentless pressure. There was no time to protest as his mouth closed over hers in a slow, sweeping kiss that tore at her reserve and shattered it. His lips were warm, and strong; without realising it her own lips had parted, and his tongue was exploring with sweet demand.

A reckless yearning seized her. For a few magical moments she forgot everything except the feel and taste of this man, who was clasping her pliant body against his own hard one. She was cast adrift from reality, into a world of sensation—a world where the faint candlelight from the gilded altar swooped and dipped as his arms clasped her tighter and his mouth so sweetly possessed hers. A soft moan started somewhere in her throat and she ached for more.

Madness. What was she doing? She'd only just met this man. She knew nothing about him. He could be dangerous... *Could* be? He'd most certainly lived the life of a rogue and a rake!

Jacques of Claremont. She'd wanted his kiss more than she'd wanted anything. Ever.

He'd drawn away. Was looking round again, coolly assessing this hallowed chapel. 'I'll start work tomorrow, then,' he said, buttoning up his coat. 'I'll meet you outside, just after six. Isn't that what you said?'

She nodded. Mam'selle Sophie, head seamstress at the Tuileries. Trying to pretend nothing of any consequence had happened, when really her whole life had just been turned upside down by this painter Jacques.

'Yes,' she said. But her voice came out like a little squeak; she pretended to cough, and said again, more calmly, 'Yes, I'll meet you outside at six. The public galleries will still be busy, which will help. But won't you need to bring paints, and brushes?'

'I've got big pockets in this coat,' he said. He was already peering at the nearest painting. 'I'll start with that one. Cupid and Venus, in dalliance.' Then he swung round to her. His smile was wicked. 'I'm looking forward to it.'

Jacques left her outside the Louvre and strolled off thoughtfully along the crowded rue de Rivoli, cheerfully brushing aside courtesans who accosted him along the way, the touts selling souvenirs of the wedding—trinkets adorned with the entwined initials of the happy couple, Austrian sweetmeats and little flags to wave on the great day.

Sophie. So lovely. So dutiful. So repressed… Until he kissed her. And then her reaction had been spectacular. His loins still throbbed at the memory of her sweetly parted lips, of her pert breasts pressing so enticingly against his chest.

And so, still musing, he got home. No artist's garret for Jacques; instead a rather luxurious four-roomed apartment in the rue du Faubourg St Honoré, where his anxious valet tutted over his scruffy clothes, and—more usefully— poured him a good large brandy while Jacques contemplated this rather intriguing adventure he'd got himself into.

Chapter Three

The wedding drew steadily nearer. Every day, Sophie supervised her small team of skilled seamstresses as they prepared the royal suite in the Tuileries Palace for the Archduchess Marie-Louise. Every day, Sophie hurried away after her work was done to visit her sick papa, seeing all around the vast preparations for the great event: the flags and garlands that were being hung all along the Champs-Élysées; the flower beds of the Tuileries that were being coaxed to exquisite perfection by hundreds of dedicated gardeners.

Poor Marie-Louise, she kept thinking. To be forced into marriage with a man she barely knew! Each evening, an hour before the Louvre closed its great doors to the crowds of sightseers, she met Jacques and together they would move, unseen, into the Salon Carré.

He was a wonderful artist, she realised: speedy yet meticulous. She'd been terrified when he'd started on the first painting. She'd seen his sketches, but this was quite different. What if his work was unacceptable? What if he *ruined* these precious masterpieces?

But he knew exactly what he was doing—had brought exactly the right brushes and tubes of oils to mutate the dark, vivacious features of Josephine into the fair prettiness of the much younger Marie-Louise. For a while, she even forgot his wicked bargain. When he gestured to her to come and examine his first completed transformation, Sophie gasped. 'You should not be a lowly street artist! You could be making money!'

He smiled, that lazy, languorous smile that disconcerted her so. 'I'm not doing this for nothing,' he drawled, looking at her in such a meaningful way that she almost felt faint.

A kiss. For each hour he spent painting.

That first kiss of his had swept all her common sense to the wind. What would the next one be like?

She waited that second night with a thundering heart for him to claim his due. Yet when he came to her at the end with his brushes and paints put away, and the candles in the magnificently adorned wedding chapel burning but dimly, he just took her hand, lifted it and gently kissed it.

She felt rather faint. With relief—or disappointment?

'Is that *all*?' she breathed.

'That's all,' he answered evenly. 'I was wrong to take advantage of you as I did last night.'

'But it was our agreement!'

'I have had payment enough, believe me.'

She gazed up at him, outwardly calm. 'Very well. We had better go. It will soon be seven, and the guards will be doing their rounds.'

So she unlocked the door to let them out, and he took

his leave. Her heart was welling with bitter disappointment. *One kiss was enough.* Was she so very unattractive? Yes must be the answer. Yes. She had simply amused him, that was all—presented a challenge, with her devotion to her task, her earnestness, her innocence!

Indeed Sophie guarded her innocence fiercely. But only because she had seen too many women in her position— lowly servants to the great—seduced, then cruelly cast aside. She had sworn that would never happen to her, and had deliberately cultivated her plain attire and her prim manner.

She had been safe until now. But Jacques the insolent artist had sparked something, unleashed something. Not just in that first kiss, but with his very presence—his casual smile, that lithe grace that emanated from every part of his powerful body, even in the shabby clothes and dusty top boots he lounged about in. She dreamed wicked dreams, every night, of being in his arms. Of his lips on her lips, and more.

How he would laugh, if he knew. Well, that was up to her. He would *not* know.

So each day, as the wedding drew closer, she dressed more severely than ever, and pulled her hair back into her demure cap, and wore her high-necked gowns. Not that he paid her appearance much attention anyway, for his eyes were always on his painting.

But he would often talk, as he painted. And Sophie would listen, enraptured in spite of herself. He would tell her the latest tales from the Paris streets. How the costumiers were running out of seed pearls because the rumour had spread amongst the grand ladies of Paris that this was what Marie-Louise would have embroidered on her wedding gown. How the builders of the Arc de Triomphe had threatened to strike unless they were paid more money. How Napoleon's outrageous sister, Princess Pauline, had fallen out with the Comtesse de Lyons over who would sit closest to the imperial couple at the wedding feast.

'How do you *know* all these things, Jacques?' she would ask wonderingly. There was gossip aplenty at the Tuileries Palace, but he seemed to know it all the minute it happened.

He turned to her, still stroking his paintbrush in the delicate colours on his palette. 'One hears everything at the Palais-Royal. One even hears how a very pretty seamstress at the Tuileries Palace has turned down one respectable suitor after another, because she is so devoted to her work, and to her father. Her name—' and now he was watching her thoughtfully '—is Sophie.'

Her cheeks burned. 'I didn't think you would stoop to pry. And besides, it is…ridiculous to say that I've turned down offer after offer, to say that I am pretty!'

'Not pretty, I agree.' He was looking at her, those dark eyes glinting again. 'I actually said…*very* pretty. And I've heard something else. That this same Sophie signed away four years of her life to work at the Tuileries, so that her father, who is ailing, did not lose his job at the Louvre. Monsieur Denon, who is hand-in-glove with the head steward at the Tuileries, wanted you to stay and reject all suitors, because you were so good at your job. Your price was that your father should keep his. Is it true, Sophie?'

Her heart was beating like a panic-stricken bird trying to get out of a cage. 'My father is excellent at his job! No one knows the collection as he does—no one cares for it as he does!'

'But he is becoming careless. Isn't he?' said Jacques the painter softly. 'That's why he didn't realise there were pictures of Josephine all around this wedding chapel, until it was almost too late. Even then, he thought there were only one or two, but it was you who spotted them all, wasn't it, Sophie?'

'You should not know this,' she said bleakly. 'No one should know it.'

'But is it true?'

Her shoulders drooped 'Yes.' Suddenly her eyes blazed again. 'But I love my father, I love my job, and besides, I have no wish to marry, to be bargained away like poor Marie-Louise!'

'Are you quite sure, Sophie?'

In the rich shadows, surrounded by the marble pillars and sumptuous hangings, the gold altar decorations and the priceless paintings, Sophie suddenly felt so full of emotion that she could scarcely breathe. He had moved closer—too close. She had not seen him put down his palette and brush, but he was here, facing her, with one hand on her shoulder, and the other cupping her chin, tilting her face towards him.

'Payment,' he said softly.

She lifted bewildered eyes to his dark, intent ones. 'But I thought you didn't want anything more from me. I thought I must repel you....'

'Repel me?' He backed away. 'Dear God, Sophie, I've been fighting for the past few nights to keep my hands off you, woman, haven't you realised?'

'No doubt it would be the same with *any* female who was young, and available!' she cried. 'You artists have a reputation after all!'

'Is that why you hired me?' he stormed. 'To test out my *reputation*?'

Her hands were on her hips. 'Believe me, I would have hired you if you were the wickedest rake in Paris, if you'd said you would fix those paintings for me!'

Suddenly he began to chuckle, very softly. 'You're in the mood for a fight, and you look lovelier than ever when you're angry. I'd like to paint you like that, Sophie. Your eyes become a darker blue, your cheeks are flushed—just a little—and your breath comes in short little sighs. And your beautiful hair has fallen down from its pins.'

Frantically she reached to push it up again. But before she could do so he was drawing her into his arms. Her lips parted in protest.

'Payment time again,' he said softly. He lowered his head, and his mouth found the sensitive skin of her throat. 'Endure it if you must, sweet Sophie. Enjoy it if you dare.'

Sensation curled up from somewhere deep inside her and began flooding her senses. It was all she could do not to groan out loud as his hands slid down her back to clasp her waist, then moved beneath the soft fullness of her breasts.

Endure, he'd said. But he must know. This sensual, experienced man must know that he only had to touch her for her body to become a mass of need. Only had to move his lips against hers for her mouth to open to him, savouring his kiss that possessed and plundered, while she clung to his wide shoulders, not only her breathing but her whole self almost out of control.

It was he who carefully drew away, though he still held her, steadying her, as his eyes glinted darkly.

Only then was she was strong enough to step back from him. Defensively she clenched her hands and stared up at him. Payment. That was all this was. He was amusing himself at her expense, toying with her. 'So,' she breathed at last. 'One more night of work to go. I trust all this has kept you entertained!'

He was watching her, his eyes unreadable. 'There is no harm in happiness, Sophie,' he said quietly. 'Sometimes you have to grasp at life, or it isn't worth living.' And he went back to his work.

But that night, when Jacques returned to his apartment in the Faubourg St Honoré, he was in such a black mood that even his valet was wary of him.

Only two nights left before the wedding, and the Tuileries Palace had been hectic all day. Though Sophie had completed her work in preparing the draperies for the empress's private chambers, she was constantly being called on for extra tasks or advice.

'Sophie, these flowers need arranging! Sophie, the curtains in the reception hall could really do with your finishing touch!' the head housekeeper would beg. 'Sophie, should these gold candlesticks—they were a wedding gift from the Tsar of Russia—be here, or here? No one knows these things as well as you, my dear!'

Sophie got away at last at six, and hurried through the still-sunny Paris evening to the Louvre where Jacques would be waiting. And her heart was heavy. These hours in the dimly lit wedding chapel had come to mean more to her than she would ever admit.

She had made a fool of herself in front of Jacques, an utter fool, by declaring that she had no time for men or sentiment, then yielding so treacherously to his kiss. Still, why worry? she told herself sadly. After tomorrow tonight she would never see him again, and no doubt he was completely happy with that arrangement. In fact, that evening he worked more swiftly than ever, applying paint with dexterity. Only once did she dare to question him about his work.

'Jacques, I did not think Josephine was in that painting!'

'Ah, but she is,' he told her calmly. 'She's lurking amongst the nymphs surrounding gallant Hercules—who just happens to be Napoleon. It won't take me long.'

Suddenly they were aware of a cacophony of sound, at the far end of the Long Gallery but drawing nearer. Sophie looked speechlessly at Jacques for guidance; he, being taller, could see better than she.

'Napoleon,' he said swiftly. 'With his courtiers, and Denon. I don't think they'll enter the chapel. He's probably checking that the gallery is ready for all his guests, and the procession. If we stand behind the pillars—here—I don't think they'll see us.'

He was right. From where Jacques guided her, she was able to see the emperor stalking up and down the gallery issuing orders, while his courtiers scurried around him, listening, nodding, making notes.

'We need more bronze eagles here,' the little emperor declaimed, 'above the place where my Imperial Guard will stand!' He pointed to another section of the hall. 'Those laurel wreaths should be more prominent. And couldn't we have the Bartolini bust of me in here?'

'Your Imperial Majesty,' said Denon quickly, 'we might be able to move the Bartolini from the Salle de la Victoire, yes, but not the Rubens painting, *The Triumph of the Victor*, that hangs so appropriately, so sublimely, above it! How can the two be separated? Be assured that all your distinguished guests will wish to view the two of them together, and indeed will be guided to them—I myself will take responsibility for it!'

For a moment the silence was ominous. Then, 'Hmm,' said Napoleon. He glanced round critically. 'Perhaps for once you are right, Monsieur Denon. Other than that, it is all good, very good. Marie-Louise will not be disappointed. Her wedding day will be the most glorious day of her life!'

Sophie had listened with bated breath, but now she had to repress the sudden desire to laugh. Jacques glanced down at her; his lips, too, were quivering with amusement. 'Emperors. They tend to have a high opinion of themselves,' he said wryly. He glanced out at the Long Gallery. 'It's all right, they've gone.'

'I feel so sorry for Marie-Louise,' Sophie blurted out. 'She is scarcely more than a child! And to be married to a man so vain, so prone to rages!'

'You feel pity for her, when she is to be married to the most powerful man in Europe? To be fêted throughout the greatest cities in the world, to be adorned with crowns and jewellery—have you seen the *parure* that Napoleon has bestowed on her?'

'I have heard of it,' she breathed. 'A necklace and tiara,

earrings and comb, all made from the finest diamonds and emeralds in the world. For myself, I do not care for show, but all the great ladies of Paris are wild with envy!' Then Jacques saw her face become shadowed. 'It's just that… she is so very young. And she must be so nervous, at the thought of the…the…'

'Of the wedding night?' His dark eyes lazily smouldered. *'Au contraire.* I believe she welcomed him rapturously to her bed. Her cries of delight were heard throughout the neighbouring chambers.'

Sophie's cheeks were filled with fierce colour now. 'They have been intimate? But how? Where?'

'He went to meet her at Compiègne, where he spent the night with her. They were—' he paused '—very happy with each other.'

'How do you *know* such things?'

He put a finger lightly to her lips. 'One hears everything at the Palais-Royal.'

Sophie thought, And our vain emperor is quite capable of spreading such stories himself. She struggled to collect herself. To remind herself that she was merely a seamstress, a spinster, and a man's touch should definitely not send rivulets of heat trickling through her. 'I'm sure one does, Monsieur Jacques,' she responded crisply. 'Now, if you have finished, we really must be locking up.'

'So I'll see you here tomorrow?'

She froze. 'I thought you had finished.'

'Not quite. The varnish needs to be applied, remember?'

'Of course.' She frowned, and stared at the painting he had just altered. 'To think that I never noticed that one!'

'It was easily missed, but we can't afford to take any

chances,' he reminded her. 'Napoleon has eyes like a hawk. Tomorrow night?'

'Tomorrow night.'

The night before the wedding. The last time she would see him, ever. And tonight he hadn't even kissed her.

But he'd wanted to. Oh, he'd wanted to. After he'd walked with her to the Tuileries, Jacques the painter pounded round Paris, until he finally settled himself in a lowly wine bar in the rue de la Baume, where men were laying wagers on how long Napoleon's bride would take to bear him a son. 'She's a Habsburg,' they were declaring. 'A fertile race, the Habsburgs, as well as possessing the bluest blood in Europe!'

Jacques closed his eyes to their increasingly raucous banter and drank too much burgundy.

Hell. How had he landed himself in this? He'd just wanted to help her, because she was lovely, an innocent. But he'd quickly realised the kisses had to cease, because her reaction to his touch brought fire to his own blood, and heated him to the point where he would not be able to stop.

For God's sake. He couldn't bear the thought of not seeing her again. But how was he going to tell her...*everything*?

Chapter Four

On the eve of the wedding the Tuileries Palace was thronged with courtiers and servants. Down in the vast kitchens, armies of cooks bustled and flapped, while outside delivery drays pulled up one after another, laden with fancy foodstuffs, exotic plants, garlands of flowers and gifts large and small from all corners of Napoleon's empire.

Sophie was eating in the servants' quarters, but couldn't understand why there was yet no sign of Fleur. No one else noticed her absence, because one of the housemaids was reading out the menu for the wedding feast tomorrow night.

'Pickled oysters. Buttered lobster. Venison in a pastry case. Mutton à la Turc. Roast lamb with cockles. Trifle and gingerbread ices—oh, my!' breathed the housemaid longingly.

'All that fancy stuff won't impress Napoleon.' A cocky young groom laughed. 'You all know what he's like over food. "Fifteen minutes is time enough for anyone to fill his stomach," says our little emperor.' He winked saucily.

'His views are exactly the same, by the way, on the subject of—ahem!—carnal relations.'

'Quiet, you cheeky young scamp!' ordered a burly cook.

Just then Fleur came hurrying in, looking white and desperate.

'Fleur!' Sophie was at her side in an instant. 'Whatever is it, my dear?'

'Oh, Mam'selle Sophie!' Poor Fleur was openly sobbing now. 'It's my Henri. They've told me he died in the fighting in Spain. He won't be coming back—ever!' She collapsed in Sophie's arms, in floods of tears.

That evening Jacques the painter was waiting for her in the usual place. His eyes narrowed. 'You look serious.'

She sighed, pulling off her hooded cloak as she unlocked the door and let him into the wedding chapel. 'Someone who works with me—a young friend—learned today that her fiancé has been killed in Spain. They were going to be married in the summer. It's so cruel for poor Fleur, with the talk of the wedding everywhere!'

'And isn't that life?' Jacques asked quietly. 'To love and to lose perhaps? Isn't that the point of living? No one can guard themselves for ever. No one can be safe for ever, whatever emotional walls they put up. We have to find happiness where we can.'

She gazed at him. His voice was so grave. As though he, too, had secrets, dark secrets perhaps. How could she bear not ever learning more about him, not ever seeing him again?

He took her hand and said gently, 'Sit, and watch me work. Only a coat of varnish, and I've finished.'

So she watched him, taking pleasure in his skill, en-

joying his calm, competent movements and smothering
her forbidden yearning for his touch, his kiss. They talked
about Paris, and their lives and hopes.

'I suppose you will want to become a successful painter
like Monsieur David,' she said. 'My father will help you if
he can.'

'My thanks.' He smiled. 'And I've enjoyed the task.
Have you, Sophie?'

She hesitated. 'I always take pleasure in seeing a job well
done.'

He laughed. 'Just as well, since you are in a position
of some responsibility at the Tuileries. I'm sure your col-
leagues respect you enormously.'

But I don't want respect, she was thinking in anguish. *I
want love. Yes, love...*

He was putting away his painting things. 'All finished,'
he said cheerfully. 'Listen, Sophie, there will be tightrope
walkers and tumblers in the Tuileries Gardens tonight.
Come with me, why don't you?'

She stood very still. The gardens at night were a place of
loose behaviour, of debauchery even. She said, as steadily
as she could, 'You might prefer to attend the celebrations
with your friends.'

'Aren't *we* friends, Sophie?' A smile tugged at the corners of his mouth. 'I'm just inviting you for a walk, in the
Tuileries Gardens, tonight, the eve of the royal wedding.'

'And my debt to you?' she whispered.

'It's been my pleasure. Consider it paid off,' he said.

She often wondered afterwards why she, a sensible twenty-
three-year-old seamstress, should have agreed so lightly.

Perhaps because so much had contributed, that day, to her emotional state. Fleur's tragedy. Her own sense of time passing. Jacques was right: she always did shut herself off from life!

But not tonight. Tonight, the warm spring air of Paris was intoxicated with the forthcoming wedding. The gardens were sweetly scented with blossom, and bright with tulips and love-in-a-mist. The fountains played, glittering in the moonlight. Other couples, happy, in love, were walking down the broad avenues and along the shrubbery paths.

Jacques took her arm, and as they strolled he told her tales of his boyhood. 'I was a little wild, I'm afraid. Rebellious.' He laughed. 'My dream was to be an artist, though my father, who died five years ago, wouldn't hear of it.'

'But he would be proud of you now!' Sophie gazed up at him earnestly. 'Your work is so beautiful!'

He was gazing down at her, something dark and fathomless in his eyes. 'Not as beautiful as you,' he said softly. 'Ah, I'm sorry, I've embarrassed you.... Tell me *your* dreams, sweet Sophie. Surely you didn't always want to be...a seamstress?'

'I'm a senior seamstress!' she protested defensively. 'It's what I do best!'

'But you've never tried anything else,' he said. 'And that's because you gave up your own hopes and dreams to safeguard your father's job.'

'That is not true! It was no sacrifice to work at the Tuileries. I have no forlorn hopes, no unfulfilled dreams!'

'Well, I have,' he said.

She stared up at him, astonished. 'What?'

He'd caught her wrist and was gently pulling her closer. 'Sweet Sophie, I dream of just one more kiss from you.'

If only it had ended there, thought Sophie in anguish as much later she stole upstairs to her dark attic bedroom. If only it had ended with a kiss! What had she been *thinking* of?

It was the warm, soft Paris night. It was the musicians, playing in the terraced gardens. It was the twinkling lights set up around the trees for the wedding; it was the scented early roses, it was...

It was Jacques, you idiot. It was Jacques. If he had set out to seduce her, he couldn't have chosen a better time or place in the whole world. And she hadn't been exactly unwilling. From the first moment his lips had touched hers, and he'd let his skilled hands slip round to cup the soft contours of each breast, she'd been lost. Utterly lost.

'Tell me,' he'd said. 'Tell me the instant you want me to stop, Sophie.'

But there hadn't been a single minute when she didn't want to be held even tighter by those strong arms, breathing in the scent of his clean skin as his lips sweetly caressed and explored. Sensation—pure sensation—leapt deep inside, and began to flood her every nerve ending, bringing her not only to life, but to awareness of burning need. Especially when his fingers found the peak of her breast beneath her gown, and teased it into hot hardness. Then, she wound her arms round his shoulders and held him, tightly. *'Jacques.'*

He looked at her once more, his eyes grave. He said,

'There is still time. I will take you home whenever you say. You must not feel obliged to continue with this, Sophie.'

'But I don't want you to stop,' she whispered. 'And, Jacques, it's nothing to do with...obligation. It's to do with you, and me, and life! I'm tired of being sensible, and responsible, and always doing the right thing. I want to do the *wrong* thing, just for once, with you, tonight!'

'You are sure?' His hands tightened round her. His breathing was harsh.

'Quite sure!' She blinked in sudden self-doubt. 'That is—*if* you want me....'

'Oh, Sophie.' He crushed her against him so she became aware, suddenly, of the hardness at his loins. Her eyes flew up to his, wide, startled.

'There,' Jacques the artist said softly, 'you have your answer.'

A reckless yearning seized her every fibre as he stroked her spine from the nape of her neck to her hips, sending shivers of desire through her. 'Imagine that tonight is a dream,' he whispered. 'Just you and me in the whole world. No duties to care about, no one else to think about, just us.' He brushed her lips with his silken mouth. 'In a dream, everything is possible.'

There was a secluded pavilion along one of the paths, and he led her there in the twilight, away from the crowds. He closed the door, then drew her close again. A kiss—a deep, cherishing kiss—and she was lost to him, being dragged deeper and deeper in a whirlpool of pleasure. She moaned softly as he slipped down the shoulder of her dress and caught one nipple between his lips, drawing up fierce kindlings of desire. She felt herself dissolving, becoming molten in his hands, and when those hands gently lowered her to the floor, when he swept up her skirts and caressed her and felt the tremors passing through her, she clutched him to her.

'Jacques. Jacques,' she breathed.

He was with her then, as one in urgent desire—freeing himself, easing himself into her, caressing and coaxing as she rose to his hand, to his steely yet silken entry. With care he began to move, guiding her body into the rhythm of love, and Sophie was only aware of him possessing her, driving her to undreamed-of delights, as she clung to him, whispering out his name, because the waves of pleasure that washed through her with each stroke made it impossible for her to do anything else.

His lips were on her mouth again, on her breast; she cried out, her whole body racked with intense pleasure, as he held her, held her so tightly, and drove himself to his own release.

Afterwards, he drew her gently to her feet and helped her to restore her disordered clothing.

'Sophie,' he said. 'I want to see you again.' His hands lingered on her shoulders. 'But tomorrow, I am busy.'

'We will all be busy, I think,' she said brightly.

'Indeed. But there is something I must tell you. Something important. And I must tell you—*soon.*'

Now she lay in her attic bed, unable to sleep, unable to concentrate on anything but Jacques as the dreary hours went by. *He wants to tell me he is married. Or has a mistress he adores. What a fool he must think me. I am twenty-three years old—and I begged him to make love to me, like a nun released from a convent. I surrendered to him in those moonlit gardens like a prostitute.*

But that was not the worst of it. The worst of it was that she had fallen in love with Jacques, the decadent Parisian artist, and she must never, ever let him know it.

Chapter Five

Early the next morning Sophie hurried through streets
that were already full of crowds eager to view the wonderful pageant of their emperor bringing his bride-to-be into
Paris. Her father was waiting for her anxiously; quickly she
reassured him.

'It's all right, Papa. The paintings have all been dealt
with.'

She saw his anxiety fade; then he tensed again. 'But the
cost! I hope it wasn't too high?'

I don't know, she murmured inwardly. *I don't know
yet.* But aloud she said brightly, 'Nothing I cannot afford,
Papa!'

He nodded, clasping her hand. 'You are a good daughter. You must go now—you will have so much to do. But
somehow—' he frowned, gazing at her face '—you look
different!'

How could he tell? Could anyone else tell?

'It's the wedding,' she told him lightly. 'It's all so exciting, and we're so very busy at the palace!'

'Of course.' He smiled and patted her hand. 'You will come later and tell me all about it, won't you?'

'Dear Papa, I'll bore you to death with it!' she teased. 'Trust me!'

Everyone at the Tuileries was in a state of near-panic. Somehow Sophie had thought—wrongly—that her part in the preparations was complete, but the housekeeper spotted her as she passed through the hall. 'Sophie! Thank goodness you're here! They need some seamstresses over at the Louvre, urgently. Some of the gold hangings in the Long Gallery have come loose.'

'But the guests will already be gathering there!'

'Yes, but it's hours before the wedding. Though you must be quick!'

Sophie took two other seamstresses, including little Fleur, hoping that being busy would distract the poor girl from her heartbreak. Swiftly and calmly she organised the repair to one of the huge silk hangings that adorned the gallery's wall, while gradually the great room filled with magnificently dressed, eagerly chattering guests—royalty and nobility from all corners of Europe. Even Fleur, gazing round wide-eyed, took an eager interest.

The Princess Pauline, Napoleon's notoriously promiscuous sister, caused the most stir by entering in a décolleté gown of almost sheer white muslin on the arm of her latest lover, a burly guardsman. The whispers began, but Sophie did not join in. *Am I any better than Pauline? For what I did with the artist, Jacques, was shameless, quite shameless....*

When their task was done, she started gathering up her

sewing things. Then Fleur was gasping. 'Mam'selle Sophie. Oh, do look. Isn't he the most handsome man of them all?'

Sophie turned idly, unimpressed by all these vainglorious peacocks. But then she saw him. Dressed in restrained but exquisite clothes, his hair black and curling. *Jacques.* Her street artist, whom she'd begged to make love to her.

And the herald, as he entered, was calling out, 'Jacques-Guillaume de Vevret, Count of Claremont...'

She walked back to the palace with the others, hating him, but hating her own naivety most of all. There were still more flowers to be placed in the empress's rooms—work, work was the answer—but little Fleur and the others dragged her out to the balcony, from where they could see the imperial procession as it progressed along the Champs-Élysées.

'Mam'selle Sophie, the carriage!' Fleur was exclaiming. 'It's all gold and glass, and, oh, I can see Napoleon's bride! She's wearing a mantle of red velvet stitched with golden thread, and her crown sparkles so much that it must be *made* of diamonds!'

All around them the crowds were cheering wildly and the bands were playing. Along the banks of the Seine the artillery were firing their guns.

Then some soldiers marched by, resplendent in their uniforms, and poor little Fleur began to weep again. 'My Henri,' she whispered. 'Oh, poor Henri, he should be here.' Silently Sophie hugged her; indeed there was a huge ache where her own heart should be. Jacques's words rang again and again in her ear: 'Sometimes you have to grasp at life, Sophie, or it isn't worth living.'

But why had he let her think he was a poor artist? He must have found it amusing, the Count of Claremont, to play the part. To make her fall in love with him.

You stupid, naïve fool, Sophie. You've less sense than Fleur.

Afterwards everyone said it was the most glorious wedding ever. The Louvre and the wedding chapel were, people said, just perfect. Napoleon had surveyed it all, sharp eyed, from his throne in there, and now that all reminders of Josephine were eliminated, nothing could be seen that would send him into one of his terrifying rages.

After the ceremony the imperial couple returned to the Tuileries, and the young empress sent for the chambermaids to thank them personally, with an accent that was charming. Now that her red velvet mantle was removed, they could see her beautiful gown, a high-waisted robe of white tulle encrusted with pearls and silver thread and adorned with a stiffened collar of finest Brussels lace. One by one the maids of the chamber curtsied before her, but she raised them quickly to their feet. 'Thank you all, so much!' she said warmly. 'These rooms, and the flowers, are exquisite!'

Fleur, as impetuous as ever, blurted out, 'We thought you would miss your home, Your Majesty! You have had to travel such a long way, we really wanted you to feel welcome here!'

Marie-Louise gazed at her. 'Sometimes, one has to endure…adventures—is that the word?—to find out what is right for oneself, I think. But I feel you are already my friends, the first friends I have made in this beautiful city!'

She sank with a little sigh into the nearest chair and eased off her lovely white satin shoes. 'Too tight,' she explained with a tiny frown, 'my poor feet, they ache so...'

'Your Imperial Majesty, we will find you others to wear, from your trousseau!'

'No.' Marie-Louise raised her small white hand and smiled. 'My husband chose them for me, and I will wear them—just a *little* discomfort, you see!—because I love him, and I love Paris, because it is the city of his heart.'

Sophie thought, She loves him. Jacques was right; she truly loves him.

That evening, as the sumptuous wedding feast took place inside the palace, Sophie stood alone on the deserted terrace overlooking the gardens, which were illuminated by thousands of lanterns. An hour ago, Fleur had come running to her, bubbling with joy.

'He is back! My Henri is back. He was wounded, not dead, and we are to be married, as soon as possible!'

Sophie had hugged her warmly. 'I'm so happy for you, my dear. So *very* happy.'

Everyone was happy. All of Paris, it seemed, was partying in the Tuileries Gardens, where last night she had urged Jacques to make love to her.

The Count of Claremont. She felt renewed anguish in her heart. Oh, what a fool she was. She'd ignored so many warning signs. His bearing, his education. The fact that he knew what Marie-Louise looked like; no doubt he'd dined with her! How he must have laughed over Sophie's assumption that he was a poor painter. Tonight he would be a guest, of course, at the imperial banquet. He might even be regaling his aristocratic friends with the hilarious tale of the virgin seamstress who thought he was an impoverished artist and begged him to seduce her....

She felt a hand on her shoulder. She whirled round. It was Jacques, looking heartbreakingly handsome in a fitted black coat and white neckcloth. Her pulse thudded sickeningly. She backed away, her hand at her throat.

'Have you come here to laugh at me again?'

'Sophie,' he began. 'I want to explain—'

'Go away.' Her anger burned. 'A poor artist. You told me you were a poor artist!'

'Wrong,' he reminded her tersely. 'You *assumed* I was a poor artist. But didn't I tell you, last night, that we needed to talk?'

'What about?' she said bitterly. Her voice was shaking. 'Were you intending to offer me payment perhaps?'

'I wanted to give you something, certainly,' he said. He held out a small trinket box. Frowning, she opened it.

Inside was a silver oval brooch, containing a miniature portrait. Of...*her.*

Her heart clenched.

'Just to show you,' he said quietly, 'that you were not altogether wrong in assuming me to be an artist.'

She clasped the box tightly. *It means nothing, nothing at all...* 'But you are also a count!'

'A penniless count,' he said, 'till recently. My father was exiled during the revolution, like so many, and lost his lands, his money, everything. So I earned my own living around the cities of Europe, by doing what I was good at— painting. When Napoleon became emperor, he recalled all his exiled nobles and restored their lands. But I'm still far from rich. My father's lands were badly neglected and there's much to be done. I came to stay in Paris for the wedding, of course, to show my loyalty to Napoleon. The last thing I expected was to fall in love.'

Love. She froze.

'With you,' he went on softly.

'You cannot. Oh, Jacques, you could have your pick of the women of the court.'

He said evenly, 'Of the near-prostitutes like Pauline, who throng Paris? I'd really rather not.' He drew closer, and took her hand. 'You see, I want someone to be my companion, someone steadfast and honest, who'll talk to me of love and life, as you have done. During our nights together in the wedding chapel, I realised. I want no one else to be my wife, Sophie.'

She was silent a moment, her heart in turmoil. 'Jacques, I will have to think. In fact, there is so much to think about....'

'Is there?' he said lightly. 'Don't you feel you've known me for ever?'

She laughed suddenly. 'Yes,' she said, 'yes, I do! But—'

'Then let me tell you, sweetheart,' he said, taking her in his arms, 'that I actually finished those paintings on the third night.'

'You can't have! We spent—oh, I don't know how many more nights there!'

He grinned, white teeth flashing. 'Because I couldn't bear to let you go. So I found a few more faces to turn into Marie-Louise. Napoleon, I think, would be delighted to know that his new bride is *everywhere* in the Salon Carré. Now, no more "buts."' He kissed her hand tenderly. 'Because tonight, I'm going to dance with you, until you say that you will marry me. Understand, my foolish, darling Sophie?'

Nearby a band was playing. In the warm night air, it seemed as if all the lovers in Paris were dancing to the glorious music, in celebration of the imperial marriage. He swept her into the midst of them, to dance, rapturously; and later, as the celebratory fireworks cascaded over the gardens and the Seine, later, as he kissed her, she whispered, 'Yes.'

Yes, to her artist, her lover, Jacques.

* * * * *

Author Note

Most people know that Napoleon and Josephine had a passionate, if occasionally quarrelsome, marriage. But sadly, Josephine was unable to bear the great French emperor an heir, and so in 1810 he divorced her and took a new bride, the shy young Archduchess of Austria, Marie-Louise.

Their sumptuous wedding in Paris provides the background for my story. The tale opens with the fiery Emperor Napoleon wanting nothing at all to remind him of Josephine in the chapel of the Louvre, where the ceremony is shortly to be held. It has fallen to my heroine, Sophie, to attend to this, though she needs the help of the handsome roving artist Jacques, whose demand for payment for his services is outrageous!

Were Napoleon and Marie-Louise happy? I think they were, and the year after their marriage she gave birth to his son. But Napoleon's exile to Elba in 1814 meant that his wife and child had to return to Austria, and Napoleon never saw them again. Marie-Louise remarried and bore more children, though her first-born, Napoleon's son, died young. Napoleon himself died alone in exile on St Helena.

The emperor was an ardent collector of paintings and sculptures, just a few of which are mentioned in my story. Canova was the most renowned sculptor of his day, producing many works for Napoleon, and Jacques, my hero, has glimpsed Canova's naked statue of *Napoleon as Mars* in Rome. When Napoleon finally saw it in 1811, he rejected it as being 'too athletic,' and the statue, ironically, came into the possession of the Duke of Wellington, who vanquished Napoleon at the battle of Waterloo. It is now on view to the public at Apsley House, London.

May this year's very special royal wedding be full of happiness!

Lucy Ashford

PRINCESS CHARLOTTE'S CHOICE

ANN LETHBRIDGE

Ann Lethbridge has been reading Regency novels for as long as she can remember. She always imagined herself as Lizzie Bennet, or one of Georgette Heyer's heroines, and would often recreate the stories in her head with different outcomes or scenes. When she sat down to write her own novel, it was no wonder that she returned to her first love: the Regency.

Ann grew up roaming England with her military father. Her family lived in many towns and villages across the country, from the Outer Hebrides to Hampshire. She spent memorable family holidays in the West Country and in Dover, where her father was born. She now lives in Canada, with her husband, two beautiful daughters, and a Maltese terrier named Teaser, who spends his days on a chair beside the computer, making sure she doesn't slack off.

Ann visits Britain every year, to undertake research and also to visit family members who are very understanding about her need to poke around old buildings and visit every antiquity within a hundred miles.

Previous novels by Ann Lethbridge:

THE RAKE'S INHERITED COURTESAN
WICKED RAKE, DEFIANT MISTRESS
CAPTURED FOR THE CAPTAIN'S PLEASURE
THE GOVERNESS AND THE EARL
(part of *Mills & Boon® New Voices…* anthology)
THE GAMEKEEPER'S LADY
(linked to *More Than a Mistress*)
LADY ROSABELLA'S RUSE
MORE THAN A MISTRESS

and in Mills & Boon® Historical *Undone!* eBooks:
THE RAKE'S INTIMATE ENCOUNTER
THE LAIRD AND THE WANTON WIDOW
ONE NIGHT AS A COURTESAN

Did you know that some of these novels are also available as eBooks? Visit www.millsandboon.co.uk

Chapter One

Lady Isabelle Fenwick saw panic in Princess Charlotte's blue eyes as she stared at her reflection. 'I w-want him to like me for myself, not only because of the crown.' The slight hesitation inherited from the House of New Brunswick was another signal of agitation.

'He will,' Isabelle soothed. 'Has he not shown remarkable constancy these past two years?'

They were speaking of His Excellency, Prince Leopold of Saxe-Coburg, the man about to become the princess's betrothed husband. Isabelle wasn't surprised at the Princess Charlotte's sudden rush of nerves. She might be next in line for the British throne after her father—the Prince of Wales, now the Prince Regent—but the past two years had been fraught with difficulties.

Mrs Louis, the princess's dresser, straightened the rose velvet bow at the back of the white satin gown and stepped back. 'You look lovely, Your Highness. His Excellency must be delighted.'

It was true. The white satin gown set off the princess's milky skin to perfection and its cut made the most of her buxom figure. The dark golden curls arranged high on her crown with a few curls teased out at the temples gave her a pleasing but youthful dignity.

The princess stamped her foot. It was an impulsive impatient gesture left over from childhood. 'Then why has he waited so long?'

Sometimes Isabelle, at twenty-three, felt ancient compared to the nineteen-year-old princess. But she did not blame her for her fears, knowing the disaster of her parents' marriage. 'The time wasn't right before now.'

Mrs Louis smoothed imaginary creases from the delicately embroidered skirts. 'Now the gloves, Your Highness.'

The princess held out one plump hand with a sigh. She glanced at the door to the dressing room through which the other ladies-in-waiting would pass when they finished their toilettes. 'I do wish I had spent more time in his company when he visited London two years ago.'

Mrs Louis put on her other glove. 'I will fetch the pearls, Your Highness.' She disappeared into the bedroom next door.

'If only my father had suggested him as a possible husband then,' Charlotte continued, 'I might not have got into a scrape with Prince Augustus.' She thrust her chin out, another unfortunate mannerism she occasionally forgot to curb. 'I am tired of being treated like a miscreant. Cranborne Lodge is little more than a prison. No one visits me there. At least this marriage is a chance to escape.'

Not the best reason to accept a marriage proposal. Guilt

pressed heavily on Isabelle's chest. 'If I hadn't left you alone with—'

Princess Charlotte put up a hand. She paced away from the mirror and swirled back to face Isabelle. 'Nothing happened. Prince Augustus flirted a little. Nothing more. It is because I would not marry that drunkard, William of Orange, that I am hidden away in the grounds at Windsor with no one to talk to but the queen.'

That was one way to look at it. But if Princess Charlotte hadn't been left alone with Prince Augustus, she might not have fallen for him, and if that hadn't happened, she might not have infuriated her father by severing her engagement to William of Orange. Topping it off with an impetuous midnight flight alone across London to her mother had sealed her fate. The princess had been confined to Windsor and all her ladies had been dismissed, except for Isabelle, who had been so new and so junior no one imagined she was responsible. In truth, it had all been her fault.

The princess had begged her to say nothing of the way she'd been led astray by her own foolish heart. Count Nikkolae Grazinsky had tricked her shamefully.

'I am sure Prince Leopold is all you seek in a husband. He always appeared very kind when we met him,' she said, bringing the princess's mind back to happier thoughts.

The princess stopped pacing and put her hand to her throat. 'My heart beats so hard it feels like a wild b-bird in my throat.' She laughed, the sound loud in the small dressing room. 'I did like him when we met, I suppose, but I met so many gentlemen, I can scarce recall him. All I know of him, I know from his letters.'

The princess had been flattered by all the attention from

foreign nobility visiting London that summer. Given the rampant neglect of her parents, it was hardly surprising she had fallen for any man who smiled her way. The quiet and serious Leopold hadn't stood a chance among the flashier noblemen, despite his impeccable lineage, handsome face and the dashing uniform of a Russian general.

Mrs Louis returned with the pearls and placed them around the princess's white throat and looped them around her wrists with a smile.

Lady Ilchester, the chief of Princess Charlotte's ladies, sailed in, her beak of a nose ready to sniff out trouble. That was her job at the Prince Regent's behest. 'It is time we went down, Your Highness. We must not keep Her Majesty waiting.'

Princess Charlotte smoothed her gloves against her arms and leaned close to Isabelle to whisper in her ear. 'I meant to mention that Count Grazinsky accompanies the prince.'

Isabelle's heart sank to the soles of her pale blue slippers. Her chest constricted painfully. Nikki was here at the pavilion? How on earth would she face him without giving her anger, her hurt, away to the world?

She must. Numb, she followed the princess out of her suite of rooms. Tightly grasping the balustrade cunningly wrought to resemble bamboo, she trooped downstairs behind the rest of the ladies.

Music greeted them as they entered the gallery which led to the staterooms. In the daytime it provided a magnificent view of the sea. Everything at the regent's seaside pavilion was either from China or designed to look as if it came from the Orient. With Chinese lanterns reflected in the mirrored doors hiding the staircases at each end, it seemed to stretch for miles. Indian cabinets and ivory sofas lined the walls. Scattered tables held illuminated lotus flowers and porcelain vases, all adding to the opulence. The guests, adorned with diamonds and other jewels, sparkled as much as their surroundings.

At the midpoint of the gallery, the Prince of Wales and his mother, the queen, waited to greet the princess. The Prince Regent in finely embroidered coats over his gargantuan stomach, welcomed his daughter with royal affability. The diminutive elderly queen acknowledged her granddaughter's curtsey with a warm smile. But everyone's eyes were on the darkly handsome and slender Prince Leopold. The silver buttons on his dark blue coat and the star on his chest gleamed as he bowed with the grace of a courtier. His stern, almost sombre expression softened when his gaze rested on the princess. Isabelle was sure she heard the ladies around her sigh in unison and she smiled her pride as her royal mistress made her stylish curtsey, showing not a morsel of the nerves she'd evinced above stairs.

One by one, the prince introduced his attendants to the princess. Isabelle's heart faltered as she watched Count Nikkolae Grazinsky achieve an elegant bow for such a big man.

Tall and dark, with sculpted features, she'd thought him beautiful the first time she saw him riding in Hyde Park with Prince Leopold two years before. Where the prince was slender, Nikki's broad shoulders strained at the fabric of his dark blue uniform. While the prince employed exquisite manners honed in the courts of Europe, Nikki exuded power and energy and the sense he would take what he wanted. He observed the world from piercing blue eyes without revealing his thoughts; yet, in the few short hours they'd spent alone, she'd thought she'd seen the man behind the uniform, a man lost and alone. She'd been horribly mistaken.

When the princess turned to introduce her ladies to the prince, Isabelle dared not look up, in case she should somehow lock gazes with Nikki and show her anger. Now was not the time or the place.

When it was her turn to curtsey, she felt quite ill. Was the prince aware of what she'd done? How she managed to remain steady as she dipped her knees, she wasn't sure.

'Lady Isabelle,' the prince said in his thick Germanic accent. 'I am glad once more to make your acquaintance.'

'Your Excellency,' she said, painfully aware of the flush on her cheeks. When she glanced up, she found the prince's expression kindly, even if his dark brown eyes were a little stern. She managed a hesitant smile before he turned his attention elsewhere.

She studiously avoided any possibility of meeting Nikki's mocking glance.

The introductions over, the Prince Regent sank into his wheeled chair, his bulk clearly too much for his gout. The footman pushed him into the dining room alongside the queen. Lady Hertford, the regent's mistress, a handsome if somewhat stout woman past the first blush of youth, followed along on Lord Castlereagh's arm, leaving her longsuffering husband to escort Lady Ilchester.

Lord Alvanley, the close friend of the prince's assigned to escort Isabelle into the banqueting room, adeptly flicked open his snuff box and inhaled a pinch with practiced dexterity. 'Such a bore, don't you know,' he said quietly. 'No wonder you look depressed. I feel like crying myself. No doubt after dinner the queen will insist upon cards and backgammon for the meanest of stakes.'

The portly dandy's mock expression of agony made her smile.

'That's better,' he said. 'No point in wearing emotions for all to see. Either you do something about your troubles, or suffer them cheerfully. Repining and sighing will do nothing but give people a distaste for your company.'

Why his lordship had chosen her to receive the benefit of his advice, Isabelle wasn't sure, but she mulled it over. *Do something about it.* All very well for him to say. He was a man.

Still, he was right. A long face would be noticed by Lady Ilchester and reported to the queen and she'd had too many reprimands already. She pinned a smile on her lips. 'This is the first time I have been to Brighton. The princess usually goes to Weymouth.'

'Good girl,' Alvanley said, escorting her down the long table to her place near the queen. 'Do tell. What do you think of Prinny's folly?'

Everyone called the Prince of Wales Prinny, but never to his face. As for his folly, many people were angered by the money he'd spent on his home beside the sea. 'It is like a visit to the Orient without the journey.'

Lord Alvanley chuckled. 'The prince would be delighted by your perspective.' He frowned at the table. 'I was sure my place was beside you.'

'My seat, I believe.' The darkly insolent drawl sent a shiver down Isabelle's spine. Nikki.

Someone had made a dreadful mistake. Blankly she

stared at the place card bearing Nikki's name beside her own.

Lord Alvanley's lips curved in a hard little smile. 'My dear Count Grazinsky, I don't suppose you know where I might be sitting?'

'I think you will find your place next to Mrs Campbell, my lord,' Nikki replied with a bow.

'I expect to collect on a debt of gratitude next time we meet, Count.'

'It will be my pleasure,' Nikki said smoothly.

Lord Alvanley sauntered away, seemingly unperturbed.

The rapid beating of her heart made thinking impossible, so when the footman pulled back her chair, she sank down beside the elderly military gentleman on her left.

'Poor Lord Alvanley,' Isabelle said, trying to look severe instead of terrified as Nikki seated himself negligently on her other hand. She could not let him see how much he affected her. She would not make a fool of herself again.

A waiter leaned between them and filled her goblet with wine. Isabelle kept her gaze fixed on the ruby liquid streaming into her glass, her heart pounding against her ribs, her tongue sticking to the roof of her mouth. Not one sensible word entered her mind. Only the question that had haunted her all these long weeks. Why had he chosen her as his pawn? Did she really want to know the answer?

This feeling of panic was ridiculous. Sooner or later she would have to face him, for he was a friend of Prince Leopold's. What could he possibly do or say in such a public venue to put her to the blush? Apart from just being there, that was. She inhaled a deep breath and met his gaze.

His face was grave. His blue eyes searched her face intently. For what? Signs of forgiveness? A wish to continue their flirtation? Never.

'Count Grazinsky,' she managed from a throat in sore need of moisture. 'You visit England at a very chilly time of year.'

There, that sounded cool enough. Distant. As if she barely remembered him. Father would be proud of her composure. Or he might be, if he ever gave her a thought. It seemed she only came to his notice when she'd committed some sin.

'It is nowhere near as inclement as Russia at this time of year,' Nikki murmured. His voice struck unwanted chords in her body, set them vibrating with pleasure and the pain of loss.

His English was perfect. His English mother had insisted he attend school at Eton and Oxford, he'd told her. But it wasn't his English heritage that fascinated her. It was the darker, more mysterious Russian side of his nature that made her heart beat far too fast and turned her into a besotted fool.

He leaned close enough for her to feel his warm breath against her cheek. 'Is that all you have for me after two long years, Isabelle? Platitudes about the weather?'

'In England the weather is always a topic of interest between friends.'

His lips twitched. A smile? Or annoyance. 'Friends? Is that how you see us?' His sapphire gaze mocked her.

'If I didn't know better, I'd think Alvanley was involved in this latest scheme of yours,' she said.

Nikki's mouth tightened. 'There is no scheme.'

Just as there wasn't a scheme the last they met. She let her face show her disbelief.

The waiter ladled lobster soup into her bowl and then into Nikki's from his other side.

'Someone is sure to notice you changed the place cards,' she said quietly.

A cynical smile lifted one corner of his mouth. 'Shall I change them back?'

'And make things worse? No doubt you would enjoy that.'

She picked up her spoon. She could not look as if their conversation was anything but trivial. She must not look guilty, no matter how she felt inside. Her heart ached as her lips smiled. 'Are you determined to court trouble with the regent?' she murmured, flashing a glance up to that end of the table.

Nikki picked up his glass and took a deep draught. An arrogant smile curved his lips. 'If I managed to survive the French, I am sure I can survive the English.'

He'd fought in battles all over Europe, including the last. Waterloo, where so many had died. Terrified he might be among the fallen, she'd scanned the papers every day for his name, her stomach in knots as she looked through the lists of casualties. 'Sometimes there is more danger in peace than in war.'

A grimace and a quick rueful laugh signified agreement.

'Where have you been since peace was declared?' she asked

'The prince required my services in Paris.'

He spoke of Paris as if it was a place a few miles distant. The way he'd spoken two years before of Vienna, and Naples and Rome. Places she longed to see and experience that he took for granted. 'How is Paris?'

'Full of Frenchmen who hate us and their king equally.'

'I read something of it in the newspapers. Is it as bad as they say?'

'Paris is always more. More dangerous. More decadent. More full of beauty.'

Beautiful women. No doubt a rake like him had sampled his share. She bit her lip. 'I thought you might have visited your grandmother, since you were so close to England.'

His jaw flickered. Resenting her questions, she presumed. 'Business kept me otherwise occupied.'

The waiter returned for their bowls. With a casual flick of his fingers Nikki indicated assent for them both. Arrogant and high-handed man. She glowered.

He smiled darkly without remorse, as if he guessed at her thoughts.

Politeness required she address a few remarks to the elderly general on her other side. She turned her shoulder to Nikki. 'The princess looks beautiful, doesn't she?'

The gentleman put a hand to his ear. 'Venison, you say? Venison? 'Tis the wrong season for venison.' The general signalled for a servant to refill his wine.

That had gone well. She smiled and nodded. 'Indeed.'

Nikki's shoulders shook with laughter. It was rather funny.

Nikki carved her a breast of pheasant and did the same thing for the lady on his other side, then offered her buttered parsnips and bright green asparagus in lemon butter. He leaned closer. 'Tell me you missed me a little,' he said with wicked seduction in his voice.

Heat stung her cheeks. 'Certainly not.' An admission of missing a rake like him would be tantamount to inviting him into her bed. He had tricked her once; she would not let it happen again. She darted another glance along the table.

Everyone seemed to be either attending to their dinner or conversing with their neighbours. She searched for an innocuous topic of conversation. 'Will you remain with the prince after his marriage?'

Oh, dear. Would he now think she cared about what he did in the future?

He regarded her steadily for a moment, his eyes impenetrable, his expression remote. He lifted his shoulders. 'It depends upon several things. What about you? Do you attend the princess?'

'No. I am to return home to Kent.' Her term of duty was over. 'I will miss the princess.' She would not miss all the intrigue at court.

'I see.' A small smile flickered across his lips. He glanced down at his plate, pushing the vegetables around with his fork.

'Did—?' she asked.

'How—?' he said.

'You first,' he said.

Her heart thundered as her lips formed the question she longed to ask. But there was something more pressing. 'Did you get my letter?'

His mouth flattened. 'I received it. How—?'

'Silence for his Royal Highness,' a steward called out.

'A toast,' the Prince Regent cried with broad smile.

Everyone rose to their feet.

'To my daughter and her future husband.'

With much cheering, the company saluted the engagement. The couple looked decidedly content as their gazes locked down the length of the table. It did Isabelle good to see it. This engagement would work. The princess had been right to brave her father's disapproval and reject the sneering Prince of Orange and instead seek a man who could bring her happiness.

It was every woman's dream, should she be lucky enough to find that man.

At her side, Nikki pushed back his chair, his expression dark and moody. 'Excuse me. My prince has need of me.' He stalked away; impressive in his isolation he looked neither right nor left. After a brief word with the prince, he left the room.

Isabelle had seen no sign of a command from the prince. Nikki was clearly using it as a reason to escape her company having realised she no longer would fall for his charm. No doubt he was off to find some more amenable lady.

Something in her chest felt as heavy as lead. She'd done the right thing. She ought to feel virtuous. Instead she felt wretched. Even cruel. For despite his faint air of amusement at their sparring, she had the feeling she might have hurt his feelings.

Hurt him? How foolish. It was her heart speaking not her head. Women did not hurt Nikki. He left them weeping. She'd learned much about him in his absence. Seducer. Libertine. Gambler. The list of his wickedness was as long as this table.

The best she could do was avoid his company, see the royal wedding through as promised and return home without bringing disgrace to her family.

'Pass the codfish heads, young lady,' the general boomed. 'They'll be removing the covers soon.'

A codfish gazed at her balefully. With a sigh, she passed the plate.

Chapter Two

Dinner over, the female guests conversed in the music room, raising their voices to be heard over the orchestra. Isabelle had never seen the princess glow as she did to-night. She was as lustrous as the pearls around her throat. While they drank tea, her eyes constantly sought the doors through which her prince would enter when the gentlemen finished their port. Isabelle prayed Nikki would not make one of their number.

Leaving Mrs Campbell's side, Princess Charlotte slipped onto the sofa beside Isabelle. 'He so much handsomer than I remembered,' she murmured. A smile curved her full lips. 'But so stern.'

She turned her lips down and frowned in imitation of Prince Leopold, then burst out laughing. Loud. Too loud. Heads turned. Lips pursed. The princess liked to laugh. Many at court thought her far too boisterous. This time she elicited a headshake from the queen.

Princess Charlotte covered her mouth with her fan.

'Oops. And the count? What on earth made you sit beside him at dinner?'

Isabelle tried not to flinch. 'It was simply bad luck.'

The princess gave her a worried look. 'Does he continue his pursuit?'

'Hardly,' Isabelle said. 'He left at the first possible moment.' His rapid departure still rankled. People must have noticed how quickly he'd tired of her company. Having put himself beside her, the least he could have done was remained until the end of the meal and feigned interest.

Lady Ilchester bore down upon them, a frown on her face. 'Your Highness, you really must mingle with your guests.' She bore the princess off in a flurry of discreet disapproval.

Leaning against a pillar in a shadowy corner, arms folded across his chest, Nikki watched his royal master bend his dark head close to the princess's golden curls as they strolled the length of the stifling and furniture-stuffed gallery. Leo's normally sombre expression lightened as he smiled at something she said. He looked more cheerful than he had for years.

A gaggle of ladies followed in the betrothed couple's wake. Hiding in their midst, Isabelle looked like a primrose amidst a bunch of overblown roses. A modest flower, with light brown hair and skin the colour of rich cream that turned a delicious rose when she blushed. She blushed a great deal in his presence. It had amused him at first. Now it drove him mad wondering if she coloured up for other men. Her features were too ordinary for great beauty, her body too slight, but there was unexpected kindness in her intelligent grey eyes. One didn't expect kindness at court, just flirtation and ambition. Not that she didn't have spirit. She did. Too much or she'd not have dared to walk with him outside.

She should know a few dragon-ladies could not protect her. Look how easily he'd changed places at dinner. His shoulders tightened. He shouldn't have done it, of course. Leo had been quick to signal his displeasure. A look, a lift of one finger, had forced Nikki to leave.

He'd been wrong to test the waters. Should not have bedevilled her. The surge of desire he'd felt when she'd entered the gallery had taken him by surprise. Shocked him. He'd thought he'd cast her from his mind when he'd scraped the mud of England off his shoes. At Leo's request, he'd thrown himself into the peace negotiations after Waterloo with the same zest he'd thrown himself into battle. He'd been too busy dealing with the pettifogging bureaucracy dividing up Europe to think about women. Or, at least, none of them had sparked his interest since he left London.

Because he still wanted this one.

Damnation. Nothing must get in the way of Leo's marriage. *'I'll not let one of your peccadilloes give her an excuse to dismiss me the way she dismissed the Prince of Orange, Nikki,'* Leo had warned on the boat across the Channel.

Only a brave man would stand between Nikki and what he wanted. But Leo was a good friend and brave comrade-in-arms. For years they'd racketed around Europe, two poverty-stricken noblemen attempting to repair family fortunes ruined by Napoleon. Leo deserved his success and Nikki owed him his loyalty.

He wished he'd never met her. Wished he'd never taken the Prussian prince's wager. He'd been quite mad that summer. Betting on anything. Drinking. The relief of knowing war was at an end. Only afterwards had he realised his careless act had spiked Leo's guns.

He'd almost thrown the prince's friendship away again tonight for the chance to make her blush. He didn't blame her one bit for her anger though. He had treated her abominably.

'As brooding as ever I see, Nikki?' Count Hardenbrook said.

Nikki cast a glance at the Dutchman, Leo's chosen equerry and a member of his small but loyal retinue.

'Certainly not,' Nikki drawled. 'Simply keeping an eye on the prince. Awaiting the scraps from his table. Like you.'

'Always the cynic, Nikki.' Hardenbrook gave a short laugh. An expression of worry crossed his normally cheerful face. 'The call to come to England could not have come at a worse time. He is still unwell and this cursed weather doesn't help.'

'He covers his indisposition well enough.' Even healthy, the prince was pale and lean. 'It is certainly clear she likes him.'

'She's so exceedingly odd,' Hardenbrook said. 'I do not understand English women. I suppose growing up with parents at loggerheads, each using her as a pawn, is bad for a child. Leo says she responds well to kindness.'

Nikki's gaze drifted back to Isabelle. He'd also made her his pawn. He'd let her glimpse joys he knew she couldn't have. Not with him. A man with no prospects was not a

good catch. Most considered him a fortune-hunter clinging
to Prince Leopold's coattails. They weren't far wrong.

He could have had her, though. Isabelle. He'd seen it in
her eyes that day in the garden. He had too much experience with women not to know she'd fallen hard.

Only with difficulty had he walked away. Done the honourable thing. With nothing to offer, he hadn't had a choice.
Just as he hadn't had a choice but to return with Leo when
requested.

But he should not have sought her out.

He pulled his gaze away from Isabelle. 'Leo has a great
deal of patience. He will make a good husband.'

Hardenbrook nodded. 'Where are you lodged?'

'Above the stables.' He grinned. 'Cheaper than an inn in
town. I claimed it as my duty as Master of the Horse.'

'Not planning an elopement, is he?'

Nikki laughed. 'Not unless he plans to start a war with
Britain. And besides, it is not needed. He has it all in hand.'

The couple turned at the end of the room and headed
back, the ladies following parted like a division of well-
trained soldiers and let them through their ranks. Isabelle
smiled at the princess. A brave smile. The same smile she'd
worn the day she met him in the garden, until he'd melted
her bravado and seen her tender heart. It had warmed
places he thought frozen out of existence by war.

Hellfire. Would he never get her out of his thoughts?

'What an extraordinary house this is,' Hardenbrook said.
'The pieces are exquisite. They must have cost a fortune.'

'It's too blasted hot, if you ask me.' Nikki tugged at his
neckcloth. 'I'm stifling. Someone should open a window.'

'The Prince Regent likes it warm. I gather he was deprived of a fire in the schoolroom as a lad and swore when he reached adulthood he would never feel cold again.'

'The man needs to have mercy on the rest of us.'

The prince and princess left the gallery and entered the music room where the orchestra still played their hearts out. 'We had better follow,' Hardenbrook said. 'In case we are needed.'

Nikki's lip curled. 'I am dismissed for the evening.' For stepping beyond bounds. 'I should already be gone.'

'Ah, yes. The horses.' Hardenbrook strolled off.

Do something about it. The words went round and round in her mind. But what should she do? If she was to have peace, she needed to tell Nikki face to face what she thought of his treachery and remind him to keep his distance.

'Are there enough rooms for all the people Prince Leopold brought with him?' she asked Mrs Campbell, the kindest of the princess's ladies.

'Most have taken rooms in town.' Well that accounted for Nikki's disappearance. No doubt he was sampling all Brighton had to offer.

'His Master of Horse apparently lodges in the stables,' Mrs Campbell said.

Nikki's official title. Hope surged in Isabelle's breast. Would his presence nearby provide her with a chance she needed? The opportunity to do something?

Looking the picture of the amiable host, the Prince Regent sat in his wheeled chair tapping his fingers on his thigh in time to the music with the redoubtable Lady Hertford standing guard, but the prince and princess were on the move. The ladies around Isabelle readied themselves to follow. One of them asked Mrs Campbell a question and she turned away.

Seeing her opening, Isabelle slipped away from the group, confident that with everyone's attention fixed on the betrothed couple, her absence would not be noticed. At least for a while.

At the end of the gallery, beyond the mirrored doors, a door led out to the gardens. And to the stables. She hesitated. Did she really want to do this?

Do something. Lord Alvanley's ironic tones echoed in her ears.

This was all she could think of to do. The green-and-red-liveried footman stationed at the door raised a brow at her approach. She resisted the urge to look back and see if anyone had remarked her departure.

'I need some fresh air,' she said, fanning her face, sure it was bright red from the embarrassment of more lies.

'It is cold out there, my lady,' the young man said in his slow Sussex drawl. 'Careful lest you catch an ague.'

'I'll only be a moment or two,' she said, stemming her impatience at his obvious hesitation to let her out.

Finally he bowed and opened the door for her to pass through. 'You take care now,' he said as she stepped outside. 'All you has to do is knock, my lady, and I'll let you back in.'

'Thank you.' Fortunately, Prinny believed in lighting his grounds. Torches flickered in iron braziers on the walls and lamp standards lined the pathways. It took only seconds for her eyes to adjust and locate the stable block a little distance off.

A strong chill wind blew off the sea only a few yards

away, tugging at her light skirts and freezing her bare arms. She wished she'd brought a shawl. But there was no going back. She would call Count Grazinsky to account and be done with him once and for all.

Taking a quick deep breath, she marched to the open stable doors. Light spilled out onto to the cobbles and she could hear the low rumble of male talk and laughter and an odd rattling sound.

A shout went up. Cries of joy and dismay.

Mouth dry, heart racing, she remained in the shadows cast by the doors and peeped inside.

A group of four men in their shirtsleeves, seated on hay bales, huddled around an open space on the floor. It was easy to see what they were about. Gold coins were heaped in piles beside their booted feet. Bottles and tankards littered the floor and a pair of die lay in the centre of the group showing a pair of sixes.

Gambling.

Perhaps this was not a good time to broach Nikki.

'Nicked it, by Gad,' one of the men said in French, nobility's international language. 'You have the devil's own luck, Nikki.'

'Demmed if I don't,' Nikki said in an arrogant drawl. 'Throw again, Dimitri. Perhaps I'll relieve you of all of that fortune of yours.'

'Not a chance,' Dimitri said. 'I'm for my lodgings in town and a chamber maid with the merriest smile you ever did see.'

'Trust you,' Nikki said, scooping up his winnings.

'Join me. I'm sure she has a friend or two. Indeed you are all welcome. Why not make a night of it?'

Isabelle's heart pounded harder at the thought of him leaving with his friends. She stepped out from the shadows. 'Count Grazinsky,' she said in English. 'I wonder if I might trouble you for a word before you leave.'

Four heads swivelled in her direction.

'Isabelle,' Nikki said, shooting to his feet. The shock, perhaps even horror, on his face was well worth the risk of this nighttime visit.

'Sly dog,' Dimitri said. 'Isn't she your—?'

His eyes blazed. 'Out,' Nikki said, his voice so cold she felt the ice of it on her skin. 'All of you. Go.'

The men laughingly grumbled and gathered their belongings.

Nikki took her arm and drew her into the shadows. 'You little fool,' he muttered.

She opened her mouth to reply. He pressed a finger to her lips as he watched, tight-lipped, as the men swaggered off into the night.

Nikki swung her around to face him. 'What in God's name do you think you are doing? Are you so careless of your reputation?'

'There speaks the man who conspired to ruin my good name,' she challenged.

A frown furrowed his brow. 'Believe me, I'm sorry for it.'

Sorry they had ever met, no doubt, judging from his rigid expression. 'You didn't seem so sorry at dinner,' she said to hide her hurt. 'I wrote and asked you to stay away from me.'

He laughed darkly, pulling her into the light, gazing

down into her face. 'It seems it is you who needs that reminder.'

She pulled her hand free of the warmth stealing up her arm towards her heart. The casually open collar of his shirt above his unbuttoned waistcoat revealed the strong column of throat and a wedge of wide chest. She dragged her gaze up to his face, met his intent sapphire eyes. 'I needed to speak to you privately.'

His expression darkened. 'Why?'

'To tell you I know you only flirted with me so Prince Augustus could see the princess alone. You could have ruined us both.' Indignation made her speak with more passion than she'd intended. Anger at herself. She'd been completely blinded by his flattery. Her stupidity made her furious.

His hands closed and then opened. 'You are right. It was a wager. Augustus was entertaining himself at Orange's expense. I certainly have no reason to love the little weasel. Nor had Leo. But he was not pleased by what I did.'

A wager. Disappointment squeezed the hope from her chest. She turned her face away, stared down at the debris left by his friends amongst the trampled straw. He was what rumour said of him, a hardened gambler. 'Tonight, I suppose Leopold dared you to distract me from my duty,' she said in a low voice

'No.' The word sounded harsh and she glanced up to see a derisive smile on his lips. ''Twas Leo who dismissed me from the table.'

'Why do you feel the need to torment me?'

'Torment?' His voice was scathing. 'You don't know the meaning of torment. The people in the countries the French conquered suffered torment. Safe here on this little island, you have no idea what real torment is. However, if my presence offends you, I apologise. It will not happen again.'

The pain in his voice spoke of suffering she did not understand.

'Your family?'

His eyes darkened. He gave the slightest of nods.

'I am sorry,' she whispered. 'But that does not give you the right to ruin my life.'

His dark eyes searched her face. He took her hand, raised it to his lips, his breath warming the chilled skin of her knuckles. A shiver ran across her shoulders. Pleasure and pain. She couldn't move.

'Isabelle,' he said softly, 'Why did you come here tonight? You know I have nothing to offer.' His dark eyelashes swept down, hiding his thoughts. 'What Bonaparte didn't destroy has been lost at Vienna or Paris.' He looked up and smiled. The hardness had gone. He looked younger. He smiled the way he had in Warwick House's garden. Open, honest, with a trace of sadness in his eyes. It had tugged at her heart then and it did so now. 'But I can swear that it was not my intent to hurt you or the princess.'

Her chest ached with the longing to believe him. Her body yearned to lean against him. She snatched back the traitorous hand that lingered in the warmth of his. He'd handed her a rose that day and she'd given him her heart. The castles she'd woven in a glow of happiness had tumbled down around her ears when she realised his reason for singling her out. Such a fool.

His gaze was fixed on her mouth. 'How long before you are missed?' His voice was hoarse. Hunger heated his eyes.

The same hunger she felt. The air in the stables changed, became so charged with electricity she could feel the prickles of it along her skin.

He reached out to take her hand.

Fearful of her response to his touch, she whipped her hands behind her back. 'For all I know they could be looking for me now.' She retreated towards the door.

He stepped in front of her, a solid wall of muscle and bone and bay-scented male. The heat from his body curled around her. Large warm hands caught her by the upper arms.

She froze.

Holding her fast with one hand on her shoulder, he tipped her face up with a knuckle beneath her chin. 'Look at me, Isabelle.'

Drawn by the gentleness in his tone, she gazed into his harshly handsome face.

'You should not have followed me,' he murmured.

'I know,' she whispered, knowing she could not have stayed away. 'I wanted to see you again.' The admission pained her when he seemed so unmoved.

Or was he?

Slowly, giving her every opportunity to pull free, he lowered his head, brushed his mouth across her lips. Once, twice, a soft velvety kiss, too pure. Too gentle. Too kind.

They would never meet again. It would be the last time she would see him alone.

Loss filled her.

She flung her arms around his neck, pressed her body against his hard muscled length, revelled in the feel of him against her soft curves. She raked her fingers through his thick black hair where it curled over his shirt. Felt his heat against her body and trembled with desire.

His tongue traced a path along the seam of her lips and instinctively she opened her mouth to taste him. Their tongues met and tangled and danced. Her heart drummed in her chest, in her ears, all through her blood. Never had she felt so alive, or so near to melting.

His large hands roamed her back, drawing her tighter against him, his hard thigh pressing between her legs, his hands cupping her buttocks, drawing her close until she felt waves of pleasure beating at her core.

He broke their kiss with a sound like a groan rumbling up from his chest. Breathing hard, he stared down at her with a faint smile on his lips. Something flickered in the depths of his eyes. Heat, yes, but also determination. 'You had better leave now.'

Her legs felt so weak, her head so dizzy, she clung to his shoulders. 'Yes.' Her feet refused to move.

He stood her away from him with gentle firmness and regret, as if he, too, felt sorry this would never happen again. The pain in her heart grew until she thought she would shatter. She shivered and rubbed at her bare arms.

'You are freezing,' he said.

Not from the chill of the evening. This icy feeling came from deep inside.

He picked up his jacket, its gold buttons and braid winking in the light of the lanterns. He placed it around her shoulders. 'Come. I will see you safely inside.'

She shook her head. 'We must not be seen together.'

His expression hardened. 'I will not let you go alone.'

Against every feeling of pride, she could not help but ask, 'Will I see you tomorrow?'

His jaw flexed. 'I leave for London in the morning.'

She ought to be glad. For her own sake. She felt empty. She nodded her acceptance.

In silence, he returned her to the side door of the house, a quiet knock and she was admitted. She didn't dare look back for fear she would see relief on his face. And what little pride she had left would not allow it.

Chapter Three

London, May 2, 1816

Two months had passed when Nikki tracked Prince Leopold down at Clarence House in St James's. The footman who took his card up returned in short order and ushered him in.

Nikki bowed low as befit his friend's newly exalted position. 'May I offer my warmest congratulations on your wedding day, Your Excellency.'

'Nikki.' Leo left his conversation with Stockmar and Hardenbrook and strode forward, hand outstretched. 'I've missed you. I have been hearing such rumours too. Are you well?'

The genuine pleasure in his old comrade-in-arm's face unknotted the hard ball in Nikki's gut. The prince was a good man and a good friend, but much had altered since they served their countries against the Corsican monster. They'd both struggled to change miserable destinies. Leo had succeeded beyond anyone's wildest dreams. 'I am well. And dibs in tune too.'

Leo frowned. 'So the rumours *are* true. You spend your time gambling and wenching.'

'Do not believe all you hear. Am I invited to your wedding?'

The frown deepened. 'You are not terribly popular with my bride. You left her little pet looking sad despite my warning.'

The hackles at the back of his neck rose at the criticism. He shrugged it off. 'We had unresolved matters between us.'

Leo's brown eyes were sombre. 'After the wedding she goes home to Kent. The princess is to have only married ladies about her.'

'And what about you? Will you have only married gentlemen?'

'Don't tell me you have fixed upon an heiress to wed?' He shook his head. 'Ah, no. Or you would not have gone to the tables every night.'

Leo knew him too well. He grinned. 'Every heiress in sight has been locked up by her papa.' Not that he wanted an heiress.

Leo grunted. 'I regret I do not have it in my power to offer you a place. There are important English noblemen vying for too few positions. The settlement approved by Parliament will not support the two houses I am granted as well as a large retinue. I will not risk going into debt.'

'Sixty thousand pounds a year is not to be sneezed at,' Nikki said with a grin. He raised a hand when Leo looked as if he would protest. 'I know. It is tied to your public duties. Do Stockmar and Hardenbrook remain with you?'

Leo nodded. 'They are unlikely to set up any backs.'

Unlike Nikki. Leo didn't have to say the words. Nikki respected his decision.

The prince shrugged philosophically. 'This English Parliament is careful and naturally so. They will want to see how well we manage, before they loosen the purse strings further. They are looking for sober respectability, not drunken orgies. What will you do now?'

'Don't worry about me, Excellency. I have my future well in hand.'

'Take care some irate Englishman doesn't cut your throat for winning his all.'

'You worry too much. Care to place a wager on the outcome?'

'Not against your luck.'

'Luck is a fickle mistress.'

'So are women.'

They sank into the comfortable silence of old friends. Outside, beyond the windows, arose a great deal of shouting and clapping. 'Sounds like a party out there,' Nikki said, glancing at the casement where Stockmar stood looking out.

'They've been at it all morning,' Leo said. 'They only stop if I make an appearance, and not for long.'

'You've done well, Leo. Got the masses on your side, and a princess to love you. The newspapers have been full of the wedding for weeks. It is quite a prize you've won for yourself, this kingdom of Britain.' Hopefully his own plans would go as well.

The prince smiled his grave smile. 'There's a wildness about you today, Nikki. I've seen that look in your eye on the battlefield. Whatever it is you are about, swear you will do nothing until my affairs are irrevocably settled. Promise me that for our friendship's sake.'

Nikki reined in his impatience. Leo should know better than to think he would do anything to harm his friend. Although, no doubt the wager he'd engaged with Prince Augustus remained as a black mark. 'I give you my word.' He grinned. 'But only if I am invited to see my old friend leg-shackled.'

Leo nodded. 'Expect an invitation at your lodgings. Be warned though, the princess defends her ladies like a mother lion. She has claws.' He sounded as if he'd been scratched a time or two.

All this while they had been speaking French. 'And how are your lessons coming along?' Nikki teased in English. Leo had practiced on him all the way to England. Now he had proper tutors.

'Cursed language,' Leo muttered under his breath, also in English. Then he gave his sweet smile. 'But I persevere. *Mein gott*, but I try.'

'You do well,' Nikki said. 'No worse than the last generation of Hanovers. Or the Prince Regent's wife, Princess Caroline.'

'Stay away from that woman, Nikki. Whatever goodness she had is long gone. She has more than once involved Princess Charlotte in her machinations. My bride confessed the whole of it.'

Nikki grimaced. 'Caroline holds no interest for me.'

'Your Highness.' Stockmar had a huge smile on his face.

'The crowds once more become impatient. Another visit to the balcony is in order.'

A pained expression crossed Leo's face.

'They love you,' Nikki said. 'I was amongst the crowd when you entered the city. I've never seen Londoners so enthused. Give them what they want. The mob becomes jaded soon enough.'

Stockmar threw open the French doors to the balcony. The noise increased tenfold. Leo shuddered, then straightened his shoulders, and Nikki was reminded of their youth, when they'd risked so much for their countries. At least his friend had made the right choices. Nikki was about to risk everything on his next play.

He clapped the prince on the back and gave him an encouraging smile, much as he had before they mounted up to ride into battle. 'At least they won't be shooting at you. I will attend you later.'

'Come here for dinner first. Dress uniform,' Leo said. He took a deep breath and headed for the waiting crowds.

Nikki smiled grimly. He was going to need more than a uniform to get through tonight. He was going to need the devil's own luck and a silver tongue.

The princess left Buckingham House for Carlton House in her open carriage at exactly half past eight accompanied by Isabelle, Mrs Campbell and two other ladies. The queen had gone ahead. 'You were right,' the princess said quietly to Isabelle when they were under way and the noise of the wheels drowned her voice. 'He is all I hoped for and more.'

'I am happy for you, Your Highness,' Isabelle whispered

back. In the past few weeks of preparations there had been no time for private conversation.

The carriage turned into the mall. Masses of people lined the roadside, cheering and waving their hats.

'Bless me,' the princess said, leaping up to wave back. She grinned. 'What a crowd.' Her father certainly never received such a warm welcome and well she knew it.

'Sit down, Your Highness, please,' Mrs Campbell said. 'The queen would never forgive me if you fell.'

The princess sat, but continued to wave with great enthusiasm to the delight of the people until they turned into the gates at Carlton House where a band played 'God Save the King' with great gusto.

Princess Charlotte was directed to the royal closet where her bridegroom, the Prince of Wales and Duke and Duchess of Orléans were waiting. The queen and other members of the royal family accompanied by selected attendants were accommodated in rooms adjacent to the throne room.

At just after nine o'clock, all the guests were ushered to the Crimson Salon. Women in gold or silver gowns superbly embroidered fanned themselves. Their feather plumes waved to and fro as they gossiped and admired one another's gowns. Many of the English gentlemen present wore the uniform of the House of Windsor, a dark blue coat lavishly embroidered across the front and high standing collar with gold bullion. Some wore military uniforms, red or blue, and they flashed and glittered almost as much as the ladies. The ambassadors and ministers from every country in Europe had their own style of magnificent dress. On her way to her seat, Isabelle kept a careful eye out for the swords they wore on their hips.

Isabelle was delighted with her own gown for the occasion. Mrs Louis kindly suggested a white crêpe off-the-shoulder gown handsomely ornamented with blond and silver lace around the neck. A pink satin sash and train finished what was the prettiest dress she had ever worn. It brought out the soft grey of her eyes. Her hair was dressed in a simple braid woven with pink ribbon at her crown and a cascade of curls around her face.

Too bad there was no one to care if she looked her best.

Seated off to one side against the wall in the crowded room, Isabelle had a good view of the crimson-covered altar bearing the ancient royal communion plate brought from the Chapel Royal in St James's Palace. Six-foot candles towered over the whole. On the floor in front of the altar dais sat a pair of crimson velvet-cushioned stools. The Archbishop of Canterbury stood ready to perform the service aided by the Bishop of London. The sumptuous room was, as usual, exceedingly hot.

Waiting at the altar, the Prince of Wales wore scarlet regimentals. Beside him Prince Leopold looked splendid in the dark blue and gilt uniform of an English general with a sword and belt studded with diamonds. His gentlemen stood proudly to attention behind him and Nikki was amongst them! She had to admit he looked dashing in his Russian hussar uniform of dark blue trimmed with gold lace, the fur-edged pelisse hanging from one shoulder. As if he sensed her watching him, his gaze found hers. A small smile played about his lips, and her heart gave a painful squeeze. Would she ever see him without feeling such hopeless longing?

Hearing the rumours about Nikki's exploits in London,

the gambling in halls, the debauchery, had been hard to bear while staying at Cranborne Lodge these past few weeks, but she was determined to present a happy face and forget Nikki and his kisses.

Every time she recalled the feel of his mouth on hers, she went hot and shivery.

She would, she told herself, be glad to go home. To put this time in her life behind her.

The queen took a chair near the front with her daughters and her own ladies gathered around her.

All was ready. A breathless hush came over the guests as Princess Charlotte walked regally into the room. Her gown of silver lamé on net over a silver tissue slip glittered with thousands of points of lights. A delicate silvery train floated from her shoulders. Rich frills of lace skimmed her generous bosom and edged the small puffed sleeves. The fabric brought out the remarkable luminescence of her pale skin. Diamonds set amongst a wreath of rosebuds flashed fire in her gold curls. She looked every inch a fairy princess in the sumptuous surroundings of crimson.

The guests gasped their appreciation of the vision she presented. Isabelle smiled proudly.

Prince Leopold stepped forward to take his place on one side, while the Prince Regent stood on the other. Hand in hand, the couple knelt before the archbishop. His words rang through the room. Charlotte spoke her responses clearly and distinctly. Leopold's voice was quieter, but no less firm. The vows over, the groom gallantly drew his bride to her feet. At that moment the Tower guns thundered the good news to the people of London.

The princess lifted her face for her father's kiss and he

bestowed his blessing with a hearty paternal hug before relinquishing her to her groom. Next came a kiss from the queen and the congratulations of her aunts. The glow of happiness on the young bride's face and the expression of love in both of the newlyweds' eyes as they smiled at each other augured well for the future.

Isabelle's heart swelled with joy for her royal mistress.

The formalities over, footmen rushed around with glasses of libation. The assembled company lifted their glasses in honour of the happy couple to much laughter and many congratulations. Not too many minutes passed before Prince Leopold drew his bride away to change for their journey. He was not so fortunate as to miss the eagle eye of the queen, who clutched at Mrs Campbell's arm. 'Go with them, Mrs Campbell. Ride bodkin between them for proprieties' sake.'

With a horrified expression, Mrs Campbell backed away. 'Not if my life depends upon it, Your Majesty.'

While the queen loudly expressed her disgust with Mrs Campbell's disobedience, the newlyweds slipped away. A carriage was waiting to take them to Oatlands, the Duke of York's house, where they would spend their honeymoon.

Nowhere in the crowded room did Isabelle catch a glimpse of Nikki's tall figure. He must have left at the ceremony's conclusion. Not that she was looking for him. She wasn't. In such a crowded room, only the very commonplace could be spoken without remark. And Nikki and commonplace did not go well together. Certainly not where she was concerned. When she was sure Lady Ilchester's attention was otherwise engaged, Isabelle made her way outside. She had earlier made a pact with Princess Charlotte to wave farewell from the garden gate.

The carriage, hitched to a team of greys sporting fluttering white favours, was already standing by. The coachman touched his hat. 'Are they nearly ready, my lady?'

'Not long now, I am sure,' she said with a smile.

A few moments later, the prince escorted the princess out of the house. Dressed in a white satin travelling cape with white fur trim over a gown trimmed with Brussels point lace and a smart satin bonnet trimmed with a plume of ostrich feathers, she looked as if she floated on air. She gave Isabelle an impulsive kiss on the cheek before the prince helped her into the carriage. Once inside, she let down the window and leaned out. 'Goodbye, dear Lady Isabelle,' she called in her boisterous way. 'Do visit us at Claremont when we are settled.'

Isabelle waved back. 'I will,' she called out, very much hoping she would be invited.

The coach lurched forward and the princess fell back, hopefully into the arms of her waiting prince.

'A hoyden to the last,' a dark voice murmured in her ear. 'He'll have his hands full, but I don't doubt he is up to the task.'

She jerked around, a palm to her fast-beating heart. 'Nikki. You startled me.' Blast, she'd used his first name. She glanced around, but they were alone in the shadows apart from the footman at the door and a stablehand sweeping the cobbles. 'Are you mad? What if someone sees us?'

'Mad for you, Isabelle. A royal bird told me I would find you here. Come, my carriage awaits us.' He cupped her face in his hands and kissed her lips. 'I want you, Isabelle.'

'You said you had nothing to offer. What has changed?'

'I've made my fortune.'

Nonplussed, she stared at him, until the import of his words made sense to her scrambled brain. 'Gambling? Who did you ruin?'

His face hardened, became almost demonic in the light of the *torchères* beside the gate. 'What? You cry pity for those who profited from the war without setting foot out of doors. Many good men died for their gain. I simply taxed them a little. No man is ruined. No tradesman or nobleman is blowing out his brains on my account.'

'And when your luck runs out, what then?'

'I'm not a fool, Isabelle. I've bought an estate close to my grandmother in Sussex. I'm tired of being homeless. Weary of death and destruction. Here in England, with you, I believe I can find peace.'

'What of Russia?'

'There is nothing left for me there.'

'And if I come with you, what will I be? Your mistress? One of your women, Nikki?'

He flashed a boyishly wicked grin. 'If you wish. Though I'd far rather you married me.' He pulled her close and their lips melded in a mind-numbing kiss.

As always, she melted into his strong embrace.

'I love you, Isabelle,' he finally murmured against her mouth. 'Please, honour me by becoming my wife.'

The words broke down her defences. Her heart fluttered wildly as his blue eyes gazed back at her with laughter in their depths and something else besides. Hope, and yes…love.

Another carriage pulled up beside the gate. A footman jumped down and opened the door.

'Come away with me, Isabelle,' he whispered with tempting seduction.

She gazed at him, stricken. 'I want to say yes. I do, with all my heart. But what of my family. My father. We must seek his blessing.'

'Now you are timid? You? My naughty adventurous girl who braved a stable full of soldiers in the dark?'

'That was different. I was angry.'

He smiled. 'Remind me never to anger you again. Trust me, sweet. It is all taken care of. Your father has given his permission and your parents even now are travelling to my grandmother's house along with the vicar and assorted guests. I have the licence in my pocket. We are to be married two days hence.'

'You arranged it all without a word to me?' Laughter fought with annoyance. ''Pon rep, it is very high-handed of you, sir.'

He gave a half laugh, half groan. 'I couldn't speak of it. I gave my word to Leo I would do nothing until his knot was safely tied. He feared I would cause a scandal. Believe me, waiting for this moment has been killing me.'

'Oh, Nikki,' she sighed. 'What if my father had said no?'

'Then I would have whisked you off to Scotland, as I am sure Prince Leo guessed.'

'I'd far rather visit Paris than Scotland.'

'We will, love. All in good time.' He tilted her chin up and looked into her eyes. 'So is it a yes, Isabelle, my love, my own true heart?'

'Yes. Heavens help me, yes. I loved you the first moment I saw you, but I believed you didn't care.'

His hands cupped her cheeks; his lips brushed hers briefly. 'I will always regret my part in that foolishness and I beg your forgiveness. But I cannot regret its bringing us together. I love you, Isabelle, and will care for you always, if you will allow.' He smiled down at her. 'Since neither of us our bound by the whims of our royal masters any longer, it is time we followed our own path. Come away with me now. Your family is waiting.'

Shaking her head, she laughed up at him. 'I'll come, because I love you, Nikki, but when we are wed, you must promise a lighter hand on the reins than you have shown this night. I'll not tolerate commands.'

'I will be your slave in all things, if you will stop arguing and get into the carriage.'

Still laughing, she let him help her in, as Leopold had helped his princess minutes before. The carriage moved off. She settled into the squabs and stared at him, so handsome, so strong and proud in the light from the lamp suspended above the door. The man about to become her husband. 'Do you think they will be happy?'

'Who?'

'The prince and princess.'

'No doubt about it. The prince is as besotted with Charlotte as I am with you.'

He pulled her onto his lap and nibbled at her lips and, when she laughed, deepened the kiss.

'Besotted?' she murmured when they broke apart thoroughly breathless.

'Utterly,' he said, and kissed her all over again.

Epilogue

November 8, 1818

Isabelle held her three-month-old baby boy in her arms, looking down into his sleeping face with love and an ache in her heart for the news they had received two days before.

She looked up as her husband of eighteen months entered the nursery. 'Did you see Prince Leopold, Nikki?'

His face was sombre, etched with deep lines around his mouth. 'I did. He is inconsolable. It happened so fast, he didn't even have time to bid her goodbye. To lose both child and mother, it is beyond reason sad. She and the babe are to be interred at Windsor in a day or so. I will go to the funeral. For Leo.'

With a heavy sigh Nikki sat beside her on the sofa and took the sleeping infant from her arms. He looked into the child's face with a sombre expression. 'If I had given any thought to the danger, I would have prevented this.'

'My darling, would you deprive us of one of the greatest joys on earth?'

'If it meant losing you, I would. I saw from Leo's face, he felt the same.'

'Sweetheart mine, I could just as easily be run over by a carriage on the streets of London—would you lock me indoors?'

He looked at her moodily. 'It's just so unfair. They loved each other. They were so damned happy. He told me she called him Doucement because—' his voice cracked a little, and he swallowed '—he always said, *"Doucement, chérie,"* when she became too excited in that way she had. She calmed instantly, he said. And she made him laugh, when he has so little laughter in his life. They were good for each other. They would have ruled this country well.'

She put an arm around his shoulders and pulled him close, until he rested his dark head on her shoulder gazing down at their child in his arms. She stroked his hair. 'I know, Nikki, I know. They brought us together. But we who knew them best will never forget them.'

* * * * *

Author Note

When reading my history books for the background to this story, I was struck how closely the story of Princess Charlotte and her prince mirrored that of her cousin, Princess Victoria, even though it did not end as well. Since Prince Leopold, later the King of the Belgians, was the man who guided Queen Victoria and the prince during their early marriage, I have the sense that he and Charlotte might well have ruled England very well indeed, had she survived the Prince Regent.

My story, while factual in the details surrounding Charlotte, her engagements and her wedding, takes poetic licence with how Isabelle and Nikki fit into those events. Isabelle is a combination of ladies surrounding the princess at this time, including Miss Knight and her bosom beaux Margaret Mercer Elphinstone, who acted as a go-between by passing on letters for Charlotte when her father tried to keep her incommunicado. The princess, like any young girl of seventeen, did engage in several flirtations during this period and, shockingly, Prince Augustus did meet with her privately. The flight to her mother at Connaught House was a major scandal, with the public supporting the princess against the Prince Regent.

While I gathered information from many sources, most of what you read here comes from my imagination and I hope you enjoy this glimpse into my version of history. If you want to contact me, I can be found at http://www.annlethbridge.com

Ann Lethbridge

WITH VICTORIA'S
BLESSING

MARY NICHOLS

Born in Singapore, **Mary Nichols** came to England when she was three and has spent most of her life in different parts of East Anglia. She has been a radiographer, school secretary, information officer and industrial editor, as well as a writer. She has three grown-up children and four grandchildren.

Previous novels by Mary Nichols:

RAGS-TO-RICHES BRIDE
THE EARL AND THE HOYDEN
CLAIMING THE ASHBROOKE HEIR
(part of *The Secret Baby Bargain*)
HONOURABLE DOCTOR, IMPROPER ARRANGEMENT
THE CAPTAIN'S MYSTERIOUS LADY*
THE VISCOUNT'S UNCONVENTIONAL BRIDE*
LORD PORTMAN'S TROUBLESOME WIFE*
SIR ASHLEY'S METTLESOME MATCH *
*Part of The Piccadilly Gentlemen's Club mini-series

Did you know that some of these novels are also available as eBooks? Visit www.millsandboon.co.uk

Chapter One

Lady Emily Sumner, only daughter of the Earl and Countess of Lynne, was hurrying down Park Lane, accompanied by Margaret, her companion. She was in great haste because she had arranged to meet Richard at Hyde Park Corner and she could not wait to see him again. It was only three days since she had last seen him, but it seemed an age.

'Oh, please don't dawdle,' she said when Margaret appeared to be holding back. 'He might not wait for me.'

'He is not the man you thought he was if he cannot wait a few minutes.' Margaret had remonstrated with her about the folly of meeting a gentleman in such a way, and if the countess ever found out about it they would both be in trouble, but Emily was too enamoured of her lieutenant to take any notice of her.

It was fortunate for Emily that the countess was away from home. She was one of Queen Victoria's Ladies of the Bedchamber, which meant she had to take her turn to be in attendance on the queen night and day for a month at a time. The countess dared not absent herself, with the result that her husband and daughter had been sadly neglected.

'I did not know the streets would be so crowded, or I would have set out earlier,' Emily said. 'Every day it gets worse.'

'Of course it does, the royal wedding is only just over two weeks away.'

No one could remember when a reigning queen had married before, if indeed it had ever happened, and the excitement was building to a crescendo. The little queen was popular with the people after they had been ruled by the Hanoverian George for so long. Her father, the Duke of Kent, had died when she was a baby and she had succeeded her uncle, William IV. She was a very young queen and tiny too, but, according to gossip, one who had a mind of her own and was very aware of her exalted position.

The question of a suitable husband for her had been muted some time before her succession and several suitors brought to England for her inspection, including her first cousin, Francis Charles Augustus Albert Emanuel of Saxe-Coburg-Gotha, who was known simply as Albert, whom she had chosen on a second visit to England after her accession. They were to be married on Saturday, the tenth of February.

The populace were not so sure about the bridegroom. He wasn't English, for a start, and from what they had seen of him on his two visits he had seemed stiff and unsmiling. Surely the Queen of England deserved a husband of a higher rank than the son of a German duke? Notwithstanding their doubts, the citizens of London were being joined by visitors from far and wide flocking to the capital in huge numbers, intending the royal wedding would be a day to remember. Flags and bunting and pictures of the royal couple were on display everywhere and shops were full of souvenirs.

There was a string of empty carriages being driven down Park Lane at walking pace surrounded by a troop of cavalry rehearsing their part in the queen's procession and it had attracted a crowd that blocked the walkway. By dint of much pushing, they reached Hyde Park Corner and waited for the procession to pass before crossing the road to the park gate.

'There he is!' Emily spotted Richard standing beneath a tree, tall and splendid in his naval uniform. He had been watching the troops but, sensing her nearness, turned towards her. She dashed forward and then stopped a few feet from him. Was she being too eager, too forward? Should she behave more coolly? But how could she when he was smiling at her like that, melting her insides?

He doffed his hat and bowed to her. 'My lady, you came, then?'

'Did you think I would not?'

'I wondered if perhaps your mama would keep you at home, considering the crowds.'

'Mama is still away from home and will be until after the wedding, but she would not have stopped me. I said I would be here and here I am.'

They were hemmed in by the crowd but it meant they could stand close together and no one would think anything of it. It was exciting just to be there with him, watching, but hardly seeing, what was going on around her. Her mind was on the man beside her to the exclusion of all else.

She had first met Richard at Constance Anderton's coming-out ball. Constance was two years younger than Emily,

who had come out in the year of Victoria's coronation two
years before, but they had known each other all their lives.
Their fathers' country estates were close enough for easy
visiting and the girls had often enjoyed outings together.
Both families were in London in the build-up to the wedding.

He had been presented to her by Constance's brother,
Frederick, and had asked her to dance, bowing over her
with his hand out to raise her from her chair, the warmth
of his smile seeming to reach out to her and envelop her
in a rosy glow of pure joy. Her mother would undoubtedly
say you cannot fall in love on sight, but she had. She had
melted inside and her legs had become all wobbly as she
rose to dance with him. It was the most glorious, the most
wonderful, moment of her whole life. She could not believe
that brief dance was all she would see of him; they were
destined to meet again and, if they did not, she would have
to give destiny a helping hand.

But fate was on their side. They had met again at Lady
Framlingham's soirée and he had crossed the room to speak
to her, bowing over her and asking how she did. 'Lieutenant, I did not think to see you here,' she said, delighted that
he remembered her. 'Are you on leave?'

'Yes, while my ship, the *Ariel*, is being readied to fetch
Prince Albert from Calais to his wedding.'

'The *Ariel*. What kind of ship is that?'

'A wooden-sided paddle steamer.'

'A steamer! How exciting. It must be very different from
a sailing vessel.'

'Yes. It does not have to rely on wind and tide, but I
think there is nothing more beautiful than a sailing ship in
full canvas.'

'I believe you must be a romantic, Lieutenant.'

He smiled. 'I suppose I must be.'

'And do you like life in the navy?'

'Oh, yes. I always wanted to go to sea, even as a small boy. We had an old rowing boat on the river near my home and I would put on a tricorne hat made of newspaper and pretend to be an admiral commanding a battle. I had no siblings so I recruited the village children for my crew. Some of them had to be the enemy, of course.'

'Did they mind that?'

He chuckled. 'No. Our cook always supplied me with ample provisions and I shared them out.'

'It sounds as if you had a very happy childhood.'

'Yes, I did.'

'Where was it?' She was aware that she was quizzing him shamefully, but she wanted to know all about him and he did not seem to mind.

'At Brentford. My father is the rector there.'

'Do you go home when you are on leave?'

'Usually I do, but this time we have been told we will be recalled at a moment's notice, so I am lodging in town.' He paused. 'What about you? Did you have imaginary dramas when you were a child?'

'Oh, yes. I was a princess and a very haughty one at that. My poor dolls were constantly bullied. I was waiting for a handsome prince to come and declare his love for me. But it was only the dream of a silly child.'

'I do not think you are silly or haughty, Lady Emily. Perhaps one day your prince will come.'

'I do not think I would like being married to a prince,' she said quickly. 'There is too much ceremony and protocol and you are in the public eye all the time. You could never

be yourself. I should be quite content with a plain gentleman if he loved me.'

'Then you are a romantic too.'

'Oh, yes. Life would be very dull without romance, don't
you think?'

He did not answer because they were interrupted by
Lady Montaine, who came in a rustle of purple taffeta to
stand between them. 'Lady Emily,' she said. 'I wonder if I
might interest you in a ticket to a concert at the Foundling
Hospital on Thursday? I am sure it will be an enjoyable
occasion. All the proceeds are to go to the hospital.'

'I believe I am free at that time but I shall have to ask
Mama,' Emily said, wishing the lady would go away and
leave her to continue her oh-so-agreeable conversation with
the lieutenant. He was standing a little aside, not wishing
to intrude, but she was glad he had not moved away.

'Where is your mama?' Her ladyship looked about the
crowded room as if searching for her.

'Mama is one of the Queen's Ladies and is on duty tonight.'

'Then who is escorting you?' She looked at Richard and
away again, as if he did not count, which annoyed Emily.

'I have my companion with me, my lady. And Lieutenant
Lawrence is most attentive.'

'I am sure he is,' the lady said repressively. 'Perhaps
your mother will be free to accompany you to the concert.
I shall send two tickets, shall I?'

'Yes, please.'

Lady Montaine had left but it was too late; Emily and
Richard had not been able to regain their former intimacy.
They parted without making arrangements to meet again
and Emily was in despair. But all was not lost because

Richard bought his own ticket and was at the concert where they contrived to sit together. Her mother was not able to go and Emily was accompanied as usual by the ever-faithful but disapproving Margaret, who stayed in the background

Naturally they could not talk during the concert, but during the interval when the audience, which was made up almost entirely of nobility and wealthy patrons, was encouraged to wander round the hospital and look at the wonderful works of art on display, they contrived to be viewing the same picture at the same time.

'How are you, Lady Emily?' Richard whispered, pretending to study one of Hogarth's portraits. 'Are you well?'

'I am very well, thank you, Lieutenant,' she said, aware that his head was very close to hers. 'And you?'

'First class.'

'You have not been recalled yet, then?'

'No, it means I have the opportunity to talk to you again and that I would not miss for worlds.'

'Oh.' She felt the colour rise in her cheeks. Could it possibly mean he felt the same as she did?

'Tell me what you have been doing since we last met,' he said, pretending to study the Hogarth portrait of the founder in front of them.'

'Oh, the usual things,' Emily said. 'I did some more work on the screen I am embroidering, which is taking me an age because I do not have the patience to sit at it. I began a new library book and went for a walk with Margaret and dreamed a little...'

'Dreamed? About the arrival of your prince?'

She laughed, hoping he would not delve too deeply into the object of her dreams. 'No, I leave that to the queen. Do you think she is getting excited?'

'If she is, would she dare show it?'

'No, I suppose she would have to appear cool even if she were bubbling inside. I know I should be.'

'Perhaps one day it will happen for you.'

A bell rang to tell them to return to their seats and they made their way back to the concert hall for the second half of the programme. It was not until after the music had ended, and everyone was setting off for home, that Richard turned to bid her goodnight and added, 'I should not like to think we will not meet again. Will you allow me to call on you?'

'I do not think it would be quite proper when Mama is away from home,' she said. 'But I am going to Hookhams to change my library books tomorrow afternoon. Do you like reading, Lieutenant?' This was added with a mischievous smile.

'Oh, excessively,' he said, stretching the truth. 'I am frequently in Hookhams and I do believe I shall find myself there tomorrow.'

She went home in a cloud of happiness.

There were more meetings after that, most of them contrived, and at each of them her love for Richard grew until she felt her heart would burst out of her. He was such good company, so interested in her and what she was doing, and regaled her with a fund of amusing stories about his life at sea. She learned about his family, his likes and dislikes, and she told him of hers. Their times together flew by. She knew she was not behaving as the daughter of one of England's foremost earls should, as Margaret frequently reminded her, but she could not help it. She was in love.

The empty coaches and the cavalry had gone but people

were still milling about, hoping for more to watch. 'Shall we take a walk?' he murmured in her ear.

They left the crowds and strolled along beside the Serpentine. She did not bother to tell Margaret she was going and her companion did not immediately miss her.

It was very cold and blustery, but she was wearing a dark blue wool coat and a bonnet trimmed with matching blue ribbon, tied fetchingly beneath her determined little chin. She carried a muff lined with swansdown but only one hand was in it, the other was tucked into the crook of his arm.

'I must not stay out too long. Papa might wonder where I am and then there would be awkward questions to answer.'

'Why, my dear? Have you not told your parents of our meetings?'

'No. Only Margaret knows.'

'But I do not want it to be a secret. I want to proclaim to the world how much I love you.'

She stopped and turned towards him, obliging him to stop too. 'Do you? Love me, I mean.'

'Of course I do, you goose. Have I not made it plain enough? I adore everything about you—your smile, your laughing eyes, your sweet mouth and your lively mind. Everything.'

'Oh, Richard.'

'I have been meeting you for weeks now and I thought perhaps you loved me a little too. I had begun to hope you might do me the honour of consenting to become my wife.'

'Richard!' Her eyes lit up and her mouth flew open.

'You are surprised?'

'Surprised and delighted. Have you spoken to my papa about it?'

'No, dearest one, I wanted to be sure that it was your wish before I did that. Have I your permission to approach him?'

'Yes, oh, yes.'

He took her hand from his sleeve and raised it to his lips. 'Thank you, my darling, you have made me the happiest man in the world.'

They walked on and it seemed she was floating on air, because her feet hardly touched the ground. She was hanging on to his arm with both hands in order to feel him close to her, well aware that it was a shocking way to behave. But she was also aware that her parents expected her to marry someone of her own rank and Richard could hardly be called that.

'You know we cannot marry immediately,' he said, almost as if echoing her thoughts. 'Although I do not have to rely on my lieutenant's pay. Admiral Grayson, my maternal grandfather, invested some of his own prize money on my behalf, which brings in a fair return, but even with that, I still could not give you the life you have been used to. And I have no title or noble connections which might make a difference.'

'I do not care about titles. I would live in a garret with you.'

He laughed. 'My darling, brought up in luxury, you can have no idea of what living in a garret is like. I promise you, you would not care for it, and as I am often away at sea you would be lonely without a companion.'

'You ask me to marry you in one breath and then tell me we cannot in the next,' she said, her joy slowly evaporating.

'I know. I should not have said anything to you, but it

has been eating away at me, day by day, until I could keep silent no longer. I simply had to speak.'

'I am glad you did. I should have been so miserable if you had not, thinking you were dallying with my affections.'

'Oh, my darling, never that. How could you think it? My hesitation was all to do with the practicalities, obstacles which I cannot see how we can overcome.'

'I am sure something can be contrived.'

'I shall tell the earl that I am aware my situation is not good, but I am hoping for promotion and then I might have something to offer a wife.'

'But I will have an enormous dowry,' she said. 'Papa is quite wealthy, you know.'

'I do know,' he said wryly. 'That is half the trouble. I do not want to marry you for your dowry. It is the last thing on my mind.'

'But it would help, wouldn't it?'

'Yes, of course it would help, but I think we should wait until I am made a captain.'

'How long will that take?'

'I cannot know. I shall have to do some daring deed of valour and be promoted for that. Waiting for dead men's shoes could take forever.'

'I don't want you to do a daring deed of valour, it sounds too dangerous. I will speak to Papa. No, on second thoughts I will approach Mama first. She will speak to Papa.'

Chapter Two

'Emily, you cannot possibly marry a nobody of a naval lieutenant,' the countess said next morning when Emily sought out her mother in her rooms at Buckingham Palace. It was no good waiting until the countess's month of duty ended; Emily was too impatient to know immediately whether she would be allowed to marry the man to whom she had given her heart.

She had pulled up a footstool close to the countess's chair and squatted down on it with the skirt of her green taffeta gown spread about her and a pleading look on her upturned face. The pose was one she had often used as a child to have her own way and it had usually worked. But not today. Her mother's answer had been disappointing but not totally unexpected and Emily, realising she had not put her case well, was determined to change her mother's mind.

'He is *not* a nobody, Mama, he is a lieutenant in Her Majesty's Royal Navy, but he is destined for great things.'

'That's as may be,' her mother said. 'I should like to

know how you met him. I cannot recall a Lieutenant Richard Lawrence being presented to me.'

'I met him at Constance Anderton's coming-out ball. You were there. He asked me to dance with him.'

'You danced with several young men at that ball,' her mother said with a faint smile, in spite of being so annoyed with her daughter. 'Quite put Constance's nose out of joint.'

'Yes, but there was only one Richard Lawrence,' Emily said. 'You must remember him. He was quite the handsomest man in the room. He has dark hair and brown eyes and a lovely smile....'

'Enough of that,' her mother snapped. 'I could hardly recall him from that ridiculous description. How old is he? What about his family? I presume he comes from good stock.'

'He is twenty-three and his father is the rector of Brentford.'

'A parson!' her mother exclaimed in horror. 'He must have been a second or third son, then.'

'No, I do not think so. Richard never said anything about having uncles, though I do believe he has an aunt on his mother's side who married a German baron. I do not recall her name.'

'Then I was right. He is a nobody. That he had the effrontery to address you on the subject of marriage on your very first encounter more than proves it.'

'It wasn't on our first encounter. It was later when we had come to know each other better.'

'Come to know each other better!' the countess almost shrieked. 'That a daughter of mine, who has been brought up to observe the proprieties and has always been properly chaperoned, could form an attachment to any young man that I do not know and have never met is beyond me. And you should certainly not have been discussing marriage before he had spoken to your papa. I cannot believe it of you, Emily, truly I cannot. I am shocked beyond telling.'

'Why, Mama? We have done nothing wrong.'

'It is to be hoped not. You had better tell me the whole. How often have you met him? Where and under what circumstances?'

'I met him a second time at Lady Framlingham's soirée, I did not know he would be there. And we were both at the concert at the Foundling Hospital. His father has some connection with it, I believe. And we met again by chance at Hookhams library and he carried my books home. I seemed to come across him at several functions after that and yesterday he was watching the cavalry rehearsing when I went for a walk in the park. It was then he asked me for permission to approach Papa, but I said I would speak to you first.'

'And where was Margaret when all this was going on?'

'Margaret was close by.'

'She has neglected her duties shamefully. She should have reported all this to me. I think perhaps she should be dismissed and someone more suitable employed to be your companion.'

'Oh, no, Mama, please don't punish Margaret. I asked her not to say anything. It is not her fault.'

'So, you knew what you were doing was wrong or you would not have asked her to keep silent on the matter. I blame myself. I should have kept a closer watch on you, but what with all the preparations for the wedding, I have been overwhelmed with things to do. I trusted you to behave properly when I am engaged with the queen, and it seems my trust has been sadly misplaced. No doubt you have been seen together and given the gabble-grinders something to get their teeth into.'

'I am sure the gossips have no interest in what I do, Mama, and we have been very discreet.'

'I had every hope you might be made a maid of honour,' the countess went on, as if Emily had not spoken. 'But if Her Majesty hears of this, it will not happen. Oh, Emily, how could you?'

'I do not want to be a maid of honour. It is a horrible job, stuck in the palace all the time.'

'There are thousands of girls who would give their right arms for that. It would guarantee you a welcome in every drawing room of note in the whole country. You could take your pick of all the eligible young men at court.'

'I have already taken my pick. I do not want to marry anyone but Richard. I love him dearly....'

'Love him, bah! What do you know of love?'

'The queen loves Prince Albert, you told me so, and she and I are of an age. And Richard is three years older than Prince Albert. If they can have a love-match, so can we.'

'Prince Albert belongs to an ancient royal family, even if he is not English, and it was all properly conducted according to protocol. It was fortuitous that they took to each other from the first.'

'We took to each other from the first too. And Prince Albert is inferior in rank to the queen—everyone knows he is—and Saxe-Coburg-Gotha is a nothing little state, hardly bigger than an English county, but it didn't stop him asking her to marry him.'

'He did not ask her. That would have been highly improper. She asked him.'

'Well, it doesn't make any difference who asked whom. No one said they could not marry because of his inferior rank.'

'Emily, for goodness' sake, do not repeat that outside this room. You will have us thrown in the Tower.'

Emily giggled at that notion.

'It is no laughing matter,' the countess went on. 'You have become far too pert for your own good. You will not see or communicate with Lieutenant Lawrence again.'

'But, Mama, if only you would see him and talk to him, I am sure you would like him....'

'Enough. I have said no and that is an end of it.'

'Yes, Mama.'

Emily decided she had better pretend to be acquiescent, because arguing with Mama was a futile exercise and would only make her more obdurate. She would not put it past her mother to give instructions that she was to be locked in her bedroom and not allowed out at all if she showed any sign of rebellion. But that did not mean she would capitulate. Richard was far too important to her to be given up at the first hurdle.

'I must go back to the queen,' the countess said, standing. 'She is having a fitting this afternoon and is in a state of anxiety about it. How did you come?'

The interview was at an end and Emily got up off the stool, dejection in every line of her body. 'I asked Grimes to bring me in the carriage. Papa gave his permission.'

'Did he know why you wanted to see me?'

'No, he did not ask and I did not say. I hoped you would tell him.'

'Not I. He will think ill of me for not being able to control my own daughter. And there is no need to say anything to him at all because the subject is at an end. You will not marry Lieutenant Lawrence and you will not meet him again. Is that quite clear?'

'Yes, Mama, quite clear.'

'There are several eminent young men with good prospects of titles and fortunes who are far more suitable, and when the queen's nuptials are over and we go back to normal, your father and I will set about introducing you to one or two. We have been far too indulgent with you over your fussiness up to now.' She was on the way to the door as she spoke, her silk gown whispering about her. 'Where is Margaret?'

'Waiting outside, Mama. I wanted to talk to you alone.'

The countess flung the door open, startling the young lady who stood in the corridor. 'Margaret, there you are. I want you to make sure Lady Emily does not see or communicate with Lieutenant Lawrence again. It will cost you your position if you allow it.'

Margaret curtsied. 'Yes, my lady.'

With that the countess sailed past her, leaving a tearful Emily to be comforted by her companion.

'What am I to do?' Emily asked. 'I cannot give Richard up.'

'I do not know, my lady, but if you are thinking of meeting him secretly, I advise you to think again. I dare not disobey her ladyship.'

'I know that, Margaret, and I will not ask it of you.' She brightened suddenly. 'I could apply to the queen.'

'Oh, no, please don't do that. The queen is too busy arranging her own wedding, and besides, she will only tell you to obey your mama. And how humiliating that would be for her ladyship. She might be dismissed from the royal presence on account of it, and then what would your papa say?'

Emily sighed. 'You are undoubtedly right. Let's go home. I hate it here. It is cold and draughty and smells of gas and goodness knows what else. How the queen can bear to live here, I don't know.'

They found their way out of the building, passing maids and footmen, all occupied on some errand or other, who took no notice of them. The palace was like a busy town, with hundreds of servants performing hundreds of different functions, not to mention people from outside—like costumiers, dressmakers, lace makers, corset makers, shoemakers, furriers, caterers and vintners—coming and going on the business of the wedding.

Speculation about what the bride would wear was rife; cloth of gold or silver, crimson velvet and purple satin and ermine were being bandied about. Emily knew, because her mother had told her, that the queen was concerned that her role on this occasion was to be that of a bride, not a queen, and she would not wear robes of state or a crown, because they would belittle her groom. But the countess was silent on exactly what the queen would wear, except to say the material for the gown had been woven in Spitalfields and the lace had been occupying the Honiton lace makers for some time.

What was occupying Emily's mind as they drove the short distance from Buckingham Palace to Upper Brook Street was not the royal wedding but her own. How could she send a message to Richard without involving Margaret? How could she meet him? She had to see him, not only because a day without a glimpse of his dear face was a day of misery, but because she needed to reassure him she had not given him up and never would. Not normally disobedient, she could not cut Richard out of her life, she just could not.

'I must let Richard know what has happened,' she told Margaret as the family coach carried them home.

'If you are going to ask me to convey a message to him, I am afraid I shall have to refuse,' Margaret said. 'Much as I love you and sympathise, I dare not go against the countess. She is already very cross with me.'

'I know.' A huge sigh followed this. 'But you could take a note to Constance Anderton asking her to call on me. Mama would surely not object to that?'

'No, but it depends on the reason for it....'

'Please, Margaret, I beg you. You need not listen to what Constance and I talk about. As far as you are concerned it is nothing but idle gossip about the queen's wedding.'

'Oh, very well, but on your own head be it.' Margaret sighed. Emily in one of her stubborn moods was difficult to gainsay.

Chapter Three

All Constance wanted to do when the two girls had settled themselves in Emily's bedroom was talk about the royal wedding and the parties they were going to attend and who was likely to be at them and what she might wear. It was some time before Emily was able to bring up the subject of Richard. Margaret was in the dressing room next door, busying herself with Emily's wardrobe, and Jeannette, Constance's companion, had gone to join her.

'Constance, can you keep a secret?' she asked when they had exhausted the topic of *that* wedding.

'A secret?' The other girl's eyes lit up. Unlike Emily, she had fair hair and blue eyes and dressed in pale pinks and blues and apple greens, whereas Emily favoured stronger colours which went well with her dark hair and hazel eyes. Today she was in yellow and green stripes. 'Oh, do tell.'

'Only if you promise not to divulge it to a soul.'

'Of course I won't.'

'You remember Lieutenant Richard Lawrence?'

'Yes, he was at my ball. Don't tell me you have developed a tendre for him.'

'More than that. He has asked me to marry him.'

'Emily! And you never said a word to me and I am your best friend.'

'He only asked me two days ago. And I'm glad you are my friend because I have a favour to ask you.'

'Oh.' This was said warily.

'Mama had forbidden me to see him and I simply have to get a message to him. Will you deliver a letter?'

'But, Emily, I hardly know him. He was a friend of my brother. They joined the navy together. He was only asked to the ball to make up the numbers. I can no more communicate with him than you can. My parents would have a fit.'

'Then what am I to do? I simply have to tell him why I cannot meet him. He will be waiting for me and when I do not come he will think I do not care for him any more. And nothing could be further from the truth. I love him to distraction.'

'Waiting for you where?'

'At the gate of Green Park.'

'I cannot simply walk up to him in the park and hand him a note. Oh, Emily, friend or not, I dare not do that.'

'Then I shall have to defy my mother and go myself. I will not give him up, I will not. I'll run away with him first.'

'Emily, I beg you not to do that. The scandal will be too dreadful and think of your poor parents. And how will you live? He is only a lieutenant, after all.'

'I know all that. He said it himself, but I was sure I could bring Mama round and I think I still could. The trouble is she has so little time for me nowadays.'

'Then be patient.'

'Oh, you are not much use at all.'

Constance was thoughtful. 'I could ask Freddie to let Lieutenant Lawrence know why you cannot meet him. More than that I dare not do.'

Emily thought about this. It meant bringing Constance's brother into the conspiracy and the more people who knew about it, the more chance there was of her mother finding out she had disobeyed her. On the other hand, it might be a safer way to communicate with Richard. 'Oh, would you? Oh, thank you, thank you. I'll give you a note to give to him.'

'I did not say I would deliver a note.'

'Oh, but you will, won't you? I must tell him in my own words, and—'

'Enough, Emily! Do not tell me any more. I do not want to know. Write your letter.'

Emily had already written it in anticipation and it was the work of a moment to give it to Constance, who stuffed it in the pocket of her skirt, just as Margaret and Jeannette put in an appearance. Emily and Constance turned to them, all innocence, and drew them into a conversation about the queen's wedding and speculation about Her Majesty's groom. He was very handsome, they conceded, but a little dour, though perhaps it was the seriousness of being the consort of the most powerful monarch in the world which made him like that; perhaps he would unbend a little when he became used to his new life. Emily's mind was only half on the conversation; she was thinking of Richard and what he would do when he read her letter.

Chapter Four

Lieutenant Richard Lawrence was sitting in a corner of Fladong's parlour, a hotel popular with naval officers, until it was time to make his way to Green Park and his assignation with Emily.

How he had come to fall in love with her, when he had told himself, and anyone else who would listen, that marriage was not for him, not until he became a captain at the very least, he did not know. But he had been bewitched by her the moment he saw her sitting on the edge of the Anderton ballroom looking delectable in a gown whose colour he could only describe as squashed raspberry. It had a boat-shaped neckline which hinted at a well-shaped bosom, and huge puffed sleeves trimmed with quantities of lace which seemed to emphasise a tiny waist he had an urge to put his hands around.

He had asked her to dance and discovered she had a lively intelligence and an independent spirit coupled with a keen sense of humour, unlike so many of the hothouse blooms he had come across that evening. She had a beautiful face too. He sat musing on this, recalling her bright hazel eyes, her pink cheeks and perfectly shaped mouth, just right for kissing, when Freddie Anderton sat down opposite him and shattered his dream.

'There you are, Dick, I've been searching everywhere for you.'

'Why? Have we been recalled?'

'Not yet. I don't think we'll recognise the *Ariel* and *Firebrand* when we get back to them, they'll be so prettied up for the prince. No doubt we'll be shoved in with the mates to make room for the entourage.' Richard was serving on the *Ariel*, Freddie on the *Firebrand*, another paddle steamer being readied for Prince Albert's use.

'No doubt.'

'What were you in such a brown study about?'

'Never you mind.'

'I can guess. A young lady. A young lady by the name of Emily.' Richard's startled look made his friend smile. 'Did you think it was a secret? It's written all over you. "I am in love." Do not deny it.'

'I am not denying it. There is a snag to our happiness though.'

'To be sure there is. The daughter of an earl and an impoverished naval lieutenant do not make a match. You must have realised that from the outset.'

'Of course I did, but we were carried away....'

'Not *too* carried away, I hope.'

'No, of course not.' Richard was indignant. 'But I did blurt out that I wanted to marry her, expecting her to turn me down, but she didn't. Freddie, she said yes.' His eyes lit up at the memory. 'But that has left me with a dilemma. She is convinced she can persuade her parents to agree to the marriage, but even if they do, we cannot live as she is accustomed to on my income.'

'Unfortunately, my friend, her parents do *not* agree.' He fished a letter from his pocket and put it on the table in front of Richard. 'This will explain.'

Richard snatched it up and skimmed through it. 'She has been forbidden to see me or communicate with me.'

'Well, she has already disobeyed one of those instructions,' Freddie said, nodding at the sheet of paper in Richard's hand.

'Yes, and prepared to disobey the other. I have only to say the word and she will come to me.'

'But you are not going to say the word, are you?'

'No,' he said gloomily. 'How can I? It will ruin her reputation.'

'And your career. Don't forget that.'

'I wish in a way we were at war and could see some action, then I might distinguish myself and earn a promotion. Instead of that we are required to sail to Calais and bring back the queen's bridegroom.'

'Perhaps after that, we'll be ordered to join a battleship or a cruiser and sent off to far-flung places. Will she wait for you, do you think?'

'She says she will but I cannot hold her to that, can I? She is young and her parents are sure to bring pressure to bear for her to marry someone they consider more suitable.'

'Then I suggest you do not answer that letter. She will get over you all the quicker if she hears nothing from you. And so will you. It is a lost cause, my friend.'

Richard gave a huge sigh. He suspected his friend was right, but he had the gravest difficulty in accepting it. He was convinced he and Emily were made for each other and somehow or other a way had to be found for them to be together. The trouble was no matter how often he teased his brain with it, no solution came to mind.

'Come on, Dick,' Freddie said cheerfully. 'It is not the end of the world. Let's go to Boodles and play a hand or two. That will take your mind off her.'

Richard knew nothing would take his mind off Emily for very long, but he agreed. Anything was better than moping, and Freddie was good company and might be persuaded to take a reply to Emily through his sister. It was no good going to Green Park. Emily had said she would not be there.

They left the hotel and made their way from Oxford Street down Duke Street, but as they reached Grosvenor Square, Richard suddenly turned left into Upper Brook Street.

'Hey, where are you off to?' Freddie asked, grabbing his arm.

Richard shook him off. 'I'm going to see if I can catch a glimpse of her.'

'Don't be a fool. You will only make it worse for yourself.'

They were approaching Lynne House when Emily came out accompanied by Margaret. They were both wrapped in warm cloaks with fur-lined hoods and were each carrying books. Richard stopped, waiting for Emily to acknowledge him. She stopped too. They looked at each other without speaking for what seemed an age, each trying to convey with their eyes and expression alone what they were feeling: love, despair and hope all mixed together. And then she smiled briefly and lifted the hand that held the books hanging from her wrist by the ribbon which bound them, before moving on. Not a word was exchanged.

'She is going to Hookhams.' Richard did an about turn and set off for Old Bond Street with Freddie in his wake.

Once in the library it took a moment or two to locate Emily; she had managed to conceal herself behind a bookcase and was pretending to study a book on exotic plants.

'Emily,' he whispered, coming up behind her. 'I received your letter.'

'Then you must know I have been forbidden to speak to you.' She was trembling, not only because she was not accustomed to disobeying her mother, but because of his nearness. His breath was tickling the back of her neck and sending the most extraordinary messages to the rest of her body.

'Is it the end between us?' he enquired in a hoarse whisper. 'Is that your wish?'

She turned towards him. 'No, Richard, how could you think it? But do you think you can be patient until after the queen's wedding? When everything has quietened down and Mama is not so stressed, I will speak to her again. If she knows how determined I am, she will change her mind.'

'Of course I will wait, is that not what I have been saying?' he said. 'It will be worth it to have you as my wife in the end. In the meantime I shall contrive to better my own lot, even if it means coming out of the service and doing something else. I hate all this hole-in-the-corner way of doing things. It goes against my nature, but it is better than nothing.'

Over his shoulder, Emily saw her companion, who had

managed to go off to another part of the shop, returning. 'Margaret is coming. I must go.'

He lifted the back of her gloved hand to his lips and smiled a little wryly. 'Adieu, my love,' he whispered. 'Be assured you are never out of my thoughts, no matter what.' Then he turned on his heel and rejoined Freddie. 'Come on,' he said. 'Let's go to Boodles.'

They spent the rest of the afternoon playing cards, at which Richard won a modest sum. It did not cheer him up. 'Lucky at cards, unlucky in love,' he said to his friend as he pocketed his winnings and returned to his lodging.

The next day they were recalled to their ships and took the stage to Dover. He did not know that Emily had been summoned to Buckingham Palace, not by her mother but by the queen.

Chapter Five

Full of trepidation Emily made her way through the draughty corridors of Buckingham Palace to the queen's sitting room, where Her Majesty was examining the lace of her veil which she had designed herself, and talking to her ladies, who sat or stood about her. Her mother, Emily noticed, was with her.

The countess stepped forward. 'Your Majesty, may I present my daughter, Emily.'

Emily dipped the deepest curtsey she had ever made and then stood waiting for the queen to speak.

'Lady Emily, I believe you are desirous of becoming one of my maids of honour.'

It was not a question but a statement and Emily did not know what to say. She could hardly deny having any such desire and knew, with certainty, that her mother had engineered the interview. 'It would be an honour, Your Majesty.'

'Do you know the duties expected of you?'

'Not exactly, ma'am.'

'I am sure your mama will enlighten you. You will, of course, be in attendance at my wedding with the other maids, after the bridesmaids and Ladies of the Bedchamber. Your gown for this will be provided for you.' She took a little box from the small table at her side and extracted a miniature of herself set in diamonds in the form of a brooch. 'You will wear this at all times while you are with me, Lady Emily. It is your badge of office.' She leaned forward and pinned it to the bodice of Emily's gown. 'Needless to say, any proposals of marriage you receive will be directed through me from the first. I trust you understand that?'

'Yes, ma'am.' Emily's heart sank. Did the queen know about Richard? Was that what it was all about? How on earth was she to meet Richard if she had to live in the palace, where her mother could keep an eye on her? Everything was conspiring against her and she felt like rebelling.

'If I approve of your choice of husband, then you will receive the usual dowry, but I do not expect that to happen in the near future. You are still very young.' Said by a woman who was the same age as Emily. 'I shall expect you to begin your duties on Monday.'

The interview at an end, Emily curtsied again and backed out of the presence to rejoin Margaret in an anteroom. 'I have to be a maid of honour,' she murmured. 'Three months living in this great barn of a place, three months at the queen's command. How am I ever going to see Richard?'

Margaret was not required to answer because the countess had followed her daughter. 'Come with me to my room,' she told Emily. 'I will go over your duties.'

'Mama, you knew I did not want this honour,' Emily said as they went. 'Is it your way of punishing me?'

'Punishing you, child? It is not a punishment, it is a wonderful opportunity. I asked the queen about it some time ago, but a vacancy has only now arisen and that rather suddenly. Her Majesty graciously remembered my request. You should feel elated. You will be part of the queen's procession at her wedding and will see everything that goes on. The dress was made for your predecessor, but can easily be altered to fit you.'

Emily followed her mother into her sitting room with Margaret a little behind them. The countess turned to her. 'You may wait outside until Lady Emily is ready to return home.' To Emily she said, 'Sit down.'

Emily obeyed and waited.

'Your duties as a maid of honour are simple enough,' the countess said. 'You will attend the queen whenever she requires it between the hours of ten in the morning and five in the afternoon, and again in the evening until she dismisses you. You might be asked to converse with her, take walks, read to her and sometimes deal with her correspondence. You will share these duties with the other maids, but you must be ready for the call at any time. Is that quite clear?'

'Yes, Mama.'

Emily returned home in the depths of despair. It seemed her loving relationship with Richard was blighted. 'I must see him,' she told Margaret in the carriage going home. 'I have until Monday and then I shall be in servitude for three months. Oh, how could Mama do this to me?'

'It is a great honour and you will be in the chapel to see the royal wedding. Think of that.'

'I would rather be thinking of my own wedding,' she said gloomily.

'Cheer up,' Margaret said. 'It is not the end of the world.'

'It seems like it to me. Margaret, will you take a note to Constance for me?'

'If you insist.'

The note enclosed one for Richard but it could not be delivered. Richard had been recalled to his ship.

Chapter Six

Prince Albert enjoyed a farewell banquet at home with his family on the twenty-seventh of January and next day left Gotha with his father, the Duke of Saxe-Coburg, and brother Ernst, in their father's travelling carriage, bound for Calais and a new life. A string of other carriages followed, sent by Victoria for his retinue and luggage, which made an impressive caravan. In spite of wet blustery weather, he was fêted all the way with crowds of people in the streets and in the windows of houses, even on the rooftops, waving flags and handkerchiefs.

When they reached Calais he found the *Ariel* and the *Firebrand* waiting for him. Both ships had been prepared so that he could choose which to use. In the event he went aboard the *Ariel*.

It was obvious as soon as they left the harbour that it was going to be a rough crossing. The *Ariel* was tossed about by gale-force winds and mountainous seas, and all the passengers were seasick, including the royal brothers. Neither was able to sample the refreshments so painstakingly prepared for them and they remained in their cabins. The prince's servants seemed incapable of doing anything to help their master and Richard found himself waiting on the young groom. He took a liking to the twenty-year-old who was approachable and grateful for anything that was done for him, including a seasickness remedy that Richard had used himself when he had first gone to sea as a cabin boy ten years before.

He found himself in conversation with the prince, who was talking to him in an effort to ignore his heaving stomach. Albert did not say so, but it was obvious that he was exceedingly nervous about the wedding and, more especially, how he would conduct himself as the wife of England's queen. He had been schooled in what was expected of him, but it was clear to Richard that the young man was not prepared to be a shadow of the queen and had very decided views on a number of subjects. He was going to need all his tact to be allowed to let his own personality shine through.

He was interested in his new country and its ways and quizzed Richard in a strong German accent about his own life as a sailor and whether he found it congenial. Richard responded by talking about life in the Royal Navy and the ships he had served on, from cabin boy to midshipman to second and then first mate. 'It is a slow climb,' he said. 'And the higher you go, the slower it becomes.'

'I think it is the same for the consort of a queen,' the prince said. 'One must tread slowly and carefully. But with determination, one may succeed.'

'I hope so, sir. I shall not be consort of a queen but I hope one day to be consort of an earl's daughter.'

'You are engaged?'

'Unfortunately, no. Her mother, the Countess of Lynne, does not consider me good enough for her daughter.' It was said with a wry smile. 'And to be honest, that is undoubtedly the case, but it does not stop me wanting her. I must make my way up, and quickly, if I am to succeed.'

'I am sure you will. But have you no sponsor, someone to speak for you?'

Richard was aware, as was everyone else, that the prince's marriage to Victoria had been engineered through their mutual uncle Leopold of Belgium. Would that he had a similar relation. And then he smiled. 'I had an aunt, who married a German baron and went to live in Coburg several years ago, but I doubt that would carry much weight with the countess.'

'Coburg, eh? Then I should know the gentleman. Tell me his name.'

'Baron Mingen.'

'Why, I know him,' the prince exclaimed. 'He is a distant relation of mine and one of my equerries. He is part of my entourage travelling on the *Firebrand*. Have you not met him?'

'No. My aunt and he were married before I was born and lived all their time abroad. My aunt died last year.'

'Then I shall see that you are introduced to him when we land. He might further your cause. Like me, he is in favour of greater ties between Germany and Britain.' He paused. 'I do believe that cure of yours is working. Already I am feeling a little better.'

'I am glad to hear that, Your Highness.'

His optimism was short-lived because the weather worsened as they reached Dover after five hours of buffeting, and entering the harbour was a hazardous undertaking.

The waxen-faced prince was uplifted by the sight of the crowds gathered to welcome him, waving flags and cheering, their earlier animosity apparently dissipated. He took his leave of the crew, including Richard for whom he had a special word, and with an effort of will staggered up on deck and stepped thankfully onto dry land to acknowledge the applause of his well-wishers.

The carriages were being unloaded to take him and his entourage to London, but before he left, he remembered his promise and sent for Baron Mingen and presented Richard to him.

The baron was a portly man, sporting a dark beard streaked with white. He had a round face with apple-red cheeks and bright blue eyes, which reminded Richard of Prince Albert. He spoke only German but as Richard had a smattering of the language they were able to make themselves understood. There was no time for any more than the briefest of exchanges, because the coaches had been landed and readied for the onward journey. 'Come and see me in London,' the baron said. 'We will have a long talk and you can tell me all about yourself. My wife, your aunt Matilda, often spoke of your dear mother and wished she had been able to see you. Alas, it was not to be.'

'I am sorry for your loss,' Richard said.

The caravan of carriages had been re-assembled and the prince and his brother were ready to continue their journey, escorted by a company of the 11th Dragoons. Richard asked for and was given leave to return to the capital and took a seat on a public coach which, unable to overtake, had to follow in the wake of the prince's entourage until they reached Canterbury.

In spite of the dreadful weather, the prince was cheered

all the way by the population who had come out to see them pass. In Canterbury it seemed the whole town was out to welcome him. He and Ernst stayed there that night and next day. Rested, though still wan from his sickness, he continued his journey, arriving at Buckingham Palace soon after four on the afternoon of the eighth of February to be greeted by his bride. There were just two days to the wedding.

Chapter Seven

The queen sent for two of her maids each day to wait on her, but had not called upon Emily. Unable to go out, unable to see Richard, she had nothing to do but mope and dream. The other maids who were not in attendance gossiped over their embroidery, and Emily, for want of anything else, started a sampler. She was working on it when she was summoned to attend the queen and took it with her.

All the arrangements for the wedding had been made, most of which were in the hands of the queen's advisors and Ladies of the Bedchamber, but the queen had taken an active interest in everything down to the last detail. Today all she had to do was await the arrival of her bridegroom. If she felt any trepidation about this she did not show it, as she beckoned Emily to a seat beside her.

'Lady Emily, have you settled in comfortably?'

'Yes, thank you, Your Majesty.'

'You have brought your embroidery, I see.'

'Yes, ma'am. I was advised to have something to do with my hands if you wished to talk.'

'Very sensible.' When the queen smiled, her whole countenance softened and Emily found herself relaxing a little. 'May I see?'

Emily handed it over for inspection. She had sketched out the design: a crown with the names of Victoria and Albert and the date of the wedding on the top half, to be done in several different stitches. The names Richard and Emily were to go on the bottom half. There was no date, but a gap in which to put it. All four names were entwined with flowers.

The queen studied it for some time while Emily wondered if she would be angry that the sampler of the royal wedding should also depict her own name and Richard's. 'Who is Lieutenant Richard Lawrence?' she asked at last. 'You have linked his name with your own.'

'Yes, ma'am. I hope one day it will be linked.'

'You know you must apply to me before that can happen?'

'Yes, Your Majesty.'

'Tell me about him.'

The opportunity was heaven-sent and Emily found herself confiding everything. It was only when she finished, she realised she perhaps should not have been so forthright.

'Your mama must surely know what is best for you, Emily.'

'Yes, Your Majesty,' she said dolefully. 'But I love him so very much.'

'Ah, that is important, I agree.' She paused. 'I think I will speak to the countess about her reasons for withholding her consent.'

'They are on the grounds of his inferior rank, Your Majesty.'

'Quite.' Victoria smiled again. 'That can be a stumbling block, but the higher in rank one is, the harder it is to find an equal, and I do not think it is as important as some would believe. It depends on the qualities of the gentleman in question and, of course, we cannot know that. He would need someone to speak for him.'

'Yes, Your Majesty.'

Emily could not believe she was having this conversation or that the queen would be so sympathetic. She wondered what her mother would say when she learned of it. The countess was being kept very busy with the final arrangements and Emily had seen little of her, but it was unlikely the queen would speak to her before Saturday, even if she remembered. And then there was the honeymoon afterwards. It sounded as if Her Majesty was offering her hope, but Emily was realist enough to know that the chances of anything coming from it were slim. But she could still dream.

Chapter Eight

Saturday dawned to pouring rain and strong winds, but the crowd were not to be deterred and early that morning began gathering in their thousands all along the route from Buckingham Palace to the garden entrance to St James's Palace. Unlike previous monarchs who had married at night to avoid the crowds, Victoria relished them and the wedding was set for one o'clock in the afternoon in the Chapel Royal. Those invited to the ceremony took their places long before that.

The cheers of the crowd grew louder as the carriage containing Prince Albert and his father and brother neared St James's. The queen had made him a field marshall the day before, and invested him with the Order of the Garter. He arrived dressed in a field marshall's uniform with white satin bows on his epaulettes and the emblem of the Order across his chest. He was a handsome man, and many were the sighs of envy of the queen. His quiet dignity commended him to the nobility, who were in their places ahead of him, arrayed in all the colours of the rainbow, wearing whatever decorations they were entitled to. He kissed the hand of the queen dowager and took his place at the altar to await the arrival of the bride.

The queen's procession left Buckingham Palace at midday, with the queen, her mother and Lady Sutherland, the Mistress of the Wardrobe, in the golden state coach, followed by her attendants in a fleet of carriages. Emily, in one of the last ones with three other maids of honour, remembered the rehearsal she had watched with Richard. Never, in her wildest dreams, had she imagined she would be part of it. All along the route the crowd cheered and waved flags, the cold rain notwithstanding.

When they arrived the queen's procession formed up to make its way to the chapel, preceded by trumpeters, members of the royal family and officers of the royal household. At last the speculation about what the bride would wear was answered. There was no cloth of gold, no silver, no crimson velvet or royal purple, no ermine. The tiny figure was all in white. Her gown was of ivory silk-satin trimmed with yards and yards of elaborately designed lace on the skirt and sleeves. It had a V-shaped waist and a full pleated skirt. Her headdress was a simple circlet of orange blossom with a lace veil. She wore the Star of the Order of the Garter. Her jewellery was a diamond necklace, diamond earrings and a beautiful sapphire brooch which Albert had given her as a wedding gift the previous evening. The very simplicity of her attire made her stand out, in spite of her small stature. There was a concerted sigh of admiration from everyone as she moved through the crowded corridors and anterooms to the chapel, followed by her twelve bridesmaids, also in white silk, holding up her train. Behind them came the Ladies of the Bedchamber and, after them, the eight maids of honour.

The galleries and seats in the chapel were filled with nobility, resplendent and glittering with jewels. Emily was hardly aware of them. She was concentrating on the simple ceremony—a bride and groom being joined in holy matrimony—and she wished she was standing at the altar with Richard by her side, giving the responses as Victoria and Albert were doing. She found her eyes filling with tears and resolutely blinked them away.

After the ceremony the royal couple went off to sign the register, while the whole procession went into reverse for the journey back to the palace. It was as she was climbing into the carriage that Emily saw Richard. He was standing right in front of the crowd, tall and upright. She could not go to him, could not even acknowledge him, but her joy lit her face when she saw him smiling at her, conveying in the warmth of it that he had not given her up. She sat back in her seat with a sigh, not exactly of happiness, but perhaps of hope. If she could not hope, what was there to live for? Tomorrow she would have another try at persuading her mother. Surely, surely, she would not continue to refuse her daughter's dearest wish?

The crowds were still cheering when the royal couple returned to Buckingham Palace for the wedding breakfast, and again hours later when the queen and her new husband set out for Windsor Castle, where they were to spend a few days' honeymoon. Longer than that the queen would not allow away from affairs of state.

It was all over; the great day had come and gone and on the whole it had passed off smoothly in spite of the dismal weather. The countess's tour of duty was over until the next time, and Emily had been given leave while the queen was at Windsor. They were both free to go home. The family carriage was to fetch them next day.

She lay awake that night going over her arguments again and again, one of which was the queen's comment: 'The higher in rank one is, the harder it is to find an equal, and I do not think it is as important as some would believe. It depends on the qualities of the gentleman in question.' Surely that would sway her mother, especially as she knew very well the queen could and would overrule her if she so chose.

Her sleepless night meant she slept late and it was her mother's maid who woke her to tell her she was wanted in the countess's room and to make haste with her toilette.

Half an hour later she made her way to her mother's room and was astonished to find the room full of people, and more astonishing still was that one of them was Richard. It looked very much as if her disobedience had been found out, and not only was she in for a scolding, so was Richard. And it wasn't his fault. She looked about her, prepared to defend him in spite of the odds stacked against her. Both her parents were standing by the hearth. A portly man with a round red face and a full beard rose from a chair at her entrance, as did another man in clerical clothes, who bore an uncanny likeness to Richard. On the sofa sat a plump, middle-aged woman with bright blue eyes; she turned towards Emily and looked her up and down with undisguised curiosity. Surely this pair must be Richard's parents?

'Emily,' her father began. 'This is Baron Mingen.' He indicated the man beside him. 'He is Lieutenant Lawrence's uncle by marriage. Baron, my daughter, Lady Emily.'

Emily curtsied and her father went on with the introductions. 'The Reverend Mr Lawrence and Mrs Lawrence, the lieutenant's parents.' Emily curtsied again, wishing they would get on with it. The suspense was making her heart beat uncomfortably fast and she was shaking all over.

She turned back to her father. 'They have come because the lieutenant has something particular to ask you,' he went on. 'He has requested and been given permission to pay his addresses to you.'

'He has?' She could hardly believe her ears. 'But...' She turned towards Richard. He was grinning foolishly, though he did not speak.

'Yes,' her father went on. 'Do you wish to receive him?'

'Oh, yes, yes,' she said, relaxing at last, though she had no idea how this great change had come about.

'Then I suggest you go into the next room and listen to what he has to say. We will wait here for you.'

Richard held out his hand and she moved forward to take it, so that he could lead her into her mother's dressing room. All her mother's clothes had been packed away to be taken back to Upper Brook Street and the room had been tidied in readiness for its next occupant. Emily hardly noticed this as he shut the door and turned towards her. She had eyes only for him.

'Richard, how—' She was stopped from saying more because Richard had taken her in his arms and was kissing her soundly on the mouth. Her queries were set aside in the pleasure of this new sensation and it was some time before both came up for air and then they were laughing delightedly.

'Richard, how did it come about?' she asked at last. 'I was forbidden to speak to you or communicate with you in any way and a wedding between us was out of the question according to Mama.'

'I know. It is all down to my German uncle. You remember I told you my aunt Matilda had married a German baron. Well, that is Baron Mingen. He is part of Prince Albert's entourage and when I was talking to Prince Albert—'

'You were talking to the prince?' Emily echoed in surprise

'Yes, we had a long conversation while we were crossing the Channel and he asked me all about myself and I told him about you. He sent for Baron Mingen before he left Dover and introduced us and I told him about our dilemma. And so after the royal wedding was over, he spoke to Prince Albert, who spoke to the queen, who gave her consent for us to wed. My parents were already in town to view the wedding procession and they and the baron met the earl and countess....'

'And all of that changed Mama's mind. Oh, I cannot believe it is true. Kiss me again, so that I might know it is.'

He obliged with alacrity. 'Baron Mingen is standing my sponsor,' he said when they drew breath. 'He and my aunt had no children and apparently I am his heir, though I never knew it. And I have been granted the promotion I need and will soon be appointed to my own ship.' He laughed suddenly. 'You are looking at Captain Richard Lawrence.'

'It is no more than you deserve.'

He hugged her to him and kissed her again. And again. And again. 'So how do you feel about becoming Mrs Richard Lawrence?' he asked.

'It feels wonderful. Oh, Richard, I can hardly believe it. Yesterday I was so miserable. The queen was having a lovely day and marrying her own choice of husband, so why couldn't I? And now it has happened. God bless the queen.'

'And Prince Albert.' He smiled and kissed her forehead and the end of her nose. 'Shall we go and tell everyone the good news?'

They returned to the countess's sitting room, where Emily was hugged and kissed by everyone and a bottle of champagne was opened for a toast. After that they settled down to discuss the wedding arrangements. An Easter wedding, they decided, and Richard's father would marry them at St George's. The bride would not go to her wedding in a golden coach with trumpets and fanfares and cheering crowds, but she would travel in an open landau, given away by her father and attended by Constance in pink. As for the gown, Emily thought the queen's choice of white had been a very happy one and she would wear white too. She was brimming with tearful happiness and could not help constantly looking at her future groom. No one, not even Queen Victoria, could be happier than she was, she decided, smiling at Richard and reaching for his hand.

* * * * *

Author Note

When I was asked to write a short story around a royal wedding for this book, I chose that of Victoria and Albert. Before that royal weddings tended to be political affairs, and to some extent so was Victoria's, but it was also a love match—as is evident from her diaries. Nevertheless, she was well aware of her status as monarch, and Albert had to tread very carefully to stamp his own personality on the reign—which he managed to do very successfully, so that Victoria and Albert have become forever inseparably linked in people's minds. Theirs was a true love story. Emily and Richard are fictitious characters, but I like to think their love endures as long.

Mary Nichols